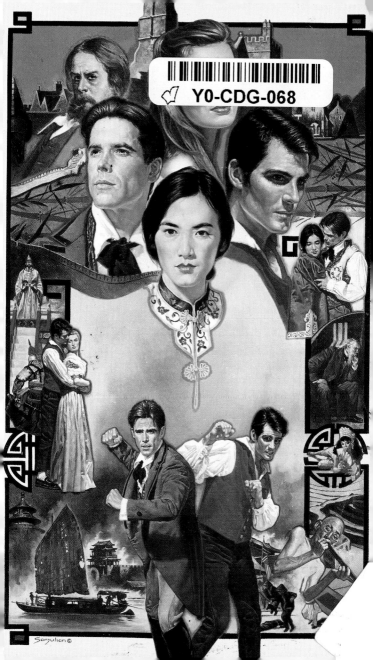

Desire (handwritten at top)

T'IEN HSIA: BENEATH THE SKY . . .

Heathen sun . . . The Reverend Samuel Outerbridge's words played through Ross Ballinger, conjuring images of this mysterious land: a barefoot coolie squatting in a dirt alley, his nimble fingers wrapped around a bowl of rice, "quick sticks" ticking their staccato rhythm . . . a terraced hillside cascading into a harbor choked with sampans and junks, flashes of blue water amid a riot of bobbing reds, blacks, and greens . . . an emaciated peasant aging into his thirties, brittle hair turning white, stomach empty but lungs filled with the fleeting satisfaction of an opium pipe. . . .

As the junk drew farther away from the British schooner, Ross glanced at the reverend, who stood at the rail, hands clasped as he whispered a private, undecipherable prayer to his God. His eyes were closed, yet Ross could feel in them a dark, zealous light.

Yes, he thought, *Outerbridge and his like are the true heathens in this land. And the gift they bear will likely come not as a savior but as a stern, unforgiving plague. And which plague will prove to be the deadlier?* he could not help but wonder. *Opium or the Cross?*

Turning back to the rail, Ross gave a slight shudder, and as if in reply, the boards of the deck creaked beneath his feet.

TWO FAMILIES BOUND
BY ONE MAGNIFICENT DESTINY

AMIDST THE RISE OF A WONDROUS EMPIRE, THE BALLINGERS AND THE MAGINNISES STRUGGLE IN THE THROES OF TREACHERY, BETRAYAL, AND FORBIDDEN PASSIONS AS AN AGE-OLD RETRIBUTION COMES DUE—AND ACROSS A BOUNDLESS OCEAN A RAGING WAR DIVIDES LIVES . . . AND LOVES

CONNOR MAGINNIS
The virile, headstrong son of a merchant, born into a world of poverty and hardship, he uses his looks and charms to survive on the shadowy streets of London. But he waits for the day he can clear his father's name . . . and exact his revenge upon the powerful family that ruined him.

ZOË BALLINGER
The beautiful, independent daughter of Lord Cedric Ballinger, she fights a battle for social reform until she succumbs to the age-old temptation of passion— and dares to fall irrevocably in love with the one man who could topple the Ballinger dynasty.

ROSS BALLINGER
The rugged, daring offspring of a prosperous merchant, he sets sail for Canton on an unforgettable journey of self-discovery into the heart and soul of the Celestial Empire—where a tragic war and the forbidden love of an Oriental beauty could spell his doom.

EDMUND BALLINGER
Forced to change his career after a sadistic twist of fate deprived his family of their rightful inheritance, he is struggling to forge his own mighty empire—

an empire his son, Ross, will one day rule. But few know the devastating price he paid for his success—and the shattering truth about his former partner.

GRAHAM MAGINNIS

Cruelly betrayed by his trusted friend and business partner, he has spent nearly two decades in a filthy London prison for a crime he didn't commit. Burning with hate, he will not rest until his good name has been cleared—and he is at long last reunited with his children.

LORD CEDRIC BALLINGER

Sole heir to the Ballinger fortune and estate, he guards the terrible secret his cousin Edmund has kept hidden for so many years. He would never expose the other man because of his loyalty and breeding—but an event Lord Cedric could never have predicted will soon force his hand.

EMELINE MAGINNIS

The gentle, delicate daughter Graham Maginnis never knew he had, she adores her older brother, Connor, and would risk anything for his welfare. Yet she is unaware of the consuming passions that drive him to deeds that could endanger them all.

MEI-LI

The lovely young niece of China's high commissioner, she makes the fatal mistake of losing her heart to valiant Ross Ballinger—a man sent to her embattled country on a mission of peace. Although she is promised in marriage to another, Mei-li's love tempts her to betray her own country's ancient empire.

BENEATH
THE
SKY

Paul Block

 Producers of **The First Americans,**
The Frontier Trilogy, and **The Holts.**

Book Creations Inc., Canaan, NY • *Lyle Kenyon Engel, Founder*

BANTAM BOOKS
NEW YORK • TORONTO • LONDON • SYDNEY • AUCKLAND

BENEATH THE SKY

*A Bantam Book / published by arrangement with
Book Creations Inc.*

Bantam edition / August 1993

*Produced by Book Creations Inc.
Lyle Kenyon Engel, Founder*

ISBN 0-553-56286-X

Published simultaneously in the United States and Canada

*Bantam Books are published by Bantam Books, a division of Bantam
Doubleday Dell Publishing Group, Inc. Its trademark, consisting
of the words "Bantam Books" and the portrayal of a rooster,
is Registered in U.S. Patent and Trademark Office and in other
countries. Marca Registrada. Bantam Books, 1540 Broadway,
New York, New York 10036.*

PRINTED IN THE UNITED STATES OF AMERICA

OPM   0 9 8 7 6 5 4 3 2 1

To my favorite travel agents—and parents—Estelle and Murray Block, who took me to forty-seven states, Canada, Mexico, Spain, and China and taught me that the greatest journey of all is that of the imagination.

```
── ──
─────
── ──
─────
```

Chên: The Shock

The shock brings good fortune.
Earthquake comes—oh, no!
Laughter is heard—ah, ha!
The quake terrifies all within a
    hundred miles,
Yet the superior man does not spill
    the sacrificial wine.

Tremor follows tremor.
Thus amid fear and quaking,
the superior man makes his house
    quiet and still
and searches his heart.

—I Ching

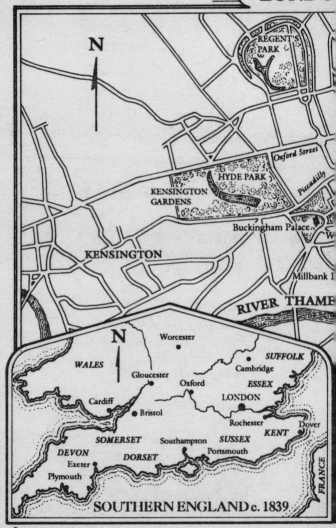

LONDO

N

REGENT'S
PARK

Oxford Street

HYDE PARK

Piccadilly

KENSINGTON
GARDENS

Buckingham Palace

KENSINGTON

Millbank I

RIVER THAME

N

Worcester

WALES

SUFFOLK

Cambridge

Gloucester

Oxford

ESSEX

Cardiff

LONDON

Bristol

Rochester

Dover

SOMERSET

Southampton

SUSSEX

KENT

DEVON

DORSET

Portsmouth

FRANCE

Exeter

Plymouth

SOUTHERN ENGLAND c. 1839

© BOOK CREATIONS INC. 1993

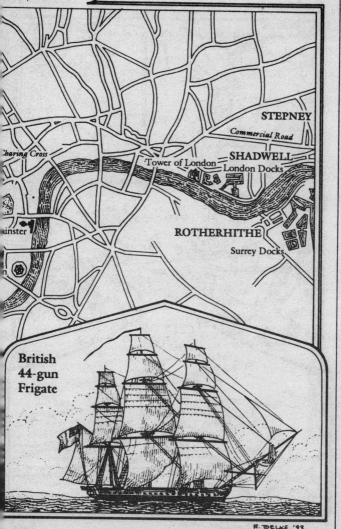

STEPNEY

Commercial Road

Charing Cross

Tower of London SHADWELL

London Docks

minster

ROTHERHITHE

Surrey Docks

British
44-gun
Frigate

R. TOELKE '93

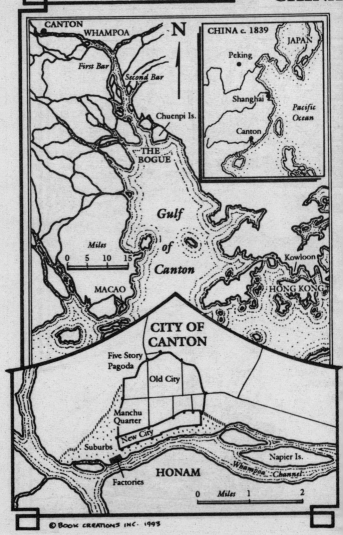

CHINA

CANTON
WHAMPOA
N

First Bar
Second Bar

Chuenpi Is.

THE BOGUE

CHINA c. 1839
JAPAN
Peking
Shanghai
Pacific Ocean
Canton

Gulf of Canton

Miles
0 5 10 15

MACAO

Kowloon

HONG KONG

CITY OF CANTON

Five Story Pagoda
Old City
Manchu Quarter
New City
Suburbs
Factories

HONAM

Napier Is.
Whampoa Channel

0 *Miles* 1 2

© BOOK CREATIONS INC. 1993

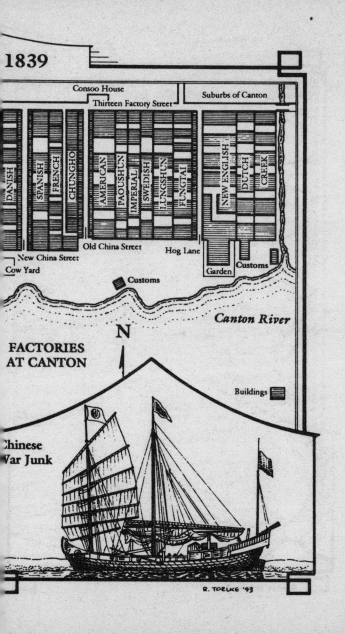

1839

Consoo House

Thirteen Factory Street

Suburbs of Canton

DANISH · SPANISH · FRENCH · CHUNGHO · AMERICAN · PAOUSHUN · IMPERIAL · SWEDISH · LLUNGSHUN · FUNGTAI · NEW ENGLISH · DUTCH · CREEK

Old China Street

Hog Lane

New China Street

Cow Yard

Garden

Customs

Customs

Canton River

N

FACTORIES AT CANTON

Buildings

Chinese War Junk

R. TOELKE '93

BENEATH
THE
SKY

Prologue

" 'Our cousins, then, were happy. Happy,
for they loved one another entirely; and on those
who do so love, I sometimes think that, barring
physical pain and extreme poverty, the ills of
life fall with but idle malice. Yes, they were
happy, in spite of the past and in defiance of
the future.'

" 'I am satisfied, then,' said my friend, 'and
your tale is fairly done!' "

As the last words of *Paul Clifford* faded on her lips,
Alexandrina dropped the novel onto the coverlet of her
bed and faced the window. Earlier that evening she had
requested that the drapes not be drawn, and though it was
too black outside to see any of the large oaks that graced
the lawns, she could hear the harsh wind rushing through
their branches.

Shivering against the cold, she again picked up the
leather-bound book, opened to the first page, and ran her
forefinger across the words written there by the author: *If
sometimes, Alexandrina, as thou go with me through these
pages, thou suffer thy humble companion to touch thy heart,
to guide thy hope, to excite thy terror, to gain thy tears—*

then is there a tie between thee and me which cannot readily be broken! I am now, as always, your most humble servant, Sir Edward Bulwer-Lytton, Bart.

Amused by the overly florid inscription, Alexandrina flipped past the preface to the story's opening: " 'It was a dark and stormy night . . . ' " she read aloud, smiling at the overly melodramatic image. " ' . . . the rain fell in torrents, except at occasional intervals when it was checked by a violent gust of wind which swept up the streets—for it is in London that our scene lies—rattling along the housetops and fiercely agitating the scanty flame of the lamps that struggled against the darkness.' "

Slapping the book closed yet again, she shook her head. "Dear Lehzen would never approve," she sighed, knowing how much her governess, Baroness Louise Lehzen, despised popular fiction like *Paul Clifford*. But she had to admit that there was something ominous, something foreboding in the air this unusually cold June night. Perhaps that was why she had felt too unsettled to read more than a few paragraphs of Bulwer-Lytton's novel and had jumped to the last page to see how it all turned out.

She looked down at the book, a present from her uncle Leopold on the occasion of her eighteenth birthday, just a month before. She briefly considered giving *Paul Clifford* one more try, then decided to put it aside and get some sleep. Placing it on the bedstand, she turned down the lamp and lay back against the pillows, listening as the wind rose and shook the heavy windowpanes.

◆ ◆ ◆

"Faster!" the man in the black wool cloak shouted, pounding the knob of his cane against the roof of the closed coach. In response, the coachman's whip cracked above the heads of the matched team of four gray geldings, and their gait quickened.

"It would do no good for us to be killed racing through

the streets like madmen on a night like this!" the second passenger called to his companion on the facing seat, shouting to be heard above the pounding of the wind and the horses' hooves. He clutched the brass handrail beside the door, stuggling to keep his seat in the bounding vehicle.

"You'll be fine, Dr. Howley! There's been enough dying already tonight for all England!" the first man called back. He smacked the cane smartly against the roof and yelled, *"Faster, man! There's no time to be lost!"*

"But Marquis Conyngham . . ." the man named Howley replied, his voice trailing off as he realized there was no slowing this coach on its harrowing journey through the windswept streets of London.

Pulling aside the leather window curtain, Howley peered outside into the predawn darkness and saw something go whipping past the vehicle—another carriage or perhaps only a branch. He quickly leaned back against the plush leather seat, clutching the handrail tighter as he closed his eyes and silently recited the Twenty-third Psalm, repeating one line in particular: *Yea, though I walk through the valley of the shadow of death, I will fear no evil: for Thou art with me; Thy rod and Thy staff they comfort me*. He tried to conjure up the image of a shepherd raising his staff to gather the flock to safety, but all he could envision was Marquis Conyngham banging his cane against the roof and exhorting the coachman to go faster.

" 'Yea, though I walk through the valley of the shadow of death, I will fear no evil: for Thou art with me . . . ' " he whispered, repeating, " 'Thou art with me . . . Thou art with me . . . Thou art with me . . . ' "

"Dr. Howley? Are you praying?" Conyngham inquired with barely concealed humor.

Opening his eyes, Howley gave his companion a petulant frown. "Isn't that what an archbishop's supposed to be doing on a night such as this?"

"Yes, your *reverence*," Conyngham replied with mock servility. "But for all England—not just for himself."

"It's not for myself that I'm praying. It's for those four gray steeds up front!" Glancing around the coach compartment, he added, "And for whichever carriage maker assembled this flimsy ark on wheels!"

As if in reply, the coach went careening around a corner and unceremoniously spilled Dr. William Howley, the archbishop of Canterbury, into the aisle between the two seats.

"Alexandrina?" a gentle voice called. "Are you awake, Alexandrina, my child?"

The young woman propped herself up on one elbow and stared with bleary eyes toward the doorway, in which stood a woman in a long dressing robe, her features framed in candlelight. "Mama, is that you?" She cocked her head and strained to make out the image.

The woman entered the room, shielding the candle's flame with her hand. "Yes, my dear. I'm sorry to awaken you so early, but—"

"What time is it?" Alexandrina asked abruptly, sitting up in bed.

"Almost six o'clock." Her mother placed the candle holder on the dresser nearest the bed and opened the clothes closet, from which she removed a long white dressing gown. "Here, this will do," she said, presenting it to her daughter.

"Whatever is going on?" The young woman felt a cold shiver run through her and clutched the gown to her chest. Outside, the wind buffeted the trees and set the windowpanes rattling.

"You must dress quickly. You have unexpected guests."

"Now?" she said incredulously. "At six in the morning?"

"The night maid told them you were in a sweet sleep and could not be disturbed, but they were insistent. I'm afraid Dr. Howley put a scare in the poor girl. You know how pompous he can be. He fixed her with that ominous eye of his and told her—" She raised her left hand, palm forward, and placed the right one on her breast, then intoned in as deep and bombastic a voice as she could muster: " 'We have come on state business, to which everything, even sleep, must give place.' " She giggled at her impersonation.

"The archbishop of Canterbury is here? To see me?"

"And with him is the lord chamberlain, Marquis Conyngham."

Alexandrina stood and began putting on the gown. "I must straighten my hair," she said a bit distractedly. "Could you send for the maid? And tell our guests I will see them in my sitting room presently."

"You look fine just as you are, Alexandrina," her mother assured her, coming closer and gently stroking the young woman's cheek. "And they've already been escorted to the sitting room."

"Are you certain I look presentable?" Alexandrina stared down at her gown as she tightened the sash around her trim waist. She gave a slight frown as she reached up and touched the long brown curls on her shoulder. "Shouldn't I take a moment to put up my—?"

"You mustn't keep them waiting. Not when they've come all this way on such a frightful morning."

The urgency in her mother's tone unsettled Alexandrina. She started to inquire further as to what was going on, then thought better of it. "I'm ready, Mama," she declared, placing her hand in her mother's and walking with her from the bedroom.

The hallway was still dark, but lamplight glowed from an open doorway. As they approached the sitting room, Alexandrina's mother squeezed her hand, then let go of it and pushed her forward. Alexandrina stepped into the doorway, saw the two men quickly rise from their chairs, then turned back to her mother with a questioning, almost frightened expression.

"It will be all right," the older woman promised. She gave a warm smile, and her eyes filled with tears. "Go ahead, my dear. They are waiting for you."

Alexandrina was certain that something was terribly wrong, but she drew in a calming breath and walked toward the visitors. The archbishop of Canterbury was not dressed in his formal attire, and he looked somehow smaller than she remembered him to be. He took a few steps, then abruptly halted and dropped to his knees, as if in prayer.

Marquis Conyngham came forward past his companion. Sweeping his black cloak off his right shoulder, he took the young woman's right hand and kissed it gently as he went down on one knee and declared, "The king is dead! Long live the queen!"

Alexandrina's jaw dropped in surprise, and she looked around for her mother, who was standing in the doorway, tears flowing down her cheeks.

"Unc-Uncle William?" the young woman stammered, turning back toward the marquis. "Uncle William has died?"

"Yes, Your Highness. King William passed peacefully in his sleep at twelve minutes past two this morning. His final thoughts were of you."

"That is true, Your Highness," Dr. Howley put in. "I was with him last night, and he spoke of you." The archbishop reached into the pocket of his cloak and withdrew a folded piece of paper. Opening it, he read, " 'I am sure that my niece will be a good woman and a good queen. It will touch every sailor's heart to have a girl queen to fight for. They'll be tattooing her face on their arms, and I'll be bound they'll all think she was christened after Nelson's ship.' " He looked up at Alexandrina. "I wrote it down as closely as I could recall."

The young woman nodded numbly. "Thank you. Uncle William was always very dear to me."

"At the end, the king's suffering was not great," the archbishop assured her. "He had directed his mind to religion and died in a perfectly happy, quiet state."

Realizing that the two men were still on their knees, she motioned them to rise, then said to the lord chamberlain, "Please express my feelings of condolence and sorrow to poor Queen Adelaide."

"Of course, Your Highness," Marquis Conyngham replied with a slight bow. "With your leave, we shall return to Windsor Castle with your message. After breakfast the Privy Council will assemble here at Kensington so that the royal oath may be administered and the declaration to the kingdom may be issued."

"Yes . . . of course," she whispered.

"Then by your leave . . ." Conyngham again kissed her hand and walked over to the doorway.

The archbishop of Canterbury approached and, performing his obeisance, declared, "May the good Lord protect you and give you strength, Queen A'_xandrina."

The new queen just stood shaking her head as the men started from the room. Suddenly she spun around and called after them, "No, not 'Queen Alexandrina.' "

The two men halted and looked back at her. "What was that, Your Highness?" Conyngham asked.

"I don't wish to be called Alexandrina. It is too . . . foreign for a British queen."

"Then what name shall you adopt?"

"Perhaps Elizabeth?" her mother asked, moving forward into the room. She turned to the two men and explained, "Her father, the duke of Kent, wanted to name her Elizabeth, but he acceded to the wishes of the tsar Alexander, who promised to stand sponsor if she were named Alexandrina."

"No, Mother, not Elizabeth." Alexandrina clasped her

hands together. "I wish to use my middle name—*your* name, Mother." She smiled at her mother, Princess Victoria Mary Louisa of Saxe-Coburg-Gotha.

"Victoria?" the two men asked in unison.

"Yes. Victoria."

"But Alexandrina . . ."

"Alexandrina Victoria," the young woman corrected her mother, "hereafter to be known as Queen Victoria."

"Yes," the archbishop put in enthusiastically. "A most English name for our new English queen."

The lord chamberlain lowered his head. "The proclamation shall be drawn up as you have indicated, Your Highness . . . Queen Victoria."

The two men hurried down the hall to their waiting coach.

"I . . . I didn't expect it to come so soon," the young queen blurted as she dropped onto the nearest seat, a plush red sofa.

"I'm so happy for you," her mother exclaimed, sitting beside her.

Queen Victoria looked up at her uncertainly. "Happy?" she muttered. "But I'm not ready. I'm too young for such a thing."

"You will do fine."

"But I don't know the first thing about—"

"There will be plenty of people to help you. And the prime minister, Lord Melbourne, will always be at your side." She stood and took her daughter's hands. "Now come along. So much must be done before the Privy Council arrives."

Alexandrina Victoria allowed herself to be led back to her room. Then her mother went off to summon the maids who would lay out the new queen's gown and to organize the staff so that Kensington Palace would be ready to receive the distinguished visitors who would administer the royal oath.

Alone in her room, the young woman stood at the window and watched the rising sun trying to break through the heavy bank of storm clouds that hung over London. "Alexandrina . . ." she whispered, touching a finger to the windowpane. "Alexandrina Victoria . . . Queen Victoria . . ."

Feeling her eyes well with tears, she wiped them with the back of her hand. She stood erect and straightened her shoulders. "Queen Victoria," she declared, listening to the wind and imagining that it was calling the name like the throngs of people who would line the streets on the day of her coronation. A resolute smile touched her lips, and she clasped her hands together.

Abruptly she turned from the window and walked to her writing desk. Her journal was still open to the latest entry, and she picked up her pen, dipped it in the inkwell, and jotted down the date: Tuesday, 20th June, 1837.

She paused a moment, staring down at the page. Finally she drew in a breath and began to write, speaking each word aloud as she did so:

"Since it has pleased Providence to place me in this station, I shall do my utmost to fulfill my duty towards my country; I am very young and perhaps in many, though not in all things, inexperienced, but I am sure that very few have more real goodwill and more real desire to do what is fit and right than I have. . . ."

Part One

ENGLAND
June 1838

I

Thursday, 28th June, 1838

I was awoke at four o'clock by the guns in the Park, and could not get much sleep afterwards on account of the noise of the people, bands, etc., etc. Got up at seven, feeling strong and well; the Park presented a curious spectacle, crowds of people up to Constitution Hill, soldiers, bands, etc. I dressed, having taken a little breakfast before I dressed, and a little after.

At half-past nine I went into the next room, dressed exactly in my House of Lords costume, and met Uncle Ernest, Charles, and Feodore (who had come a few minutes before into my dressing-room), Lady Lansdowne, Lady Normanby, the Duchess of Sutherland, and Lady Barham, all in their robes.

At ten I got into the State Coach with the Duchess of Sutherland and Lord Albemarle and we began our Progress.

It was a fine day, and the crowds of people exceeded what I have ever seen; many as there were the day I went to the City, it was nothing,

nothing to the multitudes, the millions of my loyal subjects, who were assembled in every spot to witness the Procession. Their good humour and excessive loyalty was beyond everything, and I really cannot say how proud I feel to be the Queen of such a Nation. I was alarmed at times for fear that the people would be crushed and squeezed on account of the tremendous rush and pressure.

—Journal of Queen Victoria

"Clo'! Clo'!" an old man barked, his voice muffled by the pile of clothing draped over his head and shoulders. "Good clothes to buy or sell!"

"Out o' my way, you old codger!" another voice shouted as the throng of people pushed forward down the street, nearly knocking the clothes man off his feet.

The old man staggered under the weight of his load, took another jarring blow from one of the passersby in the crowd hurrying en masse down Petticoat Lane, and came to rest against the stone wall of an adjacent building. "C-Clo'!" he shouted a final time in a weak, gravelly voice, then started to lower his bundle.

"Here, let me help you," a friendly voice offered, and a pair of strong hands reached up and relieved the man of his burden, lowering the heavy pile of clothing to the ground, still wet from the morning rain. "You really shouldn't be trying to walk about on a morning such as this," the stranger said, extending his hand. "My name's Connor Maginnis."

The clothes man was rubbing his shoulders, and he paused now and looked the stranger up and down, paying particular attention to his outfit. The young man named Connor was dressed in a neat but fairly modest brown suit that complemented his striking brown eyes and thick, dark hair. The old man reached forward with his gnarled hand and fingered the jacket lapel, then gave a low murmur of approval. Though not the outfit of a gentleman, this was by no means one of the secondhand suits bought by most commoners at the Old Clothes Exchange. The trousers were fashionably snug, though not so tight-fitting as to show the shape of the legs, like those favored by the dandies. And the outfit was nicely set off by a white waistcoat and modest cravat that held the upright points of the collar suitably close to the cheek.

Seeing that Connor was still offering his hand, the old man seized it with a surprisingly strong grip. "You lookin' for some new clothes?" he asked.

"No. Not today."

The old man harrumphed. " 'Not today,' he says. Just like all the rest." He stooped to count the items in his bundle, as if checking to make sure no one had stolen any off his back.

Connor chuckled. "Well, you can't expect to do very much business on Coronation Day. Perhaps if you were selling ginger beer or fish cakes or the like." He gestured down the lane toward the vendors who lined the buildings, selling everything from oysters to "coker-nuts" to trays heaped high with tiny sponge cakes. "But clothes? On a day such as this?"

"And why not?" the man demanded with a challenging frown. "Folks need clothes, Coronation Day or no."

"I'd say that folks are more concerned with the queen's clothing than their own this morning."

The clothes man grunted. "All a bunch o' foolishness, I say. She's been queen nigh onto a year already—since King William died last June."

"But the year of mourning is over; today's the coronation."

The man shrugged. "So what is that to me? She's just a young pup. Like yourself, I daresay."

"She's only nineteen. I'm twenty-one."

"Well, you'd best be off with you or miss the

procession. 'Tis for young folks like yourself. It means nothin' to the likes o' me."

Connor raised his forefinger to his brow as if in salute. "Well then, a good day to you, sir. And good luck with your clothes."

The man grunted again, but there was the trace of a smile as he went back to counting and sorting his clothes. Connor continued down the lane and heard the man take up his call: "Clo'! Clo'! Good clothes to buy or sell!"

◆◆◆

Ross Ballinger looked quite uncomfortable as he stood in his new blue cutaway suit under his stepmother's critical gaze.

"You're sure it's not too tight?" she asked.

"It's fine," he assured her, fidgeting slightly as she adjusted his white silk cravat.

"And the parricide—it isn't too stiff?" She touched the upturned points of his collar, commonly called a parricide because of a popular myth that a student who had taken up the fashion had returned from university in a collar so stiff that when he embraced his father, it cut the old man's throat.

"It's fine," Ross proclaimed for what seemed like the hundredth time.

"But it's going to be brutally hot at Westminster. You don't want to risk another—"

"It's been more than a year since I've had an *episode*." He emphasized the word they had used since he was a little boy to refer to his once-frequent bouts of asthma.

"Yes, but with all the commotion today, I just don't want anything untoward to happen—"

"I'm fine, Iphigenia," he said again. "And if the sight of our new queen takes my breath away, I promise to open my cravat."

"Are you teasing me?" She cuffed his chin.

"Of course." He stepped back a few feet and raised his arms to present himself. "Now tell me, how do I look?"

Iphigenia narrowed one eye and looked him up and down appraisingly. Ross was a handsome young man of eighteen who had worked hard to overcome the effects of asthma, which had left him frail and bedridden for much of his youth. During the past year he had grown considerably, and though he was still slim, he filled out his suit admirably. He was just over six feet tall, with blue eyes and sandy-brown hair, and while he exuded a calm, gentle air, it was complemented by a strong jawline and full, expressive mouth that suggested he was developing into a man to be reckoned with.

Iphigenia gave a purr of approval. "You look positively regal." She patted his wide, velvet lapels. "And this jacket brings out the color of your eyes. You're liable to go to the coronation a commoner and return home a king."

Feeling himself blush, Ross headed across the parlor toward the front door. "I'd best be going; Zoë is sending a carriage for me."

"You've plenty of time. I thought you might go over to the warehouse first. I'm sure your father would like to see how you look."

Ross frowned slightly; he knew that Edmund Ballinger was nursing a bitter disappointment at not having been invited to the coronation—an honor afforded the family of his cousin, Lord Cedric Ballinger. It was as the guest of Cedric's daughter, Zoë, that Ross would be at the event that all London—indeed all England—desired to attend.

"You *will* go to the warehouse, won't you?" Iphigenia stepped over to the door and held it open for him.

"I'm not sure that's a wise—"

"Promise Iphigenia that you will," she pressed with a coquettish pout.

Ross gave a slight sigh. "Of course, if you really wish."

"I do," she proclaimed, leaning forward to kiss the corner of his lips. "And you'll be polite to your uncle Tilford when you see him at the coronation?"

It was no secret that Ross—that all the Ballingers, in fact—intensely disliked Iphigenia's brother, who used every opportunity to capitalize on his tenuous connection to their family. Still, Ross knew that his stepmother doted on her younger brother, and he indicated with a nod that he would do as she requested.

"That's a good boy." She brushed a stray lock of hair off his forehead, turned him by the shoulders, and pointed him out the door.

Ross started down the brick walkway, then halted and looked back at Iphigenia, who stood in the doorway, her ample figure showing through her gauzy black dressing gown, her lush brunette hair hanging casually over one shoulder. Though at thirty-nine she could no longer be considered young, she wore her years well and seemed closer in age to her eighteen-year-old stepson than her forty-six-year-old husband. Ross could see why his father had been so smitten when they met only a few months after the death of Ross's mother almost ten years ago. And he could not help but wonder why his father now paid her so little attention.

"Hurry along," Iphigenia called, waving him away. "And tell Edmund not to be late for dinner."

Ross walked the few blocks between their modest home just off Commercial Road in Shadwell and the warehouse his father leased at the London Docks, just east of the Tower of London on the north bank of the Thames. It had rained earlier that morning; the sky was still overcast, and there was a bite to the air that caused Ross to raise his jacket collar. As the large brick building housing the family's import-export business loomed out of the mist, he noted that the paint was fading on the sign over the wide delivery doors. It had read Ballinger Trade Company for sixteen years, ever since Edmund had assumed full control of the Ballinger-Maginnis Import and Export Company following the conviction of his former partner, Graham Maginnis, on fraud and bribery charges.

The front door was unlocked, and as Ross let himself in, he closed his eyes briefly and inhaled the familiar, pungent odor of tea—the major import of Ballinger Trade. He passed quickly through the small entryway and into the cavernous room that dominated the building. It was darker than usual; none of the lamps had been turned on, and the soot-grimed windows filtered the muted sunlight. The room was divided into long rows of wooden chests, which were grouped in stacks as high as ten feet tall on the wide-plank floor. A network of ropes and pulleys hung from the iron beams of the ceiling, positioned over the stacks so that the heavier chests could be maneuvered down the rows and out the massive rear doors facing the docks.

Ross was surprised to find the room empty of workers. His father had given most of the employees a rare holiday in honor of the coronation but supposedly had kept a skeleton crew on hand to finish off-loading a Jardine, Matheson & Company schooner that had arrived the previous day. It would not be like him to have a change of heart and let the men off.

Ross was about to leave when he remembered that the front door had been unlocked, which would seem to indicate that his father was on hand. He started down one of the aisles until he could see the small office Edmund maintained at the back of the warehouse. Sure enough, a light was glowing behind the smoky glass window on the door.

Ross continued down the aisle, past the tall stacks of tea imported from China. Each chest was marked with a symbol, called a chop, that denoted the type of tea it contained, its quality, and the province of origin. Black tea was most popular since it held up better than the more delicate green tea, which was easily damaged by the moist sea air during the journey of four to six months. The greens were consequently far more expensive, since they had to be sealed in special lead-lined containers to maintain their quality.

Ross ran his hands along the chop marks, which he had learned by heart as a young boy. There was bohea and the more refined-tasting congou from Fukien, as well as the prized pekoe and the coarse, somewhat bitter twankay. Smaller, lead-lined chests held the delicate imperial and gunpowder greens from Chekiang, Anhwei, and Kiangsi.

Toward the rear of the warehouse were much longer, narrow crates of silk cloth, the majority of which would be transferred to ships bound for America, where it would be traded for tobacco and sugar. Smaller crates contained porcelain, lacquered boxes, and vermilion, which gave sealing wax the correct shade of red.

Approaching the office door, Ross raised his hand to knock but pulled back abruptly when he heard a strange squeal coming from the other side. His first thought was that his father was chasing a piglet around the small office, but then the squeal shifted into a woman's throaty sigh, accompanied by an even deeper moan that was indisputably Edmund's.

Ross felt a wave of nausea as he pivoted and staggered back against the wall beside the door. His throat was constricted, and he could not breathe. His body was rigid and unresponsive; though he willed himself away, he could not move from the wall, which was rhythmically pounding against his back in a crescendo that mirrored the moaning on the other side.

"No!" a voice wailed, and though it was unfamiliar and distorted, Ross realized it was his father's. "No! *No!*"

"Yes!" the woman cried as the pounding abruptly halted. "Yesssss . . ."

Ross stood there for a moment, struggling to calm his breathing. Perhaps it wasn't his father, he told himself, though he realized the foolishness of such a notion. And the certainty of who it was became undeniable when Edmund Ballinger said in his raspy, deep voice, "You'd best be out of here before the others come back. And nothing of this to anyone, mind you, or you'll be back on the street where I found you."

Ross cringed at what sounded like a sloppy kiss, followed by the clinking of coins.

"Now off with you. There's work to be done."

Suddenly Ross realized the awkwardness of his position, but before he could move, the office door opened and a woman came out. Shutting the door behind her, she turned and with a shock of recognition found herself staring at the son of her employer. Ross recognized the woman, as well. She was one of the crew of three charwomen who worked odd hours around the warehouse, handling the general cleaning duties. In her late twenties, she might have been considered modestly attractive were she not so unkempt and dirty. Her shapeless dress was of coarse muslin that once had been red but now was a faded, mottled brown. The threadbare garment had been torn and sewn numerous times and on the best of days would be considered disheveled. Today, following the activities in the cramped office, it looked even more rumpled and dreary than usual.

The woman—Ross thought he remembered her name as Clarissa—was clutching something against her breast, and as she glanced from him down to her hands, Ross caught a glimpse of several silver coins. When she raised her eyes toward him again, they were brimming with tears, and Ross could not tell if her expression of shame was due to what she and Ross's father had been doing or the disparity between the way she and Ross were dressed. But she looked so disconsolate that he wanted to reach out and comfort her. He parted his lips slightly, searching for something to say, but she abruptly hiked her skirt and scurried away down one of the aisles.

Ross waited until the woman disappeared into the supply room used by the charwomen, and then he faced

the closed office door, debating what to do. His breathing
was steady now, and he felt considerably calmer; still, he
thought it best not to present himself to his father, so he
turned on his heel and strode briskly across the room toward
the front door.

"*Ross!*" a voice boomed just as he was nearing the
entryway. "Is that you, boy?"

Halting, Ross heard the heavy footsteps of his father
coming up one of the aisles.

"What are you doing here, son?" Edmund called.

Ross turned to face his father, who appeared to have
just finished tucking in his shirt. He was not wearing his
waistcoat or suit jacket or even his cravat and collar.

"Is something wrong?" Edmund asked, his dark, bushy
eyebrows rising expectantly as he halted in front of Ross.
He was several inches shorter and far more muscular and
stocky than his son, whose features resembled his mother's.

Ross felt exceedingly nervous under his father's dark-
eyed gaze. "I . . . uh, Iphigenia wanted me to stop by before
going to . . ." The words trailed off, and he shifted uneasily
on his feet.

"Iphigenia sent you?" Edmund asked, one eye narrowing suspiciously.

Ross caught himself glancing toward the supply room
into which the charwoman had disappeared. He quickly
looked down, but not before his father realized what had
happened.

"Sent you to spy on me, I suppose," Edmund declared,
dark eyes smoldering as he clenched his hands into fists.

"No, Father." Ross's voice was a bare whisper as he
looked up at him. "It's just that I was getting ready to go
to Zoë's, and Iphigenia thought you might want to see how
my suit came out."

Edmund eyed him dubiously, then seemed to accept
the explanation. He fingered the seam along the right lapel.
"It's very fine. Who made it?"

"Henry Kleckner."

"I figured as much. You can't deny that their kind do excellent work. How much did he 'Jew' us for?"

"I'm not certain. I think about—"

"It doesn't matter," he cut in, waving off the question. "Twice what it's worth, no doubt. Every time one of those Jew tailors slips his thread through a needle's eye, we Christians end up paying through the nose." He chuckled at his attempt at humor.

"I would have gone to Mrs. Simmons, but Iphigenia thought that for today—"

"I don't want to hear about today." His scowl betrayed how bitter he felt about not having been invited to the coronation.

"I don't have to go. . . . I mean, if there's work you need done around here . . ." Ross looked around the warehouse, avoiding the room into which the woman had gone.

"No. Your cousin's expecting you to escort her."

"Zoë would understand."

Edmund shook his head. "Be off with you, now. I'm fine here by myself."

Ross wanted to ask where the other workers were but thought better of it and turned to leave.

"Ross . . ." his father called after him.

"Yes?" He halted at the door that led to the front entryway.

"I, uh . . ." He shifted uncomfortably. "Well, it's just that I was hoping you wouldn't mention anything to Iphigenia about . . ."

"Iphigenia? There's nothing to tell Iphigenia, is there?"

Edmund stared closely at his son for a long moment, then smiled broadly. "Of course there isn't." He approached again and clapped Ross on the shoulder. "You've gotten tall—become a man—without my even realizing it. That's why I've decided to send you to China."

Ross's jaw dropped. "Wh-What?"

"China, son. Haven't you been begging to go overseas for the past couple of years?"

"Yes, but I had no idea—"

"You're eighteen now." He waved a hand back toward the warehouse. "Someday all this will be yours. I'd say it's about time you got your feet wet—though not the rest of you, I hope."

"But China?" Ross asked eagerly. "When?"

"In a couple of months. There's much preparation to be done if you're going to be the representative for Ballinger Trade in Canton next spring. That is, if you want to go."

"Want to? Of course I do. But why now? You've always said I had to wait until I was twenty-one."

Edmund looked him up and down. "I guess I realized just how much you've grown . . . what a man you've become."

Ross straightened with pride. "You won't be sorry, Father."

Carefully measuring his words, Edmund replied, "I'm sure I won't."

The young man started from the room again, then halted just inside the entryway and looked back a bit uncertainly. "You really mean it, don't you?"

"About being a man?"

"About letting me go to China."

"Provided between now and August you don't do anything stupid—" he paused for effect "—anything to show me that you're still a boy. I wouldn't want to send a boy—a stepmama's boy—to China."

Looking beyond his father, Ross saw Clarissa in the doorway of the supply room. This time he did not avert his gaze but fixed it first on the woman and then Edmund. He boldly declared, "You don't have to worry about me, Father. Send me to China and I'll prove that Ross Ballinger is no mama's boy." He strode quickly from the building.

II

◆━◆━◆━◆━◆━◆━◆━◆━◆━◆━◆━◆━◆

Zoë Ballinger turned in place in front of the floor-length mirror in her dressing room, critically eyeing how she filled her coronation gown. A tight-laced corset narrowed her already trim waist, and the full skirt and puffed sleeves created the fashionable hourglass effect. Her gown had been hand tailored from Chinese gold-brocaded silk, with a flounce of ruffled blond lace at the hem. Her shoulders were bare but covered by a mantelet of white silk trimmed with ermine.

In the mirror, Zoë saw her eldest brother standing in the doorway, frowning impatiently. Austin Ballinger was a heavyset man of twenty-seven with long brown hair, parted in the middle and pulled to the back of his neck, and a full, reddish-brown beard. His dark eyes were narrowly set and just now appeared even more stern and critical than usual.

"You're just being difficult," he said, continuing a conversation they had been having all morning. "Everyone thinks Bertie a wonderful catch . . . charming, wealthy, and not too bad to look at, or so the young women seem to think."

"I know he's handsome," Zoë conceded. "But really, Austin, you must admit that Bertrand Cummington is

25

something of a fop." Turning her attention back to her outfit, she adjusted the diamond broach on the bodice.

Austin stepped into his younger sister's dressing room. "A fop?" He forced a laugh. "And your cousin Ross isn't?" Rocking back and forth on his heels, he thrust his thumbs into the pockets of his black waistcoat; he had not yet put on the formal dress coat that he would wear to Westminster Abbey.

"Ross is a sweetheart," Zoë declared, repositioning the mantelet on her shoulders. "And he's *your* cousin, too."

"People will get the wrong idea. They'll be thinking you and Ross are . . . well, more than mere cousins."

Zoë spun around, glowering at her brother. "And what if we are?"

Taken aback, Austin sputtered, "You're cousins, for chrisakes."

"Second cousins."

"Surely you've no intentions toward Ross. He's nothing but a sickly little whelp with no future but that of a common *merchant*." He spat out the word as if it were diseased.

"That's not his fault," she replied, then shook her head and declared, "as if there's something wrong with being a merchant. Why, Edmund's ships sail all over the world, from the Indies to Africa to the Orient."

"They aren't Edmund's ships—he leases space from others. And even if Edmund had a whole fleet, that wouldn't make it proper for you to be cavorting with the likes of Ross Ballinger—a mere boy."

"You'd rather I cavorted with an old lecher like Bertrand Cummington?" Turning her back on him, she started pinning up her long auburn hair.

"A *lecher*? Bertie's nothing of the sort. And he's barely thirty."

"An exceedingly old and foppish thirty," Zoë commented.

"The only thing old about Bertie is his pedigree. Lord

Henry and Lady Virginia Cummington are among the most respected—"

"I'm attending the coronation with Ross. It's settled, so there's no point in your haranguing me like this."

Austin's features softened. Lightly stroking his beard, he moved up behind Zoë and said in a soft, measured voice, "Please don't misunderstand my motives. Of course there's nothing wrong with having Cousin Ross escort you to the Abbey. But Bertie will be there, as well, and you know how fond he is of you. I only thought that if you could find it in your heart to show him a bit of attention, it might go a long way toward dispelling any false rumors about your intentions toward Ross."

"My intentions are my own business."

"Of course they are. But—"

"And as much could be said about your intentions toward our *dear* Lenora."

Austin's jaw dropped, and for a moment he could not speak.

Zoë grinned up at him in the mirror. "Don't play the innocent. I've seen the looks that pass between the two of you. So has Julian," she added, referring to their twenty-three-year-old brother.

"Me? And Lenora? Why, she . . . she's . . ."

"Tilford's wife?" Zoë chuckled. "Since when has that stopped Lenora?"

"There's nothing between Lenora and me!" Austin exclaimed. "Nothing at all!"

"Perhaps not as yet. But that woman has set her sights on you, mark my words."

"And Ross hasn't on you?" Austin asked, trying to turn the subject back to his sister's situation.

"Of course not. We're friends, nothing more."

"So why not give Bertie a chance?"

"Bertrand Cummington doesn't interest me."

"Is there anyone who does?"

Zoë gave a shrugging sigh. "Not as yet. Perhaps one day."

"You'll be an old maiden aunt before you find a man who's able to meet your unrealistic expectations."

"I'm only nineteen."

"Which is why I worry about you." Placing a hand on her shoulder, he gave a comforting squeeze. "At nineteen you ought to be thinking about marriage and children. You should be spending your time with eligible young bachelors and not with our merchant-class cousin, no matter how well-intentioned, no matter how much of a *sweetheart*"— he mimicked her voice—"he may be."

"Don't fret so about me." Turning, she pressed her palms against her brother's chest, as if to push him from the room. "Now be off with you; Ross will be here soon, and I'm nowhere near ready."

"It's not just me who worries about you, Zoë. It's Mother and Fa—"

"It's *you*, Austin, and you know it. You're afraid that Julian or I may do something scandalous and ruin your chance of one day winning a seat in Parliament." She paused, waiting for him to deny the accusation. When he did not, she continued, "Well, our brother will soon be sailing for India, and as for me, you needn't worry about a scandal. Ross and I really *are* only friends, and though I'm not keen on your friend Bertie, I'm sure the man I end up with will be equally *acceptable*."

Austin raised his hands in protest. "You misinterpret my intentions—"

"Run along now, Austin. I've a coronation to get ready for." She pushed him toward the hall.

Austin gave a slight bow of defeat. "I'll send word when your escort arrives."

"I want you to be polite to Ross when he gets here."

"Don't worry about me. I'll make sure your little *fop*— I mean friend—is properly attended."

Zoë was about to lash back at him, but Austin had already disappeared down the hall. Shaking her head in dismay, she turned to the mirror and stood looking at herself. She was indeed strikingly beautiful— tall and graceful, with a lithe figure and classic features—yet she was not pleased by what she saw. She never was. Her cheeks were a bit too prominent and high, her jawline a touch too firm. But her skin was smooth and clear, and her eyes . . . yes, she was more than satisfied with her eyes.

Of Cedric and Sybil Ballinger's three children, only Zoë had Grandfather William's green eyes— not hazel, but a striking emerald green that was both mesmerizing and disconcerting, to Zoë as well as to anyone on whom she fixed her gaze. Something in those deep, impenetrable eyes told her she must not allow her life to fall into comfortable routine. She must not settle for the likes of Bertrand Cummington but must wait for someone exciting— scandalous, even. She must await the man who could gaze into those penetrating green eyes, into that deep abiding soul, and not fear the depths of the darkness, the brilliance of the light that lay within.

Less than a mile away, Connor Maginnis joined the crowd hurrying down Petticoat Lane toward one of the larger streets along which Queen Victoria's procession would pass. Despite the persistent threat of rain, the street vendors—at least those who sold food and drink—were doing brisk business, with passersby snatching up the assorted cakes and fried fish that were the staples in this most popular of the street markets. Most vendors merely stood beside their stands, heads bobbing cheerfully as they exchanged food for coin. Some of the more enterprising went among the crowd, enticing people toward their stands with cries of "Lemonade! Raspberryade! Ha'penny a glass! Ha'penny a glass! Sparkling lemonade!"

The sellers of items such as penny scissors and pocket knives, pencils and steel pens, stockings, stationery, sponges, and "chewl-ry" were not faring nearly so well. In fact, most of them appeared to be asleep at their stands or sagely meditating on the smoke curling up from their pipes. But should anyone indicate, even by a glance, that he might be interested in the proffered goods, the vendor would be on his feet at once, diligent and attentive and promising "the best goods and price in all London—indeed, in all Her Majesty's empire!"

Connor was nearing the corner that marked the end of the Petticoat Lane business district when he saw that much of the crowd had come to a halt around something in the street. As he neared the area, he caught glimpses of what seemed to be a fight in the middle of a ring formed by curious onlookers. Some jostled for a better view, while the less interested surged around the sides and continued down the street.

Connor moved through the crowd toward the source of the commotion. All around him, women in tattered dresses and men in threadbare suits raised their fists and cheered as they egged on the combatants, who could not be discerned through the press of people. At a small pub nearby, the somewhat better-dressed patrons set aside their whiskey and beer and poured outside to see what was going on.

"Black his eye!" one particularly disheveled old Londoner yelled, foamy yellow spittle glazing his bristly chin. He smacked fist against palm, then leaned over and spat a gob of tobacco juice onto the hard-packed ground.

Connor stepped to the side to avoid the mess, then continued forward, drawn by the high-pitched squeal of whoever it was who was taking the beating—one of the local street women or perhaps a child.

"Damn Jew boy!" shouted another voice in the crowd. "Kill the damn Jew!"

Connor knew at once that the object of derision was

one of the many young Jewish street sellers who frequented the district, hawking their wares from small pushcarts or, in the case of the poorest of the lot, from canvas sacks slung over their shoulders.

As Connor pressed forward, he saw several of the onlookers clutching oranges, while other pieces of the fruit lay squashed on the ground. The boy being assaulted was obviously a costermonger of fruit, and the crowd had seized the opportunity to divest him of his wares.

"Get out o' the damn way!" a burly, relatively well-dressed man exclaimed as Connor pushed past him to the front of the crowd.

Connor glowered at the man, whose broad, flat face was a mass of veins bursting from mottled red skin. When the man grabbed Connor's sleeve to haul him aside, Connor jerked his arm free and stepped into the clearing formed by the crowd surrounding the combatants. The boy who was the object of the attack was in his early teens. He had curly brown hair that was badly tousled just now, and he wore an old but well-kept corduroy suit of the square-cut style favored by his class. His three attackers were barefoot and far more poorly dressed; Connor took them for young Irish toughs. They had the Jewish boy squatting on the muddy ground and were kicking him relentlessly, all the while shouting, "Jew bastard!" "Clipped Dick!" and "Wooden Shoe!" This last epithet had nothing to do with Jewish attire but was a popular rhyming slang for "Jew"—an indication of the widespread prejudice against anything considered foreign.

Though Connor was American by birth, his ancestry was Scots-Irish, and he had lived in England long enough to be considered a native. Still, he often felt like an outsider, which made him naturally sympathetic to the Jewish lad, who probably had been born right here in London but would always be a foreigner, an outcast in his own land. And Connor could never abide someone's being ganged up against, no matter the cause—even if it were overcharging or passing off rotten fruit as good. More than likely the Irish toughs were simply moving in on the Jewish boy's territory, and today they were driving home the point that they wanted the "Wooden Shoe" costermonger to clear out for good. It was a sight becoming all too familiar on the streets of London, with the more recent arrivals, the poorer Irish, seeking to supplant the Jews, who formerly had a monopoly on such trade in many of the districts.

"Get up and fight!" one of the toughs bleated as he kicked the squatting boy in the back, almost knocking him over. The boy gripped his canvas sack more tightly and lowered his head between his arms.

The other two toughs grabbed hold of the sack and tried to yank it off the boy's shoulder. Several more oranges and a lemon spilled out, and as the boy reached to grab them, the sack slipped from his shoulder and was wrenched away. A moment later it was tossed into the crowd and immediately torn open, the contents snatched up by eager, clutching hands.

"Enough of that!" Connor Maginnis shouted, moving into the center of the clearing.

The young toughs glanced up, then returned to their business, one of them taking hold of the boy's curly hair and twisting it, forcing him onto his back.

"You heard me! Enough!" Connor dashed forward and clasped a powerful hand around the tough's forearm until he released his grip on the hair.

"Wha' the hell?" a voice in the crowd shouted. "Leave 'em to their sport!"

Connor felt someone grab the back of his brown jacket, and he spun around to see the burly man who had argued with him before.

" 'Tis none o' yer damn business!" the man blared, staring up at Connor, who was a good bit taller and, at twenty-one, perhaps half his age.

Connor jerked his jacket free, and when the man again grabbed at him, he pushed the fellow back, not roughly but enough to warn him off. But the man would not be dissuaded; he took one step back and swung wildly at Connor's head. The younger man easily ducked the blow and, straightening up, drove his right fist into the man's ample belly, doubling him over.

An excited cry came from the crowd, and Connor knew that if he did not make quick work of the fellow, a brawl would break out. He waited until the man stopped sputtering and gasping for air. Then, when the man straightened up and moved in for the attack with both fists raised, Connor planted his feet firmly, drew back his right arm, and feinting to the left, delivered a crushing blow to the man's temple. The punch staggered him, and he went down on his knees, swaying left and right before finally crumpling to the ground.

A great cheer went up; apparently the crowd did not much care who was fighting or why, so long as there was some action to see. Connor noticed that his own fight had drawn the attention of the young toughs, who for the moment seemed to have forgotten their prey. Using their lapse to his advantage, Connor stepped toward them and shouted, "Be gone with you! Leave the fellow alone now!"

The three did not react other than to stare at one another, as if wondering what they should do. Connor took hold of the nearest one's collar and pushed him toward the crowd. "Get going! The lot of you!"

The other two hesitated. Then one of them glanced down at the boy curled up on the ground. Turning to his companions, he muttered, "Come on. We're done here." He gave Connor a smirk, then stalked off with his mates into the crowd, with many of the onlookers slapping them on their backs as they passed.

The crowd stirred, tiring of the spectacle. Connor spied the Jewish boy's canvas sack lying in a tattered heap near the edge of the crowd, and he snatched it up and took it back to where the boy was lying. Kneeling beside him, he clasped the lad's arm. "It's over. You can get up now." Realizing the boy was sobbing into his sleeve, Connor handed him the sack and said, "Wipe your face on this."

The boy did as he was told, then with Connor's assistance struggled to his feet. People paid him little attention now as they continued their march down Petticoat Lane toward the coronation route. The incident seemed all but forgotten; even the man lying on the sidewalk where Connor had downed him drew little reaction from the passersby.

The boy was choking back his tears, trying his best not to look childish. He allowed Connor to smooth his hair and even smiled faintly when his benefactor commented, "It's nothing to be ashamed of. I cried myself the last time a trio of Irishmen beat me up."

"Th-Thank you," the boy stammered.

He waved off the thanks. "Forget it. Are you injured?"

"I'm all right. They . . . didn't really hurt me."

"That's good. I'm sorry I couldn't save your goods. Did you lose much?"

Frowning bitterly, the boy looked down at the empty sack, which hung limply from his hands. "My whole stock. Near twenty shillings."

Connor straightened the lad's jacket and brushed off some of the mud, then adjusted his own cravat and collar. He noted the boy was wearing a coarse, collarless shirt several sizes too large, probably purchased at one of the stalls along the lane or perhaps at the nearby Old Clothes Exchange.

Just then the man lying on the ground nearby began to rouse, and Connor said, "Come on. Let's be off before that brute tries to finish what he started." He led the boy back into the business district of Petticoat Lane. After they had gone several blocks, he asked, "You've a family?"

"Just my grandfather, and he's mostly laid up in bed. He helps with the sellin' when he can."

"Has he got enough stock money put aside for a new sack of goods?"

The boy halted, looked curiously at Connor, and asked, "You know a lot about mongerin'. But you don't look like one."

Connor glanced down at himself. "The suit, eh? Well, don't let such things fool you. I've done my share of mongering. Still do when I have to."

"You ain't a Jew, though?" the boy asked, more a statement than a question. When Connor shook his head, the boy's eyes narrowed suspiciously. "Irish, then?"

"No. American," Connor said simply.

"I never seen me an American street monger. Nor an American, I suppose. What're you doin' here?"

Connor placed his hand on the boy's shoulder. "This is my home. My father was from Edinburgh, my mother from New York. I was born there, but we moved to London soon after. Then they . . . they died. I've made my living on the streets ever since."

They continued walking. Seeing how the boy kept glancing over at his well-tailored brown suit, Connor said, "Like I told you, don't let these clothes fool you. In my line of work, a fellow needs a good outfit."

"What do you sell?" the boy asked cautiously.

Connor's eyes brightened. "Let's just say I've learned there are things to be sold that don't need much of a stake, other than a fancy suit and a smile."

"You mean, you're a fancy man?" The boy's voice was filled with wonder. "It's all right; I'm old enough to know about those things."

Halting, Connor turned to look at him. "Exactly how old *are* you?"

The boy drew himself up tall. "Sixteen . . . in November."

"And your name?"

"Mose. . . . Mose Levison."

"Well, Mose, I'm Connor Maginnis, and I suppose when I was your age I knew as much. But I wouldn't have called someone a fancy man—at least not to his face."

Mose's face blanched. "I'm sorry. I didn't mean—"

Connor laughed and clapped him on the back. "Think nothing of it."

"But it ain't my business how you earn—"

"I said forget about it. Let's just say I'm a monger of a different sort. . . . Now, you look a mite hungry. How about a booler?"

The boy's eyes brightened. "Well, I ain't really eaten. But I wouldn't want you—"

"A booler it is, then." Coming to a halt in front of a stand that offered all sorts of cakes and cookies, Connor said to the middle-aged woman working it, "A booler for the lad. Better serve up two; I'm a bit famished myself."

The woman took a small piece of newspaper and placed on it two thin yellow cakes made from egg, flour, and candied lemon, the coloring enhanced with a dash of saffron. She handed them to Connor, who gave her a penny and thanked her. After serving one of the cakes to Mose, he quickly devoured the other in a single huge bite.

"Thank you," the boy told him as he nibbled on his cake, savoring it slowly.

As they began to walk again, Connor asked, "About that stock of yours—has your grandfather got enough money put aside to stake you to another sack?"

Mose looked down. "We spent the last we had on that fruit. We won't have any more till the end of the week. He put all our savings into commemoratives."

"Commemoratives?"

"You know . . . of the queen. We stand to make a good profit when we sell 'em."

Connor looked at him curiously. "So what were you

doing with those oranges? I'd think Coronation Day, with such crowds all over London, would be the best time to be selling commemoratives."

"We ain't got 'em yet. We bought 'em on speculation. They're booklets tellin' all the news of today's events. They'll be printed up tomorrow, and I'll sell 'em to the Saturday crowds at the park."

"I see."

"Is that what you're doin'?" Mose asked, cocking his head and examining Connor's outfit more closely. "Are you attendin' the coronation?"

Connor couldn't help but laugh. "Me? At Westminster Abbey? I should think not. I was hoping one of the queen's Ladies of the Bedchamber would send me a personal invitation, but . . ." He gave a sly wink. "No, a coronation's no place for a fancy man like me."

"She'll be passin' by in the state coach on the way to the Abbey," Mose said, his expression growing more animated. "And after the coronation's finished, she'll be ridin' back through the streets wearin' her crown and carryin' the scepter and orb."

Connor snapped his fingers. "I'll tell you what. Why don't we head over to Hyde Park Corner; the procession is going right past there. Then, if you come along with me for a while, I think I know a way to get you a fresh stake."

"You do?"

"I'd loan you the money myself, but a few pennies for boolers is all I've got. But I know someone who's got a lot more than a few pennies . . . a whole lot more."

"Are you sure?" The boy looked up expectantly at his benefactor.

"Just stick with me, Mose. We'll get that sack filled, and then some. Just do exactly what I tell you." He gripped the boy's sleeve and motioned him down the street. "Now come along. The first rule of a fancy man is to never keep a woman waiting. Especially the queen of England."

III

Thursday, 28th June, 1838

I reached the Abbey amid deafening cheers at a little after half-past eleven; I first went into a robing-room quite close to the entrance where I found my eight train-bearers: Lady Caroline Lennox, Lady Adelaide Paget, Lady Mary Talbot, Lady Fanny Cowper, Lady Wilhelmina Stanhope, Lady Anne Fitzwilliam, Lady Mary Grimston, and Lady Louisa Jenkinson—all dressed alike and beautifully in white satin and silver tissue with wreaths of silver corn-ears in front, and a small one of pink roses round the plait behind, and pink roses in the trimming of the dresses.

After putting on my mantle, and the young ladies having properly got hold of it and Lord Conyngham holding the end of it, I left the robing-room and the Procession began. The sight was splendid, the bank of Peeresses quite beautiful all in their robes, and the Peers on the other side. My young train-bearers were always near me, and helped me whenever I wanted anything. The Bishop of Durham stood on the side near me, but he was, as Lord Melbourne told me,

*remarkably maladroit, and never could tell me
what was to take place. At the beginning of the
Anthem I retired to St. Edward's Chapel, a dark
small place immediately behind the Altar, with
my ladies and train-bearers—took off my crimson
robe and kirtle, and put on the supertunica of
cloth of gold, also in the shape of a kirtle, which
was put over a singular sort of little gown of linen
trimmed with lace; I also took off my circlet of
diamonds and then proceeded bareheaded into
the Abbey; I was then seated upon St. Edward's
chair, where the Dalmatic robe was clasped
round me by the Lord Great Chamberlain.
Then followed all the various things, and last
(of those things) the Crown being placed on my
head—which was, I must own, a most beautiful
impressive moment—all the Peers and Peeresses
put on their coronets at the same instant.*

*My excellent Lord Melbourne, who stood
very close to me throughout the whole ceremony,
was completely overcome at this moment, and
very much affected; he gave me such a
kind, and I may say, fatherly look. The
shouts, which were very great, the drums, the
trumpets, the firing of the guns, all at the same
instant, rendered the spectacle most imposing.*

—Journal of Queen Victoria

As the crown was lowered onto the young queen's head, two banks of trumpeters raised their horns and sounded the fanfare, and a thunderous cheer went up from the multitude assembled within Westminster Abbey. The drums began a low, rumbling roll that grew in intensity, then abruptly cut off as the trumpeters played another fanfare, followed almost immediately by a series of loud explosions that shook the immense hall. The shock stunned the crowd into silence, but as the deafening roar trailed off, it was replaced by the muffled cry of the great hordes of people gathered outside as they shouted and sang "God Save the Queen" to their new sovereign, whose coronation had been proclaimed by the cannon blasts. Hearing the exclamations of the commoners for their queen, the audience again burst into cheering applause.

Ross Ballinger felt a hand grab his and grip it tightly, and he turned to his cousin Zoë.

"She's so beautiful!" Zoë exclaimed, leaning close and practically shouting into his ear so that he could hear her above the joyous din.

"Yes, she is!" he agreed, gazing up at the queen, who raised the heavy scepter to accept the accolade of the crowd. Indeed she looked beautiful—angelic, even—with the Dalmatic robe of gold cloth lined with ermine hanging over her gold supertunica and with the Crown of State on her head. The newly fashioned crown was encrusted with the historic jewels of the Imperial Crown, which had proved too large for Victoria's head. It glittered not only with diamonds and pearls but with a pair of sapphires, one worn by Edward the Confessor and the other by James II when he fled England, and with the great Black Prince's Ruby, worn in Henry V's helmet crown at Agincourt.

The peers and peeresses, seated in facing rows in front of the throne, had donned their diamond coronets at the same moment that Victoria was crowned, and Ross noted that the crisscrossing beams of light that reflected off all those jewels created a silent fireworks display. Seeing a slight commotion among the peers, he nudged his cousin and directed her attention to where an elderly man apparently had fallen asleep.

"It's old Lord Glenelg," she exclaimed, suppressing a giggle. "He's always dozing off."

Just then Lord Glenelg tottered forward, and his heavy jeweled headpiece fell off and went clattering to the floor.

His head snapped up, and as he blinked his bleary eyes and tried to focus, he blurted, "Oh! I have lost my nightcap!" His voice carried through much of the hall, and the resulting titter of laughter spread quickly, fueled by Glenelg's gasp of embarrassment upon realizing where he was and his subsequent clumsy attempts to retrieve the coronet from under the seat in front of him.

Victoria gave no hint of having noticed the incident but sat patiently while the peers went forward to pay her homage. As they ascended the steps to the throne, she leaned forward slightly so each in turn could touch the Crown of State before kneeling and kissing her ring.

A tall, silver-haired man rose from his seat and approached the steps, where a portly woman joined him.

"There's your father!" Ross exclaimed. "And Sybil!"

"Lady Sybil and Lord Cedric Ballinger," the herald announced. They mounted the steps, touched the crown, and paid homage to their queen, Cedric kneeling somewhat clumsily to kiss the ring while his wife executed a perfect curtsy.

When the couple was back down the steps, Ross faced Zoë, then looked beyond her at his other relatives—his older cousins Austin and Julian, his uncle Tilford York, and Tilford's young wife, Lenora. The expression of pride was unmistakable on the faces of Cedric's two sons. Tilford's look was more one of smugness at being somehow special because of his relationship to the Ballinger family and his position as a courtier in Buckingham Palace—a position secured for him by Cedric after Tilford's sister, Iphigenia, had married Ross's father.

Lenora York had an equally explicit expression, but it had little to do with pride and everything to do with passion—and just now it was directed at Austin, who was seated beside her but seemed oblivious to her hungry gaze. An attractive, well-endowed blonde of twenty-five, she was twelve years younger than her husband—and at least twice as smart and cunning, Ross figured. It was no secret that she strayed often from her marital bed; she had even tried her charms on Ross, who had made it clear that he viewed as quite unseemly any such relationship with an aunt—albeit such a young and attractive one. Apparently now she was setting her sights on Austin.

"Don't they look divine?" Zoë asked, catching Ross's attention with her warm green eyes. She was far and away Ross's favorite cousin. He considered her eldest brother, Austin, an arrogant boor, while Julian was a bit too showy and something of a dandy. "It's a shame your family isn't here to see them."

"My father? Sit in the commoners' section? And with Tilford up here with the invited guests? He'd rather be dead first."

"My father could have arranged a couple of more invitations," she pointed out.

Ross shook his head emphatically. "You know how Edmund is about these things—he took it as a personal slight that he wasn't invited by Queen Victoria. Anyway, it would have devastated him to see your father up there with the queen."

"He still holds a grudge, then."

"Not against Cedric, really. But yes, against his father for losing the title in the first place." He did not have to repeat the story; everyone in the family knew how Edmund's father, James, had scandalized the family with his notorious, much-publicized affair with a married French actress, after which he had been disinherited, the family title and fortune falling to his younger brother, William, and later to William's son, Cedric. That left James's son, Edmund, forced to earn his living in the import-export trade, feeling all the while that he had been cheated out of his rightful inheritance.

"I'm sorry," she told him, and he knew she meant it.

"It isn't your fault. It's . . . fate, I suppose." Leaning

closer, he squeezed her hand. "And if it hadn't happened, I might never have been given a chance to see the world."

She looked up at him curiously. "What do you mean?"

Ross drew in a breath, his grin broadening. "Father's finally agreed to send me to China."

"China?" she said aghast.

"I leave in August. I'll be representing Ballinger Trade in Canton next spring."

"I know you've always wanted to go abroad, but wasn't Edmund insisting you wait until you turned twenty-one?"

"It seems he's changed his mind."

"I'd always thought it would be Paris or Rome—or maybe even New York. But China?" she said skeptically. "It's so far away."

"Not really. Britons go all the time." Seeing her less-than-exuberant expression, he asked, "Aren't you happy for me, Zoë?"

She forced a smile. "Yes, of course, Ross. But I've gotten used to having you around. A trip to China—who knows how long that might take?"

"It could be a year or more. But I'll write often."

"And so will I." Suddenly her expression brightened. "At least you won't be completely alone. There'll be another Ballinger in the Orient."

"Who?"

"Julian. He's just received his orders; he'll be sailing for Calcutta next month. Perhaps you'll run into him along the way."

Ross looked beyond Zoë to her brother. At twenty-three, Julian was the image of a naval lieutenant in his dark-blue dress suit with gold piping. He sat ramrod straight, his jaw firmly set, his dark mustache trimmed just above the lip. His hands were held rigid at his sides, his eyes fixed almost without blinking on the proceedings at the front of the nave, where the long procession of peers and peeresses was still making its way to the throne to give homage to the queen.

"Perhaps," Ross replied. "Of course the Orient's a very large place."

"But if you put in at Calcutta en route, you can seek out his ship."

"And that I promise to do," he declared, masking his lack of enthusiasm. "It would be good to see someone from home."

A collective gasp from the crowd drew their attention to a commotion at the front of the hall. One of the peers had slipped while ascending the steps to the throne and had fallen back down in a tumble of white silk stockings, red velvet robe, and ermine train.

"It's poor Lord Rolle," Zoë said as two courtiers helped the aged man to his feet. "He must be past eighty and dreadfully infirm."

Lord Rolle did not seem hurt and again moved toward the steps. But there was a second gasp from the crowd, for the young queen had risen from her throne and was now starting down the steps so that the old gentleman would not have to climb them again. When the lord chamberlain signaled her that such an action was not appropriate for a queen, she exclaimed, "May I not get up and meet him?" She continued down the steps and joined Lord Rolle at the floor of the nave, to cheers of approval from the crowd.

As soon as the last of the peers and peeresses had paid homage, the young queen left the throne and removed her crown so that she could receive the Sacrament. As she knelt at the altar, a ray of sunlight came through one of the high windows and illuminated her bare head, causing her mother to burst into tears. The queen slowly rose and, taking Lord Melbourne's arm, reascended the throne while the anthem was played. At its conclusion, she stood again—the entire audience did likewise—and led a procession of her ladies and trainbearers into St. Edward's Chapel, where she would remove the Dalmatic robe and supertunica and don the purple velvet kirtle and mantle that she would wear during the final procession.

As soon as Victoria disappeared into the chapel, the crowd stirred and mingled, taking advantage of this break in the long ceremony to stretch their legs and gossip about the proceedings thus far and the manner in which the young queen was handling herself.

"Ross," a voice called, and he saw Julian leaning around Zoë. "Did you say you're sailing for China?"

"In August."

"Delightful! If you put in at Calcutta, I can show you a time."

Julian seemed genuinely sincere, and Ross wondered if his cousin's budding naval career was softening the arrogant conceit that was a trademark of Ballinger men on Lord Cedric's side of the family. Ross well remembered how as a child he had been the butt of pranks by Julian and Austin. He distrusted both of them and was cautious in his reply: "Zoë tells me that you're leaving next month for Calcutta?"

"That's right. I've been transferred to the *Lancet*." His voice had lowered, as if with reverence, when he said the name of the ship. Then one side of his mustache quirked upward, and his tone took on a familiar smugness. "I'll be sailing under 'the ffist.' "

"Fist?"

Julian made a fist and thumped it against his chest. "Surely you've heard of him. The ffist—Captain Reginald ffiske. Spells his name with a lowercase double-*F*, and he's damned proud of it. Any man who spells it wrong gets an earful of how medieval monks used a lowercase double-*F* to signify an uppercase one."

"I see. So his men call him the fist."

"With a double-*F*, of course. And only behind his back." Julian thumped his chest again. "And I'm to be his first lieutenant."

"It's quite an honor, isn't it?" Zoë said.

"Damned right it is. When the position opened up,

some two dozen officers put in—and the ffist chose me."

Zoë took Ross's arm. "Perhaps you'll meet this Captain ffiske in Calcutta."

"Just look for our ship, and I'll see to it," Julian promised.

Just then the door to St. Edward's Chapel opened, and the spectators settled back into their seats. A few minutes later, the final procession began, with Queen Victoria carrying the scepter in her right hand and the orb in her left down the long center aisle of Westminster Abbey to the resounding cheers of the assembly. After a visit to the robing room, where she was joined by her mother, the duchess of Gloucester, the duchess of Cambridge, and numerous ladies and trainbearers, the procession continued to the Abbey entrance, where the state coach waited at the head of a line of ornate, gaily beribboned coaches.

The state coach had been built for King George III in 1762. The entire body and carriage was ornamented with carved laurels and was richly gilded. The driver's box was held atop two carved figures, which appeared to be drawing the coach by cables stretched around their shoulders. The driver's footboard was a large scallop shell, ornamented with marine plants and conch shells, symbolizing the approach of the monarch of the ocean. Eight palm trees held up the coach roof, and four other trees held trophies representing Great Britain's victories in war. At the center peak of the roof stood the figures of three boys, representing the genii of England, Scotland, and Ireland. They supported the Imperial Crown of Great Britian and held in their hands the scepter and sword of state and the ensigns of knighthood.

It took the better part of an hour for the participants and guests to find their vehicles and get under way to Buckingham Palace. Zoë and Ross Ballinger were seated with Zoë's brothers in an ornate four-in-hand coach near the end of the procession, but as they rode along a circuitous route through the streets of London, the multitudes were every bit as enthusiastic as they had been when the state coach passed by at the head of the line.

"Isn't this exciting?" Zoë declared as she waved at the crowd that lined Regency Street.

"Apparently the people love their sovereign," Julian said matter-of-factly.

"It's more than that," Ross put in. "It's as if they realize a new age is beginning."

"The age of Victoria?" Austin said, his tone facetious. "I don't think so. She's too young . . . too much foreign blood." He waved politely and without emotion through the open window of the coach, his reddish-brown beard partially obscuring a disdainful frown. "Mark my words, this Victoria will never amount to much. They'll marry her off, and she'll disappear behind her husband and a brood of little princes and princesses. That is, if she even survives childbirth. She looked terribly skinny and frail to me."

"Austin, you're impossible," Zoë chided. "I thought she looked positively . . . well . . . regal."

Julian laughed. "I should hope so. She's a queen, after all."

"I doubt she'll last the year," Austin continued. "Changing her name and disarming an audience by charming an old fart like Lord Rolle isn't enough to win her a lasting place in the hearts of the people. Certainly not for more than a few months. And as for an age . . ." He snickered. "The *Victorian* age . . ." he said, his tone dripping with sarcasm. "I hardly think so."

Ross knew it was pointless to argue with his older cousin, but something about this new monarch inspired confidence in him. Perhaps it *was* how she so easily disarmed the crowd at Westminster Abbey. Or perhaps Ross was being carried away by the pomp of the ceremony and by his own excitement over the upcoming voyage to China. But whatever the cause, he was convinced a new era had indeed begun—for himself and for the whole British empire.

IV

Mose Levison stood among the bushes at the side of the big brick house on St. James Square, drawing circles in the dirt with the toe of his shoe. Every now and then he glanced up at a second-floor window. It seemed as though hours had passed since the fancy man named Connor Maginnis had signaled him from that very window to remain where he was. Mose was tired and bored, and from the sounds of cannons and cheering in the distance, he was certain that Queen Victoria was already riding from Westminster Abbey to Buckingham Palace.

It was true that he had caught a glimpse of the young queen on her way to the Abbey earlier that day, but now she would be wearing her crown and purple robes of state. He found himself wondering if it was worth waiting any longer for the few pennies Connor probably would squeeze out of the lady of the house—the woman he had been entertaining all afternoon up in that second-floor room.

Mose jumped with a start at the sound of a carriage clattering around the corner of the square. Drawing back into the bushes, he peered out at the cobbled street and saw a smart-looking black hansom cab halt in front of the same house in which Connor was "plowing his trade," as he had called it.

Mose's breath caught in his chest as the carriage door opened and a man well into his sixties emerged, looking dapper in a black cutaway coat and silk top hat and wearing the stockings and knee breeches still favored by many of his generation. Mose strained without success to hear what the man was saying to the liveried driver. The man handed the driver a coin, and the hansom cab pulled away and drove right past Mose and on around the square toward central London.

There was no doubt in Mose's mind that the well-dressed passenger was the master of the house—and of the mistress who was doing God-only-knew-what in the upstairs bedroom with Connor Maginnis.

The gentleman turned toward the house and walked briskly up the drive, his silver-knobbed cane tapping jauntily on the ground. Mose risked leaning out of the bushes far enough to see the man inserting a key in the lock of the front door. His suspicions confirmed, he ducked around the side of the house and searched frantically for some means of warning his friend. Spying the gravel surrounding a nearby flower bed, he picked up a small stone and hurled it at the window, missing by inches. He tried a second time, but his aim was even worse. Snatching a whole handful of pebbles, he let them fly, and enough struck their mark to set the pane rattling.

Mose had just let loose a second handful when the drapes were thrust aside, revealing a scowling, bare-chested man. Mose waved his arms, signaling that someone had come home and was on his way inside and perhaps upstairs. It took a moment for Connor to realize what was going on; then a sudden shock of awareness came over him—either he understood Mose's message or had heard something in the house.

Connor let the drapes drop in place and disappeared into the room. A moment later he yanked the drapes open wide and, clutching his clothing against his chest with one hand, reached up with the other to release the window latch. With some difficulty he got it unlocked and pushed the window outward on its rusty hinges. Behind Connor, Mose glimpsed the woman's corpulent, naked body as she pulled a flimsy dressing robe over her shoulders. Connor and the woman exchanged words, as if debating what to do, and then she pushed him toward the open window. Connor looked around wildly and with an expression of fearful resignation stepped over the sill and onto the narrow ledge just below the window.

Mose couldn't believe what he was seeing. Connor was stark naked, his modesty protected only by the clothing clutched against his abdomen. He cautiously moved to the right, away from the window, as the woman started to pull it shut. Abruptly she halted, dashed off for a moment, then reappeared carrying something, which she heaved outside. It was a pair of boots, which went spinning through the air and landed with a thud on the ground, one of them right-side up at Mose's feet, the other upside down a few yards away.

Mose retrieved Connor's boots, then looked up to see him on the ledge, struggling into his pants. His lady friend was still at the window, attempting to close it, when a shadowed figure surprised her from behind. Mose could almost hear her gasp. She spun around to the man behind her, blocking the window with her body while she spoke to him. Just when it appeared as if he was about to move past her to the window, she raised her arms and threw herself at him in the most passionate embrace Mose had ever seen—or imagined. The man did not seem averse to her attentions, and in a moment Mose saw the dressing robe slip off her shoulders to the floor. The man's hands sank into her copious flesh, and then the pawing figures moved back from the window.

Only a couple of feet away, Connor stood on the ledge, one leg in his pants, his gaze transfixed on the open window. Apparently he had been able to see or hear enough to know what was going on, for now, disregarding his state of semidress, he inched back to the window and leaned toward it far enough to catch a glimpse inside the room.

Abruptly he spun away from the window, as if something or someone had surprised him. Losing his balance, he teetered on his perch, his naked leg struggling to maintain its footing, the clothed leg hovering over the abyss, like a tightrope walker fighting to stay on the wire. Grabbing at the wall, he had to release the pants—along with the rest of his clothes—and as his shirt, jacket, waistcoat, and undergarments went flapping to the ground, the pants slid down his leg and hung off his foot.

Connor shook his leg to free it from the dangling pair of pants. The movement only served to unbalance him more, and with a gasp and a last desperate lunge toward the window ledge, he lost his footing and went flailing through the air.

Mose gasped as his benefactor landed unceremoniously on his rear end in the middle of a well-trimmed bush below the window. Racing to his side, the boy reached into the tangle of arms, legs, and branches, then held back as Connor opened his eyes. He looked upward and his focus returned, his eyes widening, and Mose followed his gaze to see the woman of the house framed in the partially open window. Her body was screened by one of the drapes, which she held in front of her as she grabbed hold of the window. Staring down at her lover and the youth beside him, she raised a finger to her lips and frowned, then pulled the window shut and disappeared from view.

"Help me up," Connor grunted, holding out a hand to the boy, who started to reach for it. "First get my pants."

After gathering the items, Mose carried the bundle to Connor, who was still sprawled in the middle of the bush, his skin a maze of scratches.

"Give it here," Connor directed him. "And stop all that staring."

"I—I'm sorry," Mose stammered, dropping the bundle onto Connor's midsection.

"You've seen a grown man before, haven't you?" Lifting himself up slightly, Connor shook out the pants and slipped his feet into the pant legs.

"Yes, but . . ."

Seeing what a struggle it was for the boy not to stare where he shouldn't, Connor shrugged and asked, "Well, what is it? Is something wrong?"

"Why, no," Mose insisted, flushed with embarrassment. "It's just that . . . well . . . you really *ain't* Jewish."

Looking down at himself, Connor grinned. "That's what I said, isn't it? Now help me out of here."

Mose clasped Connor's wrists and hauled him out of the bush. Connor's pants were still around his knees, and he reached down and pulled them up. Then he scooped up the rest of his clothes and quickly donned them, stuffing the undergarments into the pockets of his jacket and hastily arranging the cravat and collar.

"Let's get going." Connor prodded his young companion toward the street.

Hesitating, Mose muttered, "I guess you didn't get a chance to ask her about puttin' up my stake."

"Is that what's got you frowning?" He reached into the pocket of his waistcoat and produced a gold coin, which he presented to his young friend, whose expression lit with excitement as he turned it round and round, examining both sides. "In my trade, you learn early to get your money up front—before the husband comes home."

"But I don't want to take your—"

"That coin's for you," Connor insisted, pushing the boy's hand away. "A present from the good Lady Henrietta Wellesley. I've got my own right here." He patted his waistcoat pocket.

"But how did you convince her? What'd you say?"

"I told her that my nephew just arrived in London, orphaned and penniless. She said she's more than happy to—how did she put it?—'to help a strapping young country lad get started on the right track in life.' If I'm not mistaken, Lady Wellesley would love to tell you that herself after you've got yourself 'properly situated.'" Connor's eyes twinkled with mischief, and he cuffed the lad's chin.

"Are you suggestin' . . . ?" Mose's voice trailed off with uncertainty.

"Like I told you, there's lots of ways to earn money that don't need a stake or a sack of fruit—just the right education from a fancy sort of fellow like me." His eyes sparkled with merriment. "Something tells me a good-looking Jewish lad like you would be quite a novelty for the womenfolk." He jabbed the boy dangerously close to the groin and started to chuckle.

At first Mose looked quite uncomfortable, but then he found himself laughing, as well. He followed Connor away from the building but halted abruptly, tugging at Connor's sleeve. "Just promise me one thing." He gestured toward where Connor had landed when he fell from the ledge, and his lips quirked impishly. "If I let you show me the ways of a fancy man, you'll teach me a better way'n that to end up in the bush."

"Mose, my friend, I'll show you a thousand ways." Connor led him onto the street. "And here's your first lesson—the first rule of a fancy man: 'A bird in the bush is worth two in the hand.'"

Mose looked at him curiously. "But this mornin' you said the first rule is to never keep a woman waitin'."

"That all depends, my good man, on whether she's going . . . or *coming*."

Mose shook his head in confusion.

"Give it no mind. There're plenty of rules for a fancy man, and plenty of time to learn them . . . and to break them." He picked up the pace as they rounded St. James Square and headed into the narrower city streets. "Now let's get going. If I'm not mistaken, Emeline will have a bowl of hot soup ready right about now."

"Emeline?"

"Just about the most beautiful girl in all London." He stopped abruptly and grabbed the sleeve of Mose's brown corduroy jacket. "And mind you, not a word to her about what we've been up to this afternoon! She thinks I'm working down at the docks. If she were to learn where our money really comes from . . ." He drew the tip of his thumb across his throat. "Emeline may seem all sweetness and gentility on the surface, but beneath that pretty exterior is the heart of a lioness."

"You needn't worry about me," Mose assured him. "I'll not tell your missus nothin' about—"

"My missus?" Connor cut in, then chuckled. "Emeline is no wife of mine—nor anyone else's, for that matter. No, she's just a kid, not more'n a year older than you." He wrapped his arm around the boy's shoulder and continued down the street. "Emeline Maginnis is my sister. And a far better sister than a fancy man like me could ever hope for or deserve. Now, Mr. Mose Levison, let's go have us some of that 'Sweet Emeline Soup.' "

◆◆◆

Where is he? Emeline Maginnis worried as she stooped in front of the shallow brick fireplace and stirred the few unconsumed lumps of coal. Putting aside the bent poker, she shifted the wooden ladle to her right hand and dipped it into the blackened cast-iron pot that hung over the coals. *Wherever is that boy?*

Frowning, she stood and smoothed her coarse cotton dress, then walked over to the plain wood table that dominated the center of the small room. The only other furnishings were a low cupboard along one wall and a crudely constructed counter, which held an assortment of old but serviceable cooking utensils.

Circling the table, Emeline adjusted the angles of the two plates and spoons, lining them up directly opposite each other. Tilting her head, she eyed her work and nodded in satisfaction. Then she placed the ladle on the counter and glanced up into the jagged piece of mirror nailed to the wall over the basin that served as a sink. Her frown returning, she tucked a stray lock of her light-brown hair into place and wiped a smudge from her chin. She stood gazing at herself in the mirror, and for a moment it seemed as if her pale-blue eyes were about to well with tears, but then she forced a sigh and whispered in a motherly voice, "Pretty Emeline. Pretty child."

Turning in place, she stood with her hands on the counter behind her and looked around the room, shaking her head with worry. "Where is that boy?" she muttered, tapping the scuffed toe of her high-laced right shoe against the rough planks of the floor. With a sigh, she pushed away from the counter and crossed to the doorway that led into the apartment's other room, which served as their living and sleeping quarters.

There was a single window in the room, its glass somewhat wavy and clouded but spotlessly clean, as was the rest of the apartment. Standing at the sill, she peered down at the narrow, crowded street, filled with people as they returned from watching the coronation procession. It was quite a scene, noisy and chaotic, with an air of reverie almost like that of a carnival day.

Emeline watched the celebrants with a sense of fear and longing. Connor had offered to take her with him that morning so that she could see the beautiful new queen— the sensation of London. But she had been cautious of the crowds and had begged off. She wasn't sorry; how much better it would be to hear her brother describe the scene in all its color and pageantry. He was so good at telling stories, and she never tired of listening. No wonder he never had any trouble finding work to support them.

"If only I weren't so . . . s-so . . ." She let the words die on her lips and tried not to pout as she continued to look down into the crowd for some sign of her brother.

"Connor!" she blurted, tapping on the windowpane and waving as he rounded the corner. She thought he might have seen her as well, for he halted and waved up toward the window. But then he nudged a young man beside him, and she realized he was pointing out their third-floor apartment.

Emeline's brow creased with anxiety as her brother and the stranger strode across the street and passed through the entryway two stories below. "Oh, no, C-Connor!" she whispered, staring down at her clean but threadbare dress.

But she had no time to worry about how she looked, for a moment later there was a pounding at the door, and then it swung open to reveal her brother, arms outstretched, a broad smile on his dark, handsome face. Beside him stood a young man—a boy, really—who looked just as uncomfortable as Emeline.

"There you are!" Connor declared, bounding into the room and sweeping his younger sister into his arms. He waved a hand toward his guest. "This is my new friend, Mose Levison. I've been telling him all about you. Mose, I'd like to introduce my sister, Emeline." He stood back and raised a hand toward each of them, his brown eyes gleaming.

Emeline appeared frozen in place, leaving it to Mose to make the first move. "Uh, hello, Miss Maginnis. I . . . I'm honored to meet you." He stepped toward her and seemed on the verge of offering his hand, then thought better of it and stood with his hands clasped nervously in front of him.

Connor sensed his sister's discomfort, and he moved toward her and took her arm. "Mose is a fine young lad I met down on Petticoat Lane. Almost your age, Emeline. I thought it would be nice if he joined us for dinner."

"That is, if'n you have enough," the youth interjected.

Emeline's eyes narrowed and her lips twisted awkwardly as she forced a reply. "W-W-W-Why . . . y-y-yes." Her stutter always worsened among strangers, and as her cheeks flushed with embarrassment, she cast her gaze at the floor.

Wishing to draw attention away from her, Connor pointed toward the adjoining room and announced, "That smells like potato-leek soup."

"Stew," Emeline blurted, then looked down again.

"Wonderful!" her brother exclaimed. "And believe me, we're famished. Haven't had anything but a booler all day." He waved them toward the doorway. "Shall we?"

Emeline looked up anxiously and raised her hands, indicating they should remain where they were. She scurried into the other room and could be heard gathering an additional setting for their guest. A few moments later she reappeared in the doorway and motioned for them to enter, signaling Connor to bring along a chair from the main room.

Connor and Mose removed their jackets, and soon they were all seated around the table, the two men eagerly dipping their spoons into the savory stew and sopping up the spicy gravy with chunks of dark bread. Their conversation consisted primarily of Connor's highly exaggerated account of the queen's procession through the streets of London. While it was true that they had seen her being borne to Westminster Abbey in the state coach, they were otherwise occupied at the home of Lady Henrietta Wellesley when Victoria returned to Buckingham Palace. Connor left out that particular fact, choosing instead to describe in vivid detail the beautiful purple robes the new queen was wearing—as if he had been standing right there when the coach passed rather than struggling out of Henrietta's bush and back into his pants.

When Connor's story veered from the truth, Mose

simply concentrated on the stew, avoiding the beautiful but somewhat sad eyes of the young woman seated to his right.

"Never saw anything so majestic, have you, Mose?" Connor asked, drawing him into the conversation.

"Uh, no," the boy replied after gulping down a mouthful of leeks. "It was . . . uh, majestic, all right."

"It's too bad you weren't there, Emeline," Connor went on, dipping a crust of bread into the stew. "But you were smart to stay home. The crowds were horrendous."

"You can see it all this weekend," Mose said, forgetting his shyness. When Emeline looked over at him questioningly, he shrank into his seat, glanced uncomfortably at Connor, and muttered, "In the commemoratives."

"Yes," Connor declared. "You see, young Mr. Levison is something of a businessman. He and his grandfather will be selling commemorative accounts of the coronation, and he's promised the first one to you, Emeline."

"Why, thank you, Mr. L-L-Lev—"

"Mose," the youth insisted, blushing.

"Of course," Connor cut in. "There's no need for formalities among friends."

The teenagers looked down again, and there was a long, awkward silence. It was broken at last by Connor sopping up the last of his stew with his bread and pushing the bowl away from him. "Delicious, as always," he exclaimed, popping the dripping crust into his mouth.

"Yes, quite," Mose agreed, looking over at the cook, who smiled demurely and gathered their dishes.

"Come on out here," Connor told his guest, leading him from the kitchen. "Emeline prefers to be left alone while she cleans."

Mose turned back to the young woman and opened his mouth as if to speak. Their eyes locked for an instant, and then the moment passed. He picked up his jacket and allowed himself to be led into the main room.

"I suppose I should be leavin' soon. My grandfather'll be wonderin' what's keepin' me."

"All right. But come back anytime you want." Connor's voice lowered slightly. "And I was serious when I offered to show you around, should you ever be seeking a new line of work."

"Yes. Well, thank you," Mose replied awkwardly. "And thank your sister for that fine dinner. I'll bring the commemorative around as soon as we get 'em."

Connor showed him to the door and, with a final clap on the back, sent him on his way. Shutting the door, he went into the kitchen.

"Emeline, Mose wanted me to thank you for—" He stopped short just inside the doorway. Across the room, Emeline was standing at the counter, crying softly. Approaching her cautiously, he took her in his arms and asked, "What is it? What's wrong?"

"I . . . I'm such a big f-fool," she sobbed into his shoulder.

"Whatever has gotten into you?"

"I'm so s-s-stupid!" she whimpered.

He pushed her away slightly and tilted her head up to face him. "You're nothing of the kind. Who filled you with such foolishness?"

Jerking her head free, she looked downward. "I always was. Ever since—"

"That wasn't your fault. Aunt Beatrice said it was because Mother was so weak and took so long giving birth."

Emeline cried harder at the thought of having caused their mother's death—and indeed their father's, as well, for his grief had been so great that only months later he, too, had died.

"It wasn't your fault, Emeline—really," Connor soothed, well aware of his sister's feelings of guilt. "And you're certainly not stupid—far from it. That's why

Aunt Beatrice spent nearly every shilling she had to see that we got a proper education, despite our circumstances. You're not stupid—all you have is a little problem with your speech."

"I s-sound awful!" she groaned, burying her head in his shoulder again.

"You sound as good as gold," he insisted.

"I do not."

"Yes you do. Just have a listen."

Something cold touched Emeline's ear, and she gave a start. Pushing away from him, she reached up for his hand, but he pulled it away and waved it quickly in front of her eyes. She saw a flash of something golden, and again she snatched at his hand. But he was too quick for her.

"What's that?" she asked, forgetting her sorrow.

Connor danced away from her. "Wouldn't you like to know," he toyed, again waving his hand. Finally he opened it, revealing a gold coin in his palm.

"How much is it?" she asked eagerly.

"Enough to keep us fit 'n' fed for a week."

"But you didn't go to work today. How d-did—?"

"Never you mind." He came closer and pressed the coin into her hand. "Go put it with the others."

Emeline stared at the coin in wonder; it was rare that her brother brought home gold. Then she cocked her head slightly and looked at him suspiciously. "You didn't do anything you shouldn't have to get—"

"Me?" His eyes narrowed mischievously. "You know I'd never—"

"You promised," she cut in, frowning. "You said you'd only d-do honest work." She held the coin toward him. "I don't want money that's been—"

"Honestly earned . . . I promise." He closed her hand around the coin. "I told you I've been working at the London Docks. Well, I ran into the foreman, and he gave me this as an advance on my pay."

She looked at him suspiciously, but his ingenuous smile slowly won her over. She soon found herself giggling as he tickled her chin.

"Go on, now, put it away before I spend it on something foolish."

"You see?" she declared, holding up the coin. "I always knew you'd m-make a success of yourself—just as soon as the right opp . . . opportunity came along. Maybe this job at the docks will be it!"

Spinning around, Emeline knelt in front of the counter, under which was stacked an assortment of pots and tin cans. Rummaging among them, she found a small can with a tight-fitting lid, which she pried open. Dropping the gold coin inside, she removed two pennies, then refitted the lid and placed the can back among the others.

Standing, she held forth the copper coins and announced, "These are for you. You've earned yourself an ale or two."

"Emeline, I love you!" Connor exclaimed, sweeping her into his arms and kissing her cheek. Releasing her, he snatched the coins from her hand and clutched them in his fist as he backed from the kitchen. "I'll only be an hour— two at the most. Are you sure you don't mind?"

"Of course not." She waved him away. "Now run along. I've p-plenty of my own work to do."

She smiled as her older brother donned his jacket and hurried from the apartment, slamming the door behind him and vaulting down the stairs to the street. With a sigh, she turned back to the counter and set to work cleaning the dinner dishes.

Only a few minutes had passed when a knock at the apartment door startled Emeline, who had not heard anyone coming up the stairs. "Connor? Is that you?" she called, wiping her hands and crossing through the front room. Realizing he wouldn't have knocked, she asked, "Who is it?"

"Mose Levison."

"M-Mose?" she asked, pulling open the door. "What are you d-doing b-back here?"

The young man in the hallway looked just as uneasy as she did. He stood nervously wringing his hands, looking up at Emeline and then down at his scuffed shoes. After an exceedingly long silence, he finally asked, "Is your brother here?"

She hesitated, unsure whether to admit that she was alone. Finally deciding that she was safe enough with Mose to be truthful, she replied, "Uh, n-no. He's down at the p-pub."

"I . . . I just thought I'd let him know that I'd like to take him up on his offer."

"Offer?"

"To work with him. He's gonna teach me somethin' of his trade."

Her eyes narrowed. "His trade? You mean w-working at the d-docks?"

Mose ran a hand through his curly brown hair and peered at her uncertainly. Remembering that Emeline did not know how her brother really earned their keep, he nodded slowly and said, "Yes, at the London Docks. Connor was goin' to try to get me some work down there."

"You can tr-try down at the p-p-pub," she stammered, growing increasingly uncomfortable at being alone with Mose. "It's just two blocks d-d-down to the right. Or I could t-tell him for you, if you'd like."

"Yes, I'd like that." He backed away from the door. "Just let him know that I'll be waitin' down in the street come mornin', if he's still willin' to take me along."

"I'm sure he w-will be." She started to close the door.

"Uh, Miss Emeline," he called, raising a hand toward her. "That was a real fine supper you served tonight."

She felt her face flush with embarrassment. "Th-Thank

y-y-y-" Her lips tightened as she tried in vain to get out the words. At last she gave up and looked down in shame.

"That's all right, Miss Emeline," he said, his voice gentle and reassuring. "There's lots of folks what can speak real fine but ain't got nothin' worth sayin'."

Forcing herself to look up, she saw such a genuine smile on his face that she could not help but return it. "Thank you, Mose," she whispered.

He ran his hand through his hair. "Well, I'd best be goin'. I hope I'll see you again."

"Me, too."

He headed down the stairs.

Shutting the door, Emeline leaned back against it and sighed. She pressed her hands to her chest and could feel her heart racing, as much from excitement as fear.

"Mose," she whispered ever so faintly. She wondered how old he was—she was barely sixteen, and he looked to be not much younger. And he was so polite; other boys she had met called her names and teased her about the way she spoke. But Mose had been quite the gentleman.

"Perhaps . . ." she wondered aloud, then shook off any fantasies of romance. She had plenty of work to do and an older brother who needed caring for. Romance was best left the stuff of fairy tales—at least where Emeline Maginnis was concerned.

V

Ross Ballinger felt strangely unsettled as he walked through the lamplit London streets. He had left his cousin Zoë's palatial estate in the Castlebar Hill district, just west of Kensington, more than two hours earlier and could have been home in half that time. But he was uneasy about returning, so he had sent back the Ballingers' carriage and was walking the last couple of miles. He told himself that he simply wanted to be part of the Coronation Day revelry taking place throughout the city; in fact, it was the jarring memory of his father and that young charwoman at the warehouse that kept him from going home.

The streets were full of celebrants, and perhaps that was why Ross did not notice that he had entered one of the less-reputable parts of the city. Hawkers were still working the crowds, as were more than the usual number of petty thieves and pickpockets. Ross was still wearing his coronation suit, complete with a silk top hat and an ivory walking stick, making him a prime target of the "street artists," as they were known. But though he was jostled a number of times, he had the sense to keep his hands over his pockets and did not fall victim to their tactics.

"Dearie, how about a booler?" he heard a woman call.

"No, thanks," he muttered. Glancing in her direction, he saw a fleshy, unkempt woman about twice his age in what ten years earlier might have been a fashionable high-waisted black dress—before it had been let out with ridiculously mismatching pieces of cloth to allow for her expanding girth.

"Then how about a pair o' boolers?" She grabbed her ample breasts and lifted them from somewhere in the vicinity of her stomach to where she formerly had carried them with pride. "Go on, pup. Only a ha'penny a bite."

Turning away, Ross pushed blindly through the crowd, only vaguely aware of the woman's caustic laugh following him down the street.

"Hey! Watch out wi' you!" a man blurted as Ross stumbled into him.

"S-Sorry," he stammered, pushing himself away from the bigger man. He paused at the corner and looked around, realizing for the first time that he was uncertain of his location. Forgetting for the moment the scene he had witnessed at his father's warehouse, he decided he had better find his way home to Shadwell—or at least get out of this unfamiliar district.

"Excuse me," he said to a passing gentleman—at least what passed for a gentleman in this quarter. But before he managed a question, the man disappeared into the crowd.

Ross looked for someone else to give him directions. Feeling a hand on his shoulder, he spun around and saw an older man in a battered felt hat and worn jacket. The man's smile was warm but revealed a set of brown teeth.

"You look to be in need of assistance, mate," the man said in a thick, gravelly voice.

"Uh, yes," Ross answered weakly.

"Speak up, lad." The man slapped his arm. "We're all the queen's subjects here."

"I, uh, got turned around and—" He hesitated, then asked bluntly, "Do you know the way to Shadwell?"

"O' course, me boy. But it's lookin' like you don't."
He gave a wet laugh that spattered Ross with spittle.

Ross felt his stomach roil but forced himself not to
offend the man by wiping his face. "Could you point me
in the right direction?"

"Well, now, I can do much better'n that, son, 'cause
I be goin' in that very direction. Me name's Simon, and a
simpler fellow you'll ne'er meet." He chortled at his own
wit. "Now, come along, me lad."

He wrapped a beefy arm around Ross's shoulder and
led him around the corner and down a somewhat narrower
side street.

"Now, what is a fine-dressed young man like yourself
doin' in this part o' the city?" Simon asked.

"I was just taking a walk following the coronation."

"And a lovely one it was. But your daddy should've
taught you better'n to be alone on the streets in such a
dandy getup as this." He fingered the lapel of Ross's suit
jacket. "It's not like you was gonna be sittin' right there
in Westminster Abbey with the queen."

Ross remained silent. Feeling the man's arm tighten
around his shoulder, he felt a rush of fear, his sense of
foreboding heightened by the thinning crowd and lack of
lamps on this portion of the street.

Simon abruptly halted and turned Ross toward a lighted
doorway just across the street. "What say we head into the
Gov'ner's Crescent? You can buy me a pint o' stout 'afore
I show you the way to Shadwell."

"I really should be going," Ross replied, squirming
slightly in the older man's grip.

"But that isn't polite, now is it?" the man pressed.
"Not when good ol' Simon here has offered to point you
home."

Ross tried to pull away, but Simon held him fast and
spun him away from the street. As Ross lifted his walking
stick in defense, he glimpsed a second, shadowed figure

dart out of a doorway, and then a fist smashed into his belly, doubling him over and sending the walking stick clattering to the ground.

"Hold him up!" a new voice blurted, and Simon grabbed a fistful of Ross's hair and yanked him upright just in time to meet a crushing blow to the jaw.

Ross's knees buckled, and he slipped downward, held up only by the big man's powerful grip. He tried to twist himself free, but all that served to do was to line up his head with a vicious kick from the second man's boot.

Ross gave a pained shout as the dim light from the doorway darkened to black. He was barely conscious and felt someone going through his pockets. One of the men—Simon, it sounded like—blurted, "Be quick with you!" to which the other replied, "I can't find nothin'!" There was the tearing sound of one of Ross's jacket pockets being ripped off. Then Simon muttered, "Drag him inside. He's carryin' somethin', or he's a dead man!"

Ross moaned and for his effort received a cruel kick to the belly that took his breath away. He gasped for air, unable to defend himself as the two men grabbed his arms and proceeded to haul him across the sidewalk and up a few steps into the darkened entryway of a building. His chest felt crushed and constricted, and when at last he drew in a deep, gulping breath, it was with a piercingly loud, asthmatic wheeze.

"Shut him up, Willie!" Simon blared.

Even in the thin darkness, Ross could see the glint of a blade in the second man's hand. Still struggling for air, he had no fight left in him. He tried to pray—to recall the faces of his family and friends—but all he could envision was a cruel smile and a row of sickeningly brown teeth. He closed his eyes and waited for the inevitable thrust.

The sound of scuffling and a chorus of shouted oaths came from the two thieves, and suddenly no one was holding Ross. He looked up to see that his would-be murderers were engaged in a fight with a third person. Wheezing as he struggled up on one arm, Ross saw that it was only the smaller, knife-wielding thief who was fighting; Simon apparently had been taken by surprise, for he lay sprawled unconscious on the stairs.

Though not sure of what was going on, Ross realized that someone had come to his aid, knocking out Simon and taking on his partner. They were circling each other on the sidewalk, one man slashing wildly with his long-bladed knife, the other using Ross's walking stick like a cudgel.

"Come on, bastard!" the man with the stick taunted. "Come get me!" He waved the thief toward him, challenging him to lunge with the knife.

The fellow did just that, charging forward with a furious roar as he thrust the knife toward the other man's belly. The man was ready for him and jumped deftly to one side, swinging the walking stick and knocking the knife from the thief's hand. He followed with a series of brutal jabs to the stomach and, when the thief doubled over, finished him off with a thunderous blow to the back of the neck.

Ross had risen to his knees but was still struggling for breath when his rescuer approached him.

"Are you all right?" the man asked. He was a few years older than Ross and much darker in complexion, and he was dressed nicely though not extravagantly in a brown suit with a white waistcoat and cravat.

"Yes," Ross gasped, clutching his stomach and trying to calm his breathing.

"Here. Let me help."

The man came up beside Ross, slipped a hand under his arms, and helped him to his feet. Ross leaned against him for a minute or so, his breath slowly returning to normal.

"Thanks," he murmured as the stranger handed him his walking stick.

"Let's get out of here. They'll be rousing any minute

now." He led Ross to the sidewalk, then released his grip and said, "Just one minute, friend." Turning to where the big man was just beginning to stir, he gave him a sharp kick to the head, returning him to unconsciousness. "That's better," he declared, grinning at Ross, who found himself smiling, as well.

"I want to thank you for—"

"No thanks needed. This may be a rough area, but there are those of us who don't take kindly to ganging up on a stranger." He paused, looking Ross up and down. "You *are* a stranger to this district, aren't you?"

"I guess it shows," Ross said sheepishly.

"Where do you live?"

"In Shadwell, near the docks."

"Well, they had you going in the wrong direction." He turned Ross around, and the two men headed back to the main street. "Just walk down there about six blocks and you'll reach more familiar territory."

Ross looked up and down the street a bit hesitantly.

"There's nothing to worry about on this road. We're really a friendly lot . . . so long as you stick to the main streets and just keep walking."

"Thanks again."

"If you'd like, I could walk with you a ways."

"No, that's all right." He brushed off his torn jacket. "I'm fine now . . . really."

"Then I'd best be headed home myself." He held out his hand and gave Ross's a firm shake before heading back down the dark street where the attack had taken place.

Ross watched him disappearing into the gloom of night. Turning, he started in the direction the man had shown him, then suddenly spun around and dashed back to the corner. He could just make out the figure of a man in the shadows beyond.

"Hey! Just a minute!" he called, taking a few steps down the street. "I didn't get your name!"

The man either did not hear or chose not to respond; he kept going until he was all but lost from sight. Ross took a few more steps toward him, then glanced across the street and saw several patrons of the Governor's Crescent staring at him from the lighted doorway. He shivered involuntarily and came to a halt. Deciding it would be best to let the good Samaritan go on his way, Ross whispered a final thank-you and returned to the lights of the main street.

◆━━◆━━◆

Connor Maginnis strode quickly toward home, feeling a tinge of guilt at having left his sister for so long while he enjoyed a couple of ales at the Crescent. At least he'd have quite a story to regale her with when he returned—and a few scratches and bruises to confirm it.

Though the man Connor had assisted was only a few years younger, it was obvious that he was much less experienced with life on the streets of London. He seemed a likable enough fellow, however, and Connor wondered if he should have asked his name. *What matter,* he thought. *It's not too likely our paths will cross again.*

As he reached the corner a half block from his building, he noticed an impressive and unusual coach sitting at the curb across the street. There were plenty of carriages out and about tonight, but this was one of the new cutaway coaches modeled on the one recently built for Lord Brougham. The brougham coach, as it was quickly becoming known, was similar to a full coach, but the forward seat had been replaced with a straight wall and glass window. The driver sat outside in front of the window between two large brass lamps.

This particular brougham sported a pair of matched grays in harness and an elderly driver decked out in full livery. It was clearly not a coach for hire.

Connor was just passing the vehicle when one of the leather window curtains was pulled back and a female voice called, "Mr. McGuinn?"

Connor halted in surprise; McGuinn was the name he used in his trade as a fancy man. He turned to the brougham across the street but could not see the woman seated in the dark interior.

"You *are* Mr. McGuinn, are you not?" she asked.

Connor stepped into the street and cautiously approached.

"It's all right," the woman reassured him, leaning through the window until her face was partly illuminated by a streetlamp. She was not much older than Connor—perhaps in her midtwenties—and quite attractive, with full, smooth features, a milky complexion, ice-blue eyes, and blond hair pulled back in a chignon at the nape of the neck. "We've met before . . . at Madam Wellesley's. Don't you remember?"

Connor moved closer, slowly shaking his head as he tried to recall the woman. "You don't look familiar, and I don't know any Madam Wellesley."

The young woman gave a full-throated purr. "Very good, Mr. McGuinn. You are as discreet as my mother said. And while it's true we never met, I did in fact chance to see you on one occasion when you were departing my parents' house. Later I finagled your address from Mother." She opened the door. "Come in—there's nothing to be afraid of. Certainly not from me." She sat back, allowing him room to enter.

Connor examined the young woman more closely and saw now the resemblance to Henrietta Wellesley. He considered his options, ultimately deciding that he'd do well to determine what she had in mind. If it was some sort of blackmail scheme, she would soon discover that Connor Maginnis did not take kindly to threats. Nor did he much care if anyone found out about his financial—or intimate—relationship with Henrietta Wellesley. Of course, if it could be helped, he would rather not lose the easy source of income that Madam Wellesley provided.

"That's better," she said as he stepped into the coach. She patted the seat next to her. "Right here, so we don't have to speak loudly."

Connor complied and found himself seated to the right of an extremely well-proportioned woman of apparent means. He imagined that this was how Henrietta had looked before her ample figure had gone to fat. The woman wore an evening dress that had been *de rigueur* a decade or so earlier but was now considered a bit too risqué, given the current passion for corsets and ruffles. Fashioned of loose-hanging blue silk, it was little more than a light, extremely *décolleté* nightdress, and it revealed her natural figure to great advantage.

"Just what do you want of me?" he asked, fixing her with a steady gaze.

"Indeed," was all she replied. Leaning forward, she pulled the curtain in place over the front window, then rapped twice on the glass. Almost instantly the coach gave a lurch and started forward.

Taken by surprise, Connor blurted, "Now, see here—"

"No, *you* see here. Right *here*." So saying, she reached up and undid the lace bow at her chest. "You *will* be discreet, won't you, Mr. McGuinn? Mother promised that you would."

Connor watched in amazement as she lowered the dress; she was wearing no underclothing. She slowly revealed her full breasts, then pulled her arms free of the short, puffed sleeves and let the dress slip farther down to her hips, until she was naked from the waist up, save for a small, black leather pouch that hung between her breasts on a satin cord.

Grasping the pouch with the thumb and forefinger of her left hand, she kneaded it slowly and seductively. "This is for you, Mr. McGuinn. Mother said you give your best performances for gold."

Connor heard the clink of coins inside the pouch

and allowed himself a smile. "Gold *is* the color of love, Miss . . . ?"

"Lenora. And I care nothing for love," she added with a pout. "Ah, but *lust* . . ." Her sigh was as luxuriant as the plush leather seat.

As the brougham clattered down the street, the woman rubbed the pouch across her left breast, causing the nipple to harden. Connor noticed that she was wearing a gold wedding ring set with a ruby, and he fleetingly wondered if her husband was still alive—and what kind of a husband would drive a beautiful, brazen wife such as this to seek her pleasure with a stranger. But Connor was used to such things, especially with so many well-connected women making their marriages with far older gentlemen of means. It really was none of his concern, he reminded himself. What did concern him, however, was the pouch of gold and the all-too-inviting bosom that cradled it so seductively.

Though Connor had experienced many women, few were so audacious. Certain that she liked her men to take things firmly in hand, he braced himself against the rocking of the coach, leaned toward her, and cupped her left breast. As he took the already firm nipple in his mouth and tenderly licked it, his other hand followed the curve of her belly, pausing to feel it rise and fall as she breathed, then continuing around to the small of her back. Pulling her closer, he sucked gently at her nipple, and she gave a soft moan of pleasure.

"Yes . . . discreet . . ." she whispered into his ear. "But not so gentle." Grabbing a fistful of his thick brown hair, she pulled his head against her and leaned into him. "Bite me . . . harder . . .yes, like that," she moaned as he rolled her nipple with increasing force between his lips and teeth and flicked his tongue across the hardened tip.

As Connor's right hand continued to knead her breast, his left worked its way down her bare back and under the dress gathered at her waist. She rose up slightly off the seat, and he was delighted to discover that she was wearing nothing beneath her skirts. He gave a slight sigh of approval, his palm tracing the swell of her buttocks, his fingertips delving into the valley between them and following it down and underneath to the warm moistness below.

Lenora shuddered with pleasure as his fingers dipped into her. "Yes . . ." she urged, thrusting herself against his hand.

Shifting on the seat, Connor grabbed her buttocks and pulled her closer. As she rose up over him, her dress dropped around her muscular, shapely calves. She kicked it away and climbed on top of him, straddling him with her hips, her knees pressed into the leather seat, her arms outstretched over his shoulders as she gripped the seat back to steady herself.

Connor continued to nip at her breasts, moving deftly from one to the other. His left hand slid behind her back to brace her while his right hand circled her hip and explored her inner thigh, returning again to the soft, private spot that made her tremble with delight.

Pulling back slightly, he looked up and saw her half-closed eyes, the quiver of her lips, the strain of passion tightening her cheeks and brow. *Too easy . . . it's going too easy*, he found himself thinking and knew at once that with a woman such as Lenora he would have to be far more bold if he wanted to guarantee her continued business.

"Yes, *harder*!" she urged, pressing herself against his hand. But abruptly he pulled his hand from her, and when she looked down at him in surprise, there was an assured gleam in his eyes.

Ever so deliberately, Connor lifted his hand, wet with her passion, and touched his fingertips to his tongue. "Mmmmm," he murmured as he boldly reached up and parted her lips so that she could savor her own delight. "Taste how wonderful you are, Lenora," he whispered as he ran his fingers along her lips and tongue.

She was momentarily startled, but she began to lick

his fingers, slowly at first, then with increasing ardor, until finally she grasped the hair at the back of his neck and brought her mouth down on his, forcing open his lips, her tongue thrusting deep into his mouth.

Connor felt Lenora reach down between them, her fingers frantically opening his waistcoat and searching for the hook at his waistband. He helped her unfasten it and trembled slightly as she shoved her hand inside, grabbing hold of him and pulling him free of the confines of his pants.

She purred with excitement as she felt the size and strength of him. "I must have you!" she breathed.

He eased into her, and she arched slightly, clutching his shoulders to steady herself and gripping him with her thighs. He felt her tightening around him as he thrust upward, slowly at first, the rhythm increasing to match the rocking of the brougham as it clattered briskly through Regents Park.

"Yes!" she cried, throwing her hands over her head, her fingers clawing at the coach roof. *"Now!"*

Connor allowed himself a low, pleasured moan as he clasped Lenora's buttocks and lifted her up and down over him, plunging into her harder and faster.

"Yes! Yes! *Oh, yes!*" she cried again and again, her hands banging against the roof, matching his rhythm thrust for thrust.

Outside, the elderly coachman felt the pounding against his seat back and heard the ecstatic cries from below. With a laconic smile that held more than a hint of jealousy, he snatched up his whip and called to the matched grays, "Mistress York 'pears to be callin' for a touch o' the lash!" He deftly flipped the whip out over the horses and popped it in the air just above their heads. Responding instantly, the grays lunged forward into a gallop, the dark brougham and its passengers bounding unbridled down the parkway drive.

VI

◆━◆━◆━◆━◆━◆━◆

Emeline Maginnis was short of breath as she pushed closed the door of her apartment and leaned against it. *There's still time,* she told herself, looking down at the parcel in her hand. After hoarding pennies for weeks, she had finally collected enough inside her tick mattress to purchase a small tin of West Indian powdered cocoa and some other ingredients for this very special Saturday, the fourth of August—her brother's twenty-second birthday. She was determined to prepare Connor's favorite cake to celebrate the occasion.

Removing her brown wool shawl, Emeline hurried into the adjoining room and over to the crude counter that served as the kitchen work area. Glancing only briefly at her fractured image in the piece of mirror hanging on the wall, she placed the parcel on the counter, then leaned over the narrow brick fireplace and piled fresh coal on the embers.

She hummed softly as she set to work, untying the cloth-bound parcel and carefully taking out two eggs, the tin of cocoa, and a stick of cinnamon. From under the counter she retrieved two stoneware bowls and a cast-iron Dutch oven, then gathered flour and other ingredients from the small pantry box, which Connor had built into an outside wall alongside the counter to keep the contents as cool as possible.

"My little sweet darling, my comfort, my love; sing lullaby lully," Emeline sang, her long, delicate fingers deftly cracking and separating the eggs into the bowls. "In beauty surpassing the heavens above; sing lullaby lully."

Using a long-handled wooden spoon, she whipped the egg whites, adding a pinch of cream of tartar to thicken them. Then she added the flour, cocoa, some cinnamon shavings, and the other dry ingredients into the larger bowl containing the yolks and vigorously beat the mixture into a rich, chocolaty batter. Finally she folded in the whites, then greased the Dutch oven, added the batter, and placed it on a small grate over the fireplace coals.

"Now suck, child, and sleep, child, thy mother's sweet joy; sing lullaby lully," she continued as she washed her hands at the basin on the counter. Her singing was effortless and smooth, without a trace of the stutter that plagued her when she was speaking—especially with strangers. "The gods bless and keep thee from cruel annoy; sing lully, lully, sweet baby, lully."

Emeline was so caught up in her preparations for Connor's return that she did not at first hear the rapping at the apartment door. When the sound became more insistent, she caught her breath in surprise. Connor never knocked, and their friend Mose Levison always rapped a familiar pattern.

Unaccustomed to visitors and more than a bit uneasy, she wiped her hands on the apron of her skirt and headed cautiously through the front room. "Who is it?" she asked through the closed door.

"I'm looking for Mr. McGuinn," a woman said.

"Who?"

"Mr. McGuinn. Is he at home?"

The voice seemed determined but not at all threatening, so Emeline opened the door a crack. Peering out at the cold, dimly lit landing, she saw a fairly tall woman who was as well-dressed as she was well-proportioned. The woman stood perfectly erect and motionless, her hands holding closed the ermine collar of her pale-blue mantelet, a luxuriant sweep of blond hair framing her smooth, porcelain skin and ice-blue eyes. Emeline's gaze fixed on the woman's gold wedding ring, set with the largest ruby she had ever seen.

Quickly examining Emeline with a haughty, imperious eye, the woman asked again, "Is Mr. McGuinn here?"

Emeline opened the door a bit farther. "I . . . I'm s-sorry, but I d-don't know any Mr. Mc-Mc-McGuinn."

With each of Emeline's stutters, the other woman's lips tightened with impatience. "But this is Connor's address," she snapped as she glanced over Emeline's shoulder, trying to see into the room beyond.

"Connor?"

"Yes, that's what I've been saying. Connor McGuinn. I'm certain this is where he lives."

"Perhaps you mean my b-brother. His n-name's Connor, but it isn't Mc-McGuinn."

"It isn't? But he told me . . ." The woman paused, her eyes narrowing in thought. "I suppose I may have gotten his name wrong. This brother of yours—he has brown eyes and dark hair? Quite a handsome young man in his twenties?"

With a slight blush, Emeline gave an affirming nod.

"And you say you're his sister?"

"Y-Yes. Emeline."

"Well, I'm delighted to meet you, Emeline. My name is Lenora." She held out her hand, and the teenager nervously offered her own. "May I come in for a moment?" Lenora asked in what to Emeline seemed the warmest, most genuine of tones.

"Oh, yes," she replied apologetically, opening the door and stepping back to let the woman enter.

"What a . . . charming place you have here," Lenora commented, circling the room but taking care not to touch any of the sparse furnishings. "You say that you and Connor live here together?"

An edge of shame touching her expression, Emeline looked down and whispered that they did.

Lenora stopped a few feet away from the girl and eyed her keenly. "And that he's your brother?"

Uncertain of the intent of the question or why it made her feel so uncomfortable, Emeline replied, "Y-Yes. He's raised me ever since . . . since our Aunt B-Beatrice died."

"What about your parents?"

"Mother d-died when I was born. F-F-Father . . ." Her throat tightened with emotion.

"He passed away, too," Lenora guessed. "And your brother's been taking care of you. I always knew he was a very special young man."

Emeline's eyes widened. "Then you know him?"

"Connor and I are . . . acquainted. He's done some work for me on several occasions. He's quite talented— a real artist with his hands." Her tone was playful and incautious.

"He w-works for you? At the docks?"

"Me? At the docks?" Lenora giggled, then gracefully displayed her smooth white hands. "I should think not."

"B-But that . . . that's where Connor works."

Lenora looked confused, but then she nodded as if with understanding and said, "Why, yes, I suppose he does. But *I* don't work there. My family does. Our business is there."

"Oh," Emeline declared, her expression brightening. "Connor works for your f-family."

"That's right," Lenora replied matter-of-factly. She looked around again. "Isn't he here today?"

"He's w-working," the girl said with some confusion. "Isn't he?"

"Perhaps." She gave an offhanded wave. "I pay little

attention to affairs . . . of business. What I wanted with your brother was of a somewhat more personal nature."

"I'll t-tell him you came by."

"No, I think not," Lenora said brusquely, starting from the room. "Let's leave this little visit between the two of us. No need to bother Connor—he might think there was trouble at work." She opened the door. "I'll just plan to see him tomorrow . . . at the docks."

"Of course, Madam . . . ?"

"Lenora is sufficient. And may I call you Emeline?"

"Certainly." The youngster blushed again.

Stepping onto the landing, Lenora pulled the door toward her, then paused to look back at the fair-haired teenager. "If I'm not being too bold, may I ask your family name? I could have been certain that Connor said McGuinn."

"It . . . it's similar. It's Maginnis."

Lenora appeared somewhat taken aback and asked, "Are you able to spell it?"

Emeline did so, carefully pronouncing each letter so as not to stammer.

"Maginnis," Lenora intoned after she had finished. "That's quite unusual."

"It's really quite c-common."

"Not the name—the coincidence."

"C-C-Coinci—?"

"Yes," Lenora impatiently cut her off. "I mentioned our family business—Ballinger Trade," she said, referring to the company run by the family of her sister-in-law, Iphigenia. "It used to go under the name Ballinger-Maginnis, spelled the same way. But that was a long time ago; probably before you were born."

"My father was a businessman," Emeline announced proudly.

"But you said he died. I never met our Mr. Maginnis, but he's certainly not dead—at least that wasn't the case

the last I heard. Rotting in prison is more like it, and
from what's been said of the gent, a more fitting fate
couldn't have befallen Graham Maginnis, *Esquire*." Her
tone dripped with amusement. She gave Emeline a pleasant
if insincere smile, then pulled the door the rest of the way
closed and disappeared down the stairs.

"Graham . . ." Emeline whispered, staring at the door
and hearing the voice of her beloved Aunt Beatrice as she
whispered soothing words to a lonely child: *Your father was
a big man—an honest man. There wasn't a gentleman in
London who stood as tall or proud as Graham Maginnis.*

When Connor arrived at home, he found his sister
hunched over the kitchen table, softly sobbing. Hurrying
over, he knelt beside her and wrapped a comforting arm
around her shoulder.

"What's wrong?" he asked. "Whatever happened?"

Emeline looked at him with red, swollen eyes. "I . . .
I was thinking about F-Father."

"Now, now, that's nothing to be crying about. He's
been gone from this world many a year now, and believe
me, he's in a far better one."

Emeline abruptly clasped his arm. "Are you sure?"

"I'm certain that the next world has got to be—"

"No," Emeline cut him off. "I mean, are you sure
he . . . he died?"

"Of course I am. I was not quite six years old, but Aunt
Beatrice told me all about the funeral and all the people
who came to pay their respects."

Emeline sighed and looked back down.

"What is it, Emeline?" he asked, lifting her chin until
she looked at him. "What's troubling you?"

"Was Father . . . was he ever . . . ?"

"Ever what?"

"In . . . in p-prison?"

Connor's expression froze. He drew in a short breath and, squinting slightly, asked, "Why would you ask such a thing?"

It was Emeline's turn to reach up and touch her brother's face—ever so tenderly on the cheek. When she spoke, her voice was surprisingly firm and steady. "You haven't answered me, Connor. Was he?"

Connor stood. "I didn't answer because your question is so much foolishness. Who put such a thought in your head?"

"That doesn't matter. What matters is whether or not Father was in prison."

Crossing the room, he slowly turned back toward his sister. "Did you hear something when you were little? Is that it?"

Rising, Emeline approached where he was leaning against the counter. "It's all right. I'm all grown up now; you can tell me the truth."

He opened his mouth to speak, but words seemed to fail him.

She took his hand. "I think you've answered my question. How long have you known?"

"I'm not sure . . . since I was fairly young. I remembered some of it from when it happened, and Aunt Beatrice told me the rest."

"But why . . . why didn't you t-tell me before?"

Connor swept her into his arms. "I don't know," he whispered, holding her close. "There didn't seem to be any point in it—and Aunt Beatrice made me promise. After all, you were so young, and both our parents were dead."

"Then he *is* dead?" she asked abruptly, pulling away and looking up at him almost eagerly.

"Of course."

"But when? How?"

"He died of a broken heart after Mother passed away, just as you were told. But it was in prison, not at home.

He got into some kind of business trouble—I don't know what it was, but Aunt Beatrice always said he really didn't do anything wrong. He was sent to prison a few months before you were born—and he died a couple of weeks after Mother."

"Are you sure? Are you ab-absolutely certain?"

"Why are you asking such a thing? Of course I'm sure—the very day that he died, Aunt Beatrice came back from the prison and told me."

"But you were so young."

"Yes, but I'll never forget that day."

Emeline looked down and saw that his hands were clenched white. Taking them in her own, she caressed them until he relaxed his fists. After a few moments, she looked up at him and said, "Connor . . . there's something I have to tell you." She paused a moment. "I heard something today— about a man in . . . in prison."

"What are you talking about?" he said almost distractedly, his attention still fixed on the day of his father's death.

"A woman came looking for you this afternoon. And when I—"

"What woman?"

"You work for her family at the docks. L-Lenora . . . she didn't give her last name."

"Lenora? She came here?"

"Yes, but that isn't what's important. It's something she said when I told her our name; she thought it was Mc-McGuinn."

Shifting uncomfortably, Connor waved a hand. "That's just a name I use on the job."

"No matter," she replied, unconcerned. "But when I said Maginnis, she t-told me her family was once in business with a man by that name—and spelled the same way."

"There must be a thousand folks named Magin—"

"Graham Maginnis?"

His eyes widened. "She said that? She said Graham?" he challenged, and she nodded. "Well, that doesn't really mean anything."

"She also said that this Graham Maginnis was . . . was in p-prison," she hesitantly added.

Again Connor shrugged. "So? Even if it *is* our father she was talking about, what difference does it make? We knew he was in business once and went to prison. But that doesn't change the fact that he's dead."

She grasped his forearm and whispered, "But this Lenora . . . she said he's alive. 'Rotting in prison,' she said." Her voice rose in fear, and her eyes welled with tears. "F-F-Father . . . r-rotting in p-p-prison!" She clutched at her brother, who hugged and rocked her.

"Don't worry, my honeylamb. She must've been mistaken."

"B-B-But if she w-wasn't . . ."

"Don't worry; I'll find out the truth," he promised. "I'll find out."

Holding her closer, he began ever so softly to hum the lullaby their Aunt Beatrice had comforted them with when they were little and frightened and alone.

During the next week, Connor visited the debtors' prisons at Queen's Bench and Whitecross Street and the Holloway and Wandsworth correctional prisons. He learned quickly that the only way to get information about the identities of the prisoners at each facility was to bribe the warder of the gate, who oversaw all communication between the prisoners and the outside world. Communication was in the form of correspondence, censored by the prison officials, and severely restricted visits by family and friends. During the first year of incarceration, visits generally were allowed only once every six months. This was increased to every four months during the second year and every three months in subsequent years, provided a prisoner had not been "docked" for infractions of the strict prison code, thereby forfeiting his privileges.

The most common reason for being docked was misconduct, a determination made largely at the whim of the guards. A second cause was a prisoner's failure to receive his proper quota of marks, earned by hard labor on the treadwheel, a barbaric machine on which lines of prisoners held on to a fixed bar and "climbed" an endlessly revolving staircase, which turned a crankshaft. At some prisons the machine served a practical use—pumping water or grinding corn and flour. But at most of the penal facilities its only purpose was to keep the inmates busy, or to "grind the wind," as the prisoners referred to it.

On Monday morning, August 13—just nine days after Lenora York's visit with Emeline—Connor Maginnis arrived at the main gate of Millbank Prison, the largest convict prison in metropolitan London. It was an imposing edifice, built along the Thames just west of the Houses of Parliament. Millbank looked like a labyrinthian walled city in the shape of a flower; the "walls" consisted of long three-story buildings connected by turreted towers and pieced together to form six huge pentagons around a central hexagon. At the middle of the central hexagonal courtyard and the six surrounding pentagonal courtyards were tall, free-standing towers, affording unobstructed views of all activity below.

The front gate was set in the middle of a high stone wall that enclosed the prison grounds. The warder of the gate, an aging gent with a twirled gray mustache and bushy white brows, was more than pleased to accept the gold coin that Connor offered, but as he stuffed it into the vest pocket of his blue uniform, he mentioned that a second coin would speed up the process immeasurably, "from what I daresay could be hours—even days—to a matter of minutes." His expression, stern and officious, was belied by the mischievous light in his formerly dull gray eyes.

Connor was prepared for such a demand; his earlier encounters had taught him that two bribes were generally required, the second coin going to the chief warder, who kept the prison records.

Accepting a second coin, the old man asked, "Now, what's the name of the poor bloke in question?"

"Graham Maginnis." Connor spelled the last name.

"And when might he have gone in?"

"1822. Sometime in mid-February, I believe."

The warder lifted his gaoler's cap and scratched his bald head. "Let's see, that would make it a half year over fifteen—no, sixteen years. That would have been a year before I started here. Served twenty years at Newgate, first." His voice dripped with pride, and as he drew in a breath, he puffed up like a pouter pigeon. "Now, this Graham Maginnis, I take it he's some relation to you?"

"Yes. My father."

The warder frowned at Connor. "And you're certain he's still alive?"

"Well, not exactly. That's what I've come about."

"But he was incarcerated at Millbank?" the man pressed.

"I, uh, well, I'm not even sure of that."

The warder shook his head as he looked down at the second gold coin in his hand, then back up at Connor. "You're expecting a lot for your coin. He could be anywhere—even in Australia, I suppose."

"I'm certain he's still in London."

"If he's alive, that is," the man noted. Suddenly his expression brightened, and he stood up from his stool. "And that's what you've paid to find out." He tossed the coin in the air and caught it. "You just wait right here, while me and Cap'n Manley inspect the books."

◆◆◆◆

An hour later, Connor was escorted down a seemingly endless series of dimly lit passages that led through the prison wings to the cell where Number 8414 had spent the better part of the past two decades. Several more gold coins had purchased the rare privilege of visiting the prisoner in his cell, rather than waiting several months until the next visitors' day. The warder had made the arrangements, turning Connor over to a bulky guard named Duncan Weems, a well-dressed but poorly bathed man in his midthirties who listed to the left with every step; Connor was uncertain if this was due to the effects of alcohol or a limp.

Despite having grown up in London's poorer districts, with their inadequate to nonexistent sewage systems, Connor was unprepared for the overpoweringly foul stench of Millbank Prison. The guard was holding a handkerchief to his nose, and with a sharp glance over his shoulder, he commented, "Some o' these blokes haven't sense enough to use their chamber pots; they just squat on the floor or relieve themselves agin the wall." He shook his head in disbelief.

The cell doors were of solid wood, reinforced with flat iron bars. Each had a small window at eye level, through which the guards could peer inside. All were kept closed, however, so Connor could not tell whether a particular cell was occupied or by how many people. But he could hear their sounds: a chaotic mixture of groaning, banging, shuffling, coughing, even an off-tune drinking song that wafted like stale beer along the labyrinthian halls.

"It's just round the bend," Weems muttered, slowing his pace and jerking a thumb forward. "Your pappy?" he asked, smirking at Connor.

"I . . . I'm not sure," he replied. His legs suddenly felt wooden, and he had to force himself the few feet to where the guard had come to a halt alongside one of the doors.

The guard spit on his hand and wiped the dust off the

closed window on the door, revealing the numbers eight, four, one, and four. "Yep, here's the one." He lifted a ring of keys from his jacket pocket and fumbled with it, searching for the one that opened the cells along this corridor.

Connor felt the bile rise in his throat, and he would have run away if his entire body hadn't become so leaden. For the past few weeks, the search for his father had been something of a lark—a quest, to be sure, but rooted in the assumption that he would end up empty-handed. Now he stood at a door behind which Graham Maginnis might have spent the last sixteen years of his life.

With some effort, the door creaked open, and the guard disappeared into the darkness of the cell. Connor could hear him muttering at whoever was inside, and a moment later he reappeared and grunted, "In with you, now. We haven't all day."

Forcing himself forward, Connor approached the doorway and peered in. What illumination there was inside the cell came from a small grate high in the wall that apparently led to an airshaft, for the light was negligible. The few rays that made it down the shaft were thinned further by the thick suspended dust, giving the cell an eerie, almost foglike air.

Duncan Weems gave Connor a prod in the direction of the far wall. "There he is, over there."

Connor squinted and stepped closer. Slowly he became aware of a figure shrouded in the fog—a frail-looking man with a long white beard sitting huddled on the edge of a metal cot under the window grate, dressed in a drab, undyed muslin uniform.

"F-Father?" Connor whispered softly, as if afraid to disturb the man's meditations.

"Don't be expectin' him to talk," Weems interjected. "Not much life left in the bloke. If'n I'm not mistaken, he's been off the work line these past five years—leastways that's the case for most o' the blokes on this ward." He stomped over to the cot and grabbed the old man by the beard, jerking his head upward. "Eighty-four Fourteen, you've got a visitor." As soon as he released the beard, the old man's head lolled back down.

Starting back toward the door, the guard asked Connor, "Seen enough?"

"Can I speak with him . . . alone?"

Weems frowned, first at the prisoner and then Connor. Narrowing one eye, he said, "The warder told me to bring you here . . . to see him. Well, you've seen him. I'd say you've had your shilling's worth."

Connor fumbled in his waistcoat pocket and came up with yet another coin, which he held forth. "A few minutes, please. Alone."

The guard eyed the coin and grinned. Snatching it from Connor's hand, he tucked it in his vest and strode from the cell. "You have to be locked inside, mind you."

Connor nodded in assent.

"All right, then. I'll be back in ten minutes." He leaned against the massive door, and it creaked closed. There was a sharp rasp as the lock slid into place, then the thumping of the guard's boots receding into the distance.

For several minutes, Connor stood looking at the man on the cot, watching his features grow more distinct as Connor's eyes adjusted to the light. "Father?" he ventured once more, but the old man continued to stare blankly at the floor.

Approaching, Connor knelt in front of the cot and placed himself in the prisoner's line of sight. The man's gray eyes twitched once, but he didn't react to Connor's presence.

"Father, is it you? Are you Graham Maginnis?"

The man's head lifted slightly, and he gazed into the distance, as if recalling a distant memory. Then, in a surprisingly clear tone, he whispered, *"Maginnis."* His hands, gnarled and covered with sores, trembled as he clasped them together as if in prayer.

"Then it's you? Graham Maginnis?"

"Mr. Graham Maginnis . . ." the man intoned. Connor was about to respond, but his father raised a hand and spoke in a voice that was thin and emotionless but steady: "This court sentences you to serve thirty years at hard labor, that sentence to be carried out at His Majesty's Prison at Millbank. May God have mercy upon you, for this court has none." He lowered his hand but still did not look at the young man kneeling in front of him.

Connor's eyes welled with tears as he grasped his father's hands and gently massaged them. "Father, it's me, your son . . . Connor."

The name did not seem to register.

"I've been searching for you," he continued. "We had no idea you were alive."

"Dead . . . Maginnis . . . dead, he is."

"But you're alive."

"Eighty-fo... Fourteen," Graham whispered.

"You're Graham Maginnis . . . you're my father," Connor said, his voice weak and beseeching.

"Dead, I say!" The old man yanked his hands free and stood on wobbly feet. "Dead the fourteenth day of February in the year of our Lord eighteen hundred twenty-two. Dead and buried in Millbank. It's all recorded: betrayal, arrest, conviction, death . . . Eighty-four Fourteen!" He waved a crooked finger toward the cot, and a glimmer of light seemed to touch his eyes. Just as quickly it passed, and the old man stood unmoving, shoulders hunched, head bent forward.

Connor stood up slowly and took a deep breath as he gathered his thoughts. Finally, he said in the gentlest of tones, "Do you know that you have a daughter? She was born not long after . . . after you went to prison. It was in giving birth to her that Mother passed away."

The old man's head tilted slightly, and Connor thought for a moment that his eyes were glistening. But again he turned away, and when he spoke, his voice was a funereal hush: *"Eighty-four Fourteen . . ."*

There was a sudden clang, followed by the rasp of the lock being slid aside. The cell door creaked open, and Duncan Weems called, "We've got to be goin'. 'Tis almost time for the shift to change."

"Just a few minutes longer?"

The guard's expression was unyielding. "Not today. But I'm sure somethin' can be arranged another time . . . for the proper recompense, mind you." He held the door wide, motioning for Connor to hurry.

Connor started to leave, then looked back at Number 8414, trying to find some familiarity in his features. All he saw was an old man, living just this side of death.

"Come along, now," Weems insisted.

"Father," Connor called, pausing a moment for some sign that the prisoner recognized or even acknowledged his presence. "Your daughter . . . we named her after Mother. Her name is Emeline."

Connor hesitated as long as he could, then acceded to the guard's prodding and started down the corridor.

As the door closed, Graham Maginnis dropped onto his knees on the cold stone floor. His lips quivered, and his voice caught in his throat as he mouthed the name Emeline.

Raising his hands as if in supplication, he shook his head furiously, fighting the flood of images that danced in front of him: a woman, round of belly, her hand gripping the tiny fist of a small boy, her husband standing in the barred shadows, looking on, yearning, ever so slowly dying.

Other images superimposed themselves: a guard opening the cell door, a tall young man, strong of limb and voice, a name manifest in the present, calling from the past.

"Connor!" Graham shrieked; the only reply was the harsh thud of the lock on the cell door sliding into place.

Graham's body jerked in pain with each thumping footfall as the guard and visitor headed down the hall. "Connor!" he called again, this time a coarse whisper. He fell forward onto his hands, his voice cracking each time he gasped the name of his beloved: "Emeline! . . . Emeline! . . . *Emeline!"*

He remained there on his hands and knees, calling the name of his wife, until long after the footsteps had ceased, until his voice became so hoarse that it rasped like the cell-door lock. Finally he was quiet again. He managed to pull himself off the floor and back onto the cot.

After several minutes without moving, he slipped his right hand under the back edge of the thin tick mattress and pulled out a tattered notebook. Delicately opening the pasteboard cover, he flipped through several pages, his bony forefinger searching the pencil marks scrawled across the pages. Despite the exceedingly faint light, he was able to make out the words, and when he found the passage he was looking for, he lifted the book closer and read aloud, his voice smoother and steadier:

"June the first, eighteen hundred twenty-two. Had my first visitor today—my sister Beatrice. What should have been a ray of light has proved my darkest day, for she brings word that my dearest Emeline has died two weeks ago in childbirth. I . . . I—"

His voice broke with emotion, and he stopped reading aloud as his finger continued to trace the words he had written sixteen years earlier. He flipped the page and, smiling, read again:

"Beatrice was eager at my suggestion and will name my daughter after my dear wife. Sweet Emeline! I miss you so! I miss both of you so!"

Graham stared up at the closed cell door. His eyes were filled with tears now—the first since the day he learned that his wife had died—and he let them run freely down his cheeks. When at last he looked back down, he saw that they had stained the journal, and he ran his finger across the moistened page. Steeling himself, he continued to read:

"I will not likely be seeing the streets of London again, and I convinced Beatrice to tell Connor and his new sister that their poor father has died. She is a good woman, and I'm convinced that in time she will realize the correctness of this decision. Until then—until some future lifetime when I can again be with my beloved Emeline and Connor and our new daughter—I have taught Beatrice a lullaby to sing to the little one. It was Emeline's favorite, which she sang nightly to our son. Beatrice hasn't my wife's sweet voice, but I am certain she will make the best of her efforts. If only Emeline could be there to hold our little child and sing her to sleep."

Graham Maginnis drew in a breath and began to sing. He did not need to look at the page on which he had painstakingly recorded each verse of the lullaby. And though his voice was weak and it cracked with age and emotion, the song that filled his cell and spread through the corridors of Millbank Prison was as gentle and pure as the plaintive song of a mourning dove:

> "My little sweet darling, my comfort, my love.
> > Sing lullaby lully.
> In beauty surpassing the heavens above.
> > Sing lullaby lully.
> Now suck, child, and sleep, child, thy mother's
> sweet joy.
> > Sing lullaby lully.
> The gods bless and keep thee from cruel annoy.
> > Sing lully, lully, sweet baby, lully."

VII

◆◆◆◆◆◆◆◆◆◆◆◆◆

Lenora York had willingly paid an extra ten shillings for a private box at the Haversham, a less-than-reputable theater that featured bawdy French "bedroom farces." She enjoyed them as much for the scandalous behavior of the audiences as for the entertainments, which relied more on the charms of the scantily clad performers than on the subtleties of the plot or the sophistication of the acting.

This Saturday night Lenora was focusing little attention on either the audience or the play, which had something to do with an English maid on holiday in Paris. In fact, she could not even see what was going on, for she had closed the box's privacy curtain—one of several closed curtains that night.

"Yesss . . ." she moaned, her back pressed against Connor Maginnis's chest, her fingers digging into his knees as she pushed herself down onto him, matching each upthrust as she rode atop him in the "Woman Astride Man Seated" position from the illustrated book of lovemaking positions that she had discovered among her mother's collection of Oriental erotica.

Lenora felt Connor shift on the armless upholstered chair. His hands gripped her thighs, and ever so slowly he lifted her above him, then forcefully lowered her back down, sending an electric wave through her loins and legs. She and Connor were both dressed—in expectation she had not worn her corset and some of her underclothing—yet she felt as if they were all alone, naked in each other's arms.

"Ooohh . . ." she sighed, controlling the urge to let loose her passion, allowing herself only the slightest sounds of pleasure whenever the crowd cheered or the orchestra struck up a tune.

As the music swelled, they thrust deeper and faster; she could feel the flood rising within her and realized that Connor was yet again about to take her over the edge without him. She had come only minutes before, but he had held back his own pleasure so as to satisfy her a second time.

"No!" she whispered sharply, determined to take him with her this time.

Releasing her grip on his right knee, she reached under her dress and ran her hand up his thigh to where his pants were pulled open and she could touch his skin. Slipping her fingers between his legs, she sought and took him in her hand, touching him tenderly, almost teasingly, then cupping him just below the iron-hard shaft and pulling him upward into her. She knew what pleasured him and was ecstatic to hear him moan as she massaged him, all the while riding him up and down, pulling him toward a finish neither of them any longer could delay. When it happened, she was helpless to contain her cry, but it was immediately drowned as he turned her head and covered her lips with his own, drinking her deep within him.

For several minutes they remained in each other's arms, he pulling her to him, gently caressing her abdomen and breasts, she holding him tight within her, feeling as his powerful flesh, fully sated, softened and yielded.

By the time the stage performance ended some fifteen minutes later, Lenora had pulled back the curtain, and she and her lover were the picture of decorum. As she gently fanned herself and he politely joined in the audience's applause, she remarked in an almost formal tone, "I'm pleased you were able to meet me here on such short notice. I trust my driver explained the situation?"

"He said that your husband had been called away on business and you'd been forced to attend the theater alone." He stopped applauding and smiled suggestively at Lenora. "But don't you have tickets to the opera on Friday evenings?"

"Didn't you prefer the entertainment here? The opera can be so . . . so stuffy. And our seats are down in the orchestra—far too public."

"Whereas here I can share your box."

Returning his knowing smile, she leaned closer so as to be heard above the continued applause and cheers of the crowd. "And did you enjoy yourself in my box?"

"A more snug, comfortable one doesn't exist."

She slapped her closed fan against her hand and gave a slight pout. "I'm certain you say the same to all your theater companions."

"I assure you, Madam York, never before have I been so entertained in a box."

"Then you truly enjoyed the performance?"

"The climax in particular."

"And this was your first time . . . at the theater?"

"Which is why I came so eagerly."

"And religiously," she added.

"I thought we were discussing the theater . . . church is another matter."

"In a church? You haven't!" she scolded, poking him with the fan. "Why, you scoundrel."

He grabbed the fan and held it in place. "In truth, I haven't. But if I had, would you think less of me?"

"Only if you'd done it without me."

"Then I shall save that particular delight for the good Madam York." He gave a slight bow of the head. "After all, she brings a certain zeal to her work."

Pulling the fan free of his grip, she ran it gently up and down his thigh. "Especially when it's missionary work."

"I'd be happy to apply for that position, whenever you have an opening."

"If you are as skilled at missionary positions as at theatrical performances, I shall definitely engage your servicings again."

The performers had finished their last bow, and the audience was shuffling toward the exit doors.

"But come," she told him, rising from her seat. "I must return before Tilford gets home."

"Shall I give you a few minutes and then leave—?"

"Nonsense." She took his arm as he stood beside her. "I'm not concerned about our being seen at the Haversham. Anyone I might know would be just as eager to keep her business here private."

Connor escorted Lenora from the box and downstairs, where they made their way through the crowd milling about the lobby. The Haversham did not attract a fancy-dress audience; like Connor, the men wore the simple suits of the middle class, while the women made greater effort to be fashionable, though at moderate expense. In fact, Lenora York's blue, ermine-trimmed gown was so far above the others in style and cost—and her lush figure filled it so enviably—that she attracted approving glances from the men and jealous stares from the women.

Connor noticed one man standing across the lobby who was paying particular attention to Lenora. He appeared to be in his late twenties, a stocky fellow with stern, dark eyes and a reddish-brown beard. His well-tailored cutaway suit and high parricide collar suggested a man of some means who was out for a night on the town, an impression confirmed by the colorfully dressed woman clinging to his arm. She was a working girl, the kind who frequented taverns near the theater district and earned her wages in back rooms or gentlemen's carriages. A woman not unlike Connor himself.

Concerned that Lenora might have been recognized, Connor steered her toward the front doors, but not before Lenora saw the gentleman in question and pulled up short. There was a moment's awkward silence, and then the fellow nodded politely at them and turned to converse with his companion. Connor felt Lenora's hand tighten on his arm, but then the tension passed, and she let him lead her from the theater.

Outside, they walked to the street, where a long row of hansom cabs was taking on passengers. Almost as soon as they reached the curb, Lenora's ornately appointed brougham pulled around the line of cabs and halted in front of the theater entrance, the pair of matched grays prancing eagerly in place.

"Good evening, Giles," Connor called up to the elderly driver, dressed in full livery.

"Evenin' to you, Master McGuinn." He doffed his black cap. "And to you, Mistress York. I trust you enjoyed the theater?" He clambered down from his perch in the driver's box.

"It was a most . . . ambitious production."

"Then surely you'll be wantin' to take a ride through the park?" he asked as he held open the door of the closed cabin.

Lenora hesitated, glancing first at Connor and then back at the coachman. "I'm afraid not. I'm expecting Tilford home at—"

"Pardon my boldness," Giles cut in, "but I had occasion to return home while you were inside. Miss Sarah reports that Master York sent word he'd be spendin' the night at the Ballinger estate and would see you there tomorrow."

Lenora gave a relieved smile. "In that case, yes, Giles, we'd love a ride through the park." She accepted the old man's hand and stepped up into the coach. "A very slow ride," she added, taking her seat. "We don't want to tire the horses needlessly."

As Connor climbed in beside her, Giles returned to his perch, took up his whip, and popped it over the horses' heads. They moved out smartly through the darkened streets toward Regents Park, and soon the brougham— and its occupants—had settled into a smooth, familiar rhythm.

◆——◆——◆

It was after a second pass through the park, while Connor was buttoning his shirt and Lenora was struggling with the ties at the back of her gown, that he ventured to ask, "Giles spoke of the Ballinger estate—is that the same Ballinger you mentioned to my sister?"

She looked up at him from the seat beside him. "To Emeline? Whatever do you mean?"

Connor chose his words carefully. "When you met my sister a couple of weeks ago, you mentioned your family's business—Ballinger Trade, I believe you said."

"Why, yes, that's so." She grinned conspiratorially. "But it's really not my family's. Tilford's sister is married to Edmund Ballinger, who owns Ballinger Trade. Emeline thought you were working at the docks; I exaggerated so she wouldn't be suspicious. You're not upset, are you?"

Connor waved off her concern. "It was something else that intrigued me. You mentioned a Mr. Maginnis, spelled the same way as our name."

"Graham Maginnis, yes. He's not a relation of yours, is he?"

"I doubt it," Connor lied. "Perhaps a distant one; there aren't too many around these parts who spell their name like mine."

"Well, I hope he isn't." She finished tying her dress and adjusted the hem.

"And this Graham Maginnis was in business with your brother-in-law?"

"Quite some time ago. It was the Ballinger-Maginnis Import and Export Company back then . . . oh, at least fifteen years ago, maybe more. In fact, I think it was Maginnis's company first, until Edmund bought in. Things went fine for a while, but then the troubles began. I was only a child, mind you, maybe nine or ten, but I remember talk of investors being bilked and the company's assets at risk. Both Edmund and Graham Maginnis were arrested . . . it was frightfully scandalous."

"But only Maginnis went to prison."

"Of course. The Ballingers stepped right in and got Edmund released. That's when he took over sole ownership of the company and changed the name to Ballinger Trade. It took quite a few years to overcome the stigma, but it's thriving once again, thanks to Cedric."

"Cedric?"

"Edmund's older cousin. Surely you've heard of Cedric Ballinger."

"I think so. He's a lord, isn't he?"

"Yes. And Lady Sybil is well known for her charities— one of which, I daresay, was bailing out Edmund when his business almost sank. I'm certain Cedric would have let his cousin go under, if only to prove a point."

"Which was?"

"That the Edmund Ballingers deserve their fate, just as the Cedric Ballingers deserve their good fortune."

Connor looked at her curiously. "I don't understand."

Seeming on the verge of laughter, Lenora clasped her hands together. "It's quite a story. You see, Edmund

would have been the rightful heir to the Ballinger title
and fortune if his father hadn't taken up with a married
French actress. James Ballinger's little liaison would have
been fine if he'd been discreet, but the fop insisted on
marrying her—after she obtained a divorce, mind you. He
probably would've ended up at the altar if the woman hadn't
conveniently committed suicide. The scandal finally blew
over, but James never again spoke to his family, and in
return, he was disinherited, the lands and estate falling to
his younger brother, William."

"Cedric's father?"

"Precisely."

"Which left Cedric with the title and fortune and
Edmund empty-handed."

"Oh, Cedric has helped his cousin now and again, but
mostly at Sybil's prodding."

"Such as when Edmund was arrested?" Connor pressed.

"Cedric couldn't stand to have a Ballinger in prison—
even a guilty one."

"You mean Edmund wasn't innocent?"

"He claimed to be, but no one believed him." She
restrained a giggle. "Not that any man is ever truly innocent."

"What do you mean?"

"Come on, Mr. Maginnis. Don't play the *innocent* with
me. Every man I've ever known plays at his work just as
hard as he works at his play. And when a game is involved,
rules are meant to be bent, if not broken."

"Isn't that a bit cynical?"

She laughed aloud. "Don't be so pious. You've been
cheating ever since you were old enough to play the game."
Seeing his expression, she leaned forward and took his hand.
"Now, don't start pouting. You're a master gamesman, and
you can play me anytime you'd like."

Connor forced a smile. "Well, at least you're related
to the Ballingers . . . and if by chance a Ballinger once put

the screw to a Maginnis, this Maginnis can help even the score by putting it right back to you."

"And I intend to hold you to that promise!" She pulled him toward her and lay back beneath him on the seat.

◆━━━◆━━━◆

On Monday morning, Connor followed Duncan Weems back through the labyrinthian halls of Millbank Prison. This second visit had cost twice the first—an appropriate use of the money Lenora York had lavished upon him on Saturday night, he decided. Despite the high fee, the guard was more unsettled than he had been a week earlier.

" 'Tisn't wise to bend the rules too often, mind you," Weems observed as they approached Graham Maginnis's cellblock. "It can start raisin' questions what ain't got good answers."

Connor was afraid the man would demand another coin, which he didn't have. But the guard continued down the final hallway, drew out his ring of keys, and opened the cell marked 8414.

"You'll have to be quick with you. We've got to be clear o' this ward 'afore the hour's up." He didn't bother entering first but prodded Connor into the cell. "Ten minutes—that's all I can give you." He swung the door shut.

Inside the cell, Connor stood waiting for his eyes to adjust to the light, expecting to see the same spectral figure seated upon the cot. Instead, a firm hand took hold of his upper arm, startling him. "Father?" he blurted, turning to the shadowed figure beside him.

"Shhh!" the man insisted. His grip was surprisingly strong, but he abruptly released it. "Sit down over there," he ordered, pointing a bony finger toward the cot.

"Father, it's me—"

"Connor," the man finished, his voice coarse and trembling. "I know."

He could see the old man's features now—the sunken cheeks, the wild shock of white hair and beard, the wide, intense eyes that Connor remembered as being blue but in this light seemed a steely gray.

"You know me? You know who I am?" the young man asked, incredulous with wonder.

"Yes," Graham replied, his thin, tight lips cracking into the faintest of smiles. "But you . . . you've grown."

"Last time I was here—"

"I . . . I was confused. You were the first visitor I'd had since—since my sister died."

"Then you know about Aunt Beatrice?"

Graham nodded. "No one told me, but she was sick, and when she stopped coming, I guessed."

"Then all that time—she knew you were alive?"

"She promised not to tell. Better to have you think your father dead and buried than shut in a cell where you could do nothing but watch him wither away." There was a long pause as the two men stood looking at each other. Then Graham pointed again at the cot. "Sit. Please."

Connor complied, and as he sat down he was struck by how thin the mattress was—little more than a blanket stretched over a metal frame. He wondered how his father could sleep on it, until he looked back up at him and realized even a blanket might be sufficient to cushion a body that was little more than bones.

"Why have you come?" Graham asked, remaining near the cell door.

"To find you. To find out . . ."

"And what have you learned?"

Connor felt his eyes welling with tears. "That I still have a father. That he has a family that loves him."

"You don't even know me."

"Whenever I look at Emeline, I know you," Connor said emphatically.

"It's your mother you're seeing."

Connor wiped away a tear. "Then when I look in the mirror. Emeline and I are so different; if she looks like Mother, then I—"

"No longer. Maybe once, when I was a young man. But now . . ." He looked down at himself. "There's little left of me. Little left alive."

"Father, I want to know how it happened. Beatrice told us you were once a successful businessman. She liked to say that there wasn't a gentleman in London who stood as tall or proud as Graham Maginnis."

"I'm not so tall anymore, am I?"

"How did it happen?"

"It doesn't matter. It's . . . history."

Connor rose defiantly. "It matters to me. If Edmund Ballinger— "

"Who told you about him?" Graham blurted, stepping closer, a wild light in his eyes.

"Then it's true?"

"What have you heard?" he demanded.

Risking he might be wrong, Connor said, "That Edmund Ballinger's the one who should be in prison, not you."

As Connor made the declaration, his father's shoulders sagged and he let out a long ragged breath, as if the life were going from him.

Connor waited for a reply; when none came, he went on, "Tell me I'm mistaken. Tell me you weren't falsely accused and framed. Tell me that's not the truth."

"The only truth is that I've spent the past sixteen years, six months, and seven days here in Millbank Prison as a guest of Her Majesty's government. It doesn't matter how I got here; there is one truth for an honest businessman like me, another for the likes of Edmund and Cedric Ballinger."

Convinced now that he was not mistaken, Connor rose

and approached his father. Standing in front of him, he gripped the older man's forearms and declared, "It matters to me . . . and to Emeline."

"Does she know?" Graham asked, looking up at him with a pained expression.

"Not yet."

"Then don't tell her. She shouldn't have to bear the burden of knowing."

"I didn't plan to tell her. At least not until . . ."

Connor's voice trailed off, and Graham seemed to read meaning in his reticence.

"You haven't any crazy notions about getting me out of here, do you?" he asked.

"And why not?" the young man eagerly replied. "I know it's been a long time, but with your help I could—"

"You could get yourself into a lot of trouble." Graham pulled away and turned his back on his son. "No. It's too late to correct the past. Too many people have too much at stake to sit back and let a young whelp like you get his father out of prison."

"I'm going to try," Connor said firmly and confidently.

Graham faced him again. "I don't want you to, Connor."

"You'd do the same."

"How do you know?"

"Because you're my father . . . and I'm your son."

It was Graham's eyes that filled with tears now—the second time in as many weeks. "You mustn't do anything foolish," he implored.

"I'm just going to look into things—see where your case stands today."

"You won't try to confront the Ballingers, will you?"

"Only if I have to."

"Tell me you won't," Graham pressed.

"Why shouldn't I?"

"Because they're *powerful*, son. They wouldn't just

stand idle and let you make allegations against them. They'd see you in here with me."

"I'm not afraid of the Ballingers," Connor said firmly.

"I daresay you aren't. But you ought to be. Trust me. . . . I discovered too late."

"Then you *were* framed, weren't you?"

Graham gave a simple nod.

"Help me prove it, then."

"From in here?"

"You can tell me everything you know. I can use it to gather the evidence that will prove you innocent." When Graham shook his head, Connor added, "I'm going to do this thing—with or without you."

Graham smiled again, this time more fully. "I believe you, Connor. That's how I know you're my son."

"Then help a son who wants to help his father."

Just then footsteps could be heard coming down the corridor.

"Help me, Father. I beg you."

Graham looked his son up and down, then glanced furtively toward the cot. Hearing the rattle of a key ring on the other side of the door, Graham suddenly dashed to the cot and thrust his hand under the far side of the mattress. Pulling out his notebook, he hurried back and pressed it into Connor's hands.

"There—it's in there!" he rasped, his words punctuated by the sound of the lock sliding open.

"What is?"

"Everything. I wrote it all down. Edmund Ballinger, Cedric, the whole bloody affair."

Connor flipped open the pasteboard cover and saw that it was a journal of sorts. Closing it, he stuffed it behind his shirt. "I'm going to get you out of here, Father. Somehow, I'm going to bring you home."

Taking a step forward, Connor wrapped his arms around the frail old man. Graham's return hug was tentative at first, but his grip grew ever tighter, as if he were afraid that this had all been a dream and he would never see his child again.

"Just promise me you'll take care of your sister," he whispered, his voice breaking. "You two are all that I have left."

"Don't worry. I won't let you down."

They pulled apart just as the cell door slid open. "Time to be goin'," Duncan Weems said with a jerk of his thumb.

Stepping into the corridor, Connor looked back a final time. "Father, I . . ."

"I know, son. I know."

The door creaked shut between them.

VIII

Zoë Ballinger clutched her cousin Ross's arm as the landau coach clattered through the Rotherhithe district toward the Grand Surrey Docks, the large commercial shipping center just downriver from the London Docks and on the opposite bank of the Thames. She gazed through the window at row upon row of small factories and warehouses, the brick and stone exteriors begrimed with coal soot from thousands of rooftop chimneys, the multipaned windows almost as dark as the facades. It was stark and depressing, yet she took refuge in its familiarity and was almost afraid to turn away and look at her cousin. She knew it was because he was leaving the easy comfort of London, traveling to a land that she could hardly imagine.

"It's the strangest feeling," she remarked, forcing herself to face Ross. "I'm really quite depressed at your leaving, yet I'm also filled with excitement for you."

"It won't be so long—really," Ross tried to reassure her. "And think of the presents I'll be sending you."

"Not long? A year, maybe more?" She reached up and pinched his cheek. "And you'd better send me gifts, or else I'll board one of these ships and hunt you down! Better yet, I'll send Bertie—then I'll be free of the *two* of you."

"Is he still sniffing around?"

"Like a puppy."

"Why not simply tell him you aren't interested . . . that is, if you're really not."

"I couldn't do that; our families are the oldest of friends. And Bertie's all right—really he is. But he's just a friend."

"Friends have a strange way of becoming something more."

"Not with Bertie," she insisted, shaking her head determinedly. "And what would you know of such things? You're practically a boy." She elbowed him playfully.

"Boys don't represent Ballinger Trade in China," he declared, puffing himself up with feigned importance.

She squeezed his arm, and as she looked up at him, her eyes filled with tears. "No, they don't. I'm really so proud of you, Ross; you're a real merchantman, bound for the Orient. Just have yourself an adventure. Exercise caution, but not to the point of severity, and don't even think about us back here—" her lips quirked into a smile "—except when it's gift-buying time. Then you'd better remember who your favorite cousin is, or I really *will* book passage on one of those ships and come after you." She nodded toward the waterfront off to the left, the masts of clippers and other small and medium-sized oceangoing vessels visible above the wharf buildings that lined the docks.

"China is hardly the place for an Englishwoman."

"Nonsense. The wives of naval officers and merchantmen go there all the time, and so do missionary women."

"You're not a wife—to Bertie's great dismay, no doubt—and you're certainly no missionary."

"What do you mean by that?" she asked with a petulant frown.

Ross grinned. "Nothing untoward, believe me. You're just not a fanatic—at least about religion."

Her green eyes narrowed suspiciously. "But I *am* fanatic about other things? Such as?"

"Did I say fanatic?" He shrugged innocently. "I meant fantastic."

"That's better."

"And what will you be doing while I'm gone?" he asked.

"I keep busy; you know that. There's my Women's Committee. We're focusing on prison reform just now, and a few of us are even investigating the issue of universal suffrage—though of course Mother and her friends would quit the committee before getting involved in something as scandalous as that." As Zoë gazed through the window at the warehouses that circled the commercial docks, she added almost offhandedly, "And there's always Bertie to amuse myself with."

"He really *will* get the wrong idea if you lead him on like that."

She sighed. "I know, Ross, but he's practically the only man my parents will allow me to leave the house with— except for you and my brothers, of course. And he *is* quite a gentleman; never a misspoken word or thoughtless act. If only he weren't so . . . obsequious."

"Bertie? Obsequious? Maybe toward a respectable woman like you. To me, he always seemed a bit duplicitous."

"In what way?" she asked earnestly, turning toward him.

"I don't know. . . . It's as if his every word is measured for effect and adapted to his audience. It's really nothing; just a feeling."

"But I trust your feelings."

"Don't," he said curtly. "Not where Bertrand Cummington is concerned."

"Why not?"

Ross laughed. "I was thinking of something your brother recently told me."

"Austin?" she guessed, and he nodded. "What did he say?"

Ross hesitated, and when at last he spoke, he waved his hand, as if dismissing his words: "He thinks I'm jealous."

"Of Bertie?"

"Who else?"

"But you're my cousin."

"Second cousin."

Zoë was about to reply, then stopped herself. She looked at Ross more closely, attempting to read his expression. Finally she said, ever so cautiously, "Are you trying to tell me something?"

Ross was still lost in thought, but her comment slowly registered, and his eyes widened. "Good gracious, it's nothing like that. I *love* you, Zoë, but as a cousin. I was just wondering what she'll be like . . . the woman I eventually discover." Wrapping his arm around Zoë, he pulled her close. "I want her to be just like you."

"One day you'll find her, Ross. I promise." Leaning toward him, she kissed his cheek.

"And when you find the right man, Zoë—even if it's Bertie Cummington—there'll be no one happier for you than me." He returned her kiss.

After a moment, Zoë pulled back slightly. "We're almost there, and I haven't given you your present." Loosening the drawstring of her reticule, she reached in and withdrew a thick little book, which she handed to her cousin.

"What's this?" he asked, opening the cover.

"It's for your journey—a book of Chinese words and phrases."

"That's so thoughtful, Zoë. Thank you."

"Not 'thank you,' but *'hsieh hsieh,'* " she carefully pronounced. "Here, look." Taking back the book, she flipped through the pages, found the phrase, and showed him the Chinese equivalent. "Now, you try."

Studying the pronunciation guide, he awkwardly puckered his lips and gave it his best: "Shh . . . shhya . . . shhyeh shyeh."

"That's right. *Hsieh hsieh.*"

"Why do they say it twice?" he asked, somewhat bemused.

"Who knows? Maybe they're twice as thankful."

"Let's try another," he said as he paged through the book. *"Chih tao,"* he intoned, quite pleased with himself.

"What does that mean?"

"To know," he read.

"Know what?"

He shrugged. "Anything, I guess. Here's another: *lao-hu.* It means tiger."

"I hope you don't stumble on a *lao-hu* in China."

"I know . . . I mean *chih tao,*" he replied as he continued to look through the book. "If I do, I'll be very *k'ung-p'a.*"

"Frightened?" she guessed.

"Yes . . . to be afraid."

"How about England? What's the Chinese word for England?"

Ross flipped through the book. *"Ying Kuo,* or Eminent Country. It says that they chose *Ying* because it sounds like the first syllable of England."

"How about China?"

Ross searched for a moment, then nodded. "Yes, here it is. There are several listings: In ancient times it was called *Sin,* then *Sinoe,* and finally *Chin,* before becoming *China.* But the Chinese call it *T'ien Hsia.*"

"That doesn't sound anything like *China.*"

Ross read for a moment. "It appears to be more of a nickname, like saying the Colonies for the United States."

"What does it mean?"

"T'ien Hsia . . . Beneath the Sky."

"Beneath the Sky," she repeated, nodding.

"I guess that's the literal translation." He followed the text with his finger as he read: "From *t'ien,* the sky or heaven, and *hsia,* beneath or below. Literally 'beneath the sky'; also 'land under heaven' or 'celestial land.' "

"*T'ien Hsia* . . . I like that. It doesn't sound so far away; after all, England's beneath the very same sky."

"We're there," Ross said, looking up from the book as the coach came to a halt at one of the Surrey docks. Alongside the dock was a fairly small single-masted cutter that rode low in the water, its hold filled with goods being shipped to India and the Orient by the Ballinger Trade Company. The cutter was not going to make the long ocean voyage but was only transporting Ross and the exports down the Thames and around the Channel to Portsmouth for transfer to the much larger schooner *Celeste.*

"Are you sure you've brought along everything?" Zoë asked as they waited for the coachman to open the door.

"More than I'll ever need."

"Your medicine? It may be hard to come by in Canton."

"I've plenty," he assured her. "I'll be fine."

"It's just that I worry about you." She brushed a stray lock of sandy-brown hair from his forehead.

Pulling away from her, he said a bit curtly, "I'm going to be just fine. Iphigenia has already run through the list of every possible thing that could go wrong with me, starting with my asthma."

"I'm sorry." She gently touched his cheek, turning him to look at her. "I love you, that's all."

"And I love you."

As they embraced, the door opened, and Ross escorted Zoë from the landau, then directed the coachman to deliver his bags to the boat. The morning air was unusually crisp and damp this last day of August, and he wrapped his arm around her, warming her against the chill. They walked onto the dock with the easy familiarity of a brother and sister, perhaps seeing in each other the siblings they wished they had.

"It seems so strange seeing you off alone."

"I prefer it like this. Anyway, they'll all be at Portsmouth the day after tomorrow."

"I wish I could be there, too."

"It's better this way." Stopping alongside the gangplank, he gave her a hug. "You know how difficult Lizzie can be," he added, referring to his older sister, Elizabeth Ballinger Knox, who at twenty-five was a widow with a four-year-old son.

"Will she be bringing Oliver?"

"She doesn't go anywhere without the *boy*." He said the final word as if it had turned sour in his mouth.

"Oh, Oliver's all right."

"My nephew would be a damn sight better if his mother would just give him a little room to breathe."

"You know it's been hard on Lizzie since Frederick died so unexpectedly."

Ross let out a curt laugh. "Hard? I think not. Lizzie's been training for widowhood as long as I can remember. I think she helped ease Fred into his grave."

Zoë poked him but could not suppress a slight giggle. "Enough talk of Lizzie."

"And the boy."

"Yes, the *boy*," she agreed, exaggerating his tone. "And enough talk of China. As far as I'm concerned, you're just going off to school. You'll write regularly, won't you?"

"I promise, ma'am." He gave an obedient nod.

She adjusted the lapels of his gray traveling coat. "And you'll not get into any trouble?"

"What do you mean by trouble?"

"You know what I mean . . . trouble."

"None to speak of."

"And you'll be good?"

"Zoë, you're my cousin, not my mother." He tried to

frown, but seeing her look of sincere concern, he could not help but grin. "Yes, Zoë, I'll be good." He glanced back at the boat and saw the captain watching him from the top of the gangplank. "I really must be going. This is a working ship; the captain won't wait for the likes of me."

"But it's a Ballinger ship, and the captain works for your father."

"Not from what I've heard. These sea captains are their own men. They aren't about to coddle anyone—not a Ballinger, and especially not the son of a Ballinger."

"You say it like it's a curse."

Ross nodded toward where the stern-faced captain was standing ramrod straight on the deck of the ship. "To him, I don't doubt that it is."

Ross and Zoë were saying their final good-byes when they were interrupted by the loud clash of hooves as a cabriolet came racing down the cobbled street. "Ross!" a voice shouted. "Wait up!"

"It's Father," Ross said in surprise as the cabriolet came to a clattering halt alongside the dock.

Edmund set the brake and clambered out, a large package tucked under his arm. "I'm glad I caught you, son," he called, nodding perfunctorily at Zoë as he hurried over to where they were standing. "I've something for you." He handed Ross the package. "Go on, open it."

"You could have brought it to Portsmouth," Ross said as he undid the string that held the plain brown paper in place.

"Not possible. I'm afraid I won't be able to see you off at Portsmouth on Sunday."

Ross looked up, surprised. "No?"

"Our solicitor wants to meet on some urgent business. You know how solicitors can be." He gave Zoë what passed for a smile, his bushy eyebrows arching.

"But you're always there to see the vessels off—to make sure everything's as it should be."

Clapping his son on the back, Edmund declared, "And now I don't need to, because you'll be there." He tapped the package, which was half-unwrapped, revealing a set of ledgers. "It's all listed in here. It's up to you to make sure everything's on board. That'll be no problem for the son of Edmund Ballinger, now will it?" An undeniable look of pride stretched across Edmund's face as he rocked back and forth on his heels, flaring his wide nostrils.

Not wanting to disappoint him, Ross hid his doubts and forced a smile. "No, sir, not at all. I'll take care of everything." He held the ledgers to his chest.

"Just do it the way I've shown you—as you've seen me do a hundred times." Edmund turned to Zoë, and for the first time his expression toward her looked genuinely warm as he told her, "Your cousin's a natural merchantman, he is. And he'll make a real China trader."

"Hsieh hsieh," Ross said, remembering the phrase for "thank you."

"Well, I'll be damned. You've been learning yourself some Chinese." Edmund chuckled. "I've been to Canton four times myself, and I'll be damned if I remember even a word."

"He's doing excellently," Zoë put in, her eyes flashing mischievously. "He can even say, 'My father is the number-one man from Ballinger Trade.' Can't you, Ross?"

"Is that so?" Edmund asked enthusiastically. "Go on, boy, let's hear it."

Ross shot an angry glance at his cousin, then turned back to his father, who was eagerly motioning him to continue. After a moment's hesitation, Ross drew in a breath, then in a single stream blurted all the Chinese words he had learned, throwing in a little English for good measure: *"Chih tao Ballinger k'ung-pa lao-hu T'ien hsia."*

An extremely rough translation might have been, *I know Ballinger fears the tiger beneath the sky,"* but that did not seem to concern Edmund, who declared in delight,

"Excellent, my boy! Really first rate! You're going to get on famously in Canton. I knew I was right to send you."

It was all Zoë could do to keep from bursting into laughter. Struggling to retain his own composure, Ross covered up for his grin by saying somewhat whimsically, "I'm just worried about how you'll ever manage to get along around here without my help."

"Now, don't you worry about a thing, young man. Good office boys are easy to come by. It's real merchantmen who're hard to find."

"And you'll hire yourself an office boy if you need to?" Ross asked in a more serious tone. "You should have help with the paperwork."

"Yes, yes, if I must—at least until you get back or young Oliver is old enough, whichever comes first."

"I'll be back soon enough," Ross promised.

"Aye, that you will, my boy. And when you do, you'll no longer be a boy, but a man." Edmund's voice cracked with emotion, but he brought it under control. "Now, off with you. And remember everything I've taught you. When it comes to selling tea, those Chinamen can be craftier than any Jew." Again he clapped Ross on the back in what passed for a hug.

Ross said a final good-bye to his father and Zoë, then walked up the gangplank. At the top, he greeted the captain, then stood at the rail as the plank was lifted off the deck and lowered to the dock. The wind was sharp enough from the west to allow the cutter to leave under sail, and a few minutes later it was moving briskly down the Thames, leaving behind the Grand Surrey Docks and, beyond them, the buildings of Greater London.

Ross stood watching the figures on the dock. He could see his father wave a few times at the departing ship, then walk over to his cabriolet. He even heard the crack of the whip as Edmund steered the vehicle in a wide arc and drove back through Rotherhithe toward London Bridge. But as

Ross had expected, Zoë continued to stand there, waving farewell to her favorite cousin, whom she might not see for a year or two—or even longer.

Suddenly he felt incredibly alone. Why had he ever asked to be sent to China? he wondered. His health had never been the best, and he was not sure he was prepared for the rigors of such a journey. Even more uncertain was whether he was ready to represent Ballinger Trade in Canton, where the veteran China traders would surely view him as a young upstart.

It's too late to turn back, he told himself as the wind caught the sails and the ship gained speed. Raising his arms high above his head, he called, "Good-bye, Zoë," but did not bother to shout, since she would not hear him above the wind.

Ross Ballinger realized he was truly on his own, now. But he drew comfort from the knowledge that Zoë would be there to greet him when at last he returned from his long voyage *T'ien hsia.* . . .

◆ ◆ ◆

Two days later, Edmund Ballinger was spending his Sunday at the warehouse, waiting for his wife, daughter, and grandson to return to London after watching Ross set sail for China aboard the *Celeste*. He was not meeting with the firm's solicitor, as he had explained when excusing himself from the trip to Portsmouth. Instead he was taking advantage of there being no day crew on Sundays so as to spend an energetic hour or so with the charwoman Clarissa, who he made sure was on hand every Sunday afternoon.

When he grew tired of his sport, he sent Clarissa home, telling her she could have the evening off in exchange for the extra services she had rendered to him. He did not feel overly generous and held back the usual gold coin, giving no regard to her dejected expression as she buttoned her flimsy, tattered dress and hurried from the office.

Edmund spent another hour checking the books, awaiting the arrival of the night crew before heading to his club for a good glass of scotch. When at last he heard the workers filing into the warehouse, he donned his brown greatcoat and a fashionably low-crowned silk hat, then headed out of the office and locked it behind him.

As he started down the main aisle, Edmund looked around the cavernous, crate-filled room. About a dozen warehousemen were on hand, assembling the orders to be shipped the next morning on a schooner bound for Boston. They were working at a steady pace, thanks to the stern supervision of the night foreman, Roger Avery. Catching Avery's eye, Edmund nodded at him and received back a wave that signaled all was under control.

Passing through the front entryway, Edmund unlocked the door, stepped outside, and locked it behind him. He turned to leave and found himself confronted by a curly-haired teenager in a neat but poorly tailored black suit. The boy looked uncomfortable in his starched collar, and Edmund guessed he was a common laborer, or the son of one.

Realizing the boy was purposely blocking his way, Edmund asked, "Well? What do you want?"

"Are you Mr. Ballinger?"

"What if I am?" he grumped.

The young fellow smiled, taking the answer in the affirmative. "I'd like to come work for Ballinger Trade."

Edmund raised one bushy eyebrow. He was a stocky, powerful-looking man and dwarfed the youth, who was perhaps fifteen or sixteen and had not yet filled out. And though Edmund was but an inch or so taller, he managed to look down at the intruder as he replied, "It's the foreman who hires the dock crew. But there's no work to be had."

"I'm strong, real strong, and I'm willin' to work—"

"I said there's no work." Edmund raised a stiff hand, pushing past the boy and heading down the dark, foggy

street. He heard the youth calling after him, but he paid
no attention as he disappeared into the shadows.

Edmund was just approaching the street corner when
a looming figure came around the edge of the warehouse,
startling him. He stepped aside to let the fellow pass, but
the man halted directly in front of him. The thin light from
a nearby streetlamp revealed a hulk of a man several inches
taller and wider than Edmund with coarse, dirty features,
a rotting white bandage on his left cheek, and the foulest
whiskey breath.

"Excuse me," Edmund said far more politely than he
would have done during the day. He turned aside, but the
man matched his move, leaving Edmund with his back to
the warehouse wall. He felt a slight twinge of panic, but he
had no doubt that he could handle the situation if it became
a fight. After all, the fellow was obviously drunk.

"Gi' me your money!" the man demanded, stepping
closer and practically pinning Edmund against the wall.

"I'll do no such thing!"

"Aye, you will!"

The man stepped back quite agilely for a drunk, and
Edmund saw his hand flick into the pocket of his tattered
jacket. When it reappeared, it was with the unmistakable
glint of a knife blade—a small blade, only a few inches
long, but enough to make poor work of a man.

Edmund's eyes darted left and right, gauging the best
path of escape. Attempting to buy time and set the assailant
off his guard, he said, "Just hold on, mate. I'll gladly give
you what I've got." He fumbled with his coat pocket,
getting ready to make his move.

From off to his left came a wild shriek, and someone
bounded through the air and barreled into the assailant,
staggering him and knocking the knife from his hand. It
was the youth who had asked Edmund for a job, and he
was sputtering with rage as he flailed at the drunk and beat
him back across the sidewalk.

"Get it!" the lad cried. "The knife!"

Suddenly Edmund realized that the brute was swinging clear of the boy and scrambling to retrieve his weapon. Seeing it less than a foot from his shoe, Edmund leapt for it and snatched it up in his right hand. The enraged drunk lunged for him now, and the boy vaulted onto his back, clawing at his shoulders and arms and pinning them at his sides. This only momentarily stopped the man, who already was shaking the boy off him.

"Stick him!" the lad shouted, jerking back on the drunkard's arms so that his ample belly would present a ripe target. "In the gut! *Quick!*"

The hulking assailant gave a furious oath and twisted his shoulders, struggling to free himself from the lad's tenacious grip. Edmund saw his moment passing, and he acted, drawing back his right hand, then suddenly dropping the knife and swinging his fist in a vicious arc that caught the drunk square on his bandaged cheek. The ferocious blow knocked him from the boy's arms and threw him to the ground, his head striking the pavement with a sickening thud.

It was unclear who was more surprised, Edmund or the boy. They stood side by side staring down at the man, who lay motionless, facedown on the pavement. Edmund was rubbing the knuckles of his right hand, and he found himself grinning, then chuckling softly at his good fortune and lucky blow. The boy was thoroughly stunned. He bent over the body, examining it, then looked up at Edmund.

"You . . . you killed him, I think."

"Yes, yes—I did, didn't I?" he replied, his voice quick with excitement.

"A bad piece of business, it is," the boy muttered.

The reality of what he had done set in, and Edmund's smile faded. He looked around to see if anyone was watching, then said in an undertone, "He came at me with a knife. You saw him."

"That he did, but . . ."

"But what?"

The youth slowly looked up at him. "But you killed him."

"He tried to kill *me*. And he would've done the same to you."

"I hope the magistrate sees it the same."

Edmund felt a surge of panic. Surely any sensible person would acquit him of all responsibility, but the justice system was not always known for being sensible—or fair. The system had been twisted in his favor once before; he could not be sure it would favor him again.

"No one needs to know about this," Edmund suggested. "We'll just leave him here and—"

"They'll come lookin' around your company and questionin' everyone." The boy shook his head. "He mustn't be found here—that won't do." Rising in place, he thought for a moment, then turned to the older man, his expression brightening somewhat. "You get out of here. I'll drag him a few blocks away—down to the docks. They'll think it a waterfront brawl."

"Yes . . . yes, you do that," Edmund muttered, looking around uncomfortably, wanting desperately to be as far away as possible.

The boy knelt at the man's head and slipped his arms under the shoulders. "Go on, now. Off with you."

Taking a few hesitant steps, Edmund looked over at the boy, who was rolling the body onto its back. "Thank you," he said, and the lad waved him away. He took another step, then spun back around. "Tomorrow," he called, nodding briskly. "You come see me tomorrow about that job you wanted. I can use a quick-thinking lad like you."

The boy gave a slight smile, then went back about his business. Shivering, Edmund hurried off down the street.

The boy waited until Edmund Ballinger's footsteps had receded into the fog, and then he started shaking the body lying at his knees. All the while he cursed beneath his breath, *"Damn! Goddamn it!"*

Halting for a moment, he took hold of the bandage and unceremoniously ripped it from the man's cheek. Then he continued shaking and rubbing the man until finally he was rewarded by a slight groan.

"Connor!" he whispered. "Don't you die, damn it!"

"Mohhh," came an answering moan. "Mohhhzz . . ."

Connor managed to open his right eye; his left was swollen somewhat from the hard blow he had taken to the cheek. "Whaa . . . ?"

"It's all right." Mose Levison cradled Connor's head in his lap.

Connor clutched at his stomach. "Where . . . where did he stab me?"

"He didn't. But he landed a hard fist to your cheek. Knocked you flat."

"Damn!" Connor struggled to his elbows, then forced himself to sit up. He rubbed his sore cheek and the knot that was forming at the back of his head. "Ohh!" he exclaimed in pain. "Shit!"

"You hit the ground pretty hard. I thought you was done for."

Connor clawed open the buttons of his shirt, revealing the heavy padding of a blanket, which he had wrapped around his middle to bulk him up and protect him from the knife. Pulling it away, he removed the extra material over his midsection where the short blade was supposed to stick him. Nestled in the padding was the sewn-up casing of a sheep's stomach filled with chicken blood.

"Goddamn it, Mose," he cursed. "He was supposed to kill me."

"Don't worry—he thinks he did. After he flattened you out, you never moved; even I thought you was done for."

Connor's expression brightened. "Then it worked?"

Mose beamed. "It sure did. He wants me back tomorrow to start workin' for him."

Connor signaled the teenager to help him to his feet. Once he was standing alone on shaky legs, he waved a hand at the knife on the ground, and Mose quickly retrieved it, along with the blanket and padding.

"Can you walk?" the boy asked, coming up beside him so that Connor could steady himself on his shoulder.

"I'll be fine. Let's get going."

"It worked just like you said," the boy declared as they started down the street.

Connor squeezed his shoulder affectionately. "Did you doubt it?"

"A bit, I suppose."

"Just so long as Edmund Ballinger didn't."

"It was quite the ruse, and he fell for it—every speck of it."

"The important thing is that we got you inside Ballinger Trade. If I guess right, the old fart'll have you working right alongside him in his office."

"Where I can start checkin' his books."

"In good time, Mose. For a while I just want you to do your job and get familiar with the place—and for him to get used to having you around."

"And what about you?"

"I'll be working another angle."

"You mean His Lordship?" Mose asked, having learned the full story during the past week while he and Connor pored through Graham Maginnis's journal, which detailed how Edmund Ballinger had schemed to defraud their customers and, with his cousin's assistance, had framed Graham for his crimes.

"Cedric Ballinger. Yes." Connor was walking steadier now and picked up the pace as they headed back through the London streets. "I've been checking up on 'His Lordship' and his family, and I've an idea how to work my way in."

"I'm sure you do, Connor." Mose smiled broadly. "I'm quite sure you do."

Leaving the London Docks behind, they rolled up the blanket and unceremoniously heaved the stomach full of chicken blood into a hedge, then set out for the nearest friendly tavern, where Connor would clean himself up before going home. He did not want Emeline to know what they were up to, and he reminded Mose to keep it a secret.

"You needn't worry about me," Mose assured him. "I ain't ever heard of Graham Maginnis or Millbank Prison. And if Miss Emeline learns about Ballinger's, it's just a job I happened to find."

"Good. We'll save the surprise until we're sure—until the day my father steps out of that prison into the free air." He placed his hand on Mose's shoulder. "Come along, now. After tonight's work, I'd say you're old enough to share a mug of good English rum!"

IX

"Bertrand Cummington to see you, Miss Ballinger."
The butler held forth a silver tray bearing a calling card
with the Cummington crest on the front and Bertrand's
signature engraved on the back.

"Please inform him that I'll be ready to leave in a few
minutes," Zoë replied, examining the card and dropping it
back on the tray. "Have him wait in the front sitting room,
Desmond."

With a bow, the butler backed out of the room. As
soon as he was gone, Zoë sighed and looked at herself in
the dressing-table mirror.

"Why did I ever agree to this?" she asked herself
aloud. Her cousin Ross had been gone just two weeks,
and already she was proving that his concerns about
Bertrand Cummington had been justified. "I *am* leading
him on," she sternly admonished her image in the mirror.
Her resolute expression softened, then weakened entirely
as she whispered, "Aren't I?"

Pouting, she leaned close to the mirror and examined
her eyelids, which were highlighted with just a hint of
emerald powder, in the style of the French. She couldn't
deny that it brought out the green of her eyes, but she
wondered if it might be a little too daring.

I don't want to encourage Bertie, she tried to convince herself, picking up a handkerchief to wipe away the powder. But she reconsidered and tucked the cloth under the lace-trimmed cuff of her gold-brocaded evening dress. *I'm wearing it for me,* she told herself. *And Bertie isn't so terrible—even if he* is *thirty and a bit of a fop.*

Sitting more erectly, she narrowed one eyebrow and crooked a finger at her image in the mirror. "Now, you be a well-behaved young woman tonight," she cautioned. "The Cummingtons are our oldest friends, and as for Bertie . . ." Trying not to smile, she pinched her nose and gave an affected, nasal imitation of her brother Julian's favorite remark regarding her suitor: "The trouble with Bertie is he just doesn't know if he's a-going or a Cummington."

"He'll be a-going if he overhears you talking like that," a voice declared, and Zoë jumped in surprise to see her mother, Sybil, standing in the doorway.

"M-Mother! I'm so sorry. I was just—"

"It's all right, dear." Sybil smiled warmly as she entered the room.

"I didn't mean it. I was just remembering the way Julian would always tease about Bertrand."

Coming up behind Zoë at the dressing table, Sybil laid her hands on her daughter's shoulders. "I know that Bertie can seem a little . . . well, indecisive. But he's usually just being considerate."

"I know, Mother."

"You really ought to give him a chance. He's such a congenial young man."

Zoë acknowledged that Bertrand Cummington was congenial—almost too much so—but she did not agree with her mother's assessment as to his youth. Certainly thirty was not old, but somehow it seemed that way on Bertrand. Rather than argue, Zoë simply replied, "I'm willing to give him a chance, but we're only going to dinner. It's not as if he's come to ask my hand in marriage."

"Not just any dinner, but dinner at the Piccadilly Arms." Closing her eyes, Sybil drew in a long breath.

Zoë could not help but cringe. Ever since Bertrand had invited her to the restaurant at the Piccadilly Arms Hotel, she had harbored the secret fear that he was planning to ask for her hand in marriage, since the Piccadilly was the place where her father had asked Sybil to marry him.

"He doesn't know, does he, Mother?"

"Know what, dear?" She gazed innocently at her daughter in the mirror.

"About you and Father. You haven't gone and told him about Father's proposal, have you?" She shifted on the seat and looked up at Sybil.

"Of course not, dear. I suppose that over the years something *might* have been said to Henry or Virginia, and one of them could have told Bertie. I mean, it's hardly a secret. And it was *so* romantic."

Zoë had heard the story countless times— of how Cedric had hired a special coach drawn by a team of four white Arabians to take them to the Piccadilly Arms, where he had arranged for a private room and a string quartet to entertain them during dinner. It was during dessert, when the chef was presenting the cherries in brandy, that Sybil had seen something flashing brilliantly amid the flaming liqueur. It was a gold ring set with a large tear-shaped diamond. Cedric had said some sort of cliché about it burning like his heart, but Sybil was not really listening. Instead she was nodding and whispering, "Yes," over and over, agreeing to marry him even before he had proposed.

There had better be no such question tonight, Zoë told herself. Rising from the stool, she gave her mother a somewhat perfunctory hug and said, "If I go outside and find a coach drawn by a team of white stallions . . ."

"Don't worry—I already looked. It's a coach, all right, but it's being pulled by four dun mares."

"Then I guess I'm safe." Picking up her white cashmere

shawl, embroidered and fringed in silk, she wrapped it around her and started from the room.

"I didn't look *inside* the coach, however," her mother mischievously admitted. "I suppose he could have a string quartet hidden in there—maybe even a chamber orchestra."

Zoë looked back at her mother. "If I hear even a single violin . . ."

Sybil waved her away. "You just run along and have a good time. And give Bertie—"

"A chance. Yes, Mother, I will."

◆◆◆◆

When Zoë greeted Bertrand Cummington in the front sitting room, she had to admit that he was both handsome and well turned out in his black dinner jacket and white waistcoat. His shirt sported a ruffle at the chest, and his cravat and collar were unusually high and wide. He was holding an ivory-inlaid cane, and she did not doubt that the knob was real gold.

Bertrand was tall and fairly thin, though not at all spindly. His features were somewhat angular but in a strong, masculine way, and his eyes were large, dark, and comforting. His hair was still black, though Zoë detected a slight receding at the temples, counterbalanced by a thickening of the brows. He was undeniably attractive at thirty, but there was no guarantee that twenty years later he would still be so.

"Why, Miss Zoë Ballinger, you look absolutely . . . divine," he declared, rising from the divan and crossing the room to greet her.

Zoë held out her right hand and allowed him to kiss it. "I hope I haven't kept you waiting."

"Not at all. In fact, it gave me time to visit with Austin." Looking suddenly embarrassed, Bertrand quickly added, "I don't mean to imply that you *did* keep me waiting. It's just that I enjoyed a pleasant visit with Austin."

"I understand completely," Zoë assured him, trying to ease his obvious discomfort. "But I'm ready now, if you are."

"Why, yes, of course."

She took Bertrand's offered arm, and he led the way into the foyer, where the butler was waiting with Bertrand's black evening coat and silk top hat.

"Good night, Desmond," Zoë told the butler as he opened the door and she stepped outside.

"Have a pleasant evening, Miss Ballinger, Mr. Cummington," the butler replied as the couple descended the stairs.

The Cummingtons' family coach was parked under the protection of a carriage port that extended over the side entrance of Planting Fields Manor, which for two hundred years had been the Ballingers' estate in the Castlebar Hill district, just west of Kensington outside London. The impressive vehicle was a specially designed crane-neck coach, so named because the undercarriage curved up over the front wheels like the neck of a crane. The deep-blue, gilded coach was ornamented with carved flowers and fruit, and there were heavy velvet curtains over the door windows and venetian blinds over the windows at the ends of the facing seats. The driver's box was draped in silk with velvet trim and was set on a perch over the front axle, well in front of the coach body, which was suspended on leather thoroughbraces from four C-spring braces.

The liveried driver, a graying man in his fifties, stood at attention with the door open, ready to help Zoë into the coach. However, Bertrand said, "That's all right, Crowley," and waved him away, then offered Zoë his own hand.

A few moments later, the couple was seated side by side in the coach, the interior illuminated by two brass reading lamps. The man named Crowley climbed into the driver's box, released the brake, and snapped his whip smartly. The team of four lurched forward, then settled into a steady gait down the drive that wound along the meticulously landscaped lawns and through the famed sculpted gardens, which reputedly had given the estate its name.

In reality, the gardens had once been an ancient cemetery—a Druid one, according to legend. Long before the Ballingers had built their estate and taken up residence, the cemetery was already known as the Planting Fields by local residents, who avoided the place. All that remained of the original Planting Fields was a curious circle of stones, much like the one at Stonehenge but far smaller, which according to legend had been used by the Druids for human sacrifices, the bodies of their poor victims then being "planted" in the surrounding fields. In order to break the old superstitions, the first Ballinger owners had turned the fields into ornate flower gardens that incorporated the circle of stones, thus usurping and eventually redefining the name Planting Fields.

The third generation of Ballingers, fascinated by the ten-foot-high stones and unconcerned about archaeological integrity, had hired a team of Italian stonecutters to transform them into some sort of classical representation of the gods of antiquity. The stonecutters, perhaps influenced by the spirits of the Druids who supposedly had created the circle, claimed that the type of rock was unsuitable for statuary and instead carved simple figures and designs on the broad faces of the stones, their work inspired less by the Greeks and Romans than by the Celts. The results were both beautiful and eerie, as if the tall, rectangular stones had been transformed into giant headstones bearing Celtic crosses, figures of early Christian monks and knights, and even their hermetic Druid forebears.

The sun was just setting as the coach traversed the estate, and the stones cast long shadows across the surrounding gardens. As they passed nearby, Zoë stared through the venetian blinds, recalling how she and her brothers and cousins had loved to dance and play among those stones, hiding in the shadows, leaping out at one another like spooks on All Hallows' Day. She remembered just how safe she had felt in the "Druid Circle," as most people still referred to it.

"It's a shame about Miss Rose, isn't it?" Bertrand asked offhandedly, as if looking for some topic—any topic—to fill the quiet that had fallen between them.

Drawn out of her reverie, Zoë turned from the window and muttered, "Miss Rose?"

"Why, yes. Lady Rose Hudson. Surely you've been following the *scandal*," he whispered, referring to the Hudson affair, as it was being called around London. "She certainly has made a frightful mess of it all."

"I'm sorry, but I don't see where she's made anything at all of it. It would seem that the 'mess' has been orchestrated by a coterie of jealous maids and wagging tongues."

"I didn't mean to offend," Bertrand said deferentially, looking totally mortified that he might have upset Zoë. "But surely the other Ladies of the Bedchamber have had some reason for their accusations."

"Why? Because Lady Rose has gained some weight about the middle? That does not necessarily mean a child is in the offing."

"But when a young woman is unmarried and serves on the queen's own staff, she must be doubly careful to—"

"A woman cannot guarantee her own health. And one's health should not be the source of rumor and gossip."

Zoë surprised herself at being so forthright, but she had been particularly irked by this recent scandal, which had been stirred up by many of the women who worked in the palace, Lenora York among them. As soon as it looked as if one of their fellow Ladies of the Bedchamber was pregnant, they had accused her of immoral behavior, even going so far as to bring their charges to Lord Melbourne for investigation.

Looking somewhat chastened, Bertrand said in a gentle

tone, "Perhaps the whole affair will blow over, now that the queen's physician has personally stepped in and examined the poor woman."

"The poor woman—Lady Rose—has been completely exonerated, don't forget. Yet the tongues continue to wag, despite what Sir James Clark had to say. In fact, his examination seems only to have worsened her condition; they say she's taken to bed and is continuing to gain weight."

"Perhaps Sir James was mistaken," Bertrand mused.

"There—that's exactly what I mean. A physician—the queen's physician, mind you—declares Lady Rose's honor to remain . . . intact," she said delicately. "Yet the rumors persist. We should be sympathetic because of her condition, rather than judging her moral behavior."

"I didn't mean to imply . . ." He fell into an awkward silence.

Zoë looked at Bertrand, who seemed so thoroughly dejected that she laid a comforting hand over his. "I'm sorry, Bertrand," she said sincerely. "It's not you. It's the way the whole country has taken sides, falling in line either in support of Lady Rose or in condemnation of her supposed behavior. It's just an excuse for a witch hunt—and not just against Lady Rose."

Bertrand looked at her, his dark eyes holding a ray of hope at Zoë's kind expression. He started to place his free hand over hers, but she sensed his move and delicately withdrew hers.

"A witch hunt?" he said, resuming the conversation. "You mean against our queen?"

"There are many who are eager for any excuse to speak against the queen, just because she's young."

"And a foreigner."

"It's true she has some foreign blood, but she's as English as you or I." Zoë shook her head. "It's a shame the way they attack behind her back. This situation with the Ladies of the Bedchamber simply adds fuel to their prejudices."

"I'm afraid you're right," Bertrand agreed. "No one can deny that Victoria has acted impeccably throughout the affair, yet I sense the public turning against her. The newspapers openly proclaim that she's being unduly influenced by advisers out for themselves. Even Lord Melbourne is in disfavor for letting things get so horribly out of hand . . . and for supporting Victoria's refusal to dismiss any of the Ladies of the Bedchamber."

"No doubt the Tories and Chartists are loving every minute of it," Zoë suggested. "They've already begun to come to Lady Rose's defense; I've even heard the Chartists are circulating a petition on her behalf. Anything to make political gains at the expense of the Whigs."

"And tear down the monarchy," he added.

"No doubt."

Bertrand looked at Zoë curiously, as if seeing a new side of the young woman. "I had no idea you were so interested in politics."

She smiled demurely. "Just as I had no idea of your interest in affairs . . . of the heart."

Bertrand blushed, the redness flushing his cheeks and spreading to his ears. "Speaking of the heart . . ." he ventured, the words trailing off as he gauged her mood.

Zoë shifted uncomfortably on the seat, knowing what was coming, uncertain how to avoid the inevitable. When the silence grew oppressive, she heard herself break it with a single word: "Yes?"

"I . . . I had thought to wait until we were at the restaurant. But perhaps this is a better time. After all, the Piccadilly Arms is really your parents' special place, and I want tonight to be special for you and me."

"Bertrand," she said cautiously, "I think I know—"

"Please, hear me out," he insisted, moving off his seat and switching to the bench across from her. Leaning forward, he took hold of her hands. "We've been friends for a long time, Zoë. Our families have been close. And there's nothing that would please them more—that would please *me* more—than to see the Ballinger and Cummington lines united through the two of us."

"Bertrand . . ."

"Miss Zoë Ballinger," he went on, sliding off the seat and kneeling in front of her. "I humbly, respectfully ask your hand—no, both your hands"—he gave them a gentle squeeze—"in marriage."

"Oh, Bertie . . ." she exclaimed, not sure whether to laugh or cry. "I'm not sure this is the right time—"

"Of course it isn't. The right time is whenever you're ready to say yes. And if you're not ready today, then you must take all the time you need."

"It's not that. . . . It's just—"

"Shhh," he whispered, placing a forefinger on her lips and sitting beside her. He delicately lifted her hand and kissed it. "It's my fervent desire that you become Lady Zoë Cummington. That's what I wanted you to know, and now we shall enjoy our dinner together and speak no more about it."

Zoë lowered her eyes and smiled. She had known that the proposal would eventually come, and still she was touched by his gentle consideration. It was the first time anyone had asked for her hand in marriage, and certainly most of her friends would urge her to accept. After all, the Cummingtons were among the richest in London society, and Bertrand was considered quite a catch. He was affable enough, she had to admit. But he seemed to lack the inner fire that drove one to seize hold of life or be consumed trying. Perhaps the lack was within herself—an inability to accept and make peace with life as it was. All that she knew was that Bertrand represented everything comfortable, and for Zoë, that wasn't enough.

Zoë gazed through the window and saw that they

were nearing the end of the drive and about to make a right turn onto the main thoroughfare. It was primarily a private road connecting several estates, and traffic was rare in the evening, so the driver pulled out without first coming to a stop. There was a sudden shout, and the coach swerved violently as one of the dun mares reared on its hind legs, its front hooves pawing frantically at something in front of it.

The coach lurched forward a few feet, then jerked to a halt, throwing Zoë against Bertrand. She managed to keep her seat and, looking outside, could see a carriage in the thin evening light. It was far smaller than their vehicle— a cabriolet, perhaps—and it was parked at an angle to the coach. The driver was working the reins, urging the single black horse to back away from the rearing mare.

Crowley was also fighting his team, and as he did so, he let loose a furious string of oaths; Zoë could not tell if it was directed at the horses or at his counterpart in the cabriolet. The other driver joined in now with a few choice words himself, cursing all five "goddamn beasts!" as he inched his carriage back enough for Crowley to bring his own team under control. A few minutes later, all the horses had calmed, and the drivers set their brakes and climbed down to inspect for damage.

"Easy, now," Crowley soothed as he patted each of the four dun mares, then stooped to check their legs for injuries. "That damnable gelding didn't hurt you now, did he?"

"*My* horse?" the other driver exclaimed incredulously. "Hurt *yours*? What about what *your* beast did to *mine*? There's a gash on his flank."

The driver moved forward into the light of the carriage lantern, and Zoë saw a young man, her age perhaps, dressed in a suit of the working class. He looked as if he might be an employee at a neighboring estate.

"You could have killed us all, you know," he said.

Crowley stood and faced the younger man. "You damn near bowled us over, driving like a maniac."

"You're the maniac, I daresay, pulling out onto a road without first checking to see if it was occupied."

"Why, you swept down on us like a black cloud. If you had the proper running lamps—"

"I've a lamp, sir . . . two of them." The young man pointed toward the lamps alongside the covered seat.

"Damn puny ones," Crowley said derisively.

"Perhaps if you'd been wearing glasses," the man retorted.

"I can see just fine—but I don't think I care much for *what* I see." He took a menacing step toward the young stranger, who held his ground.

Bertrand leaned across Zoë and opened the door, calling, "That's enough, Crowley," as he stepped from the coach. "The damage has already been done; no need to make things worse."

Not wishing to miss any excitement, Zoë climbed out and approached the three men, who were facing one another in the space between the vehicles. She saw that the other carriage was a two-person cabriolet of the type for rent on the streets of London.

"Now, good sir," Bertrand said to the young man, "if there's been any injury to your horse, I'll be glad to make restitution."

"It isn't *his* horse," Crowley said gruffly. "The bloke's driving a rented rig." He made no effort to mask his disdain for either the younger man or his mode of transportation.

"Be that as it may, I'm still quite willing to correct any financial loss." Bertrand took his billfold from the inner pocket of his coat. "Just how much is this . . . this *vehicle* costing you?"

"You needn't concern yourself about me or my *vehicle*," the man said in a mocking tone. "The animal will heal, as will any damage to my purse." He glanced beyond the men and noticed Zoë, who had stepped up behind Bertrand. When he spoke again, his voice was a bit unsettled. "It appears no one was injured, so we might as well go on about our business."

"Thank you," Bertrand said with a respectful nod. He motioned for his driver to climb up onto the box, then turned to Zoë. "Come along, my dear."

He took her arm, but she held back for a moment, looking at the young man. He was not as tall as Bertrand, but he was definitely as handsome—more so, in fact, with thick brown hair and the darkest eyes she had ever seen, eyes that flashed like coal as they gazed steadily at her in the flickering lamplight.

"Zoë?" Bertrand said, and she allowed herself to be led back to the coach.

A moment later the drivers were in place, and Crowley gingerly started his vehicle forward. As the coach drew closer to the cabriolet, Zoë saw that the young driver had a firm grip on the reins. He was staring intently at her, and she had the disconcerting feeling that he knew her. Abruptly she said to Bertrand, "Have your driver stop."

"What?" he asked, confused at her request.

"Please—have him stop."

Bertrand leaned forward and pulled a silk cord that hung above the other seat back. It rang a bell on the driver's seat, and at this signal Crowley immediately reined in the horses, the cabin of the coach coming to a halt directly beside the cabriolet.

Zoë leaned through the window and smiled at the young man. "I want to thank you for remaining coolheaded. Another driver might not have maintained such control, and there might have been serious injury." She purposely did not specify whether she was referring to the initial near-collision or the ensuing confrontation between the drivers.

"That's quite all right," he replied, hands gripping the reins and foot firmly pressed against the brake. "So long as you weren't hurt or jostled too badly, ma'am."

"I'm fine," she assured him. "But I'm hardly a ma'am. I'm Miss Zoë Ballinger. My friend is Mr. Bertrand Cummington."

He nodded respectfully. "Pleased to meet you, Miss Ballinger."

"And your name? I'm afraid I didn't catch it."

The man seemed quite cautious as he eyed the beautiful woman who was addressing him. Finally he muttered something that Zoë could not quite make out.

"Excuse me?" she asked.

"Connor," he repeated. "The name's Connor."

"Well, you've been quite the gentleman, Mr. Connor. I hope the rest of your evening is far less eventful and far more enjoyable."

She turned and whispered to Bertrand, who gave two short pulls on the silk cord. As the coach started forward, Zoë looked at the cabriolet a final time, then settled in her seat.

"A curious young lad," Bertrand declared.

"Why do you say that?"

"When we were outside . . . didn't you notice?"

"Notice what?"

"His shoes—they were brown."

Zoë looked at him curiously. "I'm afraid I don't understand."

Bertrand's smile dripped with condescending amusement. "Good God, even the poorest Thames wharf rat knows not to wear brown shoes with a black suit—even a common suit such as that."

After the coach had passed, Connor Maginnis turned his rented cabriolet into the long drive that led to Planting Fields Manor. He had not expected to run into Zoë Ballinger on the road but had recognized her at once from a sketch he had seen in a back issue of *Ladies of London,* a weekly two-penny sheet devoted to the latest goings-on of London society.

It turned out that Mose Levison and his grandfather were avid society watchers, and upon learning of the connection between the Maginnises and Ballingers, Mose had pored through his magazines and collectibles and come up with information and sketches about all of Lord Cedric's family.

"Now what?" Connor asked himself as he set the gelding to a leisurely pace down the drive.

It had been Connor's plan to call upon Zoë at her home, using as an excuse the woman's involvement with the Women's Reform Committee, a group of wealthy matrons and their daughters who held Saturday afternoon teas to discuss—but do little about—various social problems. According to the magazine, the committee was currently advocating prison reform—a fashionable cause at the moment—so Connor had planned to present his father's case to what he hoped would be a sympathetic ear— sympathetic for a Ballinger, that was. He had not expected to be caught so completely off guard.

And what was he to make of the tall, well-dressed rake escorting Miss Zoë Ballinger? *Cummington,* she had called him. *Bertrand Cummington.* The name sounded familiar, but Connor couldn't place him.

Mr. Cummington will just have to wait, he told himself, suddenly pulling the reins to the right and executing a smart U-turn in the wide drive. He slapped the reins and started the gelding at a brisk trot back toward the main road.

"Good boy," he said, coaxing the horse to an even faster gait, intent upon closing the distance between his little carriage and the coach. Connor had no idea what his next move would be, but he wanted to be near Zoë should some opportunity present itself.

The cabriolet pulled onto the road, heading toward the city of London and the coach's distant, unseen trail of dust.

X

~~~~~~

    Connor stood alone at the rear of the Grand Lobby of the Piccadilly Arms, keeping to the shadows as he watched the activity in the main room of the hotel restaurant. He could see Zoë Ballinger and her escort and was pleased they were not dining in one of the private rooms, a favorite retreat for formal dinner parties and romantic liaisons.

    Every now and then Connor glanced across the lobby at the captain's desk and gave Hugh Darby what passed for a smile, receiving a perfunctory nod in return. Connor had never liked Darby, but the fellow was reliable and discreet—especially when money passed into his hands. And tonight Connor had paid handsomely to be allowed to remain in the lobby on what must surely seem dubious business.

    Connor recognized several of the women serving the patrons in the main dining room. They were affable and efficient as they presented the various courses and whisked away the finished dishes. He knew their skills were put to even greater use in the private rooms in back, where they might not only serve as waitress but as appetizer, entrée, and dessert.

    Connor waited for an opportunity to present itself, then stepped from the shadows and signaled one of the serving girls to join him in the lobby. At first she seemed confused, then nodded and disappeared into the kitchen. A few minutes later she entered the lobby through a side door and approached him.

"Connor!" the woman said with enthusiasm. She was well into her middle years and using a heavy amount of powder, rouge, and henna dye to maintain a semblance of youth. "What are you doin' here? Are you workin' some angle?"

"Sarah, do you know that couple over there?" He pulled her into the shadows and pointed into the dining room.

"Over by the fireplace?" she asked, and he nodded. "Everyone knows Bertie."

"Bertrand Cummington?"

"We girls call him Bertie's Cumming." She giggled. "He's a regular, he is."

"I thought as much."

"Some of the girls have even been up to his flat."

"Here? In London?"

"Less'n two blocks away."

"He doesn't live in Castlebar Hill?"

"His family's out that way—in Kensington, I believe. But Bertie likes to take his amusements here in town. All the single young men do. And he's one of the best—good lookin' and clean, though a trifle too quick, if you know what I mean. But so what if he's not overly generous with his attentions? He more'n makes up for it with his generous tips."

"What about the woman?" He indicated Zoë Ballinger.

"Don't know her name. But from what I've seen and heard, it's lookin' to be Mrs. Bertie Cummington soon enough."

Connor found himself frowning and was surprised by his reaction. "You're sure this Bertie fellow frequents the back rooms?"

"Sweetie, I've had him myself often enough to know . . . and a darn sight more often, I daresay, than that young, uncorked bottle of wine he's havin' dinner with in there." Sarah impulsively leaned over and kissed Connor's cheek. "I've got to be runnin', 'afore the manager sees me here with the likes of you." She started to leave.

"Just a moment, Sarah." He caught her arm and turned her toward him. "I need your help."

"What kind?" she asked suspiciously.

"I need to get rid of Bertie for a while."

Sarah squeezed his arm and grinned. "It's the virgin, ain't it? You soft on her or somethin'?"

"I just need to speak with her . . . alone."

Sarah narrowed one eye. "And I'm supposed to make that happen, am I?"

"Could you?" Taking one of her hands in his own, Connor pressed a coin into her palm. "When they're leaving, just make up some story to get him to go to his flat and send her home in his coach."

She eyed him for a moment, then glanced over at the couple in the dining room. "I may be needin' some assistance from one of the other girls."

Connor saw the way she was fingering the coin in her hand and understood at once what she meant. With a skeptical smile, he took out another coin and added it to the first. "Will that do?"

"Yes, but only because it's you." She began to turn away, then whispered, "Come back sometime when you're not workin' an angle. I won't even charge."

Connor watched her disappear through the side door of the lobby. A few moments later she was back in the dining room, circling among the tables and occasionally casting a furtive wink in his direction. He retreated deeper into the shadows and waited.

◆◆◆

"That was a delightful dinner," Zoë exclaimed as Bertrand helped her with her shawl and ushered her across the lobby.

"But you didn't eat your dessert. I had them make cherries in brandy especially for the occasion."

"Yes, I know, but I was too full from the meal," she lied, pleased at least that the flaming liqueur hadn't concealed an engagement ring. "But you shouldn't have been so polite; I know how much you like dessert."

"I'm content to wait," he said with a knowing smile. "There'll be no more dessert for Bertie Cummington until the day you say, 'I will.'"

"Bertrand, you promised. . . ."

"I'm sorry. We won't discuss it again, I promise. Not until you're ready."

"Bertie . . ."

"Sorry. Never again. Not one more word."

Approaching the large brass doors that led to the street, Bertrand put on his top hat and offered Zoë his arm. They were about to step outside when a voice called, "Bertie!" and a young woman rushed breathlessly into the rear of the lobby. It wasn't Sarah, but the expression on Bertrand's face when he turned to see who was calling his name made it obvious he was well acquainted with the woman. He tried to pretend he hadn't heard her, but then she called again, and he had no choice but to wait for her.

"Yes, what is it?" he said curtly, not bothering to introduce the woman to Zoë.

"It's your father—His Lordship is dreadfully ill."

"My father? Whatever are you talking about?"

"He . . . well, he . . ." She shrugged and nodded toward Zoë, obviously uncomfortable in her presence.

Flustered, Bertrand turned to his companion and said, "If you'll excuse me for a moment." Not waiting for a reply, he stalked across the lobby, leaving the other woman to follow. When they were by themselves, he whispered sharply, "Whatever is this about, Madeline? You know better than to interrupt me when I'm with someone. And to call me Bertie . . . If you must address me in public, it's Mr. Cummington."

"I'm sorry, Bertie, but I was upset about your father."

"What about Father?"

"He's with one of the new girls."

"Father? He's here?"

"Not here. He's at your flat."

"My flat? What's he doing there?" he said even more incredulously. He really didn't need to ask, since it was his father who had introduced him at sixteen to the back rooms of the Piccadilly Arms. Though Lord Henry Cummington was now almost sixty, he still visited often and on occasion used his son's flat to meet one of his paramours.

"What do you *think* he's doing?" Madeline said, her voice edged with exasperation.

"He's sick, you say?"

"I think so. The girl came running back a few minutes ago, said he'd been stricken or something. You should have seen her—white like a ghost. She ran off again, maybe back to your flat."

"What else did she say?" Bertrand asked, his worry showing now.

Madeline shrugged. "That's all. Said he was stricken right when they were in the middle of . . . you know."

"Damn!" Bertrand cursed, no longer caring if anyone heard. He glanced over to where Zoë was standing and saw the concern in her eyes, then turned back to Madeline. "Don't worry—I'll take care of everything."

"Shouldn't I get someone? A doctor, maybe?"

"No!" he snapped. He realized his father might be gravely ill, but before he sent for a physician, he had to be sure no young tart was on hand to stir up a scandal.

"Then I should just stay here?" she asked.

"And forget anything happened. You'll do that for me . . . and for Lord Henry?"

"Yes."

"Do you promise?" he asked, uncertain just how far he could trust her. He felt only somewhat relieved when she nodded affirmatively.

Dismissing the young woman, Bertrand hurried back to Zoë.

"What is it, Bertrand?" she asked. "What's wrong?"

"Apparently my father has taken ill; he knew I was having dinner here and sent a messenger."

"We'd better get back to Kensington right away."

"Henry isn't at home," he said, trying to mask his discomfort. "He's visiting a family friend here in London."

"I see."

"Would it be terribly inconsiderate to send you home in my coach while I stay in London and look in on Father?"

"Of course not," she assured him. "I'd be glad to accompany you, if you'd—"

"That really isn't necessary. And I might get stuck here in town overnight."

"At least have the coach drop you at your friend's house before taking me home."

"I'll go in the carriage that brought the messenger. It's waiting out back," he lied.

He led Zoë outside, opening the coach door and tenderly kissing her hand as he helped her into it. He called instructions up to the driver and stepped back, watching as the vehicle pulled away from the hotel and clattered down the road.

◆━━◆━━◆

As the coach rounded a corner several blocks from the hotel, Zoë felt a slight jolt, as if they had struck a rut. She would not have thought anything more of it had she not heard a faint voice calling her name. She assumed it was the driver and was about to stick her head through the open window of the door when instead the velvet curtain was thrust aside and a face appeared—the face of the handsome young man whose cabriolet had nearly collided with the coach earlier that evening.

Zoë jumped back on the seat. "Whatever—?"

"Shhh," he begged, his arm reaching through the open window to brace himself as he clung to the side of the coach. He glanced up nervously toward the front of the vehicle, as if making sure the coachman had not seen him from the high driver's perch. "Miss Ballinger, may I come in?"

"Come in? Here?"

"Please, Miss Ballinger," he pressed in a hushed whisper. "I must speak with you."

The sudden crack of the whip startled them, and the jolt of the coach as it increased speed caused the young man to drop down from sight. When he did not reappear in the window, Zoë slid closer, pulled aside the curtain, and ventured a look out. The man was still there, crouched precariously on the narrow iron stair, gripping the door handle. It looked as if he would be bounced off at any moment, and Zoë realized that one slight push on her part was all it would take to protect herself from him. But when he looked back up at her, his expression was so lacking in guile that she found herself smiling at his audacity. After all, she could not recall the last time someone had risked a broken neck or worse just to ride in her coach.

"Let's get you inside," she said in a low voice as she reached out and helped him up from his squatting position.

Carefully, he eased himself toward the rear of the coach, releasing the door handle and holding on to the venetian blinds that covered the window beside the seat. Zoë tried to open the door, but he was still blocking it. He had to move to the rear edge of the stair and shift one foot to the axle, flattening his body against the bounding coach body. Again Zoë tried the door, and as it swung open, it caught him on the shoulder. His rear foot slipped off the axle and struck the wheel, banging against one of the spokes and almost dragging him under. But he managed to regain his footing and pull himself back up, shifting his weight onto the axle so that his body cleared the door.

Zoë pushed it open just wide enough for the young man to slip through, and as he did so, he sprawled headlong across her lap, then onto the aisle floor. The door swung closed with a thud, followed almost immediately by the sound of the coach slowing.

A voice called down from above, and though Zoë could not make out the words, she guessed the driver was inquiring about the noise. She quickly leaned through the window and shouted, "Everything is all right, Mr. Crowley. Please continue; I'd like to get home as soon as possible."

A moment later, the coach had resumed a brisk pace down the southern drive alongside Hyde Park, past the gate of Kensington Gardens, and onto Kensington Road.

Zoë turned to the stranger, who was clambering up from the aisle floor. "We always seem to be . . . bumping into each other, Mr. Conners."

"Connor," he corrected her, easing himself onto the rear-facing seat across from her. Struggling to catch his breath, he straightened his black outer jacket and discovered a large torn flap on the sleeve, which he tried without success to press into place.

"Well then, Mr. Connor—"

"No—it's my first name." Looking up from the torn sleeve, he found himself staring into Zoë's eyes. Although the cabin's only illumination was from two small oil reading lamps, he could see that her green eyes flashed with disconcerting energy and merriment. Pulling his gaze away, he said in an undertone, "My full name is Connor Maginnis."

"I'm delighted to meet you, Connor. . . . I may call you Connor, may I not?" She held forth her hand.

"Of—of course," he stammered, lifting her hand almost to his lips, then awkwardly releasing it without a kiss.

"And you must call me Zoë."

"Yes, Miss Ballinger."

"Zoë." Her smile was warm and sincere.

"Yes. Zoë."

"And to what do I owe the honor of this most unusual visit?" she asked.

"I . . ." He hesitated, looking around the ornately appointed interior of the coach and realizing the absurdity of the situation. "I just thought . . ."

"You thought . . . ? Yes?"

"I thought I . . . I'd drop in and . . ." He grinned, and it turned into a chuckle, then an infectious laugh. A moment later, the two passengers were covering their mouths to keep their laughter from being heard.

Regaining her composure, Zoë declared, "You certainly dropped in. Is this how you usually meet young women, or do you plan to simply leave your card and drop back out?"

"I have no card," he admitted, suddenly feeling as if he was totally lacking in any of the social graces.

"And apparently you no longer have a buggy. If you needed a ride, you could have waved us down and inquired."

"I wanted to speak with you . . . alone."

"And how did you know that I *was* alone?" She examined him closely.

Connor's level of discomfort rose under her increasingly critical gaze.

"You *knew* I'd be alone, didn't you?" she asked, shaking her head in wonder. "You arranged for Bertie to be called away. You've been following me, haven't you?"

"No, not following," he blurted, raising his hand in defense. "I mean, not at first. Not until you almost ran into my carriage."

"But afterward . . . you followed us to the Piccadilly Arms, didn't you?"

"Please, let me explain. . . ."

"I wish that you would," she said, her tone somewhat curt.

"I was on my way to your home," he began earnestly. "I had hoped to visit with you."

"What about?"

"Please, if you'll let me explain—"

"I'm sorry. Go on." She waved him to continue.

"I was on my way to call on you, when our two vehicles nearly collided. And when you introduced yourself, I don't know . . . I just turned my cabriolet and followed you back here to the city."

"And arranged to have Bertie called away?" she asked.

Connor did not reply.

"That story about his father being sick; it's not true, is it?"

"No," he muttered, embarrassed.

Zoë sighed. "I suppose I should be pleased—not with you, mind you, but that Lord Cummington isn't ill."

Connor looked back up at her, his eyes beseeching. "I'm sorry. I don't know what came over me, but—"

"You know perfectly well, Mr. Maginnis. Now why don't you tell me what this is *really* about?"

He drew in an exceedingly deep breath, and for a long moment it didn't seem as if he would ever release it. Finally he said, "I need you to help me, Miss Ballinger. It concerns my father. Perhaps you've heard of Graham Maginnis?"

"Graham Maginnis . . . he's your father?" Zoë asked, a light of recognition slowly coming over her features.

"Yes. He used to be in business with your father's cousin, Edmund Ballinger."

"I know. But what has that to do with me? I'm not involved in Edmund's business. In fact, our families aren't even that close." She chose not to mention the strong bond between herself and Ross.

"I realize that, but I also realize that you may be the only Ballinger willing to help me."

"Help you how?"

Connor leaned forward on the seat and for the first time looked her steadily in the eye. "I want you to help me get my father out of Millbank Prison."

◆━━━◆━━━◆

An hour later, the Cummingtons' family coach rode across the grounds of the Ballinger estate and came to a halt under the carriage port of Planting Fields Manor. The butler was already on hand, and as he opened the coach door, he looked surprised to see Zoë seated with a stranger, rather than Bertrand Cummington.

"Are my parents at home?" Zoë asked matter-of-factly as she stepped out.

"Yes, Miss Ballinger."

She turned back to the coach as Connor emerged. "This is Mr. Connor Maginnis. Please tell my parents that I'd like them to see us in the parlor."

"Yes, Miss Ballinger." Desmond looked with undisguised disdain on the visitor's unkempt appearance. Seeing the large tear on the sleeve of Connor's jacket, he asked, "May I see to your coat, Mr. Maginnis?"

By this time, the driver, Crowley, had noticed that an extra passenger had emerged from the coach. Recognizing the man who had nearly collided with them earlier that evening, he was about to say something—from his expression, something quite objectionable—when he was cut off by Zoë.

"Thank you so much, Mr. Crowley," she called up to him, smiling demurely. "And please give my regards to Mr. Cummington and tell him I hope his father is all right." She took Connor's arm and led him toward the manor.

During the ride, Connor had detailed what he knew about his father's arrest, trial, and conviction. Realizing that Edmund was Zoë's relative and that she might wish to protect him, Connor had been careful not to be too harsh in his criticism of the man, leaving open the possibility that Edmund had not intentionally fabricated evidence against Connor's father. But point by point, Connor had tried to show that Graham was not guilty of embezzlement and had been convicted on largely circumstantial evidence.

For her part, Zoë did not doubt that Edmund might be involved in foul play. From passing comments she had heard over the years, she had long suspected that his takeover of Ballinger-Maginnis Import and Export had not been wholly aboveboard. But she had always assumed that both Edmund and his former partner had been guilty of impropriety and that Edmund's good fortune had been in avoiding prosecution himself. She had never considered that Graham Maginnis might have been framed in order to take the business away from him. She also had no idea that he had left children behind when he had been sent to prison.

"I'm not sure what I can do," she said as she and Connor entered the manor. "But perhaps my mother and father will be able to help."

"I'm not sure this is wise," he replied. "After all, your parents will be inclined to side with their cousin."

"This has nothing to do with taking sides—and anyway, my father and Edmund are far from close. No, this has to do with simple compassion. Even if your father isn't innocent, as you claim, sixteen years is surely long enough to spend locked up in Millbank Prison."

◆　◆　◆

At the end of a fifteen-minute interview with the unexpected visitor to Planting Fields Manor, Lord Cedric Ballinger told his daughter and wife, "Perhaps Mr. Maginnis and I should visit alone for a while." His expression was stiff and formal as he rose from his favorite parlor chair, upholstered in plush green velvet with a heavy black fringe across the bottom and back. "We'll only be a few minutes," he assured the women as he ushered them from the room.

"Is that all right with you?" Zoë asked Connor, who reassured her with a smile and nod. "Then I'll see to having one of the carriages brought around to take you home." She took the arm of her mother, a heavyset but still attractive forty-seven-year-old brunette.

"It was nice meeting you, Mr. Maginnis," Sybil said without emotion as she and her daughter left the room.

Following them to the door, Cedric shut it and returned to where Connor was standing. "Please, sit," he insisted, motioning for the younger man to resume his seat.

Cedric walked over to his green chair but remained standing, stroking his chest as he considered what he would say. He was a fairly tall man of forty-nine, with prematurely white hair and darker, bushy sideburns that extended halfway to his chin. Standing straight as he looked down at the younger man, he gave a regal appearance, his lithe, athletic body fluid in its movements, his steel-blue eyes still bright with youth. Turning to the small side table, he poured two glasses of brandy and brought one over to his guest.

"Thank you," Connor said, taking the offered glass.

Cedric crossed back to his chair but did not sit down. "You and I must be perfectly honest with each other," he declared at last.

"I *have* been." Connor tried not to shift uncomfortably under the man's steady gaze.

"Good." Cedric circled behind the chair and placed his hand on the backrest. "Then I will speak bluntly."

"By all means." Connor steadied the glass in his hand, willing himself to show no concern.

"You spoke eloquently of your family—of your father, in particular. But you really haven't made a case for his innocence—or my cousin's guilt. You have offered not one single piece of evidence other than the rantings of an old man some sixteen years in prison."

"Then you deny his allegations?" Connor asked, forcing his voice to remain calm as he leaned forward in the chair and took a sip of the brandy.

"Allegations? The world is full of allegations . . . and denials of those allegations, as well. Of what importance are they, in the face of a total lack of hard evidence? Do you want me to deny them? Then I do so. Would you prefer that I commiserate with you and your poor sister? With your father, even? Then yes, I'll accept his allegations as being within the realm of possibility and offer my apologies. But does any of it really matter? We are speaking of events sixteen or more years past, all closely examined by the court, which has given its ruling. It may give you comfort to think of your father as a victim; far be it from me to shatter any such illusions in the heart of a child. But in a court of law, what matters are the rules of evidence, not the concerns of the heart." Eyeing Connor closely, he asked, "Do you have any hard evidence, young man?" He waited a few moments, and when Connor did not reply, he added, "I thought not."

Stepping back around the chair, Cedric sat down, placed his hands on the armrests, and closed his eyelids partway, as if signaling an end to his consideration of the matter.

Connor put the brandy glass on the table beside him and stood. "I'm sorry to have bothered you and your family with such a personal matter. In the future I'll direct my concerns to the proper authorities."

He walked across the room toward the door but halted when Cedric whispered his name in an exceedingly gentle tone. Connor looked over at the older man, whose eyes were fully closed now, as if he were remembering some distant event.

"Connor . . ." he repeated, lifting his right hand ever

so slightly from the armrest. "I remember when your father invited me to your christening. I was unable to attend, but my wife reported that you didn't cry once during the entire ceremony. Four years later, Edmund's baby boy, Ross, cried so loud during his christening that he had to be taken away." Cedric opened his eyes and looked up at Connor, his expression warm and open. "I knew even then how much my cousin resented your father. But it wasn't really his fault. It was Emeline."

"My mother?" Connor said cautiously.

"We were all in love with her. It really couldn't be helped. She was so beautiful, so fiery. Perhaps it was because she was an American, or just because she seemed so . . . unattainable." He gave a slight laugh. "I think we all hated Graham Maginnis a bit in those days. But we didn't wish to see him in prison. You see, we realized how much Emeline loved him, and we knew it would kill her. And none of us—not even my fool of a cousin—wanted to see her gone."

Connor tried to read the older man's expression, uncertain if his sentiments were genuine. Finally, he said, "Thank you for your time."

"One thing before you go," Cedric said, rising. "It's true that I may not be sympathetic to your father's allegations; after all, I heard most of them a decade and a half ago, when the courts examined the matter and ruled against him. However, that does not mean I'm insensitive to his current situation. Why not let me look into the matter further? Perhaps something can be done to see Graham released from confinement. There's no reason he shouldn't live his remaining days in the bosom of his family."

"Thank you, Lord Ballinger." Connor accepted the older man's hand. "I'd be most appreciative."

"Millbank Prison, you say? I had all but forgotten."

"His prison number is eighty-four fourteen."

"I'll see what can be done."

Cedric escorted Connor to the foyer, where Zoë and the butler were waiting, and took his leave. When Desmond helped Connor into his coat, Connor saw that the torn sleeve had been sewn, and he thanked the butler for his kindness.

"Our coachman will take you back to London," Zoë explained, leading Connor outside to the waiting family landau, its leather cover raised against the night chill.

Just as he was about to board the vehicle, a one-horse gentleman's phaeton rounded the side of the manor a bit too sharply and clattered to a halt just behind the landau. A heavyset man with a reddish-brown beard emerged from inside the vehicle; as soon as he saw Zoë, his face lit up, and he called her name.

"Austin," she called back, leading Connor over to the phaeton. "I want you to meet a friend of mine. This is Connor Maginnis," she said, presenting Connor. "And this is my brother, Austin."

As the two men shook hands, Austin looked puzzled and asked, "Haven't we met before?"

"I don't believe so. Your sister and I met only this evening." Connor stepped back a few feet, seeking the comfort of the shadows, hoping that Zoë's brother would not remember having seen him at the Haversham Theatre the night that Connor had entertained Lenora York in her private box.

"But I'm sure . . ." Austin's voice trailed off as he continued to examine Connor and search his memory.

"I really must be going," Connor said. "It was a pleasure meeting you, Mr. Ballinger."

Zoë led Connor to the landau, and after they said their good-byes, she promised to send word regarding her father's efforts on Graham Maginnis's behalf. Connor climbed into the coach, which pulled out smartly and headed down the drive.

It was quite dark, but the moon showed through the clouds just enough to highlight the turrets and gables of Planting Fields Manor. For a long time Connor peered through the rear window of the landau, watching as first Zoë and Austin and then the great stone building faded into the darkness. Even after it had disappeared from view, he continued to stare back through the little oval window, looking for some sign, some flickering light, to show that he had really been there.

◆◆◆◆

Long after most of the lights had been doused at Planting Fields Manor, one lamp continued to burn well into the night. Lord Cedric Ballinger sat at the massive mahogany desk in his downstairs library, from where he ran the family business, which consisted almost entirely of overseeing the Ballingers' vast land holdings in London and the Lake District of northern England.

Tonight, the visit by Graham Maginnis's son had brought other business to the fore—business that Cedric had thought finished and buried many years ago. It was a distasteful affair, almost as distasteful as his "damn fool of a cousin, Edmund!" Cedric shook his head in disgust as he spat out his cousin's name for perhaps the hundredth time.

Seated on the other side of the desk in an armless, spindle-back chair, his eldest son did not bother to look up from the notes he was taking. Austin held a similar opinion of Edmund Ballinger, and unlike Cedric, it wasn't at all tempered by guilt that his branch of the family had usurped the family title and fortune. In Austin's opinion, Edmund and his brood were the commonest sort of merchants, unworthy of either his consideration or his contempt. However, Austin was a politician at heart who intended to sit in Parliament one day. To that end, it was important that the Ballinger name not be touched by scandal, and for that reason alone, Austin realized they had to help their relative.

"It would seem I should start to investigate this Mr. Connor Maginnis at once," Austin said in a dry, emotionless voice. He glanced up from his notes. "And what do you suggest I do if I discover evidence?"

Cedric gave an irritated wave of the hand. "Don't do anything; just see what he's about. So what if he's visited with his father and got his head filled with stories about being poorly treated at our hands? It's just the ravings of a lunatic, sixteen years in a Millbank cell. There's no evidence that could've survived all these years. We uncovered everything during the trial—and destroyed it." Cedric's gaze wandered around the room, scanning the books on the floor-to-ceiling shelves that lined the walls. "Nothing's left to link us to what happened. Nothing at all."

"Are you sure?" Austin pressed.

Cedric's eyes narrowed. "What exactly do you mean?"

Austin put down his pen and looked at his father. "We've never spoken much about what happened back then."

"You were just a boy of ten or twelve at the time."

"Yes, but I remember much of it—and I've heard bits more over the years. And frankly, I'm concerned."

Cedric leaned forward across the desk. "Concerned? About what?"

"It's your cousin that concerns me."

"In what way?"

"I realize you have a certain . . . fondness for Edmund."

Cedric waved off the comment. "We were boys growing up together, that's all."

"Still, you've always stood up for him, even when he didn't deserve it."

"Edmund has had a difficult life, and his business is beginning to show something for his efforts."

"With your assistance, Father."

"I help when I can—and when it's in the family's interest."

"Far be it from me to disparage a Ballinger, but Edmund is not cut from the same cloth as Your Lordship." Austin rarely used the formal title with his father; he did so sparingly and always for effect.

"But he's not stupid, either," Cedric said in defense of his cousin.

"True enough. But I must say that he strikes me as the type of man cavalier enough to hold on to any written records of his past misdeeds."

"But there was nothing left. All the records have been destroyed."

"Perhaps those relating to his role in the original crimes, but what about your subsequent efforts against Graham Maginnis?"

Cedric gave a low oath, then muttered, "Even my fool cousin wouldn't be so stupid as to have committed any of that to paper. Would he?" Cedric looked at Austin, whose doubting expression did little to comfort him. "I'll send for him in the morning."

"Let me take care of it, Father. I think a more discreet inquiry might be in order."

"What for?"

"It strikes me that Edmund would never admit such a foolhardy action to an older cousin with whom he's always competed. But perhaps privately I can convince him to hand over any potentially damaging evidence to me. Then we can determine what to do."

"Yes, that sounds like a good idea." Cedric nodded in satisfaction.

"Then it's decided. I shall begin in the morning." Austin stood to go.

"Just make sure there's nothing to connect us to what happened back then. I don't want some half-crazed old man getting out of Millbank Prison and stirring up trouble for this family. If possible, keep Edmund out of it. Under no circumstances are we going to let my damn cousin drag the rest of us through the mud."

"The Ballinger name will remain unsullied," Austin assured him.

"See that it does," Cedric declared, turning away as Austin gathered his papers and left the room.

Closing the door behind him, Austin went down the hall to the wide marble staircase that led to their bedrooms. He did not look forward to confronting Edmund, but it did not surprise him that such a course of action would be necessary. The man had always been an embarrassment, he thought as he climbed the stairway.

I'll protect him if I must, but he'll pay. . . . One way or another, he'll pay.

He was grinning when he reached the second floor, realizing the situation just might prove beneficial. After all, Edmund was no longer a poor man, and he was not badly connected, at least among the London business community. A man with a political future—a man like Austin—would do well to have a prominent tradesman in his pocket.

"And one way or another," Austin whispered, "that is exactly where Edmund is going to wind up."

XI

The following Friday afternoon, Mose Levison was working feverishly in the Ballinger Trade Company warehouse. His employer, Edmund Ballinger, had asked him to review the bills of lading left by the night foreman, Roger Avery, and he still had to go through several more pallets of crates, which had been off-loaded the previous evening from an East Indies voyage. Mose raced down the list, checking off items to verify that no crates of silk or spices had been overlooked or wrongfully charged to the company.

When he reached the final crate, he stuffed the bills into a large brown folder, tucked it under his arm, and headed swiftly toward the office, where his boss was sequestered with a visitor. Edmund had not bothered to introduce the man when he handed Mose the folder and asked him to leave them alone for a while. But Mose had recognized him from pictures in the society journals, and his identity had been confirmed when Edmund greeted the man as "Austin."

Curious why Edmund and his cousin's son were meeting at the warehouse, Mose stepped up quietly to the closed office door. This was his third week of employment as Edmund's office boy, and despite his willingness to work after hours, he had not discovered a single scrap of evidence that might support Graham Maginnis's charges of being framed and wrongfully convicted. But it had been less than a week since Connor had confronted Lord Cedric Ballinger and his family, and now Austin was paying a visit to Edmund.

Opening the folder, Mose pretended to be double-checking the bills as he stood near the door. Few workers were on hand today, but every now and then someone would pass nearby and nod or call a friendly greeting. Mose tried to look as nonchalant as possible, returning a wave and then resuming his inspection of the bills of lading.

The office door was heavy and thick, but a panel of smoky glass allowed him to hear muffled voices from inside. One of the men—Austin, Mose guessed—was detailing a list of times and places. Mose caught fragments: "Monday night . . . the theater . . . in the back of her coach . . ."

It was when he heard the name Henrietta Wellesley that he grew concerned. Then he heard what sounded like the name Lenora, followed by a furious oath and the pounding of a fist on the desk. "That bitch!" floated clearly through the closed door, and Mose recognized the voice as Edmund's. "I'll kill the bastard!"

Austin tried to calm his older relation, but then their voices became more hushed, and it was impossible to make out what was being said. Mose eased closer, until he was right beside the door, his head angled toward the window. So intent was he on trying to hear the conversation that he failed to notice the approach of a young woman.

"Why don't you just go in?" she asked, causing him to jump in surprise.

"I, uh, was just . . ."

" 'Tis all right," the woman said. "You're the new boy, aren't you?"

"Um, yes. Mose Levison." He bowed politely, and the woman giggled.

"You needn't stand on ceremony with me." She held forth her hand. "I'm just one o' the charwomen. Clarissa."

She was at least ten years older than Mose, but there was something quite young and inexperienced-looking about her. Though not overly attractive, she had a warm smile that did much to dispel the overall impression of a down-on-her-luck working girl.

Mose awkwardly took her hand, uncertain whether to shake it or raise it to his lips. Before he could decide, she withdrew it, blushing slightly as she said, "I can see you're a young gentleman, Mose Levison. And if there's anything I can do to help you here at Ballinger's, just let me know."

Mose watched as she walked toward one of the supply rooms. His reverie was interrupted by another banging fist and Edmund's gruff voice declaring, "We must get rid of him! That's all there is to it!"

There was a scuffing of chairs, and Mose quickly retreated down the aisle. A moment later, the office door opened, and Austin Ballinger emerged. Clapping his hat on his head and gripping his black gloves, he looked back at Edmund. "Tonight, then?"

The owner of Ballinger Trade appeared in the doorway. "Yes. I'll see you out."

He saw Mose, who pretended to have just finished his job. When they caught each other's eye, Mose said, "Everythin' is in order, Mr. Ballinger. Shall I file the bills?"

Edmund merely grunted, then marched toward the front doors, Austin following alongside.

Entering the office, Mose hurried around the desk and opened the top drawer of a filing cabinet, where the bills were stored. Slipping the folder in place, he looked around the room. One of the wooden chairs had been pulled over next to the desk, but nothing else seemed amiss.

Leaning over the desk, Mose at first saw nothing unfamiliar there. But then he noticed that the ink bottle was open and the pen lay across a pad of paper. Not daring to move anything, he tried to make out the words scrawled on the pad. It took him a moment to understand what he was reading, and then he realized that it was an address— and not just any address, but the address of Connor and Emeline Maginnis. A time was scrawled under it: 8:00. There was no date, but from the little Mose had heard of the conversation, he was convinced it referred to that very evening.

He was about to leave when he noticed that the bottom right-hand drawer of the desk was slightly open. It caught his attention because Edmund Ballinger never failed to lock the drawer when he left the office, even if he was going into the warehouse to consult someone briefly.

It had been Mose's plan to break into that drawer eventually and see what it contained, and now he had the opportunity, albeit a risky one. Looking toward the open office door to confirm that his boss wasn't yet returning, Mose slid the drawer open and saw that it held several folders, similar to the ones used in the office files but made of black paperboard rather than brown. Dropping to his knees, he sifted through them and found bills of lading and records of transactions. Though he realized they might be illegal transactions, it was not readily apparent how any of it could help Connor Maginnis clear his father's name and free him from prison.

Mose returned the drawer to its slightly ajar position, then stood back up and almost immediately noticed on the chair a matching black folder, which apparently Edmund had removed from the drawer during or before his visit with Austin Ballinger. Glancing out into the warehouse and drawing in a calming breath, he flipped open the folder and gazed down at a sheaf of papers, clipped together at the upper left corner. Scrawled at the top was a name: Graham Maginnis, Esq.

Mose riffled the pages and saw that they contained voluminous notes and figures, all in Edmund Ballinger's hand and on the stationery both of the Ballinger Trade Company and the earlier Ballinger-Maginnis Import and Export Company. He backed away from the desk, looking around wildly and weighing his options. Almost without thinking, he dashed to the filing cabinet and pulled out the brown folder he had just been working on. Quickly removing the bills of lading, he swapped them with the sheaf of papers in the black folder, put it back on the chair, and tucked the brown folder under his arm.

Mose heard Edmund's heavy footsteps approaching, and he hastily circled the desk and left the office, nearly barreling into his employer as he departed.

"What's the rush, Mr. Levison?" Edmund asked, entering the office and walking over to his chair. Picking up the black folder, he laid it on the desk and sat down.

"I just want to recheck one of the pallets, Mr. Ballinger." Mose stood in the doorway and gazed nervously from his boss to the folder lying just inches from his hands.

"Don't trust your own figures?"

"I just want to be sure."

"It's one thing to be conscientious," Edmund lectured, "but not if it means always doing your work twice."

Mose looked down at his feet. "I'm sorry, sir."

"Perhaps we'd better go over those bills of lading together." He gestured toward the folder under the boy's arm.

Mose's hands broke out in a sweat, and he realized how stupid he had been to make such a switch. Venturing a smile, he said in an exceedingly thin voice, "I . . . I don't think that's really necessary, Mr. Ballinger. I checked the lists closely; I'm certain they're in order."

Edmund eyed him with suspicion, then gave a perfunctory nod. "Just so you're not still rechecking everything after you've been here a few more weeks. Now, file that folder away where it belongs and have a little more faith in your work."

Mose hesitated, then reluctantly complied, crossing the room and placing the folder of evidence in the filing cabinet.

Edmund waved him away. "Now run along."

"Yes, sir."

Leaving the office, Mose walked down the aisle but halted when his employer called after him: "Mr. Levison, you're due to leave at seven this evening, aren't you?"

Returning to the doorway, Mose saw that Edmund was cradling the black folder in his hands. His heart sinking, he said cautiously, "Yes, I am."

"I'd like you to stay until eight. I have to leave a bit early tonight, so I need you to brief Mr. Avery on some things that need doing around here." When Mose did not immediately reply, Edmund asked, "That isn't a problem, is it, Mr. Levison?"

"Uh, no, sir, not at all."

"Good. Then meet me back here in about ten minutes, and I'll show you what Mr. Avery needs to do."

Nodding, Mose backed away from the door, his gaze locked on his employer, who sat looking at the folder in his hands. He seemed about to open it, but then he casually slipped it into the drawer at his knees. Mose watched a moment longer as Edmund took a key from his vest pocket, closed the drawer, and locked it. Breathing a sigh of relief, the boy hurried down the aisle.

Tonight, he thought, shaking his head in dismay. *Somethin's goin' to happen tonight at eight.* He did not know what, but somehow he had to get to the address he had seen scrawled on the paper in Edmund Ballinger's office—the address of Connor and Emeline Maginnis—and make it there before eight o'clock. But first he would have to wait until Edmund left for the evening, so he could retrieve the brown folder from the filing cabinet.

"Damn," he muttered. "Eight may be too late."

"Too late for what?" a woman asked as Mose rounded the aisle and nearly collided with Clarissa.

"I—uh . . ."

"It's all right." She tenderly touched his arm. " 'Tis the old man, ain't it?"

Mose frowned. "It's just that he needs me to stay on till eight to give some sort of message to Mr. Avery."

"And you've other plans for a Friday night?" Her smile was almost conspiratorial, and Mose blushed in reply. "Well, no need to break your plans. I know Mr. Avery quite well, and I'll be glad to give him any message you require. And don't be worryin' about Mr. Ballinger—I'll see to it he's never the wiser."

"You will?"

"Like I said, Mr. Mose Levison, you just leave everythin' to Clarissa Ferguson."

"Thank you, Miss Ferguson."

"Now, you mustn't be callin' me 'Miss.' It's Clarissa to me friends. And we *are* friends, aren't we, Mose?"

"Yes, Clarissa," he affirmed. "That we are."

"So, what is this message you want delivered?"

Mose was about to explain that their boss had not yet communicated it to him, but then a mischievous thought struck him. "Just tell him that Mr. Ballinger's givin' the night crew the rest o' the week off—with full pay. Mr. Avery and the warehousemen can lock up and leave as soon as they arrive."

Clarissa looked at him skeptically. "That doesn't sound like Mr. Ballinger."

Mose shrugged. "He said somethin' about it bein' a bet he lost—I think with that gentleman who was just here."

Clarissa nodded. "Losin' a bet—now *that* sounds like Edmund Ballinger."

"Don't tell Mr. Ballinger that I told you," Mose warned. "He's mad enough as it is; he'd have my head if he knew I was spreadin' the story."

"Don't you worry, Mose. There're some things a woman never tells a man, and one o' them is that he's a loser!" She winked knowingly.

"If Mr. Avery doubts you, just tell him that I'll take full responsibility."

"You just take off whenever you need to. Clarissa Ferguson will see to it that the night crew enjoys the fruits of Edmund Ballinger's bad luck."

As she walked off down the aisle, Mose stood there marveling at what he had just done. If stealing the folder of evidence was not enough to seal his fate at Ballinger Trade, this stunt would do the trick. But after tonight Mose had no intention of ever returning.

At precisely eight that evening, a royal blue, covered landau was parked just down the street from the three-story building housing Connor and Emeline Maginnis's apartment. It attracted occasional attention from passersby, but any who paused to examine its fine detail and polished finish were quickly shooed away by the liveried driver, an imposing man whose presence assured the occupants' privacy.

Inside the coach were two men, seated across from each other at the street-side windows, one man watching the building, the other keeping an eye on the street. Whenever another vehicle rode by, the two figures invariably withdrew into the shadowed interior so that their faces would not be illuminated by the passing carriage lanterns. Then they would again lean close to the window to see if the vehicle was parking in front of the Maginnises' building.

"Are you sure this is the place?" the older man asked in a particularly gruff voice. He took a puff on his cigar, his eyes narrowing as he gazed outside through a cloud of blue smoke.

"Yes, Edmund, I'm certain," the other man said, stroking his beard somewhat nervously.

"And your father has no idea you're here?"

"I told you—I've handled everything. He knows only what I tell him, which to date isn't much."

"Good." Edmund Ballinger smiled at his cousin's son, then took another puff, his fleshy lips caressing the fat, soggy cigar.

"Here comes a brougham ... pulled by a pair of grays." Austin moved back from the window. "It looks like Lenora."

"It had better be," Edmund said testily.

The men watched as the brougham pulled to the side of the road directly in front of the building they were watching. There was a minute's wait, and then the door opened and a young man stepped out. He spoke briefly with someone inside the coach, then shut the door and called up to the elderly driver. Turning, he walked briskly into the building, and the brougham pulled away from the curb and down the street.

"Was that him?" Edmund asked.

"Connor Maginnis," came the reply.

"The bastard. . . ." He pushed open the door and motioned for Austin to exit.

"You can handle Lenora alone?" Austin asked as he stepped outside.

Edmund frowned. "Don't worry about me, young pup. Just see to it that you take care of our good Mr. Maginnis."

Austin closed the door. "And don't you forget our agreement."

"You just make sure that Connor Maginnis pays for what he's done to our family . . . and that his damn father never breathes the air outside Millbank Prison." Sitting back from the window, Edmund rapped on the far wall of the coach, which lurched forward to follow the brougham.

Austin Ballinger watched the landau disappear around the corner, then shifted his attention to the building in which Connor and his sister lived. During the past week,

Austin had carried out quite a meticulous investigation of the younger Maginnises and had discovered why Connor looked so familiar when they'd met at Planting Fields Manor. Like other handsome young men of his station, Connor lived by his wits and the largesse of several female patrons. And as soon as Austin had connected Connor to that profession, he recalled having seen him with Lenora York in the lobby of Haversham Theatre. It was then a fairly simple matter to confirm that she was one of his most ardent customers, along with her mother, Henrietta Wellesley.

Austin grinned at the thought of Lenora paying to be serviced by Connor Maginnis. He was not really surprised, however. Money was no obstacle; Lenora always seemed to have plenty of that. She might, in fact, find it exciting to pay for her pleasure. What did surprise him was her choice of lover. After all, there was no shortage of candidates sniffing around; indeed, Austin himself had already tasted her passion on two occasions. Countless other well-connected young men would willingly share a ride in her coach or in her bed.

His smile faded as he thought of Connor Maginnis touching Lenora. She was almost a Ballinger, after all, married to the brother of Edmund's wife. And she had betrayed the family name, for Austin's investigation had made it all but apparent that a tip from Lenora had gotten Connor started on his mission to clear his father—and perhaps destroy the Ballinger name in the process.

Edmund will see to Lenora, Austin told himself, wincing slightly at the memory of how enraged Edmund had become upon learning of his sister-in-law's indiscretion. *And I will see to Mr. Connor Maginnis.*

He walked down the street to where a single-horse gentleman's phaeton was parked at the curb. It had brought him to this rendezvous, and now it would take him far from central London—to a party in Kensington, which would provide him an alibi for the night's dark business.

As he approached the phaeton, two men climbed out and stood waiting for him. He acknowledged them with a perfunctory nod, then climbed into the vehicle.

"Night, gov'ner. Don't worry about a thing," the older of the men said in a gravelly voice. Doffing his battered felt hat, he grinned broadly, revealing a set of crooked brown teeth.

"Everything's under control," the second man declared. He was smaller, his green jacket in only slightly better condition than his partner's brown one. His hand dipped into his boot and withdrew a long-bladed knife, which he caressed lovingly.

"Put that away!" Austin hissed, and the man shrugged and complied. "Now, you know what you're to do?"

The older man slapped his chest. "I hold him, my young friend sticks him," he declared, his tone almost facetious.

"What about the girl?" the younger one asked.

"Do what you want with her," Austin said coldly. "It's her brother I'm concerned about."

As Austin took up the reins, the older man grabbed hold of the horse's harness. "What about our money?"

"I've already given you—"

"I'm talkin' about the other half."

"As I told you, it will be delivered when the job's finished."

The man eyed him for a moment, then seemed satisfied with the answer. "Just to be sure we understand each other."

"We understand each other perfectly well," Austin replied, his voice tight with strain.

"Then we'll be gettin' on with our business." He poked his younger partner on the arm.

"Remember—you're to wait two hours."

"Never you worry," came the reply as the two men stepped back from the phaeton and waited for it to pull away.

Releasing the brake, Austin slapped the reins against the horse's back, steered the vehicle in a tight circle, and rode off down the street. His jaw set in anger. He was not pleased to be part of such dark business, but he was determined to put an end to any risk of scandal before it started. And he wasn't just worried about the scandal that would ensue should the truth come out about their stealing Ballinger Trade away from Graham Maginnis and sending the poor wretch to prison. It wasn't even any concern that Lenora would be unveiled as a tramp. No, what worried Austin the most was his own sister.

"Damn fool," he muttered in dismay at the thought of Zoë in the arms of Connor Maginnis. It was true that he had nothing on which to base this suspicion, but he knew Zoë well and was convinced that she was enamored with the young man. Though she swore that she had only seen him that one night, she had spoken of little else all week. And she seemed determined to help Connor find a way to free his father from prison.

"Never," he whispered, then shouted it aloud. He would see to it that Connor Maginnis never came near a Ballinger again, and that Connor's father never breathed the free air outside Millbank Prison.

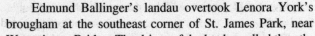

Edmund Ballinger's landau overtook Lenora York's brougham at the southeast corner of St. James Park, near Westminster Bridge. The driver of the landau called the other coachman's name and asked him to pull up, and the man complied. A minute later, Edmund stepped onto the road and walked to the other vehicle.

"Good evening, Giles," he said brusquely to the elderly man atop the brougham.

"Evenin' to you, Master Ballinger," the driver called down, doffing his black cap.

Stepping up to the coach door, Edmund pulled it open and smiled at the occupant. "Are you having an enjoyable evening, Lenora?"

"Edmund . . ." Lenora York said, pulling her black shawl around her and feigning a smile. "Whatever are you doing here?"

"I was going to ask you the same," he replied. Removing his cigar, he stared at the glowing tip for a moment, then dropped it to the street and painstakingly ground it under his shoe.

"I was visiting my mother. Tilford is working late again."

"Yes," he said without emotion, fully aware that his wife's younger brother was probably half-drunk in some London pub by now.

"And what brings *you* out this evening?" Lenora asked.

"Just enjoying the night air. When I saw your coach, I thought we might have a few words together."

"Of course. About anything in particular?"

Edmund looked up and down the street, then turned back to her. "Not here. How about going for a ride?" He held out his hand.

"I was just on my way home. I want to be there before Tilford—"

"We both know that your husband won't be home anytime soon." Again he offered his hand. "Come along; we'll take a short ride, and I'll drop you at home."

Lenora hesitated, then gave a cautious nod and accepted his hand. Stepping down from the brougham, she said to Giles, "I won't be needing the coach any longer. Mr. Ballinger will bring me home."

"Yes, ma'am," Giles replied. He watched until they reached the landau, then took up the reins and drove off.

As soon as the couple was settled inside the coach, it pulled away from the curb and drove along the road that circled St. James Park.

Edmund looked at his sister-in-law, who was seated to his right on the forward-facing bench. "Shall I take your wrap?" he asked, indicating the shawl. "It's really quite comfortable."

She clutched it more tightly around her. "I'm comfortable as I am."

"Of course."

The silence grew heavy as Edmund took out another cigar and meticulously cut off the tip with a small penknife, then folded the knife and slid it into his vest pocket. Using a silver flint-wheel lighter, he lit the end of the tobacco and drew in a long puff, which he let out ever so slowly, filling the coach with thick, cloying smoke.

"You wanted to speak with me?" Lenora asked impatiently.

Edmund sighed. "Better we speak in confidence than I find myself forced to take up matters with Tilford. He can be such a nuisance, don't you agree?" Shifting on the seat, he faced Lenora. His smile was cold, his eyes like ice.

"I'm afraid I don't understand."

"Is he good to you? Does he treat you well?"

"I really don't know what you mean," she said in a strained voice.

"When he makes love to you," Edmund said bluntly, the cigar still clenched in his teeth. "Does he please you or leave you . . . unfulfilled?"

"Edmund! My personal relationship with my husband is—"

"I'm not talking about Tilford." He took the cigar from his mouth and stared at it, his dark eyes glowing like burning coal. "I'm speaking of your lover."

Lenora's eyes widened with shock and fear.

"Your lover, Lenora," he prodded, clamping the cigar between his teeth. "Is he worth the expense? Or is *he* the one who pays? Is that it, Lenora? Have you finally found your calling . . . as a whore?"

Lenora lashed out with her right hand, but Edmund caught her wrist and twisted it cruelly. She had let go of her shawl in order to slap him, and it slid from her shoulder now. Her lavender evening dress was still half-unbuttoned from her ride with Connor Maginnis, revealing the tops of her full breasts, which swelled with each panting breath.

Shifting on the seat, Lenora lifted her other hand, but Edmund caught it, as well, and pulled her close, her face only inches from the burning cigar.

"Is that it, Lenora? You've always been a slut; now have you also become a whore?"

"You *bastard*!" she cursed, trying to wrench herself free.

He twisted her wrists a final time, then abruptly threw her backward on the seat. Her head struck the side of the coach, stunning her, and she lay there limply on her back, looking up at him in fear.

As Edmund's gaze shifted down along her body and then back up again, his eyes betrayed the swirl of emotions within him. There was no doubt that he wanted to take her, violently and cruelly. But there was another rage building within him, and it frightened Lenora even more.

"What did you tell him?" Edmund asked, barely containing his fury. When she did not answer, he leaned over her and took the cigar from between his clenched teeth. Holding it only inches above her chest, he asked the question again, adding a name: "What did you tell Connor Maginnis?"

Taken aback, Lenora stammered, "C-Connor? What are you talking about?"

"You told him about his father, didn't you?"

"I . . . I don't know what—"

"You told him! And now you're going to tell *me*. You're going to tell me how you met that bastard, everything you said to him"—his eyes widened with excitement—"and everything the two of you did!"

"N-No, Edmund," she whimpered, her eyes filling with tears as she ineffectually raised her hands. "Don't—"

"You'll tell me, damn it!" he blared, slapping her hands away.

Jabbing the cigar back in his mouth, he grabbed her partially opened dress and wrenched it downward, tearing it open to her waist. She struggled beneath him, but he smacked her hard across the face, almost knocking her unconscious. Then he snatched the penknife from his vest pocket and slid open the blade.

Lenora looked up in terror as Edmund grasped the top of her corset, pulling it down and baring her breasts. She pleaded with him to stop as he pressed the flat side of the blade against her left nipple, but he pinned her in place with his knees and lifted the knife close to her face. Then he lowered it just below her breasts and began slashing at her corset, tearing away the material until she was naked to the waist.

"Stop! P-Please stop!" she begged. "I'll tell you everything!"

"You're damn right you will!" he shouted, tossing the knife to the floor of the rocking coach and slapping her again across the face. "And you'll pay, you little slut, for betraying your own family with the likes of a Maginnis!"

Taking the cigar from his mouth, he lowered it slowly to her belly. She squirmed as some of the ashes fell on her. Then she began to writhe and scream as he pressed the burning tip against her flesh.

◆━━━━◆━━━━◆

"Let's go!" the man in the felt hat told his partner, prodding him toward the building across the street.

"It's only been ten minutes, Simon." The young man looked more than a bit nervous. "We was told to wait two hours."

"Who cares?"

"The gentleman seemed to care."

Simon looked around and grinned. "Do you see any gentleman here?"

"But he told us—"

"He ain't here, Willie boy, now is he? And I'll be damned if I'm goin' to wait two hours to get this business done with. There's a mug of ale just waitin' for me at the Gov'ner's Crescent. And I'm sure that woman o' yours'll be wantin' you home to do your husbandly duties." He chuckled.

"But the gentleman was quite insistent that we wait."

"Quite insistent?" Simon repeated mockingly. "You earn yourself a few quid from one o' them dandies and you start talkin' like 'em."

William looked down and frowned. "I don't like this . . . any o' this at all."

"Come along, Willie," his partner said with enthusiasm. "It's no different from rollin' a dandy for his purse."

"But that fellow up there"—he gestured toward the building—"ain't no dandy, and he sure as hell ain't got no purse to speak of."

"That fellow up there's the very one who knocked me over the head across from the Gov'ner's—ain't that what you said?"

"I think so," William replied skeptically.

"Well, you're the one who got a look at him that night, not me. Is he or ain't he?"

"I'm not sure. . . . I think so."

"He's not sure," Simon mocked. "Well, it don't much matter. All we gotta do is roll him and collect our purse from that dandy. Now let's get going. We already collected half the money and all but spent it."

"All right, but I don't have to like it."

"You can damn well hate it, for all I care. Just so long as you stick that blade o' yours where it belongs."

William looked somewhat heartened. "I always do, don't I?"

"That you do, Willie boy. And that is why you never see me turnin' my back to you." Wrapping his arm around the smaller man's shoulder, he led the way across the street.

"I don't have to hurt the girl, do I?" William asked.

"You just worry about her brother." Simon tightened his grip on the young man's shoulder. "I'll take care o' the girl."

William gave up his protest and shuffled along beside his partner. When they reached the building, Simon examined the front door and nodded in satisfaction. It was in rather poor shape, with signs of rot at the base, and had not seen paint in many years. It was probably unlocked; in this district, security was usually left to the tenants. However, if it was locked, it would be an easy piece of work to force it open.

"Shall we?" Simon asked, and William gave a half nod.

Simon turned the handle and felt the mechanism release. Smiling, he pushed against the door, but it held fast, the wood having swelled over the years. With a firm shove, he knocked it free of the jamb, and it opened, revealing a small entryway and a single dark staircase. Stepping inside, Simon nodded toward the doors on the left and right; there was a first-floor apartment on each side. Telling William to be quiet, he led the way up the stairs.

At the second-floor landing, there was another pair of doors, leading to two more apartments. The narrow staircase continued to the upper rear of the building and a final set of doors for the two top-floor apartments.

Reaching the third-floor landing, Simon signaled his young partner to take out his knife and wait behind him. He glanced over at the right-hand door, making sure no unusual sounds were coming from it. Then he turned to the door on the left and rapped loudly.

The two men waited, listening to the usual shuffling

sounds as someone came to answer the door. They had already decided that if the fellow named Connor answered, they would drag him out and finish him right there on the landing. If it was the girl, they would force their way in, find her brother, and make quick work of him.

"Who is it?" a man asked through the closed door.

Simon frowned. "I'm lookin' for Mr. Connor Maginnis," he said in as pleasant a tone as he could muster.

"What do you want with him?"

"I've a message from a friend."

"Then give it and be gone."

Glowering, Simon looked over his shoulder at his agitated partner, then knocked again on the door. "Will you open up, please? I've got somethin' for you."

"I'll bet you do," came the curious reply.

Sensing that something was greatly amiss, Simon motioned to William, and they stepped back slightly and rushed the door in an attempt to shoulder it open. They slammed into it, and though the frame shuddered and cracked, the door held. They crashed into it a second time, and this time it splintered and almost gave way.

With a furious oath, Simon and his partner launched themselves at the door a third time. This time the door unexpectedly swung wide, and at the same moment a dark figure rushed them from behind, knocking them through the open doorway and sending them sprawling to the floor of the apartment.

Simon was stunned but quick-witted enough to scramble to his feet and try to escape. The man who had rushed him, however, was blocking the doorway, and Simon saw now that it was the very person he had come for: Connor Maginnis. Cursing, Simon barreled into him, and they went staggering across the landing and through the open door of the vacant opposite apartment, from which Connor had launched his counterattack.

"Bastard!" Simon shouted as he clawed at his opponent.

He was a street fighter, and he fought dirty, jabbing his fingers into Connor's eyes and kneeing him in the groin.

Connor was no amateur with his fists, and he landed a vicious uppercut to Simon's belly that threw him back onto the landing, then dove on top of him. But the man managed to grab hold of Connor's neck, jerking him to the side. Connor held on, and the two men went rolling across the landing, kicking and flailing at each other as they tumbled arm-in-arm down the stairs. There was the horrific sound of bone snapping as the two went sprawling onto the second-floor landing.

At the top of the stairs a woman shrieked, and Connor caught a glimpse of Emeline standing there. It was enough of a distraction to allow Simon to break his grip, and he leapt to his feet, clutching his broken left arm as he raced down the final flight of stairs. Connor was close on his heels, chasing him out to the street, but then he heard his sister scream again and remembered there was a second attacker to account for.

Praying that he was not too late, Connor bounded up the stairs two at a time. Emeline was still standing on the third-floor landing, looking in terror through their open apartment door. Brushing past her, he raced into the room and saw two bodies lying motionless in the middle of the floor, both covered with blood. On top was the young attacker named William; pinned beneath him was the even-younger Mose Levison, who had pretended to be Connor when the two men came calling.

"Mose!" Connor shouted, dropping to his knees and rolling the other man off him.

There was blood everywhere, and for a moment Connor could not tell whether it belonged to one or both of the young men. But then he glanced over at the body of the attacker and saw the knife handle protruding from his chest. Mose had been unarmed; somehow the man must have landed on his own knife when he fell into the apartment.

"Mose," Connor called, lifting the boy and cradling him in his arms. He saw now that Mose was breathing but had been knocked unconscious when the other man landed on top of him.

Realizing that Mose was still alive, Emeline managed to compose herself and fetched some water and a cloth from the kitchen. She knelt beside Mose and wiped his brow, smiling and then crying with relief as he slowly regained consciousness.

"Wh-What happened?" the boy asked, looking up at them.

"It's all right," Connor assured him.

"D-Did they . . . ?"

Connor shook his head. "One of them's dead; the other got away, but he's not in good shape. I don't think we'll see him again."

Struggling to a sitting position, Mose looked first at the body lying a few feet away and then at the mess in the room. "It worked, didn't it?"

"Just like you said. And I've a feeling that when we get a chance to examine that folder you brought with you, we're finally going to be able to turn the tables on those bastards." He clapped the teenager on the shoulders. "Everything's going to be all right, thanks to you."

"And Clarissa," Mose added.

"Clarissa?" Connor asked.

"She's the one who's coverin' for me at work so I could get here 'afore eight."

Connor grinned. "Yes—thanks to Clarissa, too."

XII

Connor Maginnis did not even for a moment consider informing the local constabulary about the death of the young knife-wielding assailant. Though the apartments on the second and first floors of the building were occupied, the tenants had thought better than to come out and see what was going on, though surely they had heard Connor and the older man struggling on the stairs. In this part of London, it was always a better policy to mind one's own business. So with no witnesses to the incident—other than the man with the broken arm, who surely would not be complaining to the authorities—Connor came up with a plan for removing the body from the premises and disposing of it.

Less than an hour after the attack, Mose Levison had rented a two-seat phaeton and was pulling it into position in front of the Maginnises' building. Emeline was quite distraught over what she had witnessed, and Connor was with her in the vacant apartment across the hall from theirs, doing his best to explain all that had happened since the day six weeks before when they had first learned that their father might still be alive.

"B-But why?" She dabbed at her eyes with the sleeve of her dress. "Why didn't you tell me he's alive?"

Connor moved his chair closer to hers. They were

seated at a bare wooden table, which along with the two spindly chairs were the only furnishings in the apartment. "He wanted me to wait until we were sure we could get him out. He didn't want you thinking of him sitting there . . ."

"In p-prison." She began to cry again.

"It's all right," he soothed, forcing enthusiasm into his voice. "He's strong and in good spirits, and with what Mose has turned up, I'm certain we can get him released."

"You've *seen* him?" she asked incredulously.

"Twice, now."

"And you didn't tell me?" There was more than a hint of anger in her voice.

"I didn't want to upset you. Neither did Father. We wanted to wait—"

"Upset me? But it—it's my *father*. And for all these years, I—I thought he was dead."

"So did I."

She looked at him warily. "Are you sure? Maybe you've known all this time. Maybe you just didn't want to *upset* me." Her tone was uncharacteristically sarcastic, and she turned away from him.

Reaching over, Connor grasped both her hands and squeezed them firmly, forcing her to look in his eyes, which were also moist with tears. "You have to believe me, Emeline. After you told me what Lenora said about Graham Maginnis being alive, I searched all the prisons in London until I found him—in Millbank."

"M-Millbank," she repeated and shuddered. Several years before she had ridden past the large, imposing compound on the day that two of the prisoners were to be executed on the prison grounds. A large crowd had gathered for the festivities, and though she was gone from the area long before the sentence was carried out, the carnival atmosphere had left an indelibly bitter memory.

"But he's all right, I promise," Connor tried to reassure her. "That's why I didn't tell you right away—I didn't want you to worry needlessly. I had hoped to wait until he was free."

Emeline's eyes glistened with an eager light. "He's going to be released?"

Connor's shoulders slumped, and he laid his palms flat on the table between them. "I wish I could say that were true, but I just don't know. I . . . I'm trying."

Emeline rose and moved behind her brother's chair, wrapping her arms around his shoulders and resting her head against the back of his neck. "I know you are." She sighed. "We'll figure it out . . . together."

He reached up and caressed her cheek. "I'm sorry I left you out of things. I'll never do that again."

Kneeling beside the chair, she placed her hands on her brother's arm and looked up at him. "But you're sure he's all right?"

"Yes. And I'm convinced we're going to get him out of there. I've been working on a plan."

"All ready downstairs," Mose interrupted, coming through the open apartment door.

"I'll be right with you." Connor signaled Mose to wait for him in their apartment across the landing. Turning back to his sister, he said, "We'll talk more about this later. But now I want you to go next door and finish gathering your things—and mine."

"We're really leaving?" she asked.

"It's no longer safe here. You're going to spend some time with Mose and his grandfather."

"Wh-What about you?"

"Don't worry about me, Emeline. There are things I need to do . . . for Father. And I've plenty of places to stay."

"Not on the streets," she said emphatically.

"Never," he assured her. "Don't be worrying about me. You know I can take care of myself." Leaning forward, he kissed her forehead, then stood and lifted her to her feet.

"You just wait here for a minute while we get that poor fool loaded into the back of the carriage. Then you gather whatever you need, and I'll come back up and help you carry it down."

Hugging her, he went out onto the landing, where Mose was dragging the blanket-wrapped body by its feet. Connor grabbed hold of it under the arms, and together they lifted it off the floor and carried it down the stairs.

"Any idea where to take it?" Mose asked as they paused to rest at the second-floor landing.

Connor had a curious smile. "I've been thinking about that, and I've come up with just the thing. Are you game for a bit of adventure?"

"Me?" Mose's own grin broadened. "I'm always game for a lark."

"Good, 'cause I think it's about time we took the battle directly to the cousins Ballinger. And we'll start with a visit to the Ballinger Trade Company."

Hoisting the body again, they continued down to the waiting phaeton, where they unceremoniously dumped it into the rear boot.

"Poor fool," Connor muttered as he tied the leather skirt over the boot. Turning, he gripped Mose's forearm. "You keep watch here while I bring Emeline down with our things. Then we'd best be going; we've a busy night's work ahead of us."

◆━━━◆━━━◆

It was almost midnight as Edmund Ballinger's landau clattered down Bishopsgate Street. Reaching London Bridge, it turned left along the Thames and around the Tower of London, continuing along East Smithfield, which would take them past the London Docks and into the district where Edmund lived.

He was no longer smirking at the thought of Lenora York, whom he had deposited unceremoniously about a block from her home in Hoxton. He had only burned her a couple of times and bruised her a little more, but it surely had been enough to guarantee her future silence. And he did not doubt that she would do as ordered and forget who it was who had treated her so cruelly. Edmund didn't really care what she told her prig of a husband, Tilford, who was probably so drunk that he would not even notice her disheveled appearance. In fact, by Saturday morning she probably would have him convinced that he had been the one who beat her.

"Lenora . . ." he muttered under his breath. He had thought of taking her by force, as well, but she had been so hysterical that he had tired of the sport and let her go with only the beating and a warning to keep away from Connor Maginnis and his kind. At the thought of Connor, a thin smile touched his lips; by now that fancy man would be dead, and with him would die any chance of Graham Maginnis's gaining his freedom and clearing his name.

As the landau drove past the London Docks, he looked at his darkened warehouse. Suddenly it struck him that Roger Avery and the night crew should be on hand, and he called up to the driver to pull over at the building.

Minutes later Edmund was unlocking the front door, and with the driver carrying one of the coach lanterns, he led the way into the building. It was readily apparent that no one was there, despite Edmund's having left word for Avery to keep the men unloading the East Indies shipment right through the night. With the coachman following, he walked down the aisle to his office, where Avery might have left a message explaining the reason for their early departure. There was no notice on the door, however.

Fumbling with his keys, Edmund found the right one, opened the door, and stepped inside. He was startled at the sight of someone seated in his chair, and he was about to ask who it was when the coachman entered with the lantern. The bobbing light fell across a chalky white face, and Edmund gasped. The front of the young man's green jacket was soaked in blood, and a trickle of dried blood ran down his chin from the corner of the mouth. His lifeless eyes were opened wide.

The coachman pushed past Edmund, who stood paralyzed in front of the desk. Stepping behind it, the coachman grabbed the body, which lolled to one side, and pulled the chair back. The entire front of the man's shirt was drenched in drying blood, and enough of the material had been cut away to reveal a massive knife wound to the chest. A piece of paper was pinned to the shirt collar, and the coachman snatched it off and read it. Frowning, he handed it across the desk to his boss.

His hand shaking, Edmund held up the note, angling it so that it caught the lantern light. Only three words were scrawled on it: *You are next.*

Edmund felt as if he would faint but struggled to compose himself. Crushing the note, he tossed it on top of the desk.

"Shall I get him out o' here?" the coachman asked, already lifting the body from the chair.

Edmund nodded and backed to one side as the younger man dragged the corpse from the office. Looking down at his ring of keys, Edmund was about to leave the room when he thought of the locked drawer. Hurrying around the desk, he knelt and pulled on it, relieved to discover that it hadn't been tampered with. Just to be sure, he slipped the small key from his vest pocket and opened it. Inside was the usual stack of black folders; he lifted the top one and opened it.

"Wh—Whaa?" he stammered, snatching up a handful of bills of lading. He lifted the rest of the folders from the drawer and rummaged through them. When he was convinced that none contained the damaging information about Graham Maginnis, he spun around to the filing cabinet and examined the folders where the bills of lading were supposed to be kept. The most recent one was missing, and a quick inspection confirmed that the bills from it were the ones Edmund had just found in the desk drawer.

Cursing furiously, he stormed out of the office, slamming the door and hastily locking it. Something was wrong—terribly wrong—and "that little bastard" he had recently hired was somehow in the thick of it. But he would have to wait. Right now he had to see to it that the body was dumped in the Thames; then he would ride to the Ballinger estate. Despite the late hour, Austin would have to be informed about the missing sheaf of papers— papers that in the wrong hands could prove damaging, not only to Edmund, but to Austin and all the Ballingers.

Connor Maginnis was alone in the phaeton as he drove through the sprawling, manicured gardens that surrounded Planting Fields Manor. After disposing of the body, he had taken Emeline and Mose to the Levisons' apartment, which was only slightly larger than their own. It had been the first time that Connor had met Mose's grandfather, Isaac, who was quite affable though somewhat more infirm than Mose had led them to believe. He was perhaps sixty years old and suffered badly with arthritis, which had crippled his hands and feet. But he appeared to be in perennially good humor and obviously doted on his grandson; he seemed genuinely delighted to have Emeline staying with them. He even insisted they had enough room to put up Connor, though Connor turned down the offer.

As the phaeton drew closer to the manor house, Connor doused the running lamps and slowed the horse to a walk. It was almost two o'clock on a crisp, cloudless Saturday morning, and the late-September moon shone large and bright enough to illuminate the road and nearby fields.

Coming upon the Druid Circle, near the left side of the road, Connor was taken aback by the dark, towering stones, which seemed at first like a gathering of small buildings. He reined in the horse and peered into the darkness until he could discern the circle more clearly. He prodded the horse forward, then steered the carriage off the road and drove across the field.

After he pulled up in the middle of the circle, he set the brake and climbed down. For a moment he stood there, looking from one carved figure to the next, wondering how such enormous stones had ever been carried to the site and placed there in such perfect proportion.

Walking up to one of them, he ran his hand over the carving, which felt like a dragon or some sort of mythical beast at the feet of a knight in armor—St. George, perhaps. He leaned back against it and looked from one tall stone to the next. There was something safe—something almost familiar—about them, and as the wind whipped through the circle, he thought for a moment it was calling his name.

Shaking himself out of his reverie, Connor walked back to the phaeton, where he patted the horse on the muzzle, double-checked the brake, then reached under the front seat and groped around until he found a cloth-wrapped package. He opened it and removed the brown folder that Mose had brought from the warehouse. After he made sure that all the contents were intact, he placed the folder back under the seat. There was a second item in the package, and he lifted it in front of him, feeling the heft of the long-bladed knife that had killed the younger of the two assailants. Wiping the blade with the cloth to make sure all the blood was gone, he tucked the knife behind his belt, tossed the cloth onto the floor of the carriage, and started across the field to the manor house.

"Plan . . . I need a plan," he whispered aloud as he saw the building looming ahead. He had no idea what he would do if confronted; he didn't even know if guard dogs were kept on the premises, though he hadn't seen any when he had been there a week before.

Austin Ballinger, he told himself, his jaw tightening with anger. *I'm going to kill that bastard. . . . I'm going to find him and kill him!*

It wasn't much of a plan, he realized, but he felt strangely confident that he could get into the house, find his way to Austin's room, and return the knife—with a vengeance—to the man who had planned just such a fate for Connor Maginnis.

Standing below the east wall of Planting Fields Manor, Connor gazed up at the numerous turrets, towers, and windows. In the moonlight, he could make out several windows that were partway open to let in the night air. Unfortunately, none were on the first floor.

Examining the wall, he gauged the various routes of access until he found one that seemed manageable. It would be a simple bit of work, he believed—after all, he had made more than a few hasty exits through second-story windows, and a couple of entrances, as well. He walked over to the wall and felt for the knife in his belt to see that it was secure. Then, choosing his first hand- and footholds in the ornately carved granite facing, he started up.

◆◆◆

As the old wall clock gave the tinny two o'clock chime, Duncan Weems leaned back in his chair and stretched, his bulky frame nearly popping the buttons of his blue wool uniform. Normally he would be asleep at his desk at this time of the morning; Friday nights he was on duty alone in this wing of Millbank Prison, and he didn't bother to interrupt his rest until just before the day guard arrived at six o'clock Saturday morning.

"But tonight I've a pleasant piece o' business to occupy me time," he muttered, speaking aloud to help rouse himself. "Pleasant . . . and profitable," he added with a smirk.

Opening the top drawer, he removed a crude knife and held it in front of him, the jagged, hand-sharpened blade catching the glint of the kerosene lantern on the desk. It had been confiscated by Weems earlier that week from a prisoner who had fashioned it from a spoon, its handle sharpened to a point, its bowl wrapped tightly with strips of cloth soaked in a mixture of water and flour, which had hardened the material into a serviceable handle.

Weems hefted the makeshift knife. "Just the thing," he told himself as he rose from the chair, stuffed the knife into his jacket pocket, and snatched up his ring of keys. He was about to pick up the lantern, but another thought struck him, and he yanked open one of the lower drawers and took out a dented tin flask. Uncapping it, he took a deep swig of whiskey, all but draining the flask, which he closed and tossed back into the drawer. Wiping his mouth on his jacket sleeve, he grabbed the lantern, opened the office door, and went down the first of a half-dozen dark corridors that would lead him to cell number 8414.

As he entered the last of the corridors, Duncan Weems was whistling, his imagination already spending the money he would be earning for the night's work. Geoffrey Ingleby had promised fifty pounds and had delivered ten in advance—a hefty sum for dispatching one all-but-forgotten prisoner, a senile old man who had been visited only twice during the past years.

The guard had known better than to ask who wanted this dirty bit of business done. Geoffrey Ingleby was a gaunt, pinch-faced barrister of low repute who haunted the courts and the prisons, looking for whatever work might fall his way. He was undoubtedly no more than a go-between for the real person who desired Number 8414 dead, and it was likely that even Ingleby didn't know the reason why.

No matter, Weems thought as he approached the cell door. *For fifty quid, I'd kill me own mother . . . hell, I'd prob'ly kill me.* He chuckled at the thought.

The guard turned the lock and slid the bolt, then pulled open the creaky wooden door. Thrusting the lantern ahead of him, he stepped into the cell. He would make quick work of it, he told himself. Just a thrust to the belly, then leave him lying there, his lifeblood pouring onto the cold stone floor. No one would doubt Weems's story that the half-crazed old codger had come at him with a handmade knife and that Weems had heroically turned the weapon against him. *Hell, there may even be a commendation in it for me,* he thought with delight.

"Eighty-four Fourteen," he called, loud enough to rouse the prisoner but not cause a commotion in the other cells. "Up with you, matey!"

A frail, shadowy figure stirred on the metal cot.

"We're movin' you to another cell," Weems explained. His right hand dipped into his pocket, his fingers closing around the padded grip of the knife.

◆━━━◆━━━◆

Connor moved silently down the long second-floor hallway of Planting Fields Manor. He had already entered a sitting room and a study and had even stumbled into what appeared to be Sybil Ballinger's bedroom. Guessing that the adjoining room was Cedric's, he skipped it and headed farther down the hall.

Easing open one of the last doors along the corridor, he slipped into the room and pushed closed the door until it touched the jamb. His eyes were well adjusted to the exceedingly thin light; still, it was difficult to make out his surroundings. He was in an entryway of sorts, with a large room ahead—a bedroom, perhaps—and an open door to the right, probably leading to the dressing room. He entered the side room and found himself in a large walk-in closet filled with men's clothing.

Returning to the entryway, he drew a calming breath and entered the bedroom. Fortunately the drapes had been left open, and the moonlight afforded a shadowy but fairly distinct view of the room. Along the right-hand wall were a dressing table and several dressers, with a sitting area just to the left and another one under the windows.

A large canopy bed was on the far left, and as Connor ventured into the room, he heard the steady wheeze of someone asleep on it. He could see the mound of covers where the person was lying, and he hunched down lower and circled the bed. As he came around to the window side, he spied the figure of a man asleep on his back with his face toward the window. Taking care not to cast a shadow across the man's face, Connor moved closer. The moonlight shone across the pillows, highlighting the stocky features and full beard of Lord Cedric Ballinger's eldest son.

Almost involuntarily, Connor whispered under his breath, "Austin . . ." The man stirred slightly, then settled back into the pillows, still on his back and facing the window.

Holding his breath and staying low, Connor circled to the other side of the canopy bed. Cautiously rising, he reached to his belt and slid out the knife, which he lifted in both hands, the blade pointing down. He held it poised over Austin Ballinger's chest, the cool blue light reflecting off the blade and playing across the man's face, making his features seem even more arrogant and cold.

Connor's muscles tensed. He steadied his hands and his thoughts, conjuring the image of the two assailants the Ballingers had hired to kill him, remembering how the same family had betrayed his father and sentenced him to a living death in a Millbank Prison cell.

Now! a voice screamed within him. *Finish it now!*

Drawing a final breath, he raised his hands over his head and, in fury, plunged the knife downward.

Graham Maginnis stirred on his prison cot, struggling upward out of sleep as a gruff, harsh voice shouted, "Up with you, matey! We're movin' you to another cell."

Graham raised a hand against the piercing light of the lantern and saw that it was being held aloft by one of the guards—the big, unbathed one who on two occasions had brought his son to visit.

"C-Connor . . . ?" he asked in a reedy voice.

"Get up with you," the guard ordered again.

"My son . . . is he—?"

"You ain't got no visitors. You're bein' moved to another ward. Now start movin', and be quick about it."

As Graham realized what was happening, he grew even more wary. It had been more than five years since he had been taken off the work line and transferred to this cell, and from what he knew, the only way off this ward was through parole or death.

Realizing he had no option but to comply, he pushed himself to a sitting position, then rose on unsteady legs and gathered his blanket.

"Leave that stuff here," the guard told him. "Just bring any personal items."

Graham didn't have anything personal, other than a pair of leather shoes, which he used to wear on the work line. He no longer had much use for them, but he kept them tucked under the cot, perhaps as a reminder that he might one day walk out of Millbank a free man. Kneeling, he gathered them up and clutched them against his chest. Turning to the guard, he nodded that he was ready and started toward the door.

"Just a moment, there," the guard said with a cold sneer as Graham stepped past him into the corridor. "I've a present to you from an ol' mate."

Graham caught the glint of metal as a blade was thrust at his belly. He darted to the right but was stopped by the doorframe, and he felt a piercing burn as the knife slashed into his side.

His surprisingly agile movement had saved him from a fatal wound, but the burly guard quickly withdrew the blade and stepped closer, pinning him against the door and jabbing the knife upward at his midsection. Graham instinctively lowered his hands to ward off the blow, and though the shoes shielded him somewhat, the guard's thrust was so forceful that the blade went right through the sole of one shoe and buried itself in Graham's belly.

With a sighing groan, Graham slipped down along the door to his knees. The guard tried to pull the knife free, and though it easily slid out of the old man's flesh, it remained stuck in the sole of the shoe, which Graham had somehow managed to hang on to. The guard gave a furious yank, which freed the knife from the shoe but sent him staggering back across the cell.

As the guard regained his balance, Graham looked down and saw blood flowing from the wounds in his belly and side. He thought of his son and daughter, whom he had almost reclaimed but who now would be the orphans they for so long had believed themselves to be. Then he looked across the cell at the big, stocky man grinning at him, the knife raised in his hand as he prepared to finish off his victim.

"Edmund?" Graham asked, cocking his head in bewilderment. His former partner was closing in on him. He raised his blood-drenched hands in front of him, as if to ward off the inevitable, his eyes widening in shock and fear. Suddenly he gave a mournful wail, shouting, *"No!"* over and over again as he vaulted to his feet and lunged at the demon in front of him.

The big guard was taken by such complete surprise that he wasn't able to get the knife into play before Graham crashed into him, throwing both of them backward off their feet. The guard's head struck the metal rim of the cot, stunning him as he and Graham sprawled across the floor of the cell.

Graham was somewhat dazed, as well, but he shook

his head to clear the fog that threatened to envelop him. He thought he had heard the clatter of metal striking stone, and he crawled around wildly, his hands groping along the blood-soaked floor.

The guard stirred, his arms flailing as he forced himself upright against the cot. He groaned in pain and anger, his hands rubbing his eyes to clear his vision. The lantern had fallen to the floor, but it was still burning, casting eerie spokes of light across the stone.

Graham Maginnis was doubled over in pain as he dragged himself around the cell, searching for the missing knife. Turning in place, he saw the guard struggling to his feet. Then their eyes met, and the big man let out a furious oath and lunged at him.

As Graham pulled back, his hand closed around the rough cloth handle of the knife. Snatching it up, he thrust it in front of him and felt the sickening thud of blade piercing bone as it slid through the guard's sternum and punctured his heart. His body went limp, and he was dead before he hit the floor.

Rolling clear of the body, Graham tried to stand but slipped on the blood-covered stone. Crawling to the door, he grabbed it, managed to pull himself upright, and stood there for a moment, looking down at the lifeless body, then at his own wounds. Grimacing, he clutched at his belly and stumbled into the corridor.

Going to the left, he gazed down the dark hall and thought he saw a light in the distance. He felt it pulling him, and he staggered forward, dragging himself step by step toward the light. It glowed dimly at first, but it grew ever brighter, surrounding and filling him. Looking down, he saw equally brilliant rivers of light pouring from his wounds, flowing into the greater light beyond. His body was shrinking, his legs and arms receding into a single point of being, and then a voice, a hush, was calling his number . . . *Eighty-four Fourteen* . . . then

his name . . . *Graham* . . . *Graham Maginnis* . . . and he released his breath in a sighing *"Yesss!"* and entered the light.

◆━━━◆━━━◆

Connor Maginnis backed away from the canopy bed
in shock. Austin Ballinger was still wheezing in his sleep,
oblivious to what had just happened. The long-bladed knife
was buried halfway to the hilt in the mattress beside his
head, so close to him that if he rolled to the left he would
cut his cheek.

Connor was shaking with fear. He had aimed at the
detested man's chest, but something had made him pull
away at the last instant and plant the blade in the bed
instead. Even more incredible was that Austin, so deep in
sleep, had not even stirred.

Backing across the room, Connor fought to calm
himself. He had not expected it to be so difficult to murder
a man—especially one so bent on killing him. Inwardly cursing himself, he reached for the bedroom door, then pulled
away from it at the sound of heavy footsteps in the hall.

Retreating into the dark walk-in closet, Connor waited
for the footfalls to pass, but they drew closer and came to
a halt directly in front of the bedroom. Someone rapped on
the door, and a man's voice called, "Master Ballinger, are
you awake?" There was no response, and a moment later he
called again, "Master Ballinger, I'm afraid I must come in."

Connor backed deeper into the closet as the bedroom
door opened and someone stepped into the entryway carrying
a small candle lamp. The person passed quickly into the
bedroom, and for a moment Connor considered slipping
out into the hall. But he thought better of it and instead
hid behind a rack of evening jackets.

"Master Ballinger, I'm sorry to have to wake you, but
it is urgent."

Connor could hear Austin stirring—or perhaps being
stirred by the man, who sounded like the butler, Desmond.

"Whaa . . . what is it?" Austin muttered groggily.

"It's your father's cousin, Mr. Edmund Ballinger," Desmond told him. "He just arrived and said he must speak with you."

"Now? What time—?"

"Just after two o'clock. But he insists that it is urgent and cannot wait."

"All right, I suppose. Tell him I'll be right down."

"Yes, sir."

There was a pause, and then Austin snapped, "Well? What are you waiting for?"

"It's, uh, just . . ."

"Just what, man? You look like—"

"It's just that . . . that thing over there."

There was a longer, more uncomfortable pause, during which Connor tried to bury himself deeper behind the clothes. Then Austin blurted, "What the hell? Did you put this here, Desmond?"

"Me? Of course not, Master Ballinger."

"Is this a joke of some kind?"

"I don't know anything about it."

"Who's been in here?" Austin demanded. Connor could hear him circling the room.

"No one, sir. No one that I know of."

"Well, someone's been here, that's for damn sure."

"Are you sure it wasn't . . . uh, perhaps while you were sleeping . . . ?"

"Me? Are you suggesting it was me? That I got up in the middle of the night, snatched up a knife from God knows where, and plunged it into my own bed?"

"No, Master Ballinger, but—"

"Go on, get out of here. Tell that fool Edmund I'll be down as soon as I put something on."

The butler retreated from the room, closing the door behind him. Through the open closet door, Connor saw the bedroom grow brighter as Austin lit a lamp. Then without warning he appeared in the closet and began rummaging through the hanging clothes. Fortunately he had not brought the lamp, and there was barely enough light for him to make out the clothing, let along a dark figure hiding at the back of the room. He snatched some sort of dressing robe off one of the hangers and took it into the bedroom. A few minutes later, he padded out of the room and down the hall, leaving the outer door open and the bedroom lamp burning.

Connor waited until he was reasonably sure all was clear. Then he stepped cautiously from the closet toward the corridor—and almost collided with a young woman coming into the room.

"Austin?" she blurted, then realized that it was not her brother. "Connor? What are you—?"

"Zoë. I . . . I can explain," he stammered, grasping her arm and pulling her into the entryway. Closing the door, he quickly led her into the bedroom.

"What are you doing here, for heaven's sake?" She pulled her robe tighter around her.

Connor felt incredibly foolish, and he considered trying to make up some outlandish story. In the end, his shoulders slumped, and he muttered, "I came to kill your brother."

"You *what*?" she exclaimed, pulling free of his grip and backing away.

"I didn't . . . I mean, I tried, but I couldn't."

"Whatever are you talking about?"

"I . . . I can't talk about it now . . . not here."

"You'd better talk about it, or else I'm going to call—"

"Please don't," he begged her. "You've got to trust me."

"Trust you? But you said you were going to—"

"I know, but I had the opportunity and didn't."

"Where is he?" she asked, looking around in concern. "What have you done with my brother?"

"Nothing," Connor insisted. "He's fine. He's downstairs with Edmund."

"This is insane," she muttered, throwing up her hands. She started from the room. "I'm going down to get him, and we're going to find out—"

"You mustn't," Connor implored, stepping between her and the door. "Your brother . . . he . . ."

"He what?"

"He and your father's cousin—"

"Edmund?"

"Yes, Edmund. They tried to have me killed tonight."

Zoë was stunned into silence. She shook her head in disbelief, but then laid a hand on his forearm. "You're serious, aren't you?"

"Completely," he replied.

"I . . . I just can't believe that Austin would be involved in anything like that."

"Zoë, you've got to let me explain." He hesitated, then added, "You've got to meet me."

She must have seen the earnestness in his eyes. "Where? When?"

"Outside at that big circle of stones."

"Now?" she asked incredulously. "But I—"

"You must." He walked to the window and looked down. "I've got to get out of here before your brother comes back," he explained, unlocking the window and opening it. "I'll be at the circle until just before dawn. You can come alone, or you can send the others after me—but I'll be there waiting."

"No, not that way," she cautioned, moving to the window and pushing it closed. "There's an easier way— a staircase just down the hall that leads directly outside. Come with me."

He looked into her eyes and saw the utter lack of guile. Nodding, he followed her across the room and into the hall.

Almost an hour had passed when Zoë headed outside to join Connor. Before that she had sneaked downstairs and taken up a position in the dining room, from where she listened in on her brother and Edmund in the adjoining library. She had been unable to discern everything they said—they spoke in hushed tones—but she had heard enough talk of knives and hired thugs and conspiracies to convince her they were up to no good where Connor and Graham Maginnis were concerned.

Her eyes brimmed with tears as she hurried through the gardens to the Druid Circle. She wore a heavy cloak, its fur-trimmed hood pulled up over her unbrushed hair, but when she saw Connor standing beside his phaeton in the middle of the circle, she threw back the hood and ran into his arms.

"Oh, Connor, I'm so sorry!" Zoë cried, burying her head against his chest.

"It's all right." He caressed her long auburn hair, which glowed like gold in the waning moonlight. "Everything's going to be all right."

"You were right—I heard them," she sobbed. "I . . . I can't believe it. My own brother!"

"Hush, Zoë," he whispered, holding her close and rocking her gently in his arms.

XIII

Zoë Ballinger handed a few coins up to the driver of the hansom cab on his perch at the rear of the vehicle. "Please wait here for me," she told him. "I won't be long, and then I'd like you to take me to Castlebar Hill. I'll be glad to pay for your return to London, as well."

The driver looked at the generous tip in his hand and doffed his black cap. "Y'take all the time y'need, ma'am."

Turning from the carriage, Zoë looked up at the number over the doorway of the brownstone and confirmed that it was the address Connor Maginnis had given her the previous weekend when they had met at the Druid Circle. Clutching her reticule and pulling her green shawl tighter, she climbed the stoop, opened the door, and went inside.

The hallway was poorly lit, but soon she found the apartment number she was seeking. Rapping firmly on the door, she heard a flurry of voices, followed by footsteps and the voice of a man asking, "Who is it?"

"Zoë Ballinger," she said. "A friend of Connor Maginnis's."

The door immediately opened, and a young man with curly brown hair and a dimpled smile looked out at her. "Miss Ballinger? Whatever are you doin' here?"

"I'm looking for Mr. Maginnis," she explained. Peering beyond him into the room, she saw a fair-haired girl about the same age as the young man, standing a few feet away and looking nervously at her.

"I'm afraid he ain't here, but we expect him anytime now," the young man told her.

"You must be Mose Levison." Zoë gave him a warm smile. "And is that Connor's sister, Emeline?"

Mose moved to one side and glanced back at Emeline. "Yes," he replied, then quickly added, "Whatever am I thinkin'? Please come in." He ushered her into the apartment. "Emeline, this is Miss Zoë Ballinger. Miss Ballinger, Emeline Maginnis."

Zoë offered her hand, and Emeline hesitantly accepted it.

"I hope your brother mentioned me," Zoë began. "He said if I needed to find him, I should send word here."

Mose stepped between them. "Connor told us all about the other night—and how you offered to help with Miss Emeline's father."

"Yes," Zoë replied a bit somberly, walking farther into the room, which served as a parlor of sorts. It was small but nicely appointed, with framed sketches of the queen and royal family on the walls and a brown velvet couch and matching chairs.

Emeline carefully measured her words so as not to stutter: "Won't you have a seat?" She directed Zoë to one of the chairs, then sat on the couch.

"Is everythin' all right?" Mose asked impatiently as he sat beside Emeline. "Connor said you were goin' to present the court with those documents I found." From the way he was wringing his hands, Zoë could tell he was very concerned that the evidence had been turned over to a stranger—and a Ballinger, at that.

"Yes, I met this morning with the magistrate I told Connor about." She turned to Emeline and added, "The one I thought would be sympathetic to your father's case. And he . . . he was."

Emeline's formerly cautious expression brightened, but then she saw the despondent look in Zoë's downcast eyes. "Something happened, d-didn't it?"

Zoë glanced around the room uncomfortably. "You said you were expecting Connor? Soon?"

Mose nodded and started to reply, but Emeline cut him off, saying, "Please, Miss Ballinger. Tell us what happened."

"Everything went fine with the magistrate." Zoë gave a long, pained sigh, then opened her reticule and removed the brown folder Connor had given her. She placed it on a small side table beside the chair. "I presented the papers that you found, Mose, and the magistrate was quite impressed. In fact, he agreed to arrange for a hearing for your father, Emeline."

"You see!" exclaimed Mose, eagerly gripping Emeline's forearm.

"What's wrong, Miss Ballinger?" Emeline asked, responding to the lack of cheer in Zoë's voice.

"It was when the magistrate sent for your father's records at Millbank Prison. It seems that . . . well . . . something has happened."

"What?" Emeline pressed, moving forward on the couch.

Zoë shifted on the chair. "I really think I should wait—"

"Miss Ballinger," Emeline cut her off, "since last week—since I discovered that my f-father is alive—I've seen one man k-killed and my brother so filled with rage that he almost killed another." She drew in a breath and let it out evenly. "Whatever news you have, you can tell it to us now."

Zoë read the determination in the young woman's eyes and knew that, despite her stutter and reticence, she had

Connor's strength of character. "Emeline, I'm afraid that your father . . . your father . . ." Her voice trailed off.

"My father is dead," Emeline pronounced.

"No!" Zoë blurted, raising a hand, palm extended. "He isn't dead, but he almost died. He . . . he was stabbed."

"S-S-Stabbed?" Emeline stammered, her eyes wide with shock. "How? When?"

"Last Friday night. They say he attacked a guard with a handmade knife and tried to escape. They found him nearly dead in the corridor—and the guard stabbed to death in your father's cell."

Emeline was pale with shock, and Zoë leaned forward and took her hands.

"They think he killed the guard and somehow got stabbed with his own knife?" Mose said with amazement.

"That's what they claim. So now the magistrate's withdrawn his promise to investigate your charges. Instead there'll be a hearing on . . . on a charge of murder."

Emeline's lips quivered, and her hands shook uncontrollably. "N-N-No . . . oh, no!" she sobbed, then broke down in tears.

Slipping forward onto her knees, Zoë took the young woman in her arms.

Mose got up and strode across the room, shaking his head as he paced. "Friday night . . . the same night that . . ."

"I know," Zoë acknowledged, looking up at him. She, too, was unwilling to voice the thought that had tortured her all day—the possibility that her own brother and her father's cousin had arranged for Graham Maginnis to be killed.

◆◆◆◆

The next morning was a Saturday, the twenty-ninth of September, and at precisely eight o'clock Connor Maginnis and Zoë Ballinger appeared at the gate of Millbank Prison. This time Connor did not need to bribe the warder of the gate to get in, for Zoë was carrying an order she had obtained the day before from the magistrate, authorizing them to visit Connor's father in the prison infirmary.

The conditions in the infirmary were considerably better than in the cells. A large, relatively clean room, it contained a dozen metal beds with fairly thick mattresses and freshly laundered sheets and blankets. As Connor and Zoë were ushered in, they counted eight patients, two of whom were sitting up in bed, the rest stretched out on their backs or sides.

Their entrance caused quite a stir; visitors, especially female ones, were all but unheard of in this part of the prison. As they were escorted down the aisle by the hospital warder, one patient tried to reach out and touch the lace flounce that hemmed Zoë's copper-colored dress. For his efforts, he received a sharp slap to the wrist from the warder, a stern but pleasant-featured man in his forties.

"Don't mind them, ma'am. Surely you must dazzle these poor blokes," he said to Zoë by way of apology. He glanced over at one of the men sitting up and called, "You be lyin' back down, Morganroth. The doctor says to keep them legs elevated agin the gout."

Connor noted that the warder had used the man's name, rather than number—a sign, perhaps, of a kind heart. Looking around the room, he did not see his father, and he asked, "Where's Graham Maginnis? I don't—"

"Patience, me lad," the warder declared. He led them to the end of the aisle and nodded toward a door in the wall just ahead. "Mr. Maginnis is restin' his poor soul in there. The doctor didn't want him or his stitches disturbed."

Taking out a key, the man slipped it into the lock and swung the door open. The adjoining room was far smaller, with only two beds, the right-hand one empty, the left bearing the gaunt, pale body of Graham Maginnis. He looked even thinner than he had in his cell, due partly to his ordeal and partly to his long white beard and hair having been trimmed.

Connor hurried into the room and knelt beside the bed. As Zoë came up beside him, he looked up at her, and she saw the tears in his eyes. She laid a comforting hand on his shoulder and asked the warder, "May we be alone with Mr. Maginnis?"

"Surely, ma'am. You just holler when you're ready." The warder returned to the main room, leaving the connecting door open.

"Father," Connor whispered, taking Graham's hand in his own. "Father, it's me, Connor."

There was no response for a minute or so, and then the old man's eyelids fluttered open, and he strained to turn his head toward the voice. Connor quickly moved into his line of sight.

"C-Connor?" he murmured.

"It's all right, Father. I'm here."

"Connor? Is that you?"

"Yes." The tears ran off his cheek and onto Graham's hand. "How . . . how are you feeling?"

Graham forced the faintest of smiles, which cracked his parched, colorless lips. "Not quite healthy enough to be grinding the wheel," he joked, referring to the treadwheel on which the convicts performed their required hard labor. "Nor am I poorly enough to be granted early medical release. The doctor says I'm gonna heal up in plenty of time for them to tag on an extra ten years to my sentence."

"Who did this to you?" Connor asked.

"What does it matter? If they want you, they can get you, anytime they want." Graham started to shrug, but it set him sputtering and hacking. Zoë hurried around the other side of the bed and laid a hand on his chest until the coughing subsided. When Graham opened his eyes again and looked up at her, he smiled.

Realizing that he might think it was his daughter, Emeline, Connor quickly introduced his companion: "Father, I want you to meet a friend of mine. Her name is Zoë." He turned to her. "Zoë, this is my father, Graham Maginnis."

"Zoë . . ." the old man intoned, his eyes closing partway as he remembered some faraway image. "I knew a Zoë once. A beautiful little girl with a wild tangle of red locks." He opened his eyes again and stared up at her luxuriant auburn hair. "Little Zoë Ballinger was her name."

"I'm that Zoë. And I'm so happy to meet you, Mr. Maginnis."

"You used to call me Uncle Graham."

"Uncle Graham," she repeated. "Yes, that sounds familiar."

His smile softened and relaxed. "And my son was Cousin Connor. Do you remember that, as well?"

"I . . . I'm not sure." She looked over at Connor, searching his eyes for some shared memory. The only image that surfaced was of a dark-haired little terror chasing her through the gardens and in and around the stones of the Druid Circle. But then the image shifted, and she saw him standing there, tall and strong, the wind pouring through the circle of stones as he gathered her in his arms.

"We knew each other?" Connor asked in wonder, and Graham managed a nod, which set him coughing again. "Please lie still," Connor urged, rubbing his father's hand.

Zoë knelt, too, and took Graham's other hand. Her eyes filled with tears as she said, "Uncle Graham, I know what happened to you—what they did to you . . . my own father and Edmund."

Graham shook his head on the pillow, and he grimaced slightly, as if in pain. "Long time ago . . . not your fault . . ." he whispered, his eyes shut tightly.

"But it was my family, and I want you to know how sorry I am." She looked up at Connor. "How terribly sorry I am."

Connor smiled at her, then said to his father, "Zoë's been helping me with your case. She had almost arranged a new hearing for you, but then this—this thing happened." His jaw set in anger.

Graham opened his eyes and squeezed both their hands gently. "You can't change fate . . . you can't win."

"I'm going to—"

"You can't, Connor," he said forcefully. "You have to forget about me. You and your sister have to forget—"

"No!" Connor snapped, his eyes seething with hatred. "Someone paid to have you killed, and I'm going to find out which one of them it was and . . . and—" His voice caught as he saw Zoë's pained expression and realized that the person he was talking about was her brother.

It was a full three weeks later, on Monday morning, October 22, that Connor returned to the prison with his younger sister. He had been told his father would be discharged from the infirmary that day and that a hearing about the death of Duncan Weems would be held a week later. Since the crime had been committed in prison, it was not considered a civil case and therefore would be heard by a panel of three magistrates rather than a jury.

Arriving at the prison, Connor and his sister showed the warder of the gate their magistrate's order allowing them to visit Graham Maginnis.

"Sorry, but I can't let you," the man told them, handing back the paper.

"But we've proper authority," Connor insisted, waving the orders in front of him. "Signed by a magistrate. Here, look." He pointed at the signature and seal.

"I don't care if it's signed by the queen herself. I can't let you—or anyone, for that matter—visit Number Eighty-four Fourteen."

"Why not?" Connor challenged.

"Simple." The elderly man tugged at his handlebar mustache. "'Cause Eighty-four Fourteen's been discharged."

"Discharged? Are you sure?" Connor gripped his sister's hand in excitement.

The warder looked down at his ledger. "Yes. This Friday past. Got his ticket of leave and was sent packing."

"On Friday? But where did he go?"

"Go? Taken, is more like it."

"Taken? I don't understand."

"Down to the Thames, son." He ran a finger along an entry in the ledger. "Number Eighty-four Fourteen, taken down to the estuary and put aboard the *Weymouth*."

Connor leaned across the counter and tried to read the ledger entry. "Is that one of those prison hulks?" he asked, referring to the practice of using decommissioned naval vessels as floating detention centers for any overflow of prisoners—especially for those awaiting transport to one of the penal colonies, such as Van Diemen's Land, the group of islands off the southeastern tip of Australia that would come to be known as Tasmania. These hulks, notoriously overcrowded, were considered worse than Newgate, Millbank, and the other London-area prisons.

"The *Weymouth*?" The warder shook his head. "She hasn't been decommissioned—leastways not yet. No, the *Weymouth* is ocean ready and bound. She set sail yesterday for Sydney. That's in New South Wales, Australia."

Emeline tugged at her brother's sleeve. "I don't understand, Connor. Where's—?"

"Just a minute," he whispered, then turned back to the warder. "What are you trying to say? That my father has been sent to a penal colony?"

The old man gave a harrumph and nodded.

"But . . . but you said he was released."

"Discharged—that's what I said," the man snapped impatiently. "Discharged from Millbank, not released from servitude."

"What about his ticket of leave?" Connor pressed.

"Most long-sentence men going to one of the penal colonies get a ticket of leave so's they can complete their time outside prison as laborers. Course, if they break the terms of the ticket, they're subject to recall. And believe me—getting slapped in a prison in Sydney is far worse than in London."

"This can't be," Connor protested. "He's got a hearing scheduled next week. I'm planning—"

"Already happened," the warder put in. "The date was advanced to this past Wednesday, and Eighty-four Fourteen was judged guilty and shipped out Friday." The hint of a smile played across his lips. "The poor old bloke must've had some powerful friends—or enemies—to be given a hearing so fast and get shipped off to Australia before the ink's even dry on the magistrates' ruling." He paused, then added, "Now, you two better run off; there's nothing more to be done about it here."

As the man turned to leave the gate, Connor called after him, "The *Weymouth* . . . you say it's set sail?"

The warder looked back at him. "Yesterday. By now she's breezing through the Channel."

"Is she putting in at Portsmouth?"

"She's fully loaded and won't be stopping until Lisbon, at least." The warder strode away.

"Damn!" Connor muttered. Then he saw that his sister's eyes were filled with tears. He dabbed at her cheeks with a handkerchief. "Don't cry. It's going to be all right."

"But F-Father . . . he—he's gone."

"Just one day out. And I'm going to find him and bring him back." He gave her a hug. "Come along, Emeline. Time's wasting, and there's much to do."

XIV

"I don't want to go downstairs," Zoë Ballinger insisted, picking up the book she had been reading. She shifted on the settee, facing the bedroom window and putting her back to her mother, who was standing in the doorway.

"You're just being petulant," Sybil chided. Crossing the room, she reached down and snatched the book from her daughter's hand. She frowned as she read the spine. "Is Sir Walter Scott a better companion than Bertrand Cummington and his parents?"

"Far more lively," Zoë declared, reaching for the copy of *Ivanhoe*.

Her mother held it just beyond reach. "But this is a *fiction*." Her lips tightened as if she had tasted poison. "Life is much less dramatic. And I fear that yours is liable to become an old maid's tale if you don't start finding a little enthusiasm for the everyday things of living."

"Like taking tea with the Cummingtons?"

"Yes, precisely." Sybil dropped the novel onto the coverlet of Zoë's bed. "And like taking Sunday rides in the park with a suitable young bachelor."

"This is Tuesday, Mother," Zoë snapped, folding her arms across her chest.

"You know what I mean, Zoë. I'm speaking of marriage, raising your own family."

Zoë looked up at her in bewilderment. "You call those the *everyday* things of life? And you expect me to choose a husband and have this family as . . . as easily as going for a ride in the park?"

"You know what I mean," Sybil replied, her tone softening. She joined Zoë on the settee and took her hand. "You can't live in a world of fiction, my dear. Downstairs is a perfectly good, upright man who has offered his hand in marriage. I don't think you'll find another so considerate of your needs and—" her voice grew ever so delicate "—temperaments. Yet you keep him waiting more than a month for your answer—an answer, mind you, that seems perfectly obvious to everyone who loves you." She patted Zoë's hand. "Why not go downstairs and visit with the Cummingtons. They've been so gracious to come calling."

"I . . . I'm just not ready for marriage." Zoë's tone lacked conviction.

Grinning, Sybil stood and gently pulled her daughter to her feet. "No one's expecting you to go down there and take your vows. I only want you to be civil—to let Bertie know that his attentions are not altogether unnoticed."

She sighed and gave a defeated shrug. "If I must, Mother. But if the conversation turns to marriage . . ."

"I won't let it. I promise."

Zoë gently stroked the auburn curls that hung on her shoulders. "Then I'll be down in five minutes. I just want to touch up my powder and hair."

"But you look delightful," Sybil objected, then thought better of any further argument. "I'll tell them you'll be joining us presently."

She crossed the room and paused in the doorway for a moment, looking back at her daughter. Zoë was dressed in a flattering garden dress of pale green satinet that hung just off her shoulders, with a wide lace collar that provided just enough modesty without being at all severe.

"Yes, you do look delightful," Sybil repeated, then spun on her heel and headed down the hall.

With a long, disheartened sigh, Zoë looked at herself in the long dressing mirror. She ran her hands down her sides, frowning at how revealing the fitted dress was of her figure. She raised the hanging ends of the fichu-pelerine collar so that it sat higher on her shoulders, then tried to lift up and fluff the plunging lace ruffle in the front in a vain attempt to cover the swell of her breasts.

"Five minutes," she whispered, frowning at her image in the mirror.

◆━━━◆━━━◆

When Zoë swept into the formal living room fifteen minutes later, she looked both captivating and chaste in a wide-skirted dress of brown taffeta and lace, with modest bishop sleeves and a high Elizabethan collar. Her hair was pulled up in a sweep and held in place with a small bonnet of blond lace trimmed with pink satin roses.

"Zoë, you look delightful," her mother remarked as she took her daughter's arm to present her to the guests. From the way she firmly squeezed it, Zoë could tell that she was far from pleased with her daughter's change of fashion.

They crossed the room to where Lord Henry and Lady Virginia Cummington had risen from their seats. Bertrand was standing near the fireplace with Austin and Cedric Ballinger, and he whispered something to them and walked over to his parents.

"It's so nice of you to join us, Zoë," Virginia said somewhat stiffly. She was a heavyset, imposing woman who always dressed from head to toe in black, as if in eternal mourning. She looked Zoë up and down and gave a polite nod.

Henry greeted Zoë, as well, taking her hand and raising it delicately to his lips.

"I'm so pleased you're feeling better," Zoë told Henry, who looked at her cryptically, not knowing what she was referring to. "And how have you been, Bertie?" She smiled demurely at him.

"Simply wonderful," Bertrand replied, beaming. He took her offered hand and kissed it tenderly, holding it a moment before releasing it. "I trust you are well?"

As the two families made light conversation, Desmond and the kitchen staff brought in an impressive array of bread, jam, pastry, candy, and tea, all of which was laid out on a low glass table between the two large red sofas that dominated the room. Zoë and Bertrand were ushered to a matching loveseat at one end of the table, and then Sybil and Virginia sat on one of the sofas, with Henry, Cedric, and Austin taking places on the other one.

The group fell into easy banter, touching upon politics, the queen's first year and four months of reign, and the respective journeys of Julian Ballinger and his cousin Ross to the East. When the topic inevitably drifted to the approach of winter, Austin took the situation in hand.

"Bertie tells me that he's finally made his intentions known," he remarked to his sister, giving Bertrand a sly grin. "And it's about time, old fellow." Looking back at his sister and paying no attention to her venomous glare, he asked, "So, have you set the date yet?"

The question hung there awkwardly, drawing all eyes to Zoë. Her back stiffened, and she said in a calm but icy tone, "Bertrand has been gracious enough to give a young woman the time to carefully consider his proposal; would that her brother were so kind."

Austin gave an amused chuckle. "Good God, child, Bertie'll grow old, bald, and fat waiting for you to make up your mind. You'd better take him while he can still remember his own name."

"Austin, dear," Virginia Cummington put in, politely drawing the conversation away from her intended daughter-in-law. "You've never come close to marrying. Why is that?"

Austin saw his sister smirk but did not react, turning instead to the matronly Lady Cummington. "I'm afraid that's the fault of you and your husband."

"Me?" Henry protested. "How have I—?"

"My good sir," Austin declared, "my poor fate would have been altogether different had you and your wife but thought to have a daughter instead of this . . . this poor excuse for a son." He grinned at Bertie. "As it is, there's no point in looking for a wife, what with not a single Cummington lass on the market."

The Cummingtons smiled approvingly, and Bertrand took Zoë's hand and gave it a playful squeeze. She waited a moment for the sake of propriety, then unobtrusively withdrew it.

A few minutes later, Desmond reentered the room bearing a silver tray with a sealed letter. He crossed to the loveseat, excused himself for intruding, and presented the letter to Zoë, saying that the bearer insisted it could not wait and, in fact, was in the foyer, perhaps expecting a response.

Excusing herself, Zoë took the letter and went to the fireplace. Breaking the seal, she opened the single piece of foolscap and glanced first at the signature— Connor Maginnis—then at the message, written in a strong, unexpectedly formal hand:

Dear Miss Zoë,
    I have asked Mose Levison to bring word of my departure. On Monday (yesterday, as I write these words), Emeline and I appeared at Millbank Prison with the magistrate's order you so kindly obtained for us. But alas, we were not

allowed entrance, nor was such entrance required, for we were dismayed at being informed that our father, Graham Maginnis, is no longer incarcerated there but has been remanded to the naval vessel *Weymouth* already bound for New South Wales, Australia.

As you can imagine, this news of my father's fate has come as a shock to my sister and me. We had hoped to present evidence at his murder hearing next week that might lead to an eventual dismissal or pardon on all charges, but we learned that a private and secret effort was made to change the date of that hearing—an effort so heartless as to not even inform the prisoner or his family of the time or location. The outcome of that hearing was predetermined, and our father was found guilty of murder and sentenced to a life of servitude in a penal colony at Sydney.

As you can imagine, my heart is filled with bitter anger toward all who have treated my father so cruelly. While this hatred necessarily extends to certain of the Ballingers for reasons already known to you, please trust that I in no way hold you responsible for the villainy that has touched my family. But since this latest course of events puts me in earnest and eternal opposition, not only to your father's cousin and his kin, but also to your own father and brother, it is my sincere desire that you not find yourself in a position that might cause irrevocable harm to the good feelings that must exist between a daughter and her family. Therefore, I feel it best that you no longer concern yourself with me or my plight.

As it is, I shall be leaving London for the foreseeable future. I hope that your own future

holds only the happiest moments and kindest
events. I remain, as ever, your humble and
indebted servant, Connor Maginnis.

Stunned, Zoë crushed the letter in her hands. She
stood motionless, unaware that the others were staring at
her. Finally her mother ventured to approach and asked if
everything was all right.

"Wh-What?" Zoë muttered, looking at Sybil blankly.

"The letter—is it bad news?"

"It . . . it's about a friend," she said weakly. Seeing that
the butler was waiting for word of what to tell the courier,
Zoë pulled away from her mother, went to Desmond, and
asked, "Is Mose still here?"

"Mose? The name given by the courier is Emeline."

"Emeline is here?" Zoë gripped his arm, surprising
him.

"She is waiting in the foyer, Miss Ballinger." He
carefully extricated his arm from her grasp. "Shall I give
her a message?"

"No. I'll go myself." Zoë excused herself and hurried
from the room, leaving the others staring at one another in
wonder.

She headed down the hall and entered the front foyer,
surprising Emeline, who was gazing in wonder at the
large family portraits that lined the walls. Though it was
considered only an entryway, the foyer was larger than the
Maginnises' entire apartment.

"Miss Zoë," Emeline declared, spinning around at the
sound of her entrance. "I'm s-sorry if I disturbed you."

Zoë waved off her concern. Looking about, she asked,
"Is Mose with you?"

"He's with my brother. The letter was supposed to
wait until after Connor was g-gone, but I . . . I had to come
now."

"What's happened to Connor? Where is he?"

"Connor . . . he . . ." The words trailed off, and her eyes filled with tears. "Oh, Miss Zoë!" she exclaimed. "I'm so worried!"

Zoë rushed over and gathered the teenager in her arms. She held her close, whispering soothing words. As Emeline grew calmer, Zoë cautiously said, "I want to help. But you must tell me what Connor is up to."

Pulling back slightly, Emeline took a handkerchief from the inner pocket of her wool shawl and dabbed at her cheeks and eyes. Folding it but still clutching it tightly, she took a deep breath and announced, "My brother is sailing for Australia."

"Connor? Australia?" Zoë's face went pale, and the breath caught in her throat. "But . . . but why?"

"He's gone after our father."

"To bring him back?" Zoë asked incredulously, and Emeline nodded. "But when? And how did he get the money to book passage?"

Emeline lowered her eyes in shame. "He didn't. He—he's gone to Portsmouth; Mose is going to help him sneak on board a naval ship."

"Hiding aboard a ship bound for Australia? But that's insane. They'll find him and press him into service."

"He knows. He says that when he g-gets there, he'll jump ship."

"Good God, no! They'll hang him for sure!"

As Emeline started crying again, Zoë realized the horror of what she just said. Holding the girl close again, she vowed, "I won't let that happen—I promise."

"I . . . I don't want to l-lose him."

"We won't, Emeline. I swear that we won't."

◆◆◆

Lord Cedric Ballinger walked around the mahogany desk in his library and sat down, directing Austin to one chair and Zoë to another.

"This is quite irregular," he huffed, folding his hands on top of the desk. "Our guests are still here, yet you entertain that—that girl—"

"Emeline Maginnis," Zoë said firmly, still standing beside the chair. "That *girl* outside in a hansom cab is the daughter of Graham Maginnis. Surely you know who *he* is."

"Ancient history," Cedric blustered. "Graham Maginnis is no longer of any concern to me."

"No, I suppose not," Zoë conceded. "Not now that you've had him shipped off to Australia."

Cedric narrowed one eye as he looked up at her. Then he fixed his gaze on his son. "Is what Zoë says correct? Has Graham been transported to Australia?"

"Surely you knew, Father," Zoë said, but Cedric gestured for her to be quiet and to sit down, and she complied.

"Tell me, son. What have you been up to?"

Austin didn't flinch, his expression steady and resolute. "*I've* done nothing, sir. But our system of justice has prevailed, and Mr. Maginnis is being made to answer for his actions to the full extent of the law."

"And I wasn't informed?"

"I didn't think it overly important. After all, he's been in prison for—what is it?—sixteen years now? What matter is it to us if he finishes the final fourteen in a London cell or as a free convict in New South Wales?"

"Free?" Zoë raged, rising from her seat and pointing a finger at her brother. "He's being sent into servitude in an Australian penal colony. You call that *free*?"

"I've arranged for him to be a ticket-of-leave man," Austin shot back, rising to face her. "He needn't again see the inside of a prison, provided he stays in New South Wales and keeps out of trouble."

"Then it *was* you! And were you the one who paid to have him killed?"

"Enough!" Cedric bellowed, standing and raising a hand to each of them. Turning to his son, he declared, "I want the truth, and I want it now. Were you involved in this business?"

Austin looked from his sister to his father, then said in an even tone, "I had nothing to do with that business with his guard. As far as the court could tell, Graham's son got the poor man's head so filled with notions of going free that, when it didn't happen, he turned on the guard."

"Do you expect us to believe—?"

"Enough, Zoë!" Cedric motioned Austin to continue.

"As for the resultant magistrates' hearing, yes, I got word that it was rescheduled and made a point of being there." He directed his next words at Zoë. "But I didn't do anything to affect the decision, other than to assure the court that the Ballinger family would not be averse to Mr. Maginnis's being given a ticket of leave so he can live his remaining years outside a prison wall." He sat back down, a smug look of victory on his face.

Turning her back on Austin, Zoë laid her hands flat on the desk and leaned toward her father. "He isn't telling you the full story. I'm convinced that he and Edmund paid that guard to kill Graham Maginnis, just as they hired a couple of thugs to do the same to Connor!"

"Enough!" Cedric shouted, suddenly reaching out and slapping his daughter across the face. "How *dare* you accuse your own family of . . . of complicity in murder!"

Zoë pulled back, stung more by shock than pain. She stood holding her cheek, fighting to keep the tears from her eyes. She stared first at her father, who was clenching his fists and tightening his jaw in anger, then at Austin, whose impassive expression was just as telling.

Lowering her hand, she pointed an accusing finger at Cedric. "You *knew* about it, didn't you? This whole thing's a sham—all for the sake of appearances. You may not have wanted to know all the details of what they were up to, but you really knew. You may as well have plunged in the knife yourself."

Cedric's face was mottled with rage. "Get out of here!" he screamed. "Get out of my house!"

Zoë stormed from the room and down the hall, nearly barreling into Bertrand Cummington as she rounded a corner.

"Is everything all right?" he asked, grabbing hold of her. "I was just coming to see if—"

"No, everything isn't all right!" Her body was rigid with tension, but she made no effort to pull away from him.

"What is it, Zoë?" he asked tenderly, lifting her chin. "Is there something I can do?"

"No, Bertie—there's nothing anyone can do. It . . . it's personal."

"Does it involve that young man?"

She looked up at him curiously.

"You know who I'm talking about. I'm not blind, though I may be stupid. It's obvious that there's someone else in your thoughts, and from what seems to be going on . . . well, I'd have to conclude that it's that man in the carriage—the one we met on our way to the Piccadilly." When she did not answer, he said challengingly, "Tell me I'm wrong, and I'll put it out of my mind forever."

Looking up at him, Zoë gently stroked his cheek and whispered, "Oh, Bertie, please forget about me. Find yourself a sweet, loving woman and settle down."

"But it's you I want."

"You can't have me," she said in a tone that left no room for doubt.

Bertrand's shoulders sagged. "But *he* can, is that it?"

"I . . . I doubt anyone will—" her voice started to break with emotion "—will ever have me. . . ." Her eyes filled with tears, and she broke from his arms and went running down the hall.

"Zoë!" he called, starting after her. "Zoë! Wait!" But she was already gone.

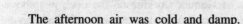

The afternoon air was cold and damp. Even in his hiding place in the hold of the *Chatham*, huddled inside a large wooden crate marked Virginia Tobacco, Connor Maginnis could tell that it was going to rain before they made open sea.

The *Chatham* listed slightly to starboard as it gained speed through the English Channel. In the dark confines of his self-made prison, Connor felt his surroundings and tried to gauge how long he would last before he would have to venture forth to relieve himself and restock his meager supplies.

Enough food for a week, he told himself, patting the oiled-canvas sack of hardtack and jerky and the flasks of water. He also had a blanket and crude mattress of pressed tobacco leaves—enough to chew all the way to Australia and back, if he wanted to take up the habit. The rest of the tobacco in the crate had been tossed overboard in the middle of the night, with the assistance of Mose Levison, who had helped spirit him on board and then sneaked back off before the ship set sail at midday on Thursday, October 25, 1838.

Connor knew it was unlikely he would make it to Australia without being found out. But he would last as long as he could, leaving his hideout only in the dead of night. And if he was discovered, he prayed that he merely would be pressed into service and not thrown overboard.

He had to lie on his side and could not stretch out in the crate, and after only a few hours, he was so stiff that he doubted he would last the day. The crate that he and Mose had chosen was at the top of a large pile of similar crates and near the back of the hold. They had pried open the top and left it so that Connor could lift it off when needed.

They had also punched a few holes in the wood, though the air inside was stifling, nonetheless.

Being near the top of the hold, Connor could hear the muffled steps of seamen working on the deck just above. Occasionally he made out what one of them was saying when they shouted commands, but usually all he could hear was the creaking of the ship as it gently heaved from side to side.

It was late in the afternoon when he realized that the noises had grown much louder. There was a great deal of banging and muffled shouts, and it sounded as if the commotion was not on the deck but somewhere in the hold. Cautiously lifting himself onto hands and knees, he pressed his ear against an air hole and, with the greatest of effort, heard snatches of conversation:

"Over there—check over there!"

" 'Tis loaded in back!"

"Tobacco, y'say?"

"Open 'em all, goddamn it!"

"Up top! Aye!"

Connor felt a cold dread. For whatever reason, they were searching for the crates of tobacco. Perhaps they just wanted to ration some to the crew and would break into one of the nearer ones. But another thought burned at him, and he curled back up and prayed they had not caught Mose earlier that morning when he had left Connor in the crate to sneak off the ship.

Good God, don't let them have taken Mose! he thought. *They'll have us both pressed into uniform or worse!*

The voices grew louder, and Connor no longer needed to have his ear at the air hole to hear them. The crate was rocking slightly, too, as a group of sailors clambered up over the crates, intently searching for one marked Tobacco.

"Here it is, mates! Virginny Tobacco!" a voice shouted, so close that Connor knew the speaker was crouched right beside him. There was a heavy thump as the sailor banged on the side of the crate. A moment later, the top was yanked off, and Connor was hauled from his hiding place.

"Drag him down here!" someone shouted, and several pairs of arms lifted him off his unsteady feet and tossed him unceremoniously from the stack of crates. He struck a few on the way down and landed on his belly on the floor of the hold, the breath momentarily knocked out of him.

"Up with him!"

Connor was dragged to his feet, still wheezing as he struggled to catch his breath. He found himself staring at the smirking face of a lieutenant, who placed one finger alongside his red, bulbous nose and declared, "Thought you'd book free to Australia, aye? Thought yourself too good to pay like the other passengers?"

"I . . . I didn't have—"

"Ain't got the money, eh? Well, we'll see what the captain wants to do about that." He turned to the two nearest sailors of the dozen or so in the hold. "Take him up top!"

The men grabbed his arms and pulled him down the aisle, then prodded him up the stairs that led to the main deck. Quite a welcoming committee awaited him there— most of the hundred or so sailors along with the dozen civilians who had booked passage, some of them emigrating to Australia of their own will, others on their way to visit relatives like Graham Maginnis who had been sent into servitude in the penal colony.

"Bring him to the captain's quarters," the lieutenant barked, motioning Connor across the deck.

A few minutes later, Connor was ushered into the small, well-appointed cabin of Captain Archibald Gaunt, who was far larger than his name suggested. A stern, gray-haired gentleman of about fifty, the captain looked as if he brooked no mischief on board his ship. When the captured stowaway was announced, Gaunt glanced up from the log he was working on and frowned.

"Name?" he finally asked, lifting his pen. "What's your name, lad?"

"Connor Maginnis."

"Spell it," Gaunt demanded, and Connor complied. Rather than write the name, the captain scanned some sort of list and made a check mark next to one of the entries. "Now, what are you doing aboard Her Majesty's frigate *Chatham*?"

"I have to go to New South Wales."

"Well, you'd be pretty stupid hiding on my ship if you had your sights set on America."

The captain betrayed the hint of a smile, and for the first time since Connor's capture, he allowed himself to hope that he would make it to Australia alive.

"Why New South Wales, son?" Gaunt pressed.

"My father's been sent there; I'm intent on finding him."

"Sent into servitude?"

"Yes."

"On board the *Weymouth,* I suppose?" Gaunt said in a disbelieving tone.

A bit disconcerted, Connor asked, "How did you know?"

"It's a captain's job to know the business of everyone on board—such as who's stowing in the hold, what story he's liable to concoct, and the like." He looked over at the lieutenant, who was standing in the doorway. "What do you propose we do with the likes of Mr. Connor Maginnis?"

The lieutenant examined the prisoner. Grinning, he suggested, "We've got us a new gangplank that needs walkin', and there ain't been nobody hauled across the keel in—what is it?—a month or two?"

"The fellow looks fit enough," the captain offered. "Couldn't you use another man working the lines?"

The lieutenant shook his head emphatically. "We've a

full crew; one more'd just mean less rum for the rest of us."

"Well, then, Mr. Maginnis, we've got us a real dilemma," the captain said, rising from his writing table. "What do you propose be done with you?"

Connor looked back and forth between the two men, unsure whether they were serious or just having some fun at his expense. Finally he said, "I'm certainly willing to work my way to Sydney."

"I don't think that will be necessary. It's against navy regulations to have a passenger work aboard ship."

"A passenger?" Connor asked, not sure of what the captain meant by calling him that.

"Yes, a passenger. Isn't that what you world travelers are called?"

"But I hid away—"

"And quite a fool's act that was—especially when you've paid good money for a ticket."

"Paid? But I—"

"Lieutenant Pettigrew, would you excuse us, please?"

"Of course, Captain." The officer departed, closing the door behind him.

"Mr. Maginnis," the captain said when they were alone, "I think we've had enough sport for one day. I don't care what size bet you had riding on that stunt of yours or how much you now stand to lose. I don't look kindly upon my ship being turned into a sporting arena for the well-to-do. So might I suggest that you get back to your cabin and save your little tricks for the good folks of Sydney?"

Connor stood there incredulous as the captain returned to his log.

"Well, are you waiting for something?" Gaunt asked impatiently.

"Uh, no, sir, I guess not."

"Good day, then." He nodded toward the door, and as Connor opened it and stepped outside, he called after him, "Don't forget—no more foolishness on board the *Chatham*."

"Of course not, Captain," Connor muttered, closing the door behind him.

He stared at the sailors milling around the deck for a full minute or so. It was obvious that he was the focus of their conversations, and more than a few were having a good laugh, probably at his expense. *But what about?* he asked himself. *Whatever's going on?*

Somehow, he must have been mistaken for one of the paying passengers, and for some unknown reason the captain had it in his head that Connor's hiding in the hold was some sort of a wager. Eventually they would discover their error, no doubt, but for the moment it had bought him some extra time.

A troubling question still bothered Connor: How did the captain know about Graham Maginnis's being shipped out aboard the *Weymouth*? It was as if someone had filled him in on all the details of Connor's "stunt," as he had called it.

Just then one of the passengers sauntered over and held out his hand. He was a fairly young fellow of about thirty, with black hair matted with oil and a long mustache twirled in pomade. "Wonderful job, Mr. Maginnis," he declared, eagerly pumping Connor's hand. "I bet two quid you'd at least last the day."

"I . . . I'm sorry, but—"

"Think nothing of it. As far as I'm concerned, it was two quid well spent, just to see that lieutenant's face when they hauled you out of there." He started to go, then said, "By the way, I'm Leslie Hart. My wife, Gabrielle, and I hope that you and your wife will join us for dinner."

From behind Connor, a soft voice replied, "We'd be delighted, Mr. Hart."

A hand slipped through Connor's arm, and as he turned in surprise to the woman who had come up beside him, Leslie

Hart bowed and said, "Then we'll see you this evening, Mrs. Maginnis." He strode away.

"Zoë!" Connor gasped.

"Shh," she hushed, squeezing his arm and steering him along the deck.

As they came up to the port rail, he looked around to make sure no one was nearby, then asked, "What is going on?"

"You didn't think you'd get away from me so easily, did you?" She smiled up at him and declared, "I'm going with you to Australia."

"But . . . but how did you—?"

"Emeline told me what you were up to, and I went down to Portsmouth and found Mose this morning. It wasn't hard; this is the only ship bound for Sydney. I got Mose to tell me where you were hiding, then booked a pair of tickets and got on board before the *Chatham* put to sea. Of course, I needed an excuse for why my husband was nowhere to be found."

"So you hatched some wild tale about my hiding in the hold as part of a wager."

"Thanks, in part, to some unsuspecting help from Mr. Hart and his companions. It's amazing the things they'll bet upon. Then I accidentally let the information slip to one of Mr. Hart's betting rivals; he passed it along to the captain so that you'd be discovered before sunset and he'd win the wager. When the captain confronted me, I was forced to confess the whole scheme, including the location where you could be found and the story you'd make up about going after your father."

"You thought all this up?" he asked in amazement.

"You didn't give me much choice. It was either invent a tall tale or see you thrown in irons or worse. I figured that a man like Captain Gaunt would think our class capable of most any foolish thing."

"*Our* class?" Connor asked.

"You're my husband, remember?" She took his hand and stood close beside him as they stared out over the water.

After a few moments, Connor asked her quite solemnly, "Do you have any idea what you've gotten yourself into, Zoë? You really don't know anything about me—about my life before . . . before all *this* happened."

"Nor you about me. But now we've got months to learn."

"But what about your father . . . your family—?"

"Shhh," she murmured, touching a finger to his lips. "I don't want to think about any of that right now. I just want to be with you." Leaning closer, she ran her hands through the tangle of dark hair at the back of his neck and raised her head toward his.

Responding to her caress, Connor started to fold her into his arms, then pulled back slightly. Looking with concern around the deck of the ship, he whispered, "People are still watching."

"We're married, aren't we? And this is how a wife greets her husband," she breathed, silencing any lingering doubts with her lips.

Part Two

CHINA
March 1839

XV

◆◆◆◆◆◆◆◆◆◆◆◆◆◆◆◆◆◆◆◆◆◆

Ross Ballinger stood on the captain's deck of the *Celeste* as the tall-masted schooner sailed past Portuguese Macao, where the China traders and their families made their home between April and October. Situated on a tongue of land at the entrance to Canton Harbor, Macao featured the impressive Praya Grande promenade of European-style buildings and had been described by one trader as "a miniature Naples, set like a jewel on the threshold of immense and unknown China."

It was the first day of March as the *Celeste* sailed up the harbor toward Canton River, a sweltering Friday morning made all the more intolerable by the humidity that presaged the coming monsoon season. Ross was wearing black duck pants and a rough blue work shirt, the sleeves rolled to reveal his tanned, sinewy arms. He had not been so muscled when he left England; the long voyage had filled out his eighteen-year-old frame, and long days in the sun had turned his sandy-brown hair almost blond.

"Nigh on seven months at sea, and you've done a yeoman's job, son," a deep voice rasped as a powerful hand squeezed Ross's shoulder.

"Thank you, sir," he replied, looking down at the ship's captain, Gregory Ailes.

The captain squinted his good right eye and laid a forefinger alongside the scarred, hollow left socket; he claimed to have lost the eye during a fight off the Tungshan coast with Chinese pirate junks that hurled flaming pitch and nearly sank Ailes's first vessel, the *Heliotrope*. "You know, you could've passeng'd your way to the Orient."

Grinning at the curious turn of phrase, Ross was about to reply when the older man continued.

"I know, passenging's for pigeons. You told me a hundred times if it warn't a day. But your pappy paid a queen's ransom to 'quester his firstborn aboard this ship, and he mightn't coddle to the notion of his young pup trimming sails and climbing—"

"Don't worry, Captain. I'll be glad to tell him I 'passenged' clear through to China and back."

"And how're you gonna explain these?" Ailes asked, grasping Ross's muscular forearms.

"I'll tell him they came from hoisting those tankards of rum you kept forcing on the officers and me."

Ailes narrowed his good eye. "And surely he'll be having me 'questered on the next ship to Australia—and not as the captain, mind you!"

"Then you'd be right at home. From what I hear, the Australians have the best rum south of the equator."

"Maybe they do, but they've also the fewest women, man for man." The captain leaned over the rail and pointed north up the harbor. "Now, son, where this vessel's bound, you won't be needing to worry yourself on that score. Canton's got more'n enough jade ladies to keep us foreign devils and the local Johnny-Cakes happy." He slapped Ross soundly on the back. "But there's still moss on your antlers, I'd daresay. You'd do best leaving them jade dragons to the likes of Captain Gregory Ailes."

"And what about the Missus Ailes?" Ross teased, then immediately regretted having brought up the topic.

"The missus doesn't much care what her master does

in foreign portals—" he winked broadly "—so long as he remembers every year or so to berth his schooner back at home. And this is one captain who knows how to snugly berth his schooner—even at ramming speed."

"Any portal in a storm, eh?"

"Not just *any*. Even after six months at sea, you won't catch me throwing any old faggot on the fire just to warm me captain's bed. That may be good enough for some of them John-and-Joans what calls themselves sailors. But for the likes of Gregory Ailes, the only portal I'll berth me ship in is the portal of Venus."

"Or China," Ross added with a knowing smirk.

"Ahh, China," Ailes sighed, his eye half closing. "Definitely China." He straightened abruptly and gave a mock frown. "Enough of this daydreaming. There's a long night of sailing ahead of us. The delta's a good forty miles up the harbor, and it's another forty up the river to Canton; we'll be lucky to make it by midday tomorrow. Till then, I'd say you've got some work to be doing."

"I thought I was passenging," Ross said ingenuously.

"I'll passenge your lazy ass all the way to Peking and back if you don't get your bum fiddle off the captain's deck and back to work!" He tried to boot Ross in the rear, but the young man was already halfway across the deck.

"If you need me," Ross called as he started down the stairs to the main deck, "I'll be in the captain's cabin making sure the portals are open wide and there's a faggot ready for the fire."

"Son of a sea cook!" Ailes shouted, spewing a string of colorful imprecations.

Ross ducked belowdecks and hurried back to his post.

◆◆◆

It was early Saturday afternoon when the *Celeste* reached Whampoa Harbor, the anchorage for Canton, which was twelve miles farther up Canton River and could only be reached by the small Chinese "chop boats" with their shallow-draft barrel hulls and mat sails.

Ross Ballinger watched as a small flotilla of these boats converged on the *Celeste*. Like the larger seagoing junks, many were a bright red or green, while others were varnished but unpainted. The Chinese sailors were dressed in simple peasant outfits, generally of blue or black cloth, with full pants, collarless jackets, and conical straw hats. They immediately set to work transferring the cargo of wool and lead from England and cotton and other goods from India to their boats for the final journey to the Jardine, Matheson & Company factory—one of thirteen such factories set up in Canton for use by foreign businesses.

The process of transferring the goods from the schooner to the fleet of Chinese chop boats would proceed throughout the afternoon, and it would be several weeks before the hold of the *Celeste* was reloaded with tea, silk, and spices for the return trip to England. Ross would not be making that trip; he would be spending up to a year in Canton as a guest of Jardine, Matheson & Company, one of the premier British shipping companies operating in the Orient. The Ballinger Trade Company had long done business with Jardine's, as it was known, and usually used their vast fleet of clippers and schooners—such as the *Celeste*—to transport Ballinger goods.

Ross watched for a while as the Chinese sailors took turns maneuvering their vessels alongside the *Celeste* to take on goods. Then he headed belowdecks and returned a few minutes later with an oiled-canvas duffel bag over his shoulder and two large valises in hand. Captain Ailes had already debarked, leaving his first mate to handle the off-loading operation while he boarded a *fu ch'uan*, or official boat. This medium-sized, double-masted junk would take him to Canton, where he would check in with the Chinese trade supervisor and obtain clearance for the goods to be delivered to Jardine's warehouse. Ross's six fellow passengers were already gathered on the raised rear deck of the junk, which was ready to make the twelve-mile journey upriver.

"Over here, lad!" a voice shouted from the *fu ch'uan* as Ross descended the gangplank that connected the two vessels.

Ross found himself accosted by the Reverend Samuel Outerbridge, a minister being sent to China by the London Missionary Society. He and his wife, Hortense, were the only other passengers who had come all the way from England, the other four having boarded a month earlier when the vessel put in at Bombay. The minister was as corpulent as his wife was slight—a pompous, overbearing man whose effusive brashness more than compensated for his wife's nervous restraint.

On numerous occasions during the voyage, Outerbridge had explained that he and his wife were bound for these "far, pagan lands," as he referred to anyplace beyond the English Channel, to "save those poor devils from their ignorance and shame." He took particular delight in having embarked on this "voyage for Christ" aboard a vessel named the *Celeste,* since "we who do the Lord's work are the true celestials." And he took great umbrage whenever Captain Ailes reminded him that the Chinese called themselves the Celestials and their land the Celestial Empire.

"You must take a look at this!" Outerbridge exclaimed as he snatched up one of Ross's valises in his fleshy hand and prodded the younger man toward the back of the junk. "It's like something out of a book—and definitely not the Good Book!" With his free hand, he scratched what remained of his thinning black hair.

Ross allowed himself to be ushered around the cabin at the center of the ship and over to the rear deck, where the minister's wife stood amid their bags. The junk, perhaps one-eighth the size of the *Celeste,* was bobbing up and down in the water, and the poor woman looked even more pale than she had during the long months at sea.

"Hortense, show Ross," Outerbridge called as they approached. "Show him what they're doing."

"Pagans and their ungodly entertainments," she grumbled as she glanced over the rail, her eyes narrowing in disapproval.

Ross knew that, at forty-two, Hortense was several years younger than her husband, but her near-constant frown had lined her face with added years, making her look more like his mother.

"Heathen games," she added, her words punctuated by a curious, rhythmic clicking sound.

Approaching the rail, Ross dropped his bags to the deck and looked over the side. Bobbing in the water just a dozen feet away was a single-masted boat, smaller than the junk but larger and more elegantly fitted and painted than the chop boats. It did not appear to be a transport vessel but rather the personal boat of a gentleman of means. Only two men were on board, and they seemed entirely disinterested in the off-loading operation. Instead, their attention was on the low red-lacquer table between them. Atop the table was a set of ivory tiles laid out in a pyramidal pattern. The men were picking up and snapping down the tiles in an ordered but completely undecipherable pattern, their movements accompanied by what sounded like lighthearted banter.

"Mah-jongg," Ross explained, gesturing toward the players.

Samuel Outerbridge's eyes widened in surprise. "I had no idea you spoke the heathen tongue," he whispered gruffly.

"I don't. But I read about this game in one of the books I brought. I believe our game of dominoes is based on it."

"Dominoes?" Hortense said offhandedly.

"Surely you've heard of dominoes. It's played in many fashionable circles in London."

The woman bristled. "Our lives have little to do with fashion."

"Not that they couldn't," her husband interjected, "if that were our desire. But the only circle fashionable enough for an Outerbridge is the circle of believers who one day will sit at the feet of our Savior."

Looking back over the rail, Ross caught the eye of one of the *mah-jongg* players, a fairly gaunt old man dressed in a blue silk robe and a curious blue cap with a scarlet crown. He was the better dressed of the two, and as he looked up at Ross, his smile revealed a set of teeth so perfect and white that Ross found himself wondering if they might be made from the same polished ivory as the *mah-jongg* pieces.

"Reprehensible," Hortense muttered, shuddering slightly as she turned from the rail.

"I hear they live on those things," Outerbridge remarked, waving his hand to indicate the various junks and chop boats that had pulled alongside the *Celeste*. "Cook their meals, raise children—" his voice lowered so only Ross would hear "—even *make* children . . . all right there on those . . . those floating dens of iniquity." He shook his head portentously. " 'Tis the work of Lucifer himself."

"Someone call me name?" Captain Ailes bellowed as he approached the trio at the rail.

The Outerbridges smiled politely, but their eyes betrayed their disapproval of the irreverent humor not only of the captain but of all the seamen they had come in contact with during the past six months.

Ailes stepped up to the rail and looked over. "Well, I'll be damned," he muttered, waving at the men in the small boat below. "Hello, friend!" he called down.

The two men turned toward the voice, and then the one in the blue and scarlet cap beamed with recognition. Standing, he waved at the captain. "Alo! Long time no see you, olo flen!"

"I see you play *mah-jongg* chop-chop, Howqua, but I wantchee you men workee chop-chop." He gave a mock frown. "I wantchee you men finish today, not tomorrow."

"No, no tomollo!" the man named Howqua promised. "Men workkee chop-chop, finish chop-chop."

The captain angled his head slightly, his good eye narrowing with concern. "You bringee me number-one men?" He looked out over the flotilla of boats. "Men no lookee first-chop. Lookee second- and third-chop."

"No, no!" Howqua protested, shaking his head forcefully. "All men first-chop!"

He turned to his friend and spoke heatedly in Cantonese, pointing wildly toward the chop boats surrounding the *Celeste*. With a curt nod, the other fellow hurried to the bow of the ship and shouted at the Chinese sailors aboard the nearest chop boats.

Howqua watched until he satisfied himself that the sailors had redoubled their efforts and the off-loading was proceeding more quickly. Turning back to the *fu ch'uan*, he nodded sagely at the captain and declared, "You will see. . . . My men finish chop-chop."

"Good work, Howqua."

The old Chinese man beamed at the compliment, then sat down to resume his game.

"He speaks English?" Ross asked in surprise.

"If you can call it that," Outerbridge said derisively.

"Not English," Ailes replied. "It's pidgin—English of a sort, with some Portuguese and even a bit of Hindustani thrown in for good measure. Like the word *chop*—that's Hindi for stamp. So when there's a load of tea all bearing the same stamp, it's called a chop of tea. But the Chinese use chop for just about everything. First-chop means first-rate. Chop-chop means quickly. And those sticks they use for eating—in pidgin they're called chopsticks, which means quick sticks."

Outerbridge frowned in confusion. "Pigeon? What's all that got to do with birds?"

"Not pigeon. It's p-i-d-g-i-n," he spelled. "The word pidgin means business, and everyone who wants to do business in Canton learns to use it—the *cohong* and *fan kuei* alike."

"*Cohong?*" Ross asked.

"That's the name for the merchant class—the *hong* merchants who control all trade with China."

"And what's a fonk . . . fonkway . . ."

"*Fan kuei,*" Ailes carefully pronounced. "Well, my young friend, that'd be us." He tapped Ross's chest. "*Fan kuei* . . . foreign devil." Chuckling, he turned to Outerbridge. "Yes, even a man of the Lord such as yourself, I'm afraid. We're all devils to them. And I can't say as I blame them for thinking of us as such. I mean, what're we bringing China but trouble?"

"Civilization," Outerbridge countered. "Civilization and religion."

Ailes shook his head. "They had both in good measure 'afore we come. No—all we're bringing is death . . . death in the bowl of an opium pipe."

"But the opium trade is legal in England," Ross noted. "The medicinal value of—"

"Medicine?" Ailes snorted derisively. "To the Chinese it ain't medicine but the devil's poison—*fan kuei* poison. They don't take it in small measures in their Godfrey's Cordial and the like. They smoke it straight and strong— and once they start, they can't give it up, even under the emperor's edict of death."

Hortense Outerbridge looked exceptionally uneasy as she muttered, "Heathen sins."

"When they come to the Lord, they'll put the Devil's poison aside," the reverend said confidently.

"Not if Parliament or the Company have any say in it."

Outerbridge eyed the captain curiously. "What's the British government got to do with it?"

"Or the East India Company?" Ross added.

"They control the China trade, is all. When we come to Canton for tea and silk, we must pay with something—and the Chinese have little use for what comes out of England. But they've plenty of use for what them coolies are unloading just now." He pointed at the *Celeste*. On the deck, the British sailors were lowering heavy mango-wood chests the size of small footlockers to their Chinese counterparts in a long, multioared boat called a *p'a-lung,* or "scrambling dragon."

Ross shook his head. "I don't understand."

"What do you think we've been carrying all the way from Bombay?" Ailes clapped Ross on the shoulder.

"Cotton, I thought."

"Aye, there's some cotton. But the better part of it is opium, son, from Patna and Ghazipur—the best kind for smoking. A hundred seventy pounds of it to the chest. It's what drives the China trade. And duties levied on the China trade drive the English government—they say the duty on tea alone pays half the expense of the Royal Navy."

"But Ballinger Trade doesn't deal in opium," Ross said somewhat defensively. "We trade British products or pay good British sterling for the goods we import."

Ailes laughed gruffly. "You've a lot to learn about the China trade, son. The Chinese don't have much use for British goods or for sterling—they especially don't like coins bearing the likeness of a foreign devil. They may take Spanish silver dollars, but there's no one wants all that silver going one way and none of it coming back. So we take your good British products, trade them in India for opium, and trade the opium here in China for silk and tea."

Outerbridge's features had hardened upon learning the contents of the *Celeste*'s cargo. He drew in a sharp breath, his face turning a mottled red as he insinuated himself between the captain and the rail of the junk. "You mean to say that my wife and I booked passage aboard an . . . an opium trader?"

Ailes laughed again but with no trace of humor. "Every British ship entering Canton Harbor's an opium trader—one way or another." His expression froze. "But I'm sure all that's about to change with the likes of you and the missus bringing Christ to the land of the Celestials."

The junk gave a slight lurch as it started away from the *Celeste*.

"If you'll excuse me, folks, I've some paperwork to prepare 'afore we reach Canton." Ailes bowed respectfully to Hortense and headed toward the cabin of the ship.

Outerbridge gave a slight sigh and frowned. "Six months at sea, and he's as disagreeable as the day we left Portsmouth." He glanced at his wife. "Pray for the poor captain, Hortense. I'm afraid he's spent too many years under this heathen sun."

Heathen sun . . . The words played through Ross Ballinger, conjuring images of this mysterious land to which he had come: a barefoot coolie squatting in a dirt alley, his nimble fingers wrapped around a bowl of rice, "quick sticks" ticking their staccato rhythm . . . a terraced hillside cascading into a harbor choked with sampans and junks, flashes of blue water amid a riot of bobbing reds, blacks, and greens . . . an emaciated peasant aging into his thirties, brittle hair turning white, stomach empty but lungs full with the fleeting satisfaction of an opium pipe . . .

As the junk drew farther away from the British schooner, Ross glanced at the reverend, who stood at the rail, hands clasped as he whispered a private, undecipherable prayer to his God. His eyes were closed, yet Ross could feel in them a dark, zealous light.

"Heathen son . . ." Ross breathed.

Yes, he thought, *Samuel Outerbridge and his like are the true heathens in this far, pagan land. And the gift they bear will likely come not as a savior but as a stern, unforgiving plague. And which plague will prove to be the deadlier?* he could not help but wonder. *Opium or the Cross?*

Turning back to the rail, Ross gave a slight shudder, and as if in reply, the boards of the deck creaked beneath his feet.

XVI

Ross Ballinger spent his first week in Canton acquainting himself with the factory district, where all of the two hundred fifty foreign merchantmen lived and worked. The district stretched for one third of a mile along the north bank of Canton River. At river's edge was an open, unpaved area approximately four hundred feet deep known as Factory Square, and the thirteen foreign factories were lined cheek by jowl along the square, facing the river. They were each about eight hundred feet long but only sixty feet wide, except for New English Factory, owned by the British East India Company, which was twice as wide, having been rebuilt in grander style following a fire in 1822.

The facades of the two- and three-story factories were an impressive, orderly sight amid the confusion of buildings in the surrounding districts. Constructed of brick and granite that had been plastered white, they sported street-level archway entrances, above which were terraces framed with ornate wrought-iron railings and bright green awnings and blinds. Each of the long, narrow factories consisted of a string of six or seven individual houses, the first fronting the square and the others reached by passing through the previous ones. The servants' quarters and cooking facilities were usually located on the ground floor of each house, while the second and third floors held the offices, bedrooms, and living quarters of the foreign merchantmen. Most factories were named after the nations that served the China trade, with the individual factory houses being owned or leased by chartered companies from those nations.

At the left, or west, end of the square was Danish Factory, with New China Street separating it from the next group, composed of Spanish, French, and Chungho factories. Old China Street ran between Chungho and the largest group of factories: American, Paoushun, Imperial, Swedish, Lungshun, and Fungtai. Then came the little street known as Hog Lane, and finally New English, Dutch, and Creek factories, beyond which was a polluted little stream that gave Creek Factory its name and marked the eastern boundary of the district. It was in this last factory that Ross Ballinger was staying as a guest of Jardine, Matheson & Company. Jardine's leased the fourth house in the factory, hence it was known as Number Four Creek House.

Bordering the factory district on both the east and west sides were the *hongs,* long brick warehouses that extended to the water's edge. Here wooden chests of tea arrived from inland China. They were inspected, the damaged tea discarded and the more-delicate green teas repacked in leaden canisters for the ocean voyages. Samples of the tea were sent to the factories, and once the foreign buyers made their purchases, the consignments were shipped directly from the warehouses to the vessels waiting in Whampoa Harbor.

The heart of the district was Factory Square, a large, open meeting area frequented by sailors, pimps, and all manner of merchants trying to sell their wares to the foreign merchantmen and new visitors to the city, who arrived at the water stairs in the river wall, across from Imperial Factory. The east end of the unpaved square was delineated by the veranda and walled garden that fronted New English, the largest of the factories. At the west end was the livestock yard in front of Danish Factory, where a few cows provided the Europeans with milk for their tea.

Old and New China streets, two of the three lanes that led from the square into the suburbs of the city, were lined on both sides with tiny shops that sold silk, ivory, lacquerware, and other curiosities of the Orient to the foreign travelers who put in at Canton. The third, Hog Lane, was designed to attract the sailor on leave from his ship. Narrower and darker, it had shops only alongside Fungtai Factory, and they featured gambling, women, and hard drink—generally a form of rice liquor known as *samshu,* often fortified with tobacco juice and arsenic. The shops advertised this elixir as "first-chop rum," and while it rarely contained any rum, it served to get the sailors rousingly drunk, divesting them of their pocket money and resulting in nightly brawls, which invariably spilled from the alley into the square.

It had taken the better part of a week for Ross to familiarize himself with the myriad comings and goings of the factory district. His father's company, Ballinger Trade, was too small to maintain a regular presence in Canton. Most of its business was handled through the offices of Jardine, Matheson & Company, which received both a commission and a shipping fee. Jardine's had similar arrangements with a number of other small importers, who assisted Jardine's by providing additional markets for their goods, especially at times when surplus crops threatened to drive down the price of tea. When supplies were poor, however, Jardine's kept the tea for itself; thus prospects for a small firm like Ballinger's were risky at best.

Since his arrival, Ross had been greatly assisted by James Matheson, whose partner, William Jardine, had sailed for England a month earlier, leaving Matheson their firm's senior representative in China. Matheson, who at forty-three was twelve years Jardine's junior, was a Scottish Highlander, educated at the University of Edinburgh and well-versed in science and the law.

Not only was Matheson better read and educated than his fellow merchantmen, he was also one of the few genuinely interested in the Chinese culture and language. Assisting him was a Jardine's clerk named Robert Thom, one of only two men in the foreign community with a thorough knowledge of Mandarin and Cantonese. It was this thin, bookish-looking young man whom Matheson assigned to serve as Ross Ballinger's guide and translator during his stay in China.

Exhausted by his long voyage and busy first week in Canton, Ross was sleeping later than usual on Sunday, March 10, in one of the dormitory bedrooms on the third floor of Jardine's Number Four Creek House. He had been dreaming, and though the images were indistinct, they hinted of home. Suddenly he was vaulted out of his reverie by a voice shouting, "Up with you, Ballinger! He's arriving!"

Ross struggled to open his eyes and raise himself on one elbow. Gazing through a fog at what appeared to be a deserted room, he sought the source of the shouting.

"Hurry up, man!" came the cry. "We're going to miss everything!"

Pushing back his wool blanket and sitting up, Ross saw a shadowed figure at the top of the stairs. A halo of light framed a thin face and shock of curly hair, and Ross recognized his guide, Robert Thom.

"He's arriving—to destroy all the opium, they say!"

"Wh-Who?" Ross stammered.

"It's the new *ch'in-ch'ai,*" Thom replied, coming across the room. He lifted a crumpled pair of trousers from the chair beside the bed and tossed them onto Ross's lap.

"Chin . . . chay?" Ross fumbled with the pants, awkwardly thrusting his stockinged feet into the trouser legs.

"The *ch'in-ch'ai ta-ch'en*. That means he's a high commissioner to Emperor Tao-kuang who has been granted special authority to clean up the opium trade. His name's Lin Tse-hsü, and his boat's approaching down the river.

Last month we got an advance proclamation that said—"
Thom gazed upward and rubbed his forehead, trying to
recall the actual wording "—it said: 'I am so determined
to strip bare and root up the opium traffic that though the
ax should break in my hand or the boat sink beneath me,
yet will I not stay my efforts till the work of purification
be accomplished.' "

Ross was already on his feet, slipping into his shoes.

"We must hurry if we hope to see the procession,"
Thom pressed.

"You say he's going to destroy all the opium?"

"No one knows for sure, but that's the rumor. We've
had quite a few incidents since the December riot."

"What riot?"

"I'll tell you about it on the way."

Ross hurriedly finished dressing and followed Robert
Thom downstairs and through houses Number Three, Two,
and One of Creek Factory, and Thom described the incident
nearly three months earlier that had almost put an end
to all China trade. It had started an hour or so before
noon on December 12, 1838. As usual, Factory Square had
been filled that Wednesday morning with an assortment of
people, the locals trying to separate the foreigners from
their coin, the foreigners trying to protect their pockets or
at least get the best value for their money. Active among
the crowd despite the early hour had been a half-dozen or
so pimps, each trying to entice the foreigners into parting
with a few shillings for one of their "clean Chinee woman,"
many of whom were actually brought in from Singapore and
even India.

As Ross and Thom circled the walled garden of New
English Factory and entered Factory Square, they were
accosted by one of those very pimps, who dashed out
of Hog Lane and insinuated himself between the two
foreigners. Ross waved a hand, signaling that he wasn't
interested, but the barefoot fellow persisted, pressing closer

and extolling the virtues of his women in barely discernible pidgin.

Stepping between the two men, Thom blurted something in Cantonese, which effectively shooed the pimp away. "Don't bother with the likes of him," Thom explained. "If you're keen to taste such wares, you'd do far better to go see the *hong* man Howqua. He knows where to find Canton's really first-chop women."

The two men continued through Factory Square until Thom abruptly halted and pointed to a spot near the entrance of Swedish Factory, halfway between Hog Lane and Old China Street. "It was here that it all started. There was a large wooden cross lying on the ground, and beside it a Chinese officer and a couple of guards were holding some poor fool by the name of Ho Lao-chin, who looked the picture of despair with a chain around his neck. They were actually planning to raise the cross and publicly strangle him with the chain—in front of all the foreign workers."

Ross looked at him incredulously. "But why?"

"He was a convicted opium dealer, and the authorities decided to execute him right here in Factory Square. It was their way of pointing a finger at our role in the opium trade."

"What happened?"

"A group of the more prominent traders—Hunter, Lindsay, Innes—even Mr. Matheson—took away the cross and put an end to the dirty business, but not before a large crowd of Chinese had gathered. They were only curious, but there were so many of them that a call went out to clear the square. It would've been fine if some of our more hotheaded countrymen hadn't taken after the crowd with sticks." Thom gave a conspiratorial grin. "The official version has it that the peasants started it, but I was here, and believe me, they were only protecting themselves from the likes of James Innes and his crowd. Mr. Matheson and the other cooler heads were drowned out in the pushing and shoving that followed. The Chinese were throwing whatever they could get their hands on—bricks, stones, big clumps of earth—and when it started getting out of control, we had to scramble for shelter in the factories."

"Were there any injuries?"

"Very nearly. It was really quite a sight, what with the lot of us making a mad dash through any doorway we could find, then barricading ourselves inside with furniture and shipping crates. Some of us took to throwing broken bottles out the windows to slow the crowd, since most of them were barefoot. And they very nearly broke in, using fence rails and the like to smash the doors. If not for Howqua and the other *cohong,* we'd've been cooked."

"They put a stop to it?"

Thom pointed to the roof of Swedish Factory. "Two of our men—Hunter and Nye—climbed out on the Number Four roof in back and crossed over Lungshun and Fungtai." His hand traced their path across the adjoining factories to the right. "They dropped down into Hog Lane and ran all the way to Howqua's house. He summoned the Nanhai magistrate, and just as the rioters were breaking through the doors, the soldiers arrived in force. The mob turned tail and fled."

Thom led Ross toward the customs house, which stood beside the water stairs. As they approached, they saw an impressive-looking *k'uai-pan,* or "quick plank boat," a sixty-foot passenger junk designed for maximum speed. This particular river junk had a large spritsail at the bow and a smaller one at the stern. Speed was accomplished by the use of four twenty-five-foot-long *yulohs,* or paddles, which extended off the stern alongside the rudder. The rudder man and four scullers stood on a raised deck and had to synchronize the movements of the rudder and *yulohs* perfectly in order to obtain a speed of up to twelve *li,* or four miles, per hour.

A group of four smaller *k'uai-pans,* each about thirty-five feet long, were docked at the river wall alongside the lead vessel, and a large party of Chinesü was assembling at the top of the water stairs. Waiting to greet the group was Howqua, the man Ross had first seen at the anchorage in Whampoa when debarking from the *Celeste;* Ross recognized him by his dark ceremonial robe and blue cap with scarlet crown. Standing beside him was a British naval officer in full dress.

"Who's that?" Ross asked, indicating the officer.

"Haven't you met the trade superintendent yet?"

"Captain Charles Elliot? No, we haven't met, though I've heard of him. I was expecting an older man."

"He's still in his thirties, but he's proven quite the diplomat, though I think he'll have his hands full with the new *ch'in-ch'ai.* That must be him now."

Ross saw Howqua bowing to a rather stout man who appeared to be in his fifties. He had a heavy black mustache and long beard and wore a green brocade robe. Standing just behind him was a petite young woman in a plum-colored robe, its sleeves and edges embroidered in bright red on black. Her feet had not been bound in the style of the upper classes, leading Ross to guess that she was a servant in Lin Tse-hsü's household.

After Howqua introduced Lin Tse-hsü to Captain Elliot, he led the commissioner and his entourage—which included a clerk, six servants, and three cooks—across Factory Square to a group of three palanquins, or sedan chairs. These were far more ornately carved and colorfully painted than the usual sedan chairs that ferried people around Canton, and each had a contingent of eight bearers. Lin Tse-hsü was escorted to the front chair, with Howqua seated second and the young woman at the rear. Then the palanquins were hoisted on the bearers' shoulders, and the procession started down Old China Street, with Lin Tse-hsü's clerk, servants, and cooks marching in formation behind.

"Let's see what's been going on," Thom said, nudging Ross toward the group of a half-dozen foreign merchantmen, who stood in animated conversation near the water stairs. Prominent among them was a man of average height with dark, thinning hair, bushy sideburns, large brown eyes, and a sensitive, intelligent expression. Ross recognized him as James Matheson.

Matheson caught sight of the two young men approaching and waved them over. "Robbie, lad, I'm glad you're here!" he called in a soft, lilting brogue as he stepped forward from the circle of men. "And how might you be doing, Mr. Ballinger? I trust Robbie and his mates are treating you properly?"

"Oh, yes, everyone's been most kind," Ross assured him.

"Good. We wouldna want to anger your father." His ready grin put Ross at ease. "What with Mr. Jardine returning to London for the sake o' his health, I'd hate for his rest to be disturbed by the wrath of Edmund Ballinger, Esquire."

"We wouldn't want that," Ross agreed.

"Now, Robbie," Matheson continued, "it looks like this Lin fellow is serious about putting an end to the opium trade—at least that is how Howqua sees it. He was certainly in a fluster when he presented Mr. Lin."

"Scared, is more like it," a gruff voice interjected from amid the gathered men, and Ross Ballinger saw that the speaker was a tall, burly man who had a remarkable resemblance to Ross's father, though he was a few inches taller than Edmund.

"In any case, Robbie," Matheson continued, "we want you to pay a visit to Howqua later today and find out the extent o' his concern. He may be more comfortable speaking in Chinese than having to use pidgin with the likes o' Mr. Innes and me." He grinned at the burly man, whose frown softened only fleetingly; Ross realized he must be James Innes, the most controversial and hotheaded of the merchantmen.

"I'd be glad to," Robert Thom replied.

Innes stepped free of the group and came over to Thom. "Just make sure you find out what this emperor's man is planning. If he means to use force—"

"Now, James, we've no reason to be expecting anything like that," Matheson countered.

Another man from the group, looking more than a bit concerned, joined them and said, "But Howqua mentioned that the new *ch'in-ch'ai* would be issuing some kind of proclamation."

"I didna think he was talking about an actual edict," Matheson replied. "Just a letter he'd be sending to the Crown."

"The audacity! Threatening the queen!" Innes blustered, and the others grumbled their displeasure at the forthrightness of Emperor Tao-kuang's new representative.

"Now, James, we dinna know any such thing," Matheson argued. "All that Howqua mentioned was a possible letter to the British government; he didna say naught about this new man making demands o' the queen, though he'd have some good arguments to make."

"Like what?" Innes challenged, eyeing the Scotsman suspiciously.

"That we're using the devil's drug to build our British Empire. That we're turning a generation o' Chinese into addicts. Perhaps the queen would want to know these things. Perhaps then she and this *ch'in-ch'ai* could figure out some other less destructive means o' payment for the tea we need."

"We've tried every conceivable product; only opium sells," Innes countered. "The Chinese want neither our textiles nor our money. They seem to think this the center of the universe—" he gave a derisive snort "—and they don't want it tainted from outside."

"But they need to unload their excess tea to protect their own market," put in Captain Charles Elliot, who as head of the Superintendency of Trade was England's highest-ranking government official in China. "So they leave it to their *cohong* and you merchantmen to work things out to your mutual benefit." He shook his head. "No, this *ch'in-ch'ai* is all bluster. The opium trade is of benefit to all concerned. The emperor sent this man merely to make a show of concern."

"I hope you're right," Matheson said, then without warning asked Ross Ballinger, "And what might you think o' this opium business? Will it be o' concern to the Crown?"

"Who's he?" Innes asked rather impudently.

"Mr. Ross Ballinger."

Innes eyed him suspiciously. "Of Ballinger Trade?"

"Yes—Edmund's son. He's a guest o' Jardine's."

"He's practically a boy," Innes said disdainfully.

"That may be so, but he was in England the most recent of any of us; he may have an idea how the Crown will react to all this opium business." He turned to Ross. "You attended the coronation, didna you?"

"Uh, yes," Ross replied, looking uncomfortably from one man to the next. It was clear they all had strong opinions on these matters, while he had been in China only a week and was far younger and less experienced in the workings of the China trade. "Well, I . . ." he began uncertainly.

"Dinna be afraid. You're among friends," Matheson assured him.

"I wouldn't presume to tell any of you how to do your business," Ross said cautiously, running a nervous hand through his sun-bleached hair, "but I agree with Mr. Matheson that this Mr. Lin has some good arguments on his side—that is, if he really intends to come down harshly on the opium trade."

"And exactly what might those arguments be?" Innes challenged, stepping closer and glowering.

"For one thing, we don't allow all that Indian opium into England, yet we don't hesitate to unload it on China."

"That's not true!" Innes pounded his fist against his hand. "England has no laws against opium."

"Not written ones, perhaps," Ross countered with growing confidence. "But while it's true that opium hasn't yet been outlawed, it soon would be if the British ever took to smoking it as they do over here."

"That will never happen," Innes declared. "We English are too civilized to take up such a vile habit. It's only heathens like these Celestials that take up the pipe—in spite of risk of execution."

"Perhaps that's because our ships return to England laden with tea, not opium."

"The lad has himself a point." From Matheson's expression, it was obvious he was enjoying the exchange.

Innes folded his arms across his barrel chest and grinned smugly. "We load our ships with whatever the market will bear—be it opium, tea, or tobacco."

"That may be so," Ross put in, "but it's also true that we make great efforts to control what each market desires." He glanced at Matheson to see if he was stepping beyond the bounds of propriety, but the older man merely nodded and motioned for him to continue. "From what you were saying before, there's very little we British export that the Chinese desire, since they're largely self-sufficient."

"Or think they are!" one of the others put in derisively.

"So in order to obtain the enormous quantities of tea our market craves, we had to find and promote a product that would balance the trade. Opium . . . the third leg of a great triangle: English textiles and goods to India, Indian opium to China, Chinese tea to England."

"Spoken like a true merchantman!" Matheson declared, slapping Ross on the back.

"Spoken more like a young pup who's got his learning from a book, rather than from life," Innes chided. "And that little speech of yours doesn't explain why the British don't use opium. If we controlled the markets as completely as you contend, we could simply leave China out of the picture and send our textiles to India and their opium back to England. It would be simpler and cheaper all around."

Ross was taken aback by the man's derisive tone; he was even more surprised by the boldness of his own reply: "That wouldn't satisfy the British craving for Chinese tea, and if we English traders didn't address that need, others would step in and do it for us. Furthermore, we know damn well that any effort to bring opium in quantity to England would result in the kind of restrictive laws that this Mr. Lin seems to be advocating here in China."

"So you're siding with the Chinaman, are you?" Innes pressed, narrowing one eye suspiciously.

"Aren't you, also?"

"Me?" Innes asked, a bit disconcerted. "In what way?"

"Not just you, but all the traders." Ross looked around at the group of men, James Matheson included. "I realize you don't want the opium trade shut down, but neither do you want it legalized. I was reading a recent copy of the *Opium Circular*," he continued, referring to Jardine's company bulletin, "and William Jardine himself had written on this very topic."

" 'If the trade is ever legalized,' " Robert Thom interjected, quoting from memory, " 'it will cease to become profitable from that time. The more difficulties that attend it, the better for you and for us.' "

"Yes, exactly," Ross declared.

"So what do you suggest we do?" Innes waved an angry hand at the surrounding factories. "Give up opium? Give up the entire tea trade?"

Ross was about to respond, but Matheson cut him off. "We're asking too much o' this young visitor if we expect him, fresh off the boat, to solve our China problem." Wrapping his arm around Ross's shoulder, he added, "I'd say 'tis late enough in the morning for a mug o' good English rum, wouldna you?"

"So long as it isn't that first-chop rum in Hog Lane."

Matheson turned to Robert Thom and chuckled. "I see that you've been teaching him the finer points o' life in Canton." He squeezed Ross's shoulder. "None o' that devilish *samshu* for you, my young friend. We'll be having our drinks on the veranda at New English Factory. Then you shall join me in their great hall for Sunday dinner. Have you dined there yet?"

"No, sir."

"There's a treat in store for you. Crystal chandeliers with spermaceti candles, the finest gold-trimmed East India Company china, servants standing at attention behind every chair seeing to your slightest desire, and a full-size portrait o' King George IV staring down from the wall."

Ross walked over to the other men and sought James Innes. "I hope you didn't take offense at—"

"Dinna worry yourself about the likes o' Mr. Innes," Matheson said jovially. "Isn't that right, James?"

"That's correct," Innes agreed with what passed for a smile. "But I look forward to continuing our conversation some other time."

"Perhaps over dinner?" Matheson suggested. "You'll be joining us at New English, won't you?"

"Of course. Captain Elliot and I wouldn't think of missing Sunday dinner."

"Then we'll see you gentlemen at noon." Matheson placed one arm around Ross and the other around Robert Thom and started toward Creek Factory. "Come along now, good fellows. I daresay you'll want to change into something a bit more festive for the occasion."

Thom looked somewhat uncomfortable. "I, uh, I'm not sure I'm free for dinner—"

"O' course you are, young man," he insisted. Realizing that Thom was begging off because he was merely a

Jardine's clerk, Matheson added, "I wouldna think of inviting young Ross here without bringing along his interpreter."

"But everyone will be speaking English," Thom noted.

Matheson gave a sly grin. "Still, I wouldna be surprised if a good measure of interpretation be needed the next time the likes o' James Innes and his crowd come up against the son of Edmund Ballinger!"

The next afternoon, Ross headed alone through Factory Square to Old China Street, which was lined on both sides with shops that were in actuality little more than open-air stands. He had been writing regularly to his family—most especially his cousin Zoë. Now he wanted to send each of them some memento of his stay in China.

The first shop he visited featured carved lacquer boxes, the proprietor an old Chinese gentleman with thin white hair and a ready smile. His face was as intricately lined as the boxes, and he kept holding them up against his cheek and pointing, laughing merrily as he chattered away in Cantonese, apparently comparing his face favorably to the boxes—or perhaps the other way around. When at last Ross picked the one he wanted—an oval-shaped red box with a lotus carved into the lid—the gentleman took out a piece of newsprint and wrapped the box so deftly that no string was needed to hold it in place.

It took several minutes to figure out how much to pay the man, and in the end Ross was convinced he had overpaid horribly—especially when he discovered how the other merchants pounced upon him as he continued down the lane. But by English standards it had been a bargain, and he eagerly made his other purchases: an assortment of ivory brooches, cloisonné napkin holders, and even a delicate pair of jade chopsticks.

When his load began to grow precarious, Ross purchased a silk scarf—a bit too florid for his taste but of heavy material and sturdy craftsmanship—and used it to tie all the purchases into a convenient bundle with a handle of sorts, through which he slipped his left wrist. Then he turned around and struggled his way back through the gauntlet of shops.

He was moving from the shadows of Old China Street into the relatively bright haze of Factory Square when he collided with a sailor hurrying in the opposite direction. Ross was nearly bowled over and lost his grip on the bundle, which fell to the hard-packed ground with a clattering thud. Not bothering to look up at the sailor, Ross quickly muttered, "Excuse me"— though in truth the accident was more the other man's fault. Dropping to his knees, he opened the bundle and searched its contents, pleased to see no apparent damage.

It was just as he discovered that one of his purchases was indeed broken—the chopsticks had shattered into a dozen shards of green jade—that the sailor who had barreled into him started laughing, at first a mere chuckle but soon a chest-thumping bellow.

"Well, I'm happy you're amused," Ross said, retying the bundle. "But I don't see—" The words caught in his throat as he looked up and recognized the familiar face of his cousin. "Julian! What are you doing here?"

"Why, l-looking—" Julian broke into laughter again, then managed to stammer, "Looking for you!"

"Me?"

"But of course." Julian helped Ross to his feet and pumped his hand in greeting. "Whom else would I be hunting for in Canton?"

"Then you knew I was here?"

"I received word that your ship wasn't putting in at Calcutta but had sailed on to China. And when the *Lancet* was reassigned—"

"Your ship is here? In Canton?"

Again Julian laughed. "You didn't think I'd swim the China Sea just to visit my poor, clumsy cousin?"

Ross found himself grinning. He was genuinely pleased to see a familiar face—even if Julian had never been one of his favorites back home.

"I knew you'd be staying at Jardine's," Julian explained, "so I went there directly upon arriving and was told you'd gone shopping. Captain ffiske has given me two days on shore, and I intend to make the most of them. I take it you'll show me around?"

"Of course I will."

"Then how about we get started with a couple of mugs of rum? The ffist doesn't much take to his men drinking on board, so he keeps the supply horribly watered; I haven't enjoyed a really stiff drink since Calcutta." Seeing Ross's hesitant expression, he added, "The drinks are on me, little cousin. It's the least I can do to make up for any damage I caused." He nodded at the silk-wrapped bundle.

Ross thought of the broken jade chopsticks, then recalled the countless times Julian and his older brother, Austin, had made their "little cousin" the butt of their pranks.

The trace of a smile touched Ross's lips. "Yes, that *is* the least. And I know just the place for good rum—first chop, all right."

"First what?"

"Never you mind. Trust me—there's a little place over in Hog Lane where the rum's got so little water in it . . . why, it's so stiff, my good cousin, you'll swear you're drinking Yorkshire pudding." Hoisting his bundle, Ross took Julian by the arm and led him to the nearest *samshu* bar.

It was probably close to midnight, and Ross wasn't sure where he was or how he had gotten there. A kerosene lamp was turned down low on a chest across the room, providing just enough light to make out the squalid surroundings. He was stretched out on some sort of divan; the only other objects in the room were the dark, bare chest of drawers and a washstand that held a chipped porcelain pot.

As Ross lifted his head to look down at himself, pain shot through his temples, and the divan seemed to slide across the floor. "Damn!" he muttered, the single word sending another needle stabbing through his head. The divan continued to shift and toss, and the pitching of his stomach suggested that he had imbibed more than his share of first-chop rum.

Ross forced himself upright on the divan. He was still wearing his clothes, though his jacket was gone and his shirt was unbuttoned to the waist. He couldn't be sure, but he was fairly certain he had managed to keep them on all evening. He vaguely remembered his cousin, the picture of energetic enthusiasm, being led upstairs by the proprietor of the *samshu* bar and urging his "little cousin" to follow. Everything afterward was a blur; Ross could only guess what escapade he might have been involved in.

A figure appeared in the doorway—a short Chinese man dressed in a simple blue jacket and slacks with a long black queue that hung over his right shoulder. Padding into the room, he gushed, "Ah, you feelie better!"

"Where am I?" Ross asked, pressing his hands against his temples.

"Feelie better!" the man repeated, raising the wick on the lamp.

Ross closed his eyes against the piercing light. When he opened them, the man was gone. In his place stood a plump young woman, somehow managing to look both innocent and brazen as she eyed Ross on the divan.

"I . . ." The word died on his lips as the woman entered the room and shut the door. She slipped out of her sandals. Her red silk robe was far shorter than would be considered proper on the streets of Canton, and from the way her body moved freely as she approached, Ross realized that it wasn't only her shapely legs that were bare beneath the robe.

"I don't—" he started to say, but she pressed one hand against his lips and undid the sash of her robe with the other. He would have tried to get up, but she was already straddling one of his legs, and as the robe pulled away, he found himself staring at her full, round breasts.

"God," he whispered, unable or unwilling to look away. He thought her breasts—her lush body—the most magnificent he'd ever seen. But he had little means of comparison, for other than a few sketches in a medical text that had been purloined and passed around by one of his cousins—Julian, as a matter of fact—this was the first woman he had seen "in the flesh," so to speak.

The woman seemed fascinated by his blond hair, and she ran her hands through it, all the while sliding back and forth on his leg, purring gently as she rubbed against the coarse material of his pants. Then she pulled his shirt open wider and ran her hands down his chest, her nails digging into the skin and flicking across his nipples.

Suddenly Ross became aware—almost painfully so—of the passion building inside him. He felt the incessant throbbing in his pants, and it took the greatest of effort not to tear open his waistband and plunge himself into her. She was riding his leg even faster now, her breasts swelling with desire, the large, dark nipples protruding and hardening.

Ross found himself fighting a flood of sensation, praying to be continents away from this woman while at the same time begging never to leave her arms. Her hands were more than educated; they were instinctive, as if they could read his every desire and wanted only to fulfill. They followed his imaginings down along the muscular curve of his stomach to the front of his pants, the fingers expertly tracing, rubbing, molding his passion and his pride.

Strange pictures played through his mind, and Ross fought them all: his stepmother picking out this very suit for his journey, his cousin Zoë seeing him off at the ship and whispering good-naturedly that he should "exercise caution, but not to the point of severity." He even caught the fleeting image of the Reverend Samuel Outerbridge, calling fire and brimstone down upon Ross for "defiling yourself with lustful, heathen flesh." Outerbridge's stern, disapproving visage transformed into that of his wife, Hortense, who also was castigating Ross, but in a far different tone, calling him "you godless devil . . . oh, you wanton, depraved man!" and worse as she rode on top of him, sacrificing her own body to save his eternal soul.

Ross shook his head, clearing away the crowding, intrusive thoughts. This was neither dream nor nightmare sitting astride him; it was a woman, a stranger, a lover.

"God," he moaned again as she slipped her hand around his neck and pulled his mouth against her breasts, her other hand still deftly massaging him through his pants. She whispered something in Chinese; Ross had no idea of the words but knew the meaning, and he nodded yes, his lips searching her breast and finding the nipple, his tongue tasting it, drawing it into his mouth.

The woman pulled back slightly and let her robe drop off her shoulders to the floor, leaving her completely, deliciously naked. Sliding off his leg, she lay back on the divan, spreading her legs and pulling him to her. As he lifted himself over her, she wrapped her legs around his hips and drew him closer, her hands reaching for the top of his pants, searching for the buttons that would release him, that would make him hers.

Ross wanted it as he had never wanted anything before. The feeling, the yearning, was so overpowering, as if he were careening down a river, plunging toward some great fall of water. And then he was there, riding the waterfall, flailing at the very edge, the immense power of the stream too great to hold back. It came without warning or control, a wild, throbbing, ecstatic rush.

Realizing at once what had happened, Ross jumped back and pulled the woman's hand away from his waistband. She did not seem to understand; indeed, her hunger, if it was not a skillful act, was still growing in intensity, and she did not want his own passion to end prematurely. Wrapping her legs tighter around him, she thrust her hips upward even more forcefully and groped for the buttons of his pants.

"No!" he shouted, his voice a harsh gasp that nearly took away his breath. Panting and wheezing, he pulled himself free and struggled to his feet, unceremoniously dumping her back onto the divan. Fighting to control his breathing, he saw her hurt, confused expression and tried to say something reassuring. But it was plain that she understood no English, and about the only appropriate Chinese expression he could think of was "thank you," which he stammered repeatedly as he buttoned his shirt and backed toward the door.

"Hsieh hsieh," he muttered a final time as he opened the door and stumbled into the hall. Slamming the door behind him, he leaned against it, his wheezing breath racing with his heart.

"Don't look so glum!" a voice called, and he turned to see his cousin coming out of another room, tucking in his shirttail, his jacket and shoes cradled under one arm.

"Julian!" Fighting the panic, he forced himself to speak slowly. "I . . . I mean, did we—?"

"Your first time, eh?" Julian asked, his smug grin betraying that he already knew the answer. "Consider it a present from your favorite cousin. I'd daresay that a jade tigress is sufficient recompense for some broken jade chopsticks, wouldn't you?"

"I, uh—"

"No need to answer. That moony look on your face says it all."

Still clutching his shoes and jacket, he came over and wrapped his arm around Ross, then led him down the hall toward the stairs.

"I believe this calls for a little celebration," Julian pronounced. "We'll hoist a mug of first-chop rum to your newly attained manhood. May it never flag or falter!" He pounded Ross on the back. "Aye, mate. Long may it wave!"

XVII

━━━━━━━━━━━━━━━━━━━━━━━━━━━━━━━━━━

Leaving Jardine's through the rear, Ross Ballinger passed through Number Five and Number Six houses and emerged on Thirteen Factory Street, which ran behind the foreign factories. Across the street were two enormous wood-frame buildings owned by the *hong* merchants. The one directly in front of Ross was as wide as the four easternmost factories, and its neighbor, the *hong* guild hall known as Consoo House, was even larger.

The street was busy this Monday morning, the eighteenth of March. A few foreigners were using the back route to pass between factories, but mostly the street was filled with Cantonese going about their business, some pulling small, overladen carts, others carrying large bundles perched on their backs or slung from poles balanced on their shoulders. The men were dressed in blue peasant slacks and jackets, and most were barefoot; a few wore the conical straw hats favored in the countryside. The only women in sight were two teenage girls assisting a matronly woman as she hobbled down the street, her feet incredibly small and disfigured from being bound as a child into the confines of fashion. She apparently had been of the upper class, some of whom practiced the custom. That she was forced to walk rather than be carried by palanquin indicated that her family had fallen on difficult times.

"Ross! Over here!" a voice called.

Robert Thom was standing on the footbridge traversing the foul little stream that ran alongside Creek Factory. Ross waved at him and headed down the street to the bridge.

"Sorry to keep you waiting," he said.

"I've only been here a moment," Thom assured him. "We'd better get started; Commissioner Lin is expecting us precisely at ten."

With no time to spare, Ross and his companion walked briskly the two hundred yards to Petition Gate, which stood at the southwest corner of the wall, twenty-five feet high and six miles long, that encircled central Canton. Foreigners were generally prohibited from entering the walled city, but Thom had a special permit signed by Commissioner Lin to present to the guards.

After he and Ross passed through the gate, they entered a rabbit warren of temples, flagpoles, and little houses with red-tile roofs that were home to half a million people. Two pagodas, each over a hundred feet high, surveyed the city, the taller being Five-Story Pagoda, a red tower that rose from a hill near the center of the north wall.

Ross could not discern any formal plan to the city, no avenues or parks or public squares to provide points of reference. Yet Robert Thom seemed quite familiar with the winding lanes that twisted through Canton. He led them expertly through jostling throngs of people, ignoring their curious stares and whispered mutterings. The citizens were plainly surprised at seeing a pair of *fan kuei* outside the foreign district.

As they walked through the central city, Thom told Ross what he had learned about Lin Tse-hsü during the past week. Lin was fifty-three and had been born in Hou-kuan in Fukien province to a family that had produced many statesmen and government officials. In his early twenties he had been employed by the governor of Fukien and had quickly worked his way up the ranks of government, becoming governor of Kiangsu in 1832 and governor-general of Hu-Kuang in 1837.

Lin was a particular favorite of Emperor Tao-kuang, who relied on him as a scholar as well as a statesman. Lin belonged to the *chin-wen,* or modern-text, school, which maintained that Confucius had been a reformer; therefore, the *chin-wen* scholars followed the practice of *t'o-ku kai-chih,* or "finding in antiquity the sanction for present-day changes." A leading proponent of this school of thought, Lin had been in the forefront of developing a new, progressive approach that he called *ching-shih chih-yung chih-hsueh,* or "knowledge for the development of the state and for practical use in the world." What was so revolutionary about this system was that it encouraged classical scholars to incorporate a world view not limited to the boundaries of the Celestial Empire.

Lin Tse-hsü was held in such esteem that already people likened his journey from Peking to Canton to a swift military operation, which would surely end in the defeat of the *fan kuei* opium traders. He had made the arduous journey of twelve hundred miles in sixty days, averaging twenty miles per day. Not wishing to overburden the finances of local governments, he had traveled with his own cooks and supplies and had sent word ahead that any meals prepared for him should be *chia-ch'ang fan-ts'ai,* or ordinary fare, rather than full-course feasts. The citizens of a small village on the Kan River were particularly impressed when at dawn on New Year's Day, February 14, Lin Tse-hsü held a ceremony to honor his ancestors and made the gesture of giving a *kowtow* in the direction of Peking to wish Emperor Tao-kuang a happy new year.

"I'm afraid we're dealing with an entirely different sort with this new commissioner," Thom suggested as they entered a less-crowded district where the streets were slightly wider and far better kept. "Lin's a student of world affairs and they say damn-near incorruptible—not an arrogant boor like Teng T'ing-chen, who thinks he can eradicate opium by convincing us that England would perish if China cut off all trade with us."

Ross had heard about the warning letters that had been issued to the merchantmen by the governor-general of Kwangtung and Kwangsi provinces, who administered his office from Canton, the capital of Kwangtung. In these letters, Teng had threatened to cut off the supply of tea and rhubarb, without which the foreign economies supposedly would collapse, leading their governments to hunt down and execute the opium dealers who had created such a calamity. The letters had been largely dismissed by the foreigners, who were amused by the long-held belief of the Chinese that without imported rhubarb, foreigners would die of constipation. The notion came from the Europeans' penchant for purgatives, most of which contained rhubarb root.

"So you'd better direct your comments to Lin Tse-hsü rather than Teng," Thom continued. "From now on, Lin's the man to watch, that's for sure."

The two young Englishmen started down a fairly wide street, on either side of which was an eight-foot wall that lent privacy to the buildings hidden behind. Heavy wooden gates in the wall marked the entrance to each residential compound.

"This is Governor-General Teng's home," Thom said as they passed a long section of solid wall. The distance before they reached the gate indicated the vast size of the estate, and the ornate carved dragons, inlaid with ivory and jade, that ornamented the massive wooden doors of the gate attested to the prominence of its occupant.

Hanging alongside the right-hand door was a braided silk cord, which Thom yanked twice, tripping a bell inside the residence.

"So this is where Commissioner Lin is staying," Ross remarked.

"No. He's taken quarters at Yueh-hua Academy near Consoo House."

"Then why did we come all the way over here? Consoo House is right there on Thirteen Factory Street."

"All I know is that he sent word he wants to see you here, at the governor-general's home."

Ross adjusted his white cravat and waistcoat, then smoothed the lapels of his gray outer jacket. "Do you have any idea why he sent for me?"

Thom shrugged. "For the past week he's been at the academy interviewing city officials, *hong* merchants and clerks, even the heads of some of the foreign trading companies. It's becoming more and more apparent that he's serious about suppressing the opium traffic."

"And now he wants to talk to me?" Ross said incredulously.

Thom grinned. "Perhaps he heard about your debate with Mr. Innes the day he arrived."

Ross was about to reply when one of the doors swung inward, and a young man dressed in the simple outfit of a clerk ushered them into the compound. They were led along a serpentine path between two large buildings, through a keyhole archway, and into the central garden, where they were shown to a grouping of stone seats. The clerk spoke briefly with Thom in Chinese, then bowed and departed.

"He asked us to wait here," Thom explained, motioning Ross to sit. "And he apologized that the governor-general has been called away unexpectedly. Commissioner Lin will be meeting with you alone."

"Alone?" Ross said in concern. "What about you?"

"I'll be here, too, but as an interpreter. And one other thing—he said the commissioner's looking forward to hearing all about Queen Victoria's coronation."

Ross looked relieved. "So that's why he summoned me."

"Most likely. A firsthand account of the coronation would be of great interest to the emperor."

"I wonder how he found out I attended."

"Any number of people could've told him—Mr. Matheson, perhaps."

The two men fell into an awkward silence as they waited for the commissioner to appear. A few minutes later the clerk returned and said something in a formal tone. Ross picked out the words Lin Tse-hsü and *ch'in-ch'ai ta-ch'en*. And then the emperor's representative came through the keyhole archway and entered the garden.

Dressed in a formal black robe, he was not tall but was imposing nonetheless, with a steady gaze and serious expression that was complemented by a surprisingly warm smile as he bowed to the two young men. He straightened, stroking the end of his long black goatee, which hung midway down his chest and was braided like a queue. It was a gesture he repeated frequently and was perhaps his only real affectation, other than a tendency to lower his highly arched eyebrows when listening or deep in thought.

The two Englishmen returned the commissioner's bow, with Thom positioning himself just behind Ross, the invited guest of honor.

Lin spoke first, his voice deep and mellifluous. Ross, of course, had no idea what he was saying, but Thom, who understood perfectly, smiled broadly, approached Lin, and offered his hand. When the two men had shaken hands, Thom said to Ross, "Mr. Lin wants to greet you in the Western style." He motioned Ross forward to shake hands. Complying, Ross noted that Lin's grip was firm and sure, and while he was quite stout, his hands were not at all soft or fleshy.

Lin whispered something to his clerk, who bowed and disappeared through the archway that led to the buildings. Then he showed his two guests around the garden, pausing every few feet to discuss the various plants and rock settings. Thom translated as best he could, though he did not always know the English equivalent for the more obscure flora.

The tour ended at a group of four white cane chairs arranged in a circle beside a small lotus pond. As Ross took the seat indicated for him, he noticed the flashing oranges, blues, and whites of the large *koi* fish in the shallow pool.

Lin sat directly across from Ross, with Thom taking the seat to Ross's right. Ross assumed that the fourth chair, to his left, was for the clerk, but when the man returned a moment later, he remained standing behind Lin. That led Ross to guess that the vacant chair had been placed there for the absent Governor-General Teng.

Lin began the formal interview at once, inquiring first about Ross's family and then requesting details of Queen Victoria's coronation. He seemed genuinely interested both in Ross's personal history and in his elaborate account of the events at Westminster Abbey the previous June. Every now and then Lin politely interjected a question about a particular aspect of the ceremony; he was especially impressed by the incident in which the young queen descended from her throne to assist the elderly Lord Rolle when he fell on the stairs.

It took quite some time for Ross to finish his account, made doubly long by the need for Thom to translate everything into Chinese. From Lin's approving nods, it was apparent that Thom was doing an excellent job, though he often struggled to find appropriate words for Ross's detailed description of the costumes, setting, and ceremony. The commissioner was totally captivated by the entire report, and while he and the clerk took no notes, Ross did not doubt that Lin would be able to recount the conversation to the emperor down to the tiniest detail.

Although Ross did not understand Chinese, he was won

over by Lin's keen attentiveness and warm smile, and he found himself liking the man. He could not help but wish Lin a certain amount of success in what surely would be delicate negotiations with the English and other foreigners. For his part, Ross did not wholly approve of his countrymen's dealing in opium, and he was too young and naive to comprehend fully how integral the practice was to the entire China trade and to the prosperity of his own family's business.

Ross soon was confident that Lin Tse-hsü liked him, as well. It was nothing in particular that Lin did or said, but rather the way a sense of familiarity developed during their discussion, despite the presence of an interpreter. Ross had been in China less than three weeks, yet he realized how unusual this was—especially with a government official. Most dealings between the Chinese and the *fan kuei* were kept at the most formal level. The few Chinese who broke that barrier, such as *hong* men like Howqua, adopted an almost deferential tone. But with Lin Tse-hsü, Ross felt as though he was being treated as an equal—rare enough in England and almost unheard of in China.

During a natural pause in the conversation, Lin gestured to his clerk, and the young man came forward and handed Lin a scroll, rolled up and tied with a red ribbon. Lin spoke for a few moments to Thom, then handed him the scroll.

"Mr. Lin wants me to read this to you," Thom explained to his companion. "I think it's some sort of proclamation."

Wondering if this might be a formal edict banning the import of opium—something all the foreign merchantmen had been expecting—Ross sat back and clasped his hands in front of him. He would remain calm, he told himself, no matter what the proclamation said or how disruptive to the foreigners it might prove to be.

Thom untied the ribbon and carefully unrolled the scroll, which was about two feet long. He scanned it up and down—the Chinese characters were written vertically—

then glanced at Ross in surprise. "It isn't a proclamation. It's a letter . . . to Queen Victoria herself."

Lin waved a finger at the scroll, indicating that Thom should translate his words.

Thom drew in a breath and began:

" 'To Her Majesty Queen Victoria. The Way of Heaven is fairness to all; it does not suffer us to harm others in order to benefit ourselves. Men are alike in this all the world over: that they cherish life and hate what endangers life. Your country lies twenty thousand leagues away; but for all that, the Way of Heaven holds good for you as for us, and your instincts are not different from ours; for nowhere are there men so blind as not to distinguish between what brings life and what brings death, between what brings profit and what does harm.

" 'Our Heavenly Court treats all within the Four Seas as one great family; the goodness of our great Emperor is like Heaven, which covers all things. There is no region so wild or so remote that he does not cherish and tend it. Ever since the port of Canton was first opened, trade has flourished. For some hundred and twenty or thirty years the natives of the place have enjoyed peaceful and profitable relations with the ships that come from abroad. Rhubarb, tea, silk are all valuable products of ours, without which foreigners could not live. The Heavenly Court, extending its benevolence to all alike, allows these things to be sold and carried away across the sea, not grudging them even to remote domains, its bounty matching the bounty of Heaven and Earth.

" 'But there is a class of evil foreigner that

makes opium and brings it for sale, tempting
fools to destroy themselves, merely in order
to reap profit. Formerly the number of opium
smokers was small; but now the vice has spread
far and wide and the poison penetrated deeper
and deeper. If there are some foolish people who
yield to this craving to their own detriment, it
is they who have brought upon themselves their
own ruin, and in a country so populous and
flourishing, we can well do without them. But
our great, unified Manchu Empire regards itself
as responsible for the habits and morals of its
subjects and cannot rest content to see any of
them become victims to a deadly poison. For
this reason we have decided to inflict very severe
penalties on opium dealers and opium smokers,
in order to put a stop forever to the propagation
of this vice.

" 'It appears that this poisonous article
is manufactured by certain devilish persons
in places subject to your rule. It is not, of
course, either made or sold at your bidding,
nor do all the countries you rule produce it,
but only certain of them. I am told that in your
own country opium smoking is forbidden under
severe penalties. This means that you are aware
of how harmful it is. But better than to forbid
the smoking of it would be to forbid the sale
of it and, better still, to forbid the production
of it, which is the only way of cleansing the
contamination at its source. So long as you do
not take it yourselves, but continue to make it
and tempt the people of China to buy it, you
will be showing yourselves careful of your own
lives but careless of the lives of other people,
indifferent in your greed for gain to the harm

you do to others; such conduct is repugnant to human feeling and at variance with the Way of Heaven.

" 'Our Heavenly Court's resounding might, redoubtable to its own subjects and foreigners alike, could at any moment control their fate; but in its compassion and generosity it makes a practice of giving due warning before it strikes. . . . ' "

Thom paused and shared a glance with Ross, whose concerned expression mirrored Thom's. These two young men, one little more than a clerk, the other a fledgling merchantman, were being afforded a rare glimpse of political brinksmanship.

Looking back down at the scroll, Thom continued:

" 'Your Majesty has not before been thus officially notified, and you may plead ignorance of the severity of our laws. But I now give my assurance that we mean to cut off this harmful drug forever. What it is here forbidden to consume, your dependencies must be forbidden to manufacture, and what has already been manufactured Your Majesty must immediately search out and throw it to the bottom of the sea, and never again allow such a poison to exist in Heaven or on Earth.

" 'When that is done, not only will the Chinese be rid of this evil, but your people, too, will be safe. For so long as your subjects make opium, who knows but they will not sooner or later take to smoking it; so that an embargo on the making of it may very well be a safeguard for them, too. Both nations will enjoy the blessing of a peaceful existence, yours on its side having made clear its sincerity by respectful obedience to our commands. You will be showing that you understand the principles of Heaven, and calamities will not be sent down on you from above; you will be acting in accordance with decent feeling, which may also influence the course of nature in your favor.

" 'The laws against the consumption of opium are now so strict in China that if you continue to make it, you will find that no one buys it and no more fortunes will be made. Rather than waste your efforts on a hopeless endeavor, would it not be better to devise some other form of trade? All opium discovered in China is being cast into burning oil and destroyed. Any foreign ships that in the future arrive with opium on board will be set fire to, and any other goods that they are carrying will inevitably be burnt along with the opium. You will then not only fail to make any profit out of us, but ruin yourselves into the bargain. Intending to harm others, you will be the first to be harmed.

" 'Our Heavenly Court would not have won the allegiance of innumerable lands did it not wield superhuman power. Do not say you have not been warned in time. On receiving this, Your Majesty will be so good as to report to me immediately on the steps that have been taken at each of your ports.

" 'Your humble servant, Lin Tse-hsü.' "

Finishing, Thom rolled up the scroll, retied the ribbon, and returned it to Lin. There was a long period of silence, broken finally by Lin, who asked through the interpreter, "I am interested, Mr. Ballinger, in how you expect your queen to respond to my letter."

Shifting on his seat, Ross stroked his chin before replying, "I'm afraid I don't know the queen personally."

"But she is English, like you," Lin said, with Thom interpreting. "And she is quite young—very close to your age, I believe. Any insight you might have would prove invaluable—both to my emperor and your Crown."

Ross thought for a moment, then asked, "May I speak in strict confidence and in complete candor?" He looked closely at Thom, wondering if Thom would think that the comment was directed at Lin or at himself. But Thom had fully assumed the role of interpreter, and he translated the question without responding to Ross.

"I would be honored if you would," came the reply. "And do not be concerned; I would never break the confidence of a friend." As Thom translated, Ross felt the warmth and sincerity of Lin's smile.

"It seems to me," Ross began, "that your words were spoken from the heart, and I am convinced that our queen will sense that and will be favorably disposed. My concern comes when you warn the queen that she must forbid her dependencies from manufacturing opium. I am neither politician nor lawyer, but I believe that may go beyond the power of even our queen."

Listening to the translation, Lin looked somewhat perplexed. "But she is the queen. There is nothing in the Celestial Empire that our emperor does not see and control."

"You said I may speak openly, and so I must ask if your emperor sees and controls the opium trade that has been carried out here in Canton for many years."

Lin nodded. "Emperor Tao-kuang sees, and he controls what and when he chooses. With the opium trade, he has benignly looked to one side—until today, that is. The emperor has decreed that the time for control—for suppression—is now."

"That may be so," Ross continued, "but that time has not come to the British Empire. In your letter you

state that in our country opium smoking is forbidden under
severe penalties. I'm afraid that isn't the case. Opium is
not illegal, though it's true that very few people smoke it.
Many consume it in liquid form, however, in cough tonics,
stomach bitters, and other medicinals."

"Then you do not believe we should outlaw this
poison?" Lin asked, leaning forward and eyeing Ross
closely, his arched brows narrowing severely.

"I didn't say that. In fact, I'm convinced that if we
British ever took to the opium pipe in any sort of numbers,
the trade would be outlawed immediately and totally."

"Under penalty of death?"

"Perhaps. More likely, those who continued to trade
in opium would be sent to a penal colony such as those in
Australia."

"Then let them deal their poison to the Australians,
not the Chinese." Lin leaned back in his chair, his arms
folded across his chest. After a moment, he glanced over
his shoulder and spoke to his clerk, who bowed and padded
quickly from the garden.

Turning back to Ross, Lin said, "When you return
to your factory, you will learn that I have issued several
edicts this morning. The first is to the people of Kwangtung
province, ordering them to surrender their opium pipes or
face the severest judgment of the law."

Thom did not have to add an explanation to his
translation; Ross was well aware that in China a capital
crime was punishable by strangling or decapitation.

"The second edict is to the forces who patrol our
waters. During the past week, it has come to my attention
that many of them are accepting bribes in the form of
portions of the opium they are supposed to be confiscating.
They must cease such unlawful activities, or their fate
will be worse even than that of the opium users
and dealers."

Ross did not know what fate could be worse than

decapitation, but he took Lin at his word and nodded that he understood the significance of both edicts.

"It is my third edict that will most greatly interest your agency houses. I have ordered the heads of all the foreign shipping concerns to surrender to my authority all their stores of opium, with not the smallest item concealed or withheld, so that these stores may be destroyed. Furthermore, they must sign a bond never to import opium again, for if they do, they will also suffer the extreme rigor of the law. And in a final edict, I have given the *hong* merchants three days to arrange for the surrender of the opium. If they fail to comply, I will seek permission from the emperor to confiscate all their property and execute the most notorious opium dealers among them."

Ross and Thom sat in stunned silence. They and their countrymen were prepared for some move against the opium trade, but Lin was threatening to execute any merchantman who continued to deal in the drug.

Just then the clerk returned, followed by two common laborers who carried between them a heavy wooden chest, which they set in front of the two young Englishmen. The clerk was holding a cloth-wrapped bundle, and he placed it on top of the chest, then took up a position behind Lin Tse-hsü and signaled the laborers to depart.

"I thought it might be helpful if you better understood the situation that faces us," Lin said, with Thom continuing to translate. "Please, Mr. Ballinger, if you would be so kind as to unwrap the bundle."

Leaning forward, Ross pulled back the corners of the cloth package, revealing a curious assortment of plant cuttings, tools, and tin canisters. The plants had long stalks, at the ends of which were hard, bulbous pods. The tools consisted of several knives, some with hook-shaped metal blades and others fashioned from large mussel shells.

"Poppy," Lin intoned, as Ross and Thom examined the plants. "It is grown in India by your British East India

Company, which controls the best tracts of land throughout that country. The soil is plowed three times and weeded, then scored with irrigation dikes. The seeds are sown in November, by your calendar, and at this time of year the flowers have shed their petals, leaving the seed cases ready for harvest."

Lin lifted one of the stalks and grasped the seed pod. Taking up a hooked knife, he deftly drew it across the pod several times. Almost immediately, thick white sap oozed through the slits.

"The seed cases are cut in the evening, and the juice seeps out all night. The next day, the hot sun hardens the juice into a dark, sticky gum. Then it is scraped off the seed cases and delivered to the East India Company factories."

Putting down the pod, he opened one of the tin canisters and used the tip of the knife to scoop out some of the hardened sap.

"At the factories, it is pressed into cakes about this size. . . ." He held up a fist to indicate the size. "The cakes are wrapped in dry poppy leaves and packed in chests of mango wood, like this one."

He nodded to the clerk, who lifted the objects off the top of the chest and opened it, revealing the leaf-wrapped opium cakes.

"Each of these chests weighs about one hundred twenty-five pounds," Lin explained, handing Ross one of the opium bundles. "That is enough opium to supply eight thousand addicts for a month."

Ross thought of all the chests identical to this one he had seen being unloaded at the anchorage in Whampoa Harbor. How many had contained opium, and how many addicts had been served by the arrival of the *Celeste*?

"I had no idea. . . ." was all he could mutter as he returned the wrapped opium to the chest.

"You can see how seriously we view this problem," Lin went on. "By my estimate, there are some twenty thousand chests of opium in Canton right now, either on the boats or in the warehouses, waiting for distribution throughout China. I have also estimated the opium population in my country, and I am distressed to say that it is at least twelve million people. That means the twenty thousand chests hold enough opium to supply all the addicts in China for a year."

Ross sat for a long time just staring at the open chest in front of him. Finally he looked up and solemnly asked, "Is there some reason you're telling me all this? Is there something you want me to do?"

Listening to Thom's translation, the commissioner nodded. "Most perceptive," he declared. "Yes, I had hoped a young man like yourself—a man as yet untainted by this opium trade—would help me in my effort to convince the English government of the seriousness of the situation. It is true that our past lack of action has encouraged the opium trade. But the English must not mistake past inaction for lack of present resolve. Emperor Tao-kuang has decreed that the opium trade must stop, and believe me when I say that it will. The Celestial Empire will not allow itself to be debased any longer by this . . . this foreign scourge."

"And what would you have me do?" Ross asked.

"I would like you to carry my letter, and my sincere concerns, to your new queen. I would like you to convince her to call a halt to this sad business so that our two nations can continue as partners and friends, without a demon such as opium between us."

"But I—I don't know the queen," Ross stammered. "You should send your letter with someone official—Captain Charles Elliot, perhaps."

"I do not trust official channels—especially when they consistently prove themselves to be in complicity with the opium interests. No, I prefer someone like yourself. After all, by your own account, your cousin is a lord, part of the royal family."

"A very distant relation."

"But well-connected enough to arrange for you to deliver my letter and my concerns personally."

"I . . . I suppose so," Ross admitted, rubbing his forehead.

"Good. Then I can count on your help in this matter?"

Ross hesitated a moment before replying, "I would like to give it some thought."

"But of course." Lin rose. "I realize that you had planned to stay longer in Canton and that what I have told you has been something of a shock. But in weighing your decision, please consider what the sages have written: 'Though the shock confuses and distresses him, he can remain free of misfortune by taking action.' "

"I'm not sure I understand."

"That is because the shock is mired in the mud, and all movement is crippled. But in the end, the quake that terrifies all within a hundred miles will bring good fortune, provided you do not spill the sacrificial wine." He smiled cyptically.

Ross stared at Thom, as if questioning the translation, but Thom merely shrugged and nodded, indicating that those were Lin's exact words. Finally, Ross said to Lin, "I'm sorry, but I really don't understand."

As Thom translated Ross's comment into Chinese, Lin Tse-hsü chuckled and waved his hand, as if dismissing his earlier comments. "There is nothing to understand, for it is also written: 'The superior man makes his house quiet and still and searches his heart.' In searching your heart, rather than your mind, you will discover the action you must take."

Ross stood and bowed to the commissioner. "I will try to follow your advice."

"Pay attention not to my advice but to your own heart." Lin returned Ross's bow. "Perhaps we can meet again six days from today?"

"On Sunday?"

"Yes. Would nine in the morning here in the garden be all right?"

Ross glanced at Thom, who nodded. "Nine would be fine," Ross replied.

"Good. I will see both of you gentlemen on Sunday."

The three men bowed again, and then Lin walked across the garden and entered one of the buildings. The clerk showed the two visitors to the gate, bowed as they passed through it, and closed the heavy wooden doors behind them.

Robert Thom was already walking down the street when Ross grasped his arm and stopped him.

"What did you think of all that?" he asked, shaking his head incredulously.

Thom forced a slight grin. "Think? With my head or my heart?"

"I'm serious."

"When I'm interpreting, I'm not supposed to think."

Ross frowned. "Come on, Robert . . . I want to know."

Thom shifted from one foot to the other and finally shrugged. "I think he was quite serious."

"About putting an end to the opium trade?"

"Yes. And he intends to use force, if necessary."

"Against the Royal Navy?"

"Against any government that fails to heed China's demands." Thom looked back at the gate that led into the governor-general's compound. "Yes, he was serious. It wasn't just the things he said but the tone he used. Lin Tse-hsü is not a man to be taken lightly." He gave Ross's sleeve a tug. "Let's go—I've got to get back to work."

As they headed through the streets of Canton toward the foreign district, Ross kept thinking of Lin Tse-hsü's final words. He could almost hear the distinguished Chinese official reciting them in English in his own, mellifluous voice: "The superior man makes his house quiet and still and searches his heart."

But how does one search his heart? Ross asked himself. *How does one become a superior man so that the shock will bring good fortune? And what kind of shock is he referring to, anyway?*

Ross thought of the crate filled with opium, of the ships laden with crates, of the harbors filled with ships. A shudder—a shock—went through him, and he felt his breath catch in his throat . . . *oh, no!* But just as suddenly it passed, replaced by the strange, overpowering urge to laugh . . . *ah, ha!*

Ross halted abruptly. Had he heard that gasp of shock? And was it Lin Tse-hsü laughing in reply?

As if in answer, a voice like Lin's, yet speaking English, sounded within him: *Thus amid fear and quaking, the superior man makes his house quiet and still and searches his heart.*

"What is it?" Robert Thom asked, looking back at his friend, who stood motionless in the middle of the street.

Ross opened his mouth to speak, but the words caught in his throat as the inner voice spoke again:

Tremor follows tremor . . .

Ross shook his head to still the voice. He told himself that it was just his imagination, for this inner voice was adding words that Lin Tse-hsü had not used.

"Is something wrong?" Thom asked, returning to where Ross was standing.

. . . thus amid fear and quaking, the superior man makes his house quiet and still . . .

"Uh . . . no," Ross forced himself to reply, again shaking his head to clear it.

"Then let's go. I'm late enough as it is."

"Yes, of course." Somewhat hesitantly, Ross started down the street, his pace slowly quickening to match that of his companion.

. . . and searches his heart.

XVIII

◆◆◆◆◆◆◆◆◆◆◆◆◆◆◆◆◆◆◆◆

The situation grew increasingly tense in Canton's foreign district following the March 18 announcement of Lin Tse-hsü's edict demanding that the agency houses surrender their opium stores. The English chief superintendent of trade, Captain Charles Elliot, was in Macao at the time, so the merchants sent a message to him describing Lin's action and requesting his advice. As the highest-ranking government official in the region, he would have to approve of any military response; without such action—or the threat of such action—the merchants could do little but negotiate with the Chinese as best they were able.

The very next day, Robert Thom was invited to a private meeting of the six most powerful merchantmen, James Matheson among them. The *hong* leader Howqua attended the opening of the meeting and informed them that until the demands of the edict were met, the Chinese superintendent of customs would not allow foreigners to travel to Macao. He also presented the full text of the edict, which Thom translated for the group. Though Howqua pressed them for an answer, they refused, and after he left, they voted to call a meeting of the full chamber of commerce on Thursday, the final day given by Lin Tse-hsü to meet his ultimatum.

On Thursday morning, the forty members of the chamber met to debate the issue, with several *hong* leaders in attendance. Sentiment was strong to refuse to comply with the commissioner's demands, but some members argued in favor of making a token gesture, perhaps relinquishing a thousand chests out of the total twenty thousand. The final vote was twenty-five to fourteen against any such action, and the *hong* representatives were given a message for Lin Tse-hsü, informing him that his edict had been received with great respect and would be considered by the group for at least another week.

By late afternoon, the *hong* leaders returned from meeting with Lin Tse-hsü and reported that he was furious; he was threatening to execute several of them—Howqua among them—if they failed to sway the foreigners. He had even used the famous quote from the Duke of Chou: *"Hsing luan-pang, yung chung-tien,"* or "To rule a chaotic state, severe punishment must be imposed."

At ten o'clock, the chamber of commerce was hastily reconvened, and the *hong* men were questioned at length to make sure they had met with the high commissioner himself and not one of his subordinates.

When asked what had taken place during the interview, Howqua told them through a translator, "We took your letter to the *ch'in-ch'ai ta-ch'en,* and upon hearing it read, he said that you have been trifling with the *hong* merchants but should not do the same with him. He declared that if no opium is delivered up, he will be at Consoo House at ten o'clock tomorrow morning to show us what he will do."

"How many chests do you require?" asked Lancelot Dent of the firm Dent and Company.

"About one thousand."

"And what security can you give that he will be satisfied with that quantity?" Dent pressed.

Howqua looked first at the other *hong* merchants, then replied, "None. But we believe if that much opium is given up, he will be satisfied that his order has been obeyed; but whether more will be required or not, we cannot answer."

A final question was then put to Howqua, as it had been to the other *hong* leaders they had interviewed: "Seriously and solemnly, are you in fear for your lives?"

"I am," Howqua answered, as each of the others had done.

The chamber was finally swayed to take action by this testimony, and an agreement was reached to surrender one thousand chests—a quarter of them owned by Jardine, Matheson & Company—worth over three hundred thousand dollars. The foreigners hoped that would assuage the high commissioner. Many assumed his edict was designed to fill his own purse, and they were confident that a thousand chests would do the job admirably. Others, such as James Matheson, were not so sure; Lin Tse-hsü showed every sign of being serious in his determination to "strip bare and root up the opium traffic."

For the time being, life returned to some semblance of order, with one disconcerting exception: an increase in surveillance throughout the district by members of what was being called Lin Tse-hsü's "coolie guard." No one was sure if the commissioner had been appeased, but at least the gesture by the foreigners appeared to have saved the *hong* leaders from reprisals, for ten o'clock came and went without Lin Tse-hsü appearing at Consoo House to carry out his threat.

Later that afternoon, Ross Ballinger was walking down New China Street, admiring the array of exotic goods in the small shops. He wondered if he should do some more shopping; rumors persisted that the Chinese shops in the foreign district would soon be closed and that the foreigners might even be ordered to leave Canton.

He was examining the intricate detail of a carved ivory

rose when he was startled to hear someone calling his name. He turned to see the Reverend Samuel Outerbridge huffing down the lane. His clerical collar was undone and hung precariously from his neck, and he was waving at Ross with a flimsy paper fan. Ross put down the carving and stepped away from the booth to meet him.

"Mr. Ballinger!" Outerbridge wiped the sweat from his forehead with a handkerchief, then fanned himself. "This heat . . . it's no wonder the Orientals are so addled."

"How is your wife bearing up?" Ross asked as Outerbridge caught his breath.

The reverend shook his head ruefully. "She's in Macao . . . got stranded there when the travel ban was announced. At least Macao catches the ocean breeze."

"It won't be long before the whole foreign community migrates down there for the season—if the travel ban is ever lifted," Ross noted. "I hear that only a couple of dozen foreigners remain in Canton during the summer months."

"I'll still be here, so long as there's work to be done," Outerbridge declared almost defiantly.

"And how is that work coming?"

"It's a slow process, but we work soul by soul." The reverend gave a bitter frown. "And then, just when we think we've won another one over to the Lord, the Papists get in their hooks and steal them away!"

Ross suppressed a grin. "At least the Catholics aren't pagans."

"Might as well be. To hear those Carmelites speak, you'd think they'd embraced Buddha as one of the twelve disciples."

"Is it really that bad?"

"You don't believe me?" Outerbridge challenged. "Then come along; I'll show you."

"Where?"

"To the mission—the Catholic mission behind the factories. I've got an appointment with one of the friars."

Seeing Ross's confused expression, he added, "I don't approve of the Papists, but sometimes we have to work together for the sake of . . ." He rolled his eyes upward, indicating heaven. "The really awful thing is that the poor heathens can't seem to tell us apart. They call Roman Catholicism the Religion of the Lord of Heaven, and all we Protestants are lumped together as the Religion of Jesus." He gave Ross an eager smile. "Why don't you come along; you might find it interesting."

"Well, I suppose I could—"

"Good! It will give us some time to renew our friendship."

Ross wanted to ask what friendship the effusive minister was referring to but thought better of it and went along meekly as Outerbridge led the way down New China Street to the rear of the factories. Turning onto Thirteen Factory Street, they walked past Consoo House and up a small alley.

"It's back this way," Outerbridge said, "alongside Yueh-hua Academy—that's where the *ch'in-ch'ai* is staying, you know."

"I see you're picking up the language."

"I've learned a few words," he beamed, puffing himself up. "Enough to start gathering the sheep."

For the slaughter, Ross thought but kept silent.

"Here we are." Outerbridge nodded at a door in the alley wall that would have been indistinguishable from all others in Canton had it not been for a heavy iron crucifix hanging on it. "Go ahead, knock," he added, indicating the door.

Stepping up to it, Ross raised his fist, but the reverend grabbed his arm and said, "Use that." He was grinning as he pointed at the iron crucifix, acting as if he were offering his young companion a great honor.

Realizing that the crucifix was a door knocker, Ross took hold of Jesus by the legs, lifted him several inches from the cross—he remained hinged at the hands—and let him bang back down against the cross.

" 'And I tell you . . . knock, and it will be opened to you,' " Outerbridge quoted from the Scriptures, then shook his head in dismay and muttered, "Sacrilegious!"

Ross rapped two more times, and then the bolt slid free and the door opened to reveal a nun in full habit. She was quite short and looked like any number of nuns Ross had seen in London, until she lifted her head and smiled at the visitors.

A Chinese nun, the astonished young Englishman thought. He returned her smile and entered the mission behind the Reverend Samuel Outerbridge.

The men were led into a small anteroom off a much larger one that looked as if it served as a makeshift chapel. The nun did not speak English, and by a series of hand gestures she directed them toward two chairs in the anteroom, then disappeared into the chapel, closing the door behind her.

"Only Papists allowed in there, I suppose," Outerbridge commented, looking around the anteroom with undisguised disapproval. The walls were lined with gilt-framed portraits of the saints—undoubtedly the work of a local artist, since most of the subjects had decidedly Oriental features. One of them, in fact, purported to show Jesus at the Last Supper but had two of the disciples using chopsticks.

A minute later, the chapel door opened and a handsome, dark-complected man in a brown monk's cowl strode in. *"¡Hola!"* he declared. *"¿Cómo están?"*

Rising, Samuel Outerbridge held out his fleshy hand. "Fray Luis Nadal, I'd like you to meet a countryman of mine, Mr. Ross Ballinger."

"So pleased to meet you," Luis said in almost perfectly accented English. He shook Ross's hand.

"Fray Luis is quite a linguist, aren't you?" Outerbridge said, turning to the cleric.

"It is true that I know several languages, but closest to my heart is Valenciano, the language of my family in Játiva, Spain."

"The home of princes, popes, and scoundrels—isn't that what you told me, Luis?"

The cleric blushed slightly. "It is true that some of the Borgia family of Italy came from my town, including Rodrigo de Borja y Doms, who became our Pope Alexander II."

"Well, Ross and I come from the little town of London, where we've got our share of princes and scoundrels but nary a pope, I'm afraid."

"Ah, except for your own great Alexander: the poet Alexander Pope. I have enjoyed him in both Spanish and English, and perhaps someday in Mandarin." Turning to Ross, Luis asked, "Are you also with the Protestant mission?"

"No, I'm a merchantman. The Outerbridges and I shared passage to Canton."

"Then you're old friends. Delightful." He gestured toward the adjoining room. "Perhaps you'd like to wait in the chapel while the good reverend and I conduct our business in my office? There is so much common ground between our faiths that it would be a pity to allow small differences to stand in the way of introducing our Lord of Heaven to this Celestial Empire on earth."

Ross allowed himself to be ushered through the doorway, and then the two men left for the cleric's office. Alone in the chapel, Ross walked down the small center aisle of the five rows of benches and stepped up to the altar, a simple lectern draped in purple velvet. Other than a few paintings on the wall behind the altar, the only real decoration was the view through the windows of a small garden.

As Ross gazed out at it, he noticed two women seated at a small stone table in the center of the courtyard. One was the nun; she was preparing tea and serving it to a much younger Chinese woman, who wore a traditional robe of gold-brocaded silk—the outfit of an upper-class Chinese. The filtered sunlight that poured over the roof of the chapel danced playfully across the young woman's face, sparking against her brocade robe.

Mesmerized by the elaborate tea-pouring ritual, Ross drifted over to an open door beside the windows and stepped into the courtyard. He stood there in the shadows watching the two women, the older nun slowly and deliberately rotating the teacup in her hands, then handing it across the table to the young woman, who held it almost reverently before taking a sip.

After a few minutes, the nun glanced over and saw Ross standing there. She did not seem at all surprised and waved for him to approach. Ross was hesitant at first, but the woman persisted, and finally he moved out of the shadows and walked down a small rock path to the table. Four stone benches surrounded the table, and the nun signaled him to take the one to the young woman's left. As he sat, Ross tried not to stare at her, but he was struck by her beauty and the abiding calmness that she seemed to emanate.

They remained silent as the nun repeated the ritual of grinding tea leaves in a mortar and pestle, pouring them into a cup, then slowly adding hot water. Turning the cup several times in her hands, she presented it to Ross, and he tried to imitate the way the young woman had held and drunk from her cup. The tea was dark and bitter, but at the nun's prodding, Ross finished the contents, leaving only the wet flakes of tea in the bottom. When he set the cup down, the nun pulled it toward her, then did likewise with the young woman's empty cup.

For a long time, the nun just gazed into the bowl of Ross's cup, her eyelids half-closed and fluttering. Then she spoke in a high, sweet voice. It was in Chinese, so Ross had no idea of what she was saying, but it sounded like the most pleasant music he had ever heard.

He was shaken out of his reverie by an equally melodic voice, this one speaking in near-perfect English: "Sister Carmelita see man sitting in large, empty room on faraway island."

Turning in surprise to the young woman, Ross was about to speak, but she raised a hand to silence him, then nodded at the older woman, who was still staring into the teacup. He remained quiet, unwilling to interrupt her meditation. Neither was the young woman, who seemed to be waiting for the nun to speak again.

When she did, it was with a single, disconcerting word: "Edmund."

For a moment Ross thought he had heard wrong; perhaps the nun had said something in Chinese that sounded like Edmund. But then she continued in her own language, and again Ross heard the name Edmund amid the Chinese words.

When the nun grew silent again, the other woman said to Ross, "Sister Carmelita ask if this Edmund is your father."

Ross numbly replied, "Yes."

The nun spoke for a while longer, after which the young woman told Ross, "Carmelita say that this man suffering from great weight that threaten his entire family. She see two boys, one born in poverty, the other in wealth. They are brothers in spirit, yet they face each other like warriors upon field of combat." She whispered something in Chinese to the nun, who did not open her eyes as she gave her reply. Then the young woman looked back at Ross and continued, "Not until each of these young men willing to sacrifice himself for the sake of other will balance be restored to their households. Only then will weight that is crushing their fathers be lifted."

While Ross contemplated the strange message, Sister Carmelita put down his teacup and picked up the other one.

After another minute or so, she closed her eyes and spoke. The young woman listened closely, nodding every now and then and finally saying, *"Hsieh hsieh."* Her expression was solemn and concerned.

Abruptly the nun opened her eyes and smiled at the two people sitting across from her. She pushed the cups away and leaned across the table, taking the young woman's hands and speaking rapidly to her, all the while glancing at Ross. When she finished, she motioned for her words to be translated.

"Sister Carmelita wonder if you ever saw a Chinese nun," the woman told him, and he shook his head. "She didn't think so, because of way you stared at her when she let you into mission. Her actual words were that she never see a 'round eye' with such round eyes."

Ross found himself smiling, as well. "Would you mind asking what led her to become a Christian?"

The two women conferred for a moment, and then the young woman gave the nun's answer: "She say that she has put on robe of foreign devil so she may vanquish the one true *fan kuei*—Lucifer. Before becoming Christian, she was fortune teller, and she does not understand why her new church frown on such useful skill. At least Fray Luis appreciate it, since it bring many people to his church. They come seeking future in her tea leaves, and every now and then one of them stay on."

"Like you?" Ross asked somewhat boldly.

She lowered her head. "I am not Christian."

"I'm sorry if I offended you."

"There can be no offense when one speak from the heart." She looked back up at him and smiled.

"I . . . I should introduce myself," Ross said, a bit disconcerted by her beauty and her words. "My name is Ross Ballinger."

"I am Mei-li."

"Mei-li . . ." he repeated, savoring the sound. "You speak English beautifully."

"I studied many years in Fray Luis's school for the Chinese. My uncle is very forward thinking; he encouraged all nephews and nieces to study English."

Sister Carmelita rose and gathered the teapot and cups onto a tray. As she picked it up, she spoke to Ross, and he sensed that she was taking her leave. Standing and bowing, he said "good-bye" and "thank you" in the best Chinese he could muster.

"We must go into chapel," Mei-li announced when they were alone. "It not seemly for us to be alone in garden."

Ross waited for her to go first, but she waved him ahead of her. He made his way across the garden and through the open door, with Mei-li walking several feet behind. As he stepped into the room, he found Fray Luis Nadal and Samuel Outerbridge waiting for him.

"I see that our little Carmelita has been serving you tea," Luis noted with a somewhat reproving expression. But then he smiled and added, "I hope it was to your liking."

"Yes, it was—very much so."

"Good. You must return and have tea with us again."

"I'd like that." Ross turned to look at Mei-li, but she was just leaving the room through a doorway behind the altar.

"I trust that Mei-li introduced herself," Fray Luis said. "She was perhaps my finest student. It is so good to see her all grown up."

"Does she live in Canton?" Ross asked.

"Her family is from Peking; she spent four years here being schooled, but now she lives at home. Her father passed away quite a few years ago, and she is under the charge of her uncle. She is accompanying him on a visit."

"I'd say we've taken enough of your time," Outerbridge interjected, looking a bit impatient. "I'll pass along your suggestions to the Protestant mission, and we'll see if we can't come up with some sort of arrangement."

"Yes, of course," Luis agreed as he led them from the chapel. "I'm sure there's room enough in China for

Reformers and Papists alike." His smile was genuine and disarming.

Much to Ross Ballinger's chagrin, his cousin Julian had developed a taste for *samshu.* Ever since that first night when Ross had thought to teach him a lesson by plying him with the infamous local concoction, Julian had taken every opportunity to revisit the establishment, pressing Ross to accompany him. Generally Ross complied, but he learned to make a single glass of rum last the evening and to decline any attempts to drag him upstairs.

On Saturday night, Ross was seated alone at the *samshu* bar, nursing his drink while his cousin was upstairs "plowing Chinese waters," as the young naval lieutenant none-too-delicately referred to it. Julian was on two-day leave from the *Lancet,* which remained at anchor twelve miles away in Whampoa Harbor; he was staying at Ross's quarters in Creek Factory and hoped to spend the time roaringly drunk.

Every now and then the bartender tried to pour Ross another drink, but Ross would cover the glass to indicate he had had enough. Then the man would point upstairs and suggest in pidgin, "First-chop Chinee woman?" to which Ross would invariably reply, "No wannee."

He had about finished his drink and was considering leaving, when at last Julian came weaving down the narrow staircase, his shirt partly undone, his naval jacket slung over one shoulder.

"Set me up another," Julian called to the barkeep, who didn't know the words but understood the meaning and quickly poured a glass of *samshu.*

"You've had enough," Ross said, going over to steady his cousin.

"I'm all right," Julian insisted, pushing the younger Ballinger away. He straightened up and walked without assistance to the counter. Picking up the glass, he raised it to his lips and downed it in a single gulp, then slapped it back on the bar. Sitting down on the stool, he signaled the barkeep to fill it yet again.

Ross looked at him in dismay. "Are you sure you want—?"

"I always know exactly what I want—unlike you, li'l cousin. Tonight, for instance . . ." He waved an arm at the stairs. "I wanted to go upstairs, so that's what I did, while you stayed down here, even though you wanted to just as much."

"I did not."

"The hell you say!" Julian blurted, leaning back a bit unsteadily. "All you done all evenin' was blather on about some jade princess who's got your fire all kindled, but when a real Canton beauty"—he nodded toward the stairs—"wants you to make her chimney smoke, you shrivel up and hide down here."

"*You* can pay for it if you want, but I—"

"We *all* pay for it, li'l cousin," Julian cut him off. "Whether it's with a wife, a mistress, or a flat-back whore, we all pay, some through the nose, others up the ass. But one way or another, we end up payin'. Believe me, that slope-eyed Mary you're stuck on'll be no different, if she's even willin' to get her chimney swept."

"Shut the hell up!" Ross snapped, more in irritation than anger.

Julian leaned closer to his drinking partner. "Then you *are* sweet on her, are you?" When Ross did not reply, Julian raised his glass and announced, "Let's drink to Ross's little lotus flower. What's her name?"

"Mei-li," Ross muttered and immediately regretted having said it.

"Ahh, Mei-li . . ." Julian sighed and downed the second drink, then wiped his mustache with his sleeve. "If Miss Mei-li's morals are anythin' like the rest of her countrymen's, maybe you won't have to pay after all." He smirked at Ross.

"Shut up, damn you!" Ross smacked his fist down on the bar.

"Oh, he's got his dander up!" Julian teased. "You'd best watch out, li'l cousin, or you may get smote by the very princess you're smitten with."

Ross shook his head in disgust and rose to leave.

"Just a minute!" Julian called after him. Standing, he fumbled with his jacket, managed to come up with a coin from one of the pockets, and tossed it onto the counter. As he struggled into the jacket sleeves, he observed, "You're right, li'l cousin—I *have* had more'n enough. We'd better get this salty dog back to his ship!"

Ross waited somewhat reluctantly for Julian to join him at the door. Then they left the bar and started down the lane toward Factory Square.

"If a body meet a body, comin' thro' the rye," Julian chanted off-key. Gesticulating wildly with his left arm, he wrapped his right one around Ross's shoulder and sang even more loudly—"If a body kiss a body, need a body cry?"— all the while poking Ross in the ribs until at last he joined in: "Ev'ry laddie has his lassie, nane, they say, hae I! Yet a' the lassies smile at me, when comin' thro' the rye!"

By the time they reached the end of Hog Lane, Ross had all but forgotten his annoyance at Julian's comments about Mei-li. After all, it was the *samshu* speaking, as much as anything else, he told himself. Julian wasn't all that terrible. At least he was family, and the rest of Ross's family was thousands of miles and many months away.

As they stumbled into the lamplit square, Ross noticed a disturbance near the water stairs across from Imperial Factory. Two sailors were jostling someone, backing him over to the stairs, which led down to the river. Ross could not see the third man clearly, but from the imprecations of the sailors, it was apparent that he was Chinese.

"Goddamn Johnnie Pigtail! Watch where the hell you're walkin'!" one of the seamen shouted as he roughly shoved the man into the other sailor.

"Fuckin' canary!" The second one pushed him away and knocked off his conical rattan hat. His partner immediately snatched it up and sent it spinning into the darkness of the river.

The two men closed in on either side of their victim, towering over him and pushing him back and forth between them. "Rice belly!" one of them shouted, the other one echoing, "Yellow-belly bastard!"

Ross had come to a halt, watching the commotion at water's edge. His cousin, standing more steadily on his feet now, pulled at his sleeve and urged, "C'mon, let's go."

Ross gestured toward the brewing fight. "But—"

"It's none of our concern," Julian insisted.

"But there's two of them."

"It's a Chinaman."

"Yes, but—"

"They're simply havin' some sport."

Just then the bigger of the two sailors knocked the Chinese man onto his back. As the poor fellow struggled to his hands and knees, the big man exclaimed, "Throw 'im in the river, Scully!" and the other responded with a savage kick to the Chinese man's chest, sending him reeling backward toward the stairs.

"Enough!" Ross hollered, running across the square. *"Enough of that!"*

The two seamen turned to see who was shouting and found themselves confronted by a young man in the well-tailored suit of a merchantman.

"Let him up!" Ross demanded, stepping over to where the man was sprawled half-conscious on the top few stairs.

" 'Tis none o' your business!" the bigger sailor declared, grabbing Ross by the shoulder and roughly pushing him aside. "He had it comin'!"

Ross faced the man. "Whatever he did, it's no excuse for the two of you ganging up on him."

With a smirk, the sailor named Scully came up beside his bigger friend. "Would you rather Virge and I ganged up on you?"

"Yeah, coolie boy." Virge gave Ross a harsh shove to the chest. "If you love that yellow belly so much, you oughta be floatin' in the river beside him." He shoved Ross again, this time toward the Chinese man, who still lay stunned on the stairs.

Ross tottered at the edge of the river wall, the water some ten feet below, but managed to keep his balance. Realizing they were about to rush him, he raised his fists and planted his feet as firmly as he could.

"If anyone's goin' to be lyin' in the river, it'll be you two sorry sea dogs!" another voice shouted.

"Why, you . . . !" Virge sputtered, but his friend grabbed his arm.

"He's an officer," he whispered. This took a little of the starch out of the big man, who still stood with fists clenched, glowering at Julian, who was circling around to where Ross was standing.

"That Chinaman called us a name," explained the more coolheaded Scully.

"What name?" Julian challenged.

He shrugged. "How the hell should I know? It was in Chinee."

"How do you know it was a name?" Ross asked as Julian stepped up beside him.

"It was the *way* he said it."

Julian grinned malevolently. "You mean, it wouldn't matter if I was to call you, say, a fart-catchin' toady for that fat-assed knobhead—" he nodded toward Virge "—just so long as I said it politely?"

The big man's fists came up. "What the—!"

"An *officer*!" Scully hissed, holding him back.

Julian's naval coat was still unbuttoned, and he took it off, tossed it to the ground, and waved the big man toward him. "Come on!" he challenged. "I'm no officer now."

It was all the encouragement the sailor needed. With a harsh growl, he lowered his head and charged, swinging wildly as he slammed into Julian. The two men almost went flying off the river wall, but Julian managed to hold his ground, warding off the blows from Virge's flailing arms and getting in a few solid punches to the gut.

Ross was soon drawn into the fray, for the other sailor came at him. Ross circled warily, the two men facing off at the wall's edge. Scully got in the first good punch, a vicious uppercut that landed on Ross's right cheek and snapped his head back. He followed with a flurry of jabs to Ross's belly, doubling him over in pain. As Ross tried to catch his wheezing breath, the sailor moved in for the finish, a left-right combination to the jaw. But Ross saw it coming and ducked low, charging at the man's midsection. There was a howl of surprise when Ross's head connected with Scully's belly, and then Scully went stumbling over the edge of the river wall, his arms and legs beating at the air. He hit the water on his back and sank like a stone.

Ross was still catching his breath as he stood at the lip of the river wall. In the lamplight of the square, he could just make out the inky surface of the water, and he waited for the sailor to reemerge. Long seconds passed, and suddenly Ross realized that the man was not coming up. Tearing off his jacket and boots, he drew in the deepest breath he could manage and dove into the blackness.

The water was cold and seemed to draw Ross into its depths. He could feel the slow, sure current seizing him, and he relaxed into it, letting the river spiral him ever deeper downriver as he reached in vain for the man.

His breath was giving way, and he knew he had to fight the current and swim to the surface. He opened his eyes, but it was too black to be sure which way was up, so he kicked his feet and started in what he hoped was the right direction, praying that he was rising.

He took several powerful strokes, and his right hand struck something. At first he thought it was the river wall, but the object was moving, floating in front of him. Groping around, he felt an arm, then a leg. The body was spinning limply in the current, either unconscious or dead.

Grabbing onto one of Scully's arms, Ross kicked for the surface, his hands and feet numb with the cold, his chest feeling as if it would burst. He was not sure if he was headed up or down, but he just kept going, aware that he had only seconds before his lungs gave out. And then he could hold his breath no longer; it went out of him in a furious spray of bubbles, and he involuntarily took a deep gulp.

Just as the water began entering his lungs, his head cleared the surface, and he gasped for air. Water came out of him in a hacking sputter as he struggled to catch his breath, all the while hanging on to the sailor's body.

"Ross!" a voice shouted from off to his left. Julian was clambering along the edge of the river wall, following as his friend floated slowly downstream.

Ross took another gulp of air and started for shore. At the end of the square was a second set of stairs, and he could see Julian racing over and bounding down them to the water's edge. A few more strokes brought Ross within reach of the stairs, and Julian leaned out and hauled him in.

Moments later they had Scully laid out on his back at the top of the stairs. Water dribbled from the corner of his mouth. Rolling him onto his stomach, they pressed on his back and watched the water gurgling out of him. For several seconds there was no other movement to his body, but then he gave a sudden gasp and wheezed for air, then started choking and coughing up the river.

Julian and Ross watched as the lucky sailor slowly regained consciousness. Finally, Ross looked around and asked, "Where's his friend?"

"Flat on his back. He won't be waking up anytime soon." Julian jabbed a thumb over his shoulder in the direction of the other set of stairs.

"And the Chinese man?"

"Took off running as soon as the fight began. What'd you expect? Thanks from a Chinaman? Hell, they don't care if we foreign devils live or die."

"Maybe," Ross acknowledged. "But perhaps if we *fan kuei* cared a little more about them, they'd return the favor."

Julian jabbed him playfully in the chest. "Always had a soft spot, didn't you? Good thing your father runs a merchant house. You'd never make a real sailor, like Scully here, or Virge."

Scully seemed to hear his name. He lifted his head off the ground and muttered, "Wh-Where am I?"

Clapping the sailor on the shoulder, Julian proclaimed, "Back in the land of the living, matey. Hell, better'n that. You're in China, Scully, my good friend. Canton, China." He chuckled. "And I'd say that calls for another glass of *samshu* all around!"

XIX

Ross Ballinger was awake early on Sunday, March 24. He had a morning meeting with Lin Tse-hsü, so he decided to let Julian sleep off the effects of the *samshu* he had continued to down after their encounter with the English sailors the night before. For his part, Ross was feeling remarkably fit; he had not imbibed nearly as much of the local rum as his cousin and had only a slightly bruised cheek from his scuffle with Scully and their subsequent swim in Canton River.

After washing and dressing, Ross took a brisk walk around Factory Square, then joined Robert Thom for a light breakfast of eggs and toast in the dining room on the second floor of Number Four Creek House. By half-past eight they were on their way to the governor-general's home for their nine o'clock meeting with Lin Tse-hsü.

They had plenty of time this morning and were able to walk leisurely through the walled city. Again they were the object of much attention, since it was rare that *fan kuei*—especially such a fair-haired one as Ross—were seen in central Canton. Having Thom along livened the journey considerably, because he stopped periodically to converse with men on the street, always being careful to observe proper etiquette and not speak to a woman unless spoken to first.

Ross was impressed with how friendly the people were after some initial reticence. Though he knew hardly a word of their language, they communicated with gestures and through Thom, when needed. Almost everyone wanted to know how many brothers and sisters Ross had and what size house his family owned. Apparently word had already spread through the populace that England was an island of relatively small families living in huge mansions.

At precisely nine o'clock, the young men arrived at the governor-general's compound and were greeted at the gate by the same clerk who had met them before. This time, however, he did not immediately usher them into the garden but stood talking to Thom for a few minutes. Finally Thom nodded and turned to Ross to explain.

"It's really quite irregular, but Commissioner Lin has asked if you would meet alone with him. Apparently he's arranged for one of his own interpreters to be on hand."

"What about you?" Ross asked, looking somewhat skeptical.

"I'm to return to the foreign compound."

"But I'm not sure I can find—"

"They'll have a guide take you back," Thom reassured him, patting him on the arm. "Is that all right with you?"

"I suppose so," Ross said without conviction.

"It's really quite an honor."

"But why doesn't he want you here?"

Thom shrugged. "Perhaps because I work for Jardine's."

"But you'd never let that interfere."

"We know that, but the commissioner doesn't. Ah, well, you can always tell me all about it when you return." Thom spoke again to the clerk, then shook hands with Ross and departed.

Ross was escorted through the garden to the chairs beside the little lotus pond. This time Lin Tse-hsü was already on hand, and to Ross's great astonishment, so was Fray Luis Nadal and the young woman named Mei-li.

"So good to see you again, Mr. Ballinger," she said, rising with the others as he approached. "My uncle looking forward to this visit."

"Your uncle?" Ross said in surprise as the commissioner greeted him with a bow. "Commissioner Lin is your uncle?"

"Didn't I tell you that?" Fray Luis asked, looking somewhat embarrassed.

"You said that Mei-li was traveling with her uncle, but you never mentioned his name."

"I'm so sorry," Luis apologized.

"My full name Lin Mei-li," the young woman explained.

"The beautiful plum," Luis added, smiling. When Ross looked at him curiously, he explained, "That's what Mei-li means—beautiful plum."

Ross bowed to Lin Tse-hsü and greeted him in Chinese, much to the commissioner's delight.

"Good day to you, Mr. Ballinger," Lin carefully pronounced in English, shaking hands in the Western style.

"Luis and I teach my uncle a few expressions this morning," Mei-li explained, "but I'm afraid his English not extend beyond simple greetings."

"Please tell him that I'm pleased to see him again," Ross said, and Mei-li translated.

As on Ross's previous visit, the four chairs were arranged in a circle beside the pond. Lin Tse-hsü directed Ross to the empty chair across from his, and the four of them sat down.

With Fray Luis translating, Lin Tse-hsü began the meeting: "I hope you have given serious thought to my request that you deliver my letter to your queen. I fear the situation here in Canton is growing more difficult by the day, and we must do everything we can to avert full-scale war. It is not the desire of the emperor to bring ruin upon your nation."

"As I am sure that our Crown would not wish to bring ruin upon yours," Ross replied.

Lin's expression was both fatherly and sympathetic. "Our Celestial Empire has existed since the beginning of time, while I have heard that your own history dates back but a mere seven or eight hundred years. When the sun no longer marches across the heavens, China will still be standing beneath the sky. You English may wish to extend your empire from one reach of the sun to the next, but China will always remain at the center of heaven."

Knowing that argument was futile, Ross nodded politely and said, "I've given your request much thought, and I've decided that it is my duty as an Englishman and a friend of China to relay your thoughtful concerns to Queen Victoria."

As Luis translated, Ross looked at Mei-li and found himself marveling at what he had just done. Until that very moment, he had not had any idea what his decision would be, and he had hoped to rely on Robert Thom's counsel when the time came. But the words had just come out, and as he gazed at the beautiful young Chinese woman, he knew why. Though he had an even greater reason for wanting to remain in Canton, now that he had met Mei-li, it was also true that he would circle the earth for her, if such was her desire.

When Luis finished the translation, Lin Tse-hsü clapped his hands. "I am so pleased," he said. "When I met you, I felt confident that you were a man who could be trusted to listen to his heart."

As Luis translated Lin's comment, Ross recalled the words the commissioner had used the previous week: *The superior man makes his house quiet and still and searches his heart.*

The commissioner waved a hand toward the Spanish cleric. "My good friend Fray Luis Nadal tells me that you met my niece at his mission near Yueh-hua Academy. Yet you do not strike me as being religious." He turned to the cleric and added, "Wouldn't you agree?"

Luis seemed a bit uncomfortable as he told Ross, "I must confess that I did not take you for a religious man."

Ross looked first at Luis, then at Lin Tse-hsü. Finally he shrugged. "I attend church, if that's what you mean."

"Ah, but have a hard time finding your God there, is that not so?" Lin asked.

The commissioner's expression was so whimsical that Ross could not help but smile. "It often does not seem as if God is attending on the same day that I do."

Listening to the translation, Lin chuckled and nodded. "It is the same with me," he agreed. "I go to the temple, I make the proper obeisances, yet the only God I find there is that of silence. The God who speaks does not allow himself to be contained within our walls." He turned to Luis. "Is that not what I have often told you?"

"Our church is the Lord's home," Luis explained; he spoke in English for Ross's benefit and allowed Mei-li to translate for her uncle. "That does not make him a prisoner; he comes and goes of his own accord. It is not for us to determine where and when God may be found. And it is sometimes at the darkest, emptiest moments that he shows his face."

Mei-li joined the conversation now, saying to the cleric in English, "You speaking of your great saint, Juan de la Cruz, are you not?" She immediately translated into Chinese for her uncle.

"Saint John of the Cross," Luis replied in English. "Yes, I suppose that I am. I must be a Carmelite to my very soul."

"And what does this Saint John have to say about God?" Lin asked.

Leaning back in his chair, Fray Luis Nadal closed his eyes and recited:

> " 'En una noche oscura
> con ansias en amores inflamada,
> ¡oh dichosa ventura!
> salí sin ser notada,
> estando ya mi casa sosegada.' "

Almost effortlessly, he translated the verse into Chinese for Lin Tse-hsü, then again into English for Ross:

> " 'On a dark night,
> hungry for that burning love,
> Oh happy fortune!
> I slipped away unnoticed,
> my house at last quiet and still.' "

Luis continued to recite from memory the next five verses of "The Dark Night of the Soul," composed in 1578 by the guiding spirit of his Carmelite order, Saint John of the Cross, finishing with the final two verses:

> " 'When the wind from the castle
> parted his hair,
> he touched my neck
> with his serene hand,
> suspending all my senses.

> " 'I diminished and abandoned myself,
> resting my face on the Beloved.
> All ceased, and I left my being,
> leaving my cares
> forgotten among the lilies.' "

There was a hush as he finished the poem. When at last Luis opened his eyes, he saw that Lin Tse-hsü was smiling peacefully and nodding ever so gently.

"Your John has the soul of a Taoist," Lin observed, his niece translating. "He understand we must leave ourselves in order to discover our true self. And he know the dark nights our spirit must pass through to climb the secret ladder. Yet when we attain the peak, we discover that grace was always there, whispering in the darkness and the light."

"I have heard of this *Tao*," Luis said, "and of Lao-tzu, the great saint who brought it to your people."

Listening to Mei-li's translation, Lin shook his head vigorously. "No," he declared in English, then continued in Chinese: "Lao-tzu not bring the *Tao*, for it always there. The *Tao* not religion or set of rules. It cannot be codified and debated. The *Tao* simply is."

Ross looked at Mei-li uncertainly as she finished translating her uncle's words. Thinking that she had missed something, he asked, "The *Tao* is . . . what?"

Mei-li did not bother to translate but answered the question herself:

" 'The *Tao* that can be told is not the eternal
    Tao.
The name that can be named is not the eternal
    name.
The nameless is the source of all being.
The named is the source of all individual things.
Without desire, you discover the mystery.
Within desire, you see only the manifestations.
Mystery and manifestation are born of the same
    mother; she is called darkness.
Darkness within darkness: the gateway to en-
    lightenment.' "

Mei-li whispered something in Chinese to her uncle, apparently telling him what she had been reciting, and he nodded approvingly. Then she said to Ross, "Five hundred years before your New Testament, that was written by Lao-tzu in his *Tao Te Ching*—in your language, *The Book of the Way*."

"And the *Tao* is the Way," Ross concluded.

Mei-li answered with a smile.

Ross tried to mask his bewilderment, but it must have been apparent to Lin Tse-hsü, for he conferred with his niece for a moment, and then she said to him, "My uncle say he can see your head swimming with all this talk of dark nights and the *Tao*. He suggest you think of it as a great journey from shock of birth, to darkening of the light that guides our path, and finally to the ascent of Keeping-Still Mountain—the friar's Mount Carmel—where we see the *Tao* and the Cross as faces of the same One."

The commissioner clapped his hands, and the clerk appeared as if from nowhere, holding the scroll that contained Lin's letter to Victoria.

"And now it is time to begin that great journey," Lin announced, with Fray Luis resuming the translation.

Ross was uncertain whether he meant the journey of the soul or the one Ross had agreed to make to England.

"We have provided an English translation," Lin continued, and the clerk showed that there was a second scroll rolled up inside the original.

"When would you like me to leave?" Ross asked.

Lin listened to the translation, then nodded sagely and said, "But today, of course."

"Today? But that's impossible. I still have work to do for my company, and there are arrangements to be made and things to be packed."

"Arrangements have all been made, and your possessions are being gathered even now and will be waiting for you on the boat."

"But I—I can't just pick up and—"

"I'm afraid you must," Mei-li interjected, her expression quite sober.

"I don't understand. You can't expect me to leave just like . . . like *that*. What will Mr. Matheson and the others think?"

"I doubt they will notice," she told him. "There will be other things to occupy their minds."

Fray Luis Nadal also looked somber, and he said to Mei-li, "Perhaps if you told him . . ."

She nodded and said something to her uncle, who motioned for her to continue. "Even as we sit here, city guard is closing off foreign district. No one permitted to enter or leave without special permit, and all commercial business must come to a halt."

Ross looked at her incredulously. "Your uncle is imprisoning all of the foreigners?"

"Detaining," she corrected, "until they come to their senses and hand over all opium under their control, not just a thousand chests."

"And forever cease dealing in the poison," Luis added.

"And if they do not?"

Mei-li's expression was full of pain despite her attempt to smile. "Please understand, Mr. Ballinger, that emperor, through his *ch'in-ch'ai ta-ch'en,* will take whatever actions are deemed necessary to put halt to opium trade."

"Even if it means war?" Ross asked.

"The Imperial Navy is ready," she said solemnly. "My uncle beg you to go to your queen and urge her to comply with the emperor's edicts. If she does not, she bring ruin upon her people; no nation can withstand might of the Celestial Terror."

"May I speak to him?" Fray Luis asked Lin Tse-hsü in Chinese, and the commissioner nodded. "Mr. Ballinger," Luis began, "I, too, must urge you to put aside your personal business and undertake this mission. I have been in China for many years, and I have seen the might of the Celestial Terror, as the emperor's forces are called."

"But they have not seen the might of the Royal Navy."

"You misunderstand," Luis continued. "These forces are equipped as they have been for hundreds of years. Why, they still use the traditional bow and sword and consider the use of muskets by us Europeans as a sign of moral weakness. They even believe your soldiers will be unable to fight because of their tight, buttoned uniforms; if they were to fall down, they'd be unable to get up again."

"I'm not sure I understand."

"In truth, the emperor's force is hopelessly outdated, and the ranks are riddled with graft. For instance, the cannons overlooking the port of Canton are fourteenth-century bronze. When Commissioner Lin recently inspected them, he discovered that the gunners have sold most of their gunpowder to English smugglers and are using a mixture that is mostly sand."

"But if that's true, why does the commissioner risk engaging the Europeans?"

"I believe he understands the danger China faces. I, too, fear what may come if some understanding is not reached. The Celestial Terror has never faced a modern, well-armed force, and I pray that it never has to. It could mean the destruction, not only of an army, but of an entire nation. That is why I beg you to go—to help Commissioner Lin Tse-hsü plead his case."

"I am not sure I'm capable of pleading anyone's case. I've only been in China a few weeks, and I've never been a student of politics—English or Chinese."

"My uncle does not expect you to negotiate on his behalf," Mei-li interjected. "He only wish you to bring his letter and introduce his representative to the queen."

Ross's expression brightened somewhat. "Then he will be sending someone along to speak for him?"

She nodded. "He has chosen someone he hopes will help your new queen understand what this opium trade is doing to our people and our nation."

"And who might this person be?" he asked, glancing around the garden to see if someone was about to be presented.

Rising from her seat, Mei-li announced, "Why, Mr. Ballinger, *me,* of course."

Ross looked at her in stunned silence. He was only vaguely aware of Luis also standing and saying, "Sister Carmelita and I shall be accompanying you as chaperones."

◆◆◆◆

Early that evening, Ross Ballinger and Fray Luis Nadal were taken under heavy guard to the Catholic mission just outside the foreign district. As they passed over the creek bridge and headed down Thirteen Factory Street, Ross was shocked at how the area had changed since morning, when he had walked unescorted out of the factories and through the suburbs to the city gate. Now the street bordering the district was filled with armed coolie guards, and Ross was told that more than five hundred of them were patrolling the area. The guards wore loose blue trousers and jackets, grass sandals, and conical straw hats with Chinese words painted on them; most were armed with pikes and staves and carried heavy rattan shields.

The factories had also undergone a transformation, their back entrances and windows boarded over. Hog Lane and New China Street were barricaded, and all traffic had to pass through Old China Street, which was being guarded by a contingent of regular soldiers armed with matchlock guns. Only those with a special wooden permit tied around their waist were allowed entrance, and no foreigners were permitted to leave. A steady stream of Chinese was flowing out of the lane, however, and Ross noted that it consisted mostly of cooks, houseboys, and other servants employed by the agency houses. They had been given orders to evacuate the district and were doing so as if running from the plague, their arms and backs weighted down with bundles of clothes and other personal effects. Ross wondered if his own belongings had been spirited out of Creek Factory on the back of one of Jardine's servants, the secret order having been passed along by the *hong* leaders, who were the real bosses of the Chinese who worked for the foreign companies.

Ross and Luis were taken to the mission, where final preparations for the journey were already well under way. Luis conferred for a while with one of the other friars, who would oversee things while Luis was gone, and Sister Carmelita finished packing the items they would need for the voyage.

At dusk, Lin Tse-hsü and his niece appeared and briefed Ross on the travel arrangements. It was crucial that they not risk intervention by the frigate *Lancet*, which was at the Whampoa anchorage with the merchant ships, or by any other English or American gunboats that might be in the deep-water channel of the Gulf of Canton near Macao. Therefore the group would travel by land to the area known as the Bogue, where Canton River flowed into the gulf. There they would board a small fishing junk, which would slip through the gulf, avoiding Macao with all its foreigners and putting in near Hong Kong Island forty miles away on the eastern shore.

A natural harbor at Kowloon, just across from Hong Kong, was becoming a popular dropping-off point for the opium traders, and Commissioner Lin had arranged for a small fleet of war junks to drive any merchant ships away and secure the harbor. The travelers would rendezvous with the junks, one of which would take them on the first leg of the journey—to Batavia on the island of Java in the Dutch East Indies—where they would book passage as unobtrusively as possible on a European merchant ship bound for England.

Lin Tse-hsü was anxious that they leave at once; the chief superintendent of trade, Captain Charles Elliot, was still in Macao, and no one could be sure what he would do when he learned that foreigners were under siege in Canton. As the English government's top representative in the region, his reaction could resolve the crisis or initiate war.

Lin thanked Fray Luis Nadal and Ross Ballinger for their assistance and took special pains to assure Ross that the Chinese did not expect him to do anything that might be construed as compromising his own nation. He was merely escorting a diplomatic envoy in the hope that the two great powers might be able to reach a mutually satisfactory accord.

Earlier that afternoon, Ross had written a letter to James Matheson explaining where he had gone and a more personal one to his cousin on board the *Lancet*. He now handed them over to Lin Tse-hsü, who promised to see that they were delivered just as soon as he was certain the travelers were beyond the reach of English warships in the area. In the interim, any inquiries into Ross's whereabouts would be met with a simple declaration that, having been outside the district when the siege began and having seen the extent of the fortifications and troops under the commissioner's command, he would be housed for the time being at the Catholic mission so that he could not pass along that information.

There was the clatter of hooves as three pony-drawn carriages proceeded down Thirteen Factory Street, rounded the corner of the *hong* headquarters at Consoo House, and halted in front of Yueh-hua Academy, where the travelers were waiting with their bags and trunks. The first and last vehicles were little more than open-topped carts, each with two side-facing benches that held a half-dozen guards, dressed in plain peasants' outfits. The middle vehicle was an English coach that had been a gift to the governor-general from the foreign merchantmen—not overly ornate, but plushly upholstered inside.

After Lin Tse-hsü and his niece shared a tender good-bye, Lin escorted the group to the coach. Mei-li and Sister Carmelita climbed in first and took their places on the forward-facing seat. Then Lin shook hands with each of the two men and bowed deferentially as they climbed in and sat across from the women. The commissioner consulted with the driver, then raised his hand and signaled the carriages to pull out.

Lin Tse-hsü stood, his hand raised as if in benediction, and watched the coach disappear into the gathering darkness. When it no longer could be seen or heard, he lowered his arm and clasped his hands in front of him. He felt a tear gathering under his right eye, but he let it sit there, gaining strength and then running down his cheek and dropping to the earth. Slowly shaking his head, he whispered the words of the *Tao Te Ching:* "Do your work, then retire; such is the Way of Heaven."

◆◆◆

At the same time that Lin Tse-hsü was returning to Yueh-hua Academy after seeing Ross and the others off, the head of the English Superintendency of Trade was nearing Canton. Upon receiving the merchants' message informing him of Lin's edict and how their district had been sealed off from the outside world, Elliot had left Macao at once aboard the seventy-five-ton cutter *Louisa.* He had taken along four crewmen and the landing gig from the eighteen-gun corvette *Larne*—the only English man-of-war other than the forty-four-gun frigate *Lancet* currently in the gulf—and had left the *Larne*'s master, P. J. Blake, temporarily in charge at Macao. Blake was to send a call for assistance aboard all merchant ships leaving

Macao to any warship of the Royal Navy that they happened upon. And if he did not hear from Elliot within six days, he was to assume full control and handle the situation as he saw fit. However, under no circumstances was he to attempt to break through to the hostages in Canton until reinforcements arrived.

Reaching Whampoa earlier that Sunday, Elliot had directed Captain ffiske to keep the *Lancet* at anchor there and await word from him before taking any action. Then he had continued on to Napier Island, four miles downstream from Canton, where he anchored the *Louisa*. Now, dressed in full uniform, he was completing the final leg to the city in the small, single-masted gig, hoping to slip through any barricade of ships that might be blocking the river.

The winds were relatively calm, and the crew of four had to use a combination of sails and oars to traverse the final four miles. As they drew closer to the river wall along Factory Square, Elliot counted only a half-dozen *fei-hsieh,* or "fast crab" gunboats, each sporting a single small bow-chaser cannon. They were stretched in an arc about fifty yards from the shore along the length of the river wall. A few other chop boats bobbed nearby, but they did not seem part of any concerted blockade and did not concern him.

Realizing that his arrival could do much to boost the morale of the hostages and sensing that he would have no trouble making it past the gunboats, Elliot ordered one of the sailors to hoist the flag. As he watched the English colors rising up the mast, he felt both a stirring of pride and a sense of betrayal at the high commissioner's actions, taken as they were while he was away from Canton. He also blamed himself for what he had to admit was a gross miscalculation.

Following Lin's arrival in Canton, Elliot had become convinced that he would make his first strike against the opium trade at the outer anchorages of Macao and Hong

Kong, where most of the opium was waiting to be off-loaded from the merchant vessels. Very little of it was distributed in Canton itself, and Elliot did not believe that Lin would take overt action against the agency houses there. What he had been expecting was some show of force against a few of the cargo ships, perhaps a shipment seized and burned. He never considered such a bold, dangerous move against the heart of the trade: the foreign community in Canton.

Elliot had carefully positioned the gig behind the gunboats, and as soon as the flag was hoisted, he signaled to turn to starboard and make a dash to shore. The wind began to pick up, but the crewmen continued to row, the gig creaking against the lapping water as it punched through the arc of boats.

Two of the Chinese boats saw the little English vessel coming, and the sailors scrambled to raise their anchors and hoist their blue-and-white vertically striped lugsails. They tried to cut off and intercept the gig, but it slipped right between them and raced directly for the main water stairs, slamming into them and almost tearing a hole in the hull.

Two of the crewmen were jarred off their seats by the force of the impact, but Elliot managed to keep his dignity, and he quickly moved to the bow and stepped up onto the stairs. As he ascended to Factory Square, he saw several Englishmen racing toward him; they had seen the colors flying, and word was already spreading through the district that ships from the royal fleet were pushing through to Canton to rescue the foreigners. Though Elliot was forced to point out that there weren't enough guns on the few English ships to attack Canton effectively, he did make a great show of raising the English flag over the square. Then he stood on the steps of Lungshun Factory, where the Superintendency of Trade maintained an office, and spoke briefly to the gathering crowd, assuring the merchantmen that he had returned to Canton "to stand between England's loyal subjects and these Chinese oppressors!"

Later that evening, an open meeting was held in the great hall of New English Factory. Almost all of the two hundred fifty Englishmen and other foreigners were on hand. Even Howqua and some of the other *hong* leaders were there, and they listened impassively as Elliot told the merchants to prepare for a mass exodus from Canton. It was no longer safe or honorable for them to remain there, Elliot insisted, and he had already sent word to Governor-General Teng demanding passports for all who chose to leave. If the passports were not issued by Wednesday, Elliot would consider it an act of open hostility against the British Crown. He did not elaborate on whether that meant war would follow or how he might carry out such a war given his limited resources in ships and troops.

"I know the situation is anxious," he exhorted the crowd, "but it is not desperate, and I will remain with you to my last gasp! Thank God we have two British men-of-war outside, small though they may be! But I offer all here assembled the protection of their flag. And within hours I expect the arrival at Macao of the American warships *Columbia* and *John Adams*. I do not doubt that when their masters learn of the perfidy that has this day been enacted upon us, we can count on their support!"

"That you may surely do!" shouted one of the Americans in the hall, to the cheers of the assembly.

Spying the man who had shouted, Elliot called to him, "And while our two great nations have had differences in the past, it is essential that we now unite arms against the dark treachery of what is daily proving itself to be our common foe!"

As he finished his speech to the thunderous applause of the crowd, James Matheson rose and declared, "I speak for us all when I say that we are grateful to you, Captain Elliot, for your brave arrival in Canton and for your heartening words. Surely now the Chinese will see that we are earnest in our refusal to bend under the unfair strictures o' these imperial decrees. We are British subjects and American citizens; we *kowtow* before no man—be he *ch'in-ch'ai ta-ch'en* or the emperor himself!"

◆◆◆◆◆

Captain Elliot sincerely expected his demand for passports to scare Lin Tse-hsü and the governor-general into backing down and ending the blockade. He assumed they would not want to see the foreign traders leave China forever, nor would they want to risk war with the English. He was so confident of his position that he went to sleep Sunday night fully expecting the next morning to find the coolie guards disbanded and the barricades removed.

What Elliot and the others discovered was that the noose around their district had, in fact, been tightened. The coolie guards, now deployed right in Factory Square, were marching up and down in front of the arched entrances of the factories. Makeshift bridges now connected the *hong* buildings on one side of Thirteen Factory Street to the foreigners' buildings on the other, and a large contingent of guards had crossed over, taking up positions on the rooftops of the agency houses. And the small fleet of six gunboats had mushroomed into several dozen junks bearing more than three hundred armed soldiers. The boats were anchored in a formation of three concentric arcs, about one hundred feet apart, the first two being made up of large tea boats and the third of smaller chop boats. It was an impressive, impenetrable barrier that all but sealed the foreigners' fate.

It did not take long for the foreigners to comprehend fully their predicament. Not only were they cut off from the outside world, but perhaps most troublesome of all, they were without their vast army of more than eight hundred Chinese servants, who kept the factory district running smoothly. Many of the foreigners had never seen the kitchens of their agency houses, and now they were forced to cook, clean, launder their clothing, and draw enough river water for it all. Drinking water was generally delivered in jars from the city, and they could only pray that this essential supply would not be cut off, as well. And while they were well stocked with beer, coffee, jams, pickles, biscuits, ham, salted beef, and other nonperishable foods brought from England, all fresh meat and produce was purchased locally by their cooks. If the siege should last, the fare at New English and the other factories would be severely restricted.

When the standoff continued for another day, Elliot slowly realized that his show of bluster had failed miserably. His greatest fear was that the eight hundred or so seamen aboard foreign vessels at nearby Whampoa might attack the twelve hundred Chinese guards in an attempt to rescue their fellow countrymen; that, Elliot knew, would prompt the Chinese to retaliate against their hostages. He had to act quickly if he was going to avoid the shedding of blood— quite possibly his own.

Concerned that his request for passports had been worded too sternly, he sent another request to Governor-General Teng in a far more conciliatory tone. When that, too, was met with firm refusal, he begged for an audience but was told that the governor-general was otherwise occupied. The *hong* leaders were also hesitant to meet with him, and he knew that only one person could be behind such an affront. Until now, Elliot had been careful not to confront that person directly, so that neither of them would be pushed into taking a position from which he could not retreat. But now it was becoming all too obvious that Elliot could no longer avoid his real opponent: the *ch'in-ch'ai ta-ch'en.*

This realization was driven home on Tuesday morning, when he and the other foreigners awoke to find large public notices tacked on the factory doors. When the message was translated, they discovered that it was from Lin Tse-hsü, who reaffirmed his order to surrender their opium. The tone was both conciliatory and condescending as it laid out his terms: All of the opium under the control of the foreign merchants—not just the one thousand chests previously turned over—was to be delivered as soon as possible. When the first quarter was received, the servants would return to the factories. When half the chests were handed over, travel between Canton, Whampoa, and Macao would be allowed to resume. The guards and barricades would be removed from the factory district upon receipt of three-quarters of the chests. And when the remaining opium in the Canton region was in the hands of the Chinese authorities, all aspects of the China trade would return to normal.

The notice concluded with a stinging jab at Elliot himself: "If the chief superintendent cannot stop his own English subjects from bringing opium to China and selling it, I would ask what it is that he superintends?"

The next morning, when it was clear that Elliot's deadline for receiving the passports would not be met, he answered Lin's question with a surprising show of authority that took the entire foreign community by surprise. He issued his own edict, not to Lin Tse-hsü or the Chinese, but to the foreign agency houses. The text of the order began:

> Constrained by paramount motives affecting the safety of the lives and liberty of all the foreigners here present in Canton, and by other very weighty causes, I, Charles Elliot, Chief Superintendent of the Trade of British Subjects in China, do hereby in the name and on behalf of Her Britannic Majesty's government enjoin and require all Her Majesty's subjects now present in Canton forthwith to make a surrender to me for the service of Her said Majesty's government, to be delivered over to the government of China,

of all the opium belonging to them, or British
opium under their respective control; and to hold
the British ships and vessels engaged in the trade
of opium subject to my immediate direction.

The edict went on to explain that Elliot, under the
powers vested in him by the Crown, was committing
the British government to reimburse the merchants for
the opium's full value, to be determined at a later date.
Each company was to draw up an inventory of its supply
by six that evening and submit it to Elliot, who then
would assume responsibility for delivering the opium to
the Chinese. Furthermore, any company that failed to list
all of its supply would forfeit any reimbursement due it on
the crates it did surrender.

The edict met with general approval, since any losses
by the agency houses would be covered by the Crown—
and ultimately by the Chinese government, from whom
the Crown undoubtedly would demand reimbursement.
Inventories were quickly assessed, and by six o'clock the
trade superintendent was able to inform Lin Tse-hsü that
he possessed and was prepared to surrender an additional
20,283 chests. This was only on paper, however, with most
of the stock still lying in the holds of ships at anchor at
Whampoa and in the Gulf of Canton. And while Elliot
was pleased at the success of his action and hoped that
it would avert an even more costly war, he realized
he was probably only buying time. For even as the
current stores of opium were being emptied and destroyed,
additional shipments were being packed and loaded aboard
vessels that would soon be on their way to refill the
supply.

As an added measure of security, Charles Elliot
summoned one of the English sailors who had been
trapped in Canton when the Factory District was sealed
up over the weekend. The young man was an officer on

the *Lancet,* and at seven that evening he arrived in full dress uniform at the office of the Superintendency of Trade at Lungshun Factory.

"Lieutenant Ballinger?" the superintendent asked, looking up from some papers he had been reading.

"At your service, sir." Julian gave a brisk salute, which Elliot returned.

"I have a delicate assignment that needs a volunteer." He indicated a chair across the desk to Julian. "You serve on the *Lancet* under Captain ffiske, do you not?"

"Yes, sir."

"Good. I have a message I'd like you to bring to him." He folded the papers in front of him. "I'm afraid that with such a cordon of ships blocking the river, it's going to be a tricky matter to sneak you out. Do you think you're up to it?"

"I'll swim, if I have to."

"I don't think that will be necessary," Elliot assured him. "There are enough Chinese willing to hide a man aboard their boats or in their carts, provided the money is right."

"I can leave whenever you'd like," Julian replied.

"Excellent. I'd like you to go as soon as arrangements are finalized—perhaps within the hour." He poured some sealing wax on the back of the letter and affixed his seal, then handed it to Julian. "You must see to it that this reaches Captain ffiske. I am sending your frigate back to England on urgent business. The letter contains my report and recommendations on the situation here in Canton, along with copies of the various edicts issued against our people by the Chinese government."

"Do you think there'll be war?" Julian asked bluntly, placing the papers in the jacket pocket of his uniform.

Elliot drew in a long breath. "I believe we will escape this current crisis. But within the year, war will come; I am convinced of it."

The superintendent stood and held forth his hand. Julian rose, and the two men shook hands across the desk.

"Get anything you need to take, and meet me here in half an hour," Elliot told him.

The two men saluted a final time, and Julian departed from the room.

"Lieutenant Ballinger," Elliot called after him. "When next I see the *Lancet,* I hope it is with a full British force at its side."

XX

Just over two thousand miles southwest of Canton, a former Royal Navy ship of the line was plowing the storm-tossed waters of the Indian Ocean. In its prime the vessel had been outfitted with seventy-four guns on its two main decks, but five years earlier it had been refitted as a troop transport and now saw most of its service carrying convicts and supplies to various penal colonies, such as those in Van Diemen's Land and New South Wales. Its guns had been reduced to twenty-four, mounted twelve on each side of the top deck, and the lower deck had been refurbished into living quarters for the passengers— or prisoners, as was the case on April 1, 1839, when the vessel was traveling toward the Keeling Islands thirteen hundred miles northwest of the continent of Australia.

Captain Malcolm Finn had charted a course that should have taken them much farther to the south, but they had been driven north by increasingly bad weather, and now he feared they might not make the safety of the islands before the full brunt of the storm hit.

Finn was in his cabin completing a final entry in his ship's log when someone knocked on the door. "Come in," he called.

The chaplain, Newell Proctor, an intelligent-looking but rather slight man of thirty, entered. He was being transferred to New South Wales.

"Yes, what is it, Mr. Proctor?" Finn asked a bit testily, thinking the man had no doubt come to intercede on behalf of a convict. With this storm building, Finn was in no mood to argue rights and conditions aboard his vessel.

"I've been belowdecks, sir," Proctor began cautiously, holding on to the doorjamb to steady himself against the heavy rolling of the ship. "I'm afraid the situation has become untenable."

"So has the weather," Finn muttered, closing his log and rising to leave.

"I understand, but we simply mustn't have men shackled in irons when there's a chance . . ." He looked down, as though afraid to voice his fear.

"A chance we're going down? Not likely," Finn grunted. "This ship and I have seen far worse in the China Sea. Those typhoons make this storm seem a London shower."

"But some of the crew—"

"I don't care what they're saying," Finn snapped, circling the desk and striding to the door. He was an imposing figure with a heavy gray beard and badly broken nose that gave him a deep whine when he spoke. He towered over the chaplain, and he liked to use his size to gain advantage. Placing his hand on the smaller man's shoulder, he gave it a friendly but intentionally sharp squeeze. "Why not go back down there and see that the poor blokes are as comfortable as possible."

"But it's quite impossible."

Just then the boat heaved to starboard, and Proctor was thrown against the doorframe. Finn, however, had no trouble keeping his balance. "What's so impossible?" he challenged.

"The prisoners are sick and getting worse. Many have never been to sea before—"

"They've been at sea these past five months."

"But never in weather like this. Why, they're deathly ill—every last one of them. And with the pitching of this vessel, they're about mad with fright."

"And these are the very men you suggest I set free to go scampering about the ship?" Finn snorted derisively. "And what for? Even if we *did* go down, what good would it do them? We've only six lifeboats and twice as many sailors as they'll hold. If I were to release them from irons, it would be worse than a mutiny. It would be chaos."

"It *is* chaos down there."

"Down *there*," Finn repeated resolutely. "And that's exactly where I plan to contain any trouble. If you don't like it, just stay right here." He stormed from the cabin.

For a moment, Proctor was too stunned to move, other than whatever movement was necessary to keep his balance. Then he marched down the corridor and onto the open deck. The wind was whipping across the ship from the southwest, hitting them in the stern and propelling them far too quickly to the northeast. Proctor knew almost nothing about sailing— this was his first ocean voyage—but it seemed that the captain should be bringing the vessel around, facing it into the wind to ride out the storm. Some of the sailors had spoken of islands nearby that might provide shelter, and Proctor guessed that Finn was making a run for them before the storm reached its peak.

They would have to hurry. Though he was ignorant about sailing, Proctor had studied weather patterns of the world at university. From what he could tell, this was no ordinary ocean storm but a cyclone of perhaps hurricane strength. North of the equator, cyclones rotated around a center of low pressure in a counterclockwise direction, whereas here below the equator they rotated clockwise. A cyclone advancing from the south, as this storm was doing, would strike them with southwesterly winds. And if Proctor was right about the intensity of the storm, those winds would increase dramatically in the next hour or so, bringing heavy rains and even higher seas.

The chaplain staggered across the deck toward the stern, fighting the drenching, wind-whipped spray. With some difficulty he found one of the hatches used to gain entry to the lower deck, but this particular hatch was closed. He signaled a nearby crewman to help him open the cover.

Proctor descended the ladder and was almost overcome by the stench, an ungodly mixture of sweat, urine, and vomit. The old gunports had been closed off, leaving almost no ventilation, and the air was so thick and cloying that he gagged. He stood for a moment at the bottom, trying to steady his breathing and calm his churning stomach— trying not to be overwhelmed by the piteous wailing of the poor souls trapped in this godforsaken hell.

As he always did when he visited belowdecks, Proctor gave a silent prayer, then smiled as best he could and started across the deck. Whereas the fore section of the lower deck had been divided into smaller compartments, each housing a half-dozen or so soldiers, the aft had been left a single compartment designed to house seventy-five prisoners. On this voyage, however, it held twice that number. They were lying directly on the deck on hard straw pallets, with only a few inches for passage between them. Heavy metal rings were bolted in four rows the length of the deck, with a weighty chain laced through the rings and through iron cuffs on the convicts' right ankles.

At least five guards were usually on duty, but all available hands had been called on deck, so only one was left below, a burly sailor named Merrick who had a reputation for taking pleasure in his work. The prisoners were too frightened of him to make an official complaint, but on several occasions they had confided to the chaplain about Merrick's sadistic penchant for buggery. Proctor had voiced his concerns about the man to Captain Finn on several occasions, but he had never been able to catch Merrick in the act.

Merrick was seated at the guards' table at the foot of the main ladder that led to the upper deck. He frowned at the chaplain, then went back to what he was doing, which appeared to be nothing.

For the next fifteen minutes, Proctor moved among the convicts, comforting those who would let him or merely bringing water to those suffering the worst. It was obvious that many of the men were dehydrated; a number had already succumbed to the effects of diarrhea and had been buried unceremoniously at sea. Others were delirious, moaning or calling out in fear and pain. The ones who concerned Proctor the most were the men who just lay on their backs, staring up at the swaying planks overhead, their eyes open but seeming lifeless.

Despite the cacophony of the prisoners, Proctor could feel the storm gaining power. The wind was howling now, accompanied by the steady pounding of driving rain. The deck was pitching and rolling so furiously that it was almost impossible to stand or walk, so he crawled up and down the narrow aisles between the pallets, speaking or praying with some, holding the hands of others, trying to comfort them with his presence.

"Don't worry yourself with me," one of the convicts muttered when the chaplain came near. "I've seen worse— far worse."

Proctor placed a hand on the man's thin, pale arm. He was one of the older ones—in his fifties, at least—with white hair and beard and intensely gray eyes.

"Were you in the navy?" Proctor asked.

The man shook his head. "Spent my time at Millbank."

"And that was worse than this?"

"Yes . . . being so near home, yet unable to be with my family. Out here, it's like I'm already gone." The convict closed his eyes.

"What's your name?" Proctor asked.

"Does it matter?"

"It does to me."

The man looked up at the young chaplain. "Yes, I believe it does," he whispered.

"I'm Newell Proctor," the chaplain offered with a pleasant smile. "I've been in the navy for ten years, but this is my first time at sea."

"I wasn't in the navy," the convict replied, "but I spent my youth on merchant ships from the Indies to China. This'll be my first time to Australia—if we make land."

"Don't you think we will?"

"Not if he doesn't bring this wreck around."

A moment later, a deep, ominous tremor ran up the spine of the hull. The ship seemed to lift right out of the water and hang there; then it dropped back down and heaved mightily to one side. Proctor's face went white, and many of the men screamed.

The white-haired convict reached up and gripped the chaplain's upper arm. "He must've heard me. He's trying to bring her around."

The ship rocked violently, and then there was an explosion of thunder, followed by a shuddering snap that felt as if the vessel had split in two.

"The mast!" someone yelled, and the others frantically took up the cry. Those who were fit enough sat up or struggled onto their hands and knees, shouting for someone—anyone—to undo their chains and give them a chance to survive.

Scrambling to his feet, Proctor staggered down the aisle toward Merrick. Some of the prisoners clawed at his legs, beseeching him to help them, and he had to swat their hands away. The ship rolled so far to starboard that it almost capsized, then came rolling back to the other side. Proctor was knocked off his feet several times, but he managed to get back up and fight his way across the deck.

Merrick was already standing, looking about wildly as if he expected the ship to break up at any minute. When Proctor stumbled over to him, he said, "Up top—better get up top!"

"The prisoners!" Proctor called back, shouting above the din of thunder and splitting wood. "We've got to unlock their chains!"

"The hell you say!" Merrick shouted back at him, dashing over to the ladder.

Proctor went after him, grabbing the back of his jacket and spinning him around. "The keys!" he yelled. "Give me the keys!"

Merrick pushed the chaplain away and clambered up the ladder to the closed hatch above. As he reached for it, Proctor grasped his ankle, pulling him back down. With a furious oath, Merrick tried to jerk his leg free, but Proctor held on, climbing the ladder behind him.

The boat took another roll to starboard, and Proctor lost his footing, but he managed to cling to Merrick's leg, pulling the big man's feet off the ladder. Merrick hung from the rungs, trying to keep his grip, but as the ship rolled back the other way, his hands slipped, and he fell hard on the deck, his head striking the planks with a sickening thud.

Proctor pushed himself free of the man and lay there catching his breath, waiting to see if Merrick would get up. But he didn't; he was either unconscious or dead. Proctor didn't bother trying to figure out which but instead rolled him onto his back and started going through his coat. The key ring was in one of the front pockets, and Proctor grabbed it and raced over to the hall, where several deck chains were secured to a heavy ring.

There were two padlocks on the chains, and he fumbled with the half-dozen keys until he found one that opened the first. He yanked it off the chains, then started working on the second lock. As he was trying one of the keys, the ship lurched violently, its stern rising up at an almost forty-five-degree angle. Proctor lost his footing and grabbed hold of a chain to keep from being thrown across the deck. All around him, prisoners were shrieking as they slid off their pallets, their shackles jerking against the chains and keeping them from sliding toward the sinking bow of the ship.

With a wrenching groan, the bow came back up, and the ship leveled off slightly. Letting go of the chain, Proctor scrambled to his knees and reached for the remaining padlock, only to discover that he was no longer holding the key ring. He looked around frantically, checking the locks and chains, but it was gone.

As he scurried around the deck, searching for the missing ring, he could not help but wonder if this was all but a futile gesture. After all, there would be no lifeboats for the prisoners, even if they did manage to gain their freedom. But he could not bear to think of so many poor souls plunging helplessly to their deaths. He would rather they went down fighting; and maybe a few could survive by clinging to pieces of the ship, which was breaking up now in the heavy waves.

An excited shout came from one of the men, who stood and waved the key ring. He tossed it over to Proctor, who dashed back to where the chains were secured to the hull and hurriedly tested the keys, finally finding the one that fit. Jerking the lock open, he pulled the chains free, and immediately the men started feeding them through the deck rings and ankle cuffs. As the chains snaked around the deck, the freed prisoners charged the ladders and poured onto the upper deck.

The ship tossed and pitched, and the stern slowly rose up again. It was clearly sinking now, for water poured into the compartment and flooded the forward end of the deck. Proctor fought the incline as he raced from pallet to pallet, rousing the prisoners who were too weak to stand. He felt someone tugging at his arm; it was the white-haired convict, urging the chaplain to give up his efforts and head up top.

"Go! Save yourself!" Proctor yelled at him, the water

swirling around his ankles now. It was already several rungs up the main ladder; Merrick's body had floated away.

"You've done enough—!"

"Go!" Proctor shouted again, pushing the convict toward the ladder at the stern.

A few feet away, one of the sick prisoners rolled off his pallet and slid toward the forward end of the deck. Proctor scrambled after him, grabbing his arms and pulling him away from the water that was rapidly flooding the compartment. Glancing up, he saw the white-haired man caught in the crush of people at the sternmost ladder, which was still well out of the water. The convict looked back at Proctor, and for a moment their eyes locked, and then he gained the ladder and was gone.

As Graham Maginnis scrambled through the hatch onto the deck of the *Weymouth,* he was hit by a cold blast of wind and spray that almost knocked him off his feet. The stern rail was about ten feet away, and he crawled up to it and joined a half-dozen other convicts who were holding on, looking down at the sinking ship. The deck was pitched at an almost thirty-degree angle, while the bow was already underwater.

Graham guessed it was about noon, but it was almost as dark as night, the only illumination the near-constant flashes of lightning. He could see that the mainmast had been split and charred by one of the bolts, and there was considerable damage toward the bow; either they had struck something or had broken up in the waves. He pulled himself up on the rail and looked out over the sea, where the waves were at least fifteen feet high. Something was bobbing on top of them—a lifeboat, which looked to be dangerously overloaded. As he watched, a huge wave broke over the little boat, capsizing it and tossing all of the sailors into the churning sea.

There was a commotion down near where the deck was sinking under the pounding waves. Graham could make out what was probably the last of the lifeboats; it had been cut from its davits and dragged down along the deck, and a crowd of sailors was trying to launch it. Not only were the waves threatening to capsize it, but as the convicts poured up from belowdecks, they rushed the boat and attacked the seamen, clawing and beating at them in a desperate attempt to save themselves. Two convicts near Graham at the stern rail also saw the lifeboat, and they let go and slid down the deck, joining the riot.

Knowing there was no hope of saving himself in such a mob, Graham searched the deck for another means of escape, his gaze finally settling on the large cover of the hatch from which he had emerged. Apparently it had broken free from one of its hinges in the crush of prisoners clambering over it, and it hung precariously from the remaining hinge. He took a last look at the lifeboat and in the flashing lightning saw that it was launched—with close to a hundred men hanging all over it. But even as he watched, the vessel capsized, and they were thrown into the raging sea.

Graham let go of the rail and slid down the deck, working his way to the hatch. The flow of escaping convicts had halted; only the dead and dying were left below. Graham jammed one foot against the edge of the hatch to steady himself and grabbed hold of the cover to twist it free. It was quite heavy, and though he could bend the hinge, he was unable to break it loose.

He looked around for something to give him leverage but saw only the water creeping closer up the deck. Most of the others were gone now; those still alive were clinging to whatever scrap of wood they could find, bobbing up and down in the water. The few who remained on deck were working at breaking loose anything that might float.

Graham considered getting someone to help him, but then he glanced through the hatch and saw the chaplain

kneeling up to his waist in water at the foot of the
ladder, his arms hooked through the rungs as he prayed.
Graham shouted down at him, calling his name over and
over until finally the man looked up. It took a few moments for him to react, but then he pulled himself upright
and climbed the ladder.

"I—I can't swim!" he shouted into Graham's ear.

"Quick!" Graham yelled back, pointing at the hatch
cover and motioning what had to be done. Newell Proctor
understood at once, and the two men took hold of the cover
and slowly twisted it off its remaining hinge.

Struggling together, they dragged the makeshift raft to
the starboard rail, then slid it down the steeply angled deck.
As they neared the water, Graham signaled that they would
have to toss the raft over the rail and leap after it if they
wanted to keep from being pounded against the deck by the
waves. They started to lift the heavy cover, but not before
two men came scrambling down the deck toward them.

Graham knew there would be trouble; at best, the cover
would hold two, possibly three. The two convicts did not
seem to care that Graham and the chaplain had done all
the work, for without warning the bigger man attacked,
knocking the chaplain to the deck and pulling away the
cover. Graham was no match for the two younger convicts,
and he stood by helplessly as they hoisted the cover over
the rail and prepared to jump. He knew that he could make
the jump with them, but he doubted they would allow him
on board. Instead, he let go of the rail and slid down the
deck to where the chaplain was lying stunned near the edge
of the crashing waves.

Graham grasped the young man around the chest and
braced himself as the *Weymouth* slipped ever more quickly
below the surface. A wave crashed against their legs, and he
hung on to the chaplain, trying to summon a suitable prayer.
All he could think of was his wife's lullaby, and in a halting
voice, he sang:

"Now suck, child, and sleep, child, thy mother's
sweet joy.
    Sing lullaby lully.
The gods bless and keep thee from cruel annoy.
    Sing lully, lully, sweet baby, lully."

The next wave pounded them against the deck, then lifted them clear of the ship and spilled them into the cold sea. Sputtering for air, Graham fought to keep his head above water, all the while clasping the chaplain to him. But Proctor jerked free and began flailing wildly, his head dipping beneath the churning waves as he raged against death. Graham felt himself being pulled under and held his breath, still trying to find the younger man. For an instant their hands met, and then the chaplain was gone.

Graham struggled back to the surface, took another gulp of air, and went under, knowing it would only be a few moments before he, too, was swallowed by the sea. He tried to conjure an image of his wife and son and the daughter he had never seen. He tried to let go, to breathe in the cold, death-giving water, but his body was not yet willing to give in, and it beat at the ocean, forcing him up again for air.

As his head broke the surface, his arm smacked something heavy and solid. Unable to see what it was, he groped at it, trying to gain a secure hold. It felt like a large piece of wood, and with great effort he pulled himself partway onto it.

With his chest flattened against the wood and the bottom half of his body still floating in the water, he clung to the raft, riding out the brunt of the storm. He did not dare move but just hung there for what seemed like hours, counting the waves as the wind slowly lessened and the clouds started to part.

When at last he could make out his surroundings, he was shocked to discover that he was clinging to the very hatch cover he had tried to use as a raft. And he was not alone; lying asleep or unconscious on the far side of the cover was the bigger of the two convicts who had stolen it away—the one who had hurt Newell Proctor. His partner was nowhere around. In fact, nothing was in sight for as far as Graham could see, save for a few floating, unmanned remnants of the sunken ship.

The convict seemed unaware that someone was holding on to his raft, and for a moment Graham debated whether or not to attack him first. But then it was too late, for the man rolled over and saw him. For a long moment they stared at each other, the young man rising to his hands and knees, Graham still floating half in the water. Then the convict peered out at the desolate seascape and shook his head in dismay. Apparently he thought better of finishing off the intruder—or perhaps he considered the older convict a potential source of nourishment should things become desperate—for he crawled across the large hatch door, grabbed hold of Graham's forearms, and hauled him on board.

"Jus' you an me, mate," was all he said as he lay back down, the water lapping gently over the surface of the raft.

◆◆◆

It had been a difficult night aboard the frigate *Chatham* as the ship was tossed about by wind and high seas. But as morning approached, the weather grew considerably calmer, the big storm off to the south apparently having veered away.

Connor Maginnis had slept fitfully, and he woke at dawn and lay listening to the waves against the ship's hull. He wondered if his father's transport had already reached Australia, and he prayed that the *Weymouth* had been nowhere near the vicinity of the storm. Connor did not yet have a plan for what he would do once he found his father; something was driving him onward, and he'd figure out a course of action when the time came.

Rolling onto his side, he gazed at Zoë Ballinger, lying with her back pressed against him. The bed was really too narrow for two, but it suited them perfectly, and they never tired of being in each other's arms.

"Zoë," he whispered, not to waken her but simply to hear the sound of her name. He touched her long, auburn hair, let the curls fall through his fingers, then slid his hand under the blankets and down along her bare shoulder and arm, feeling the curve of her waist and hips.

Zoë moaned gently and leaned back against him, her hand reaching around and touching his leg. Neither of them had on any nightclothes; they had worn them the first night but since then had not even bothered with any pretense of propriety.

Connor was accustomed to women who were plumper than Zoë, for his upper-class patronesses adhered to the common prejudice that excess weight was a sign of wealth, then spent much of their time corseting that fat into a more fashionable shape. But it had only taken him moments that first night out of Portsmouth to discover how incredibly beautiful his new lover was. She had no need of a corset, for her body was muscular, yet soft and exquisitely curved. And she took such warm delight in their passion, that each time they made love, it was as if it were their first.

With a gentle sigh, Zoë rolled over and faced him, her hands slipping behind his head and pulling him to her. His lips sought her neck, and she nibbled at his ear, then whispered, "I missed you last night."

"I was here—all night long," he replied, his lips searching, caressing.

"Yes, but I wanted you so badly."

"But the storm . . ."

"I know," she breathed, her fingers laced through his dark, tangled hair.

"It's over now," he told her, his hand cupping, kneading her breast, his tongue tracing the curve from the base of her neck to the hardened tip of her nipple.

"No, Connor, it isn't." Her fingers dug into his back. "I can feel the storm rising. . . ."

Pulling him on top of her, she wrapped her legs around his hips and drew him in, opening to his passion as she gave cry to her own.

◆◆◆

Later that morning, when the young couple emerged on the deck as Mr. and Mrs. Connor Maginnis, they were surprised to discover land in sight. "Australia!" Connor declared, hurrying to the ship's bow.

"No. Java," corrected a sailor, his arm stretched toward the vast sweep of rugged hillsides and densely forested volcanic mountains.

The passengers soon learned that the cyclone to the south had driven them off course. The sails and rudder had suffered some damage, and Captain Archibald Gaunt had decided that they would head for Batavia on the northwest coast of Java, where they could make repairs and take on supplies before completing the voyage to Sydney.

The next morning, the *Chatham* entered the deep-water harbor at Batavia. It was the first landfall the ship had made since India, and the passengers were delighted to be able to go ashore and wander around. The flavor of the bustling town was quite Dutch, with numerous canals, drawbridges, and Dutch-style homes. The East Indies had come under Dutch control in 1610, when they ousted the Portuguese. That rule had remained unchallenged except from 1811 to 1814, when the islands were occupied by the English during the Napoleonic Wars. Batavia itself had been the headquarters of the powerful Dutch East India Company until the company was liquidated in 1799, and it was still the largest city in the region.

After visiting the Portuguese Church, completed by the Dutch in 1695 and housing an enormous pump organ, Connor and Zoë had a pleasant lunch at an inn that looked out on Sunda Kelapa, the Javanese name for the harbor. It was during lunch that they overheard some British sailors at a nearby table discussing the situation in Canton, where the foreign community was under siege by the Chinese authorities. With Zoë's cousin Ross representing the Ballinger Trade Company in Canton, she was naturally concerned, and she asked Connor to find out as much information as he could.

He joined the sailors for a few minutes, then returned to the small table where Zoë was sitting. "Apparently the Chinese want to end all trading of opium in their country. The merchants—your cousin included, I suppose—" he tried to mask his distaste for the other Ballingers "—have refused to comply with an order to surrender all their stores of it."

"But Ballinger Trade doesn't deal in opium."

Connor chose not to argue the point; he had heard enough about the China trade during the voyage to know that virtually every company doing business there was involved at some level or another. He also did not want to get into a discussion of Ballinger Trade, knowing how sensitive the topic was to Zoë. Instead, he leaned across the table, took her hand, and said, "There's been no violence—at least up until the time those sailors' ship was dispatched to England."

"That's where they're headed?" she asked.

"Yes. Their frigate is on its way to London to report on the situation and bring back reinforcements."

"Warships?" she said hesitantly.

"If the Chinese don't back down, it looks like war."

"My God," she muttered, tears coming to her eyes.

"Now, don't be worrying about your cousin. He's just a merchant. They're putting pressure on the merchants, but any fighting will be done with the Royal Navy."

"That's what I'm afraid of," she explained. "My brother . . . he's in the navy."

"Oh, yes. But he's in Calcutta."

"But if they're sending for help, the *Lancet* could be reassigned—"

"Lancet?" he interrupted. "Your brother's on the *Lancet*?"

"Yes. Why?"

"Those sailors—their ship is the *Lancet*."

Zoë gripped his hands. "The *Lancet*? In Java?"

"They've put in for supplies; they sail in the morning for England."

"My God! Julian . . . here in Batavia!"

An hour later, they were being ushered aboard the *Lancet,* which sat at anchor on the far side of the harbor from the *Chatham*. They had already decided that for the time being they would not tell Julian what had happened back in London but would continue their pretense of being married and on a honeymoon journey to see Connor's father in Australia—leaving unsaid that his father was a convict.

Julian Ballinger had no warning that his sister was boarding the ship, and when he saw her racing across the deck, he almost fainted with shock. As she ran into his arms, he swept her into the air and spun her around, lowering her slowly back down and kissing her tenderly.

"Good God, little sister, what are you doing here?"

"You'll never believe what's happened!" she exclaimed. Grabbing his hand, she pulled him over to where Connor was standing. "Julian, I want you to meet my husband, Connor Maginnis."

"Husband?" he asked incredulously, looking back and forth between them. "I thought you and Bertie . . ."

"Oh, he was just a friend," she said, waving her hand as if dismissing the entire Cummington family. "But I've finally met someone and fallen in love."

Julian looked down at his sister. "Yes, but marriage—and so abrupt—"

"No it isn't. You've been away."

"I guess I have!" he declared. Forcing a smile, he turned back to Connor and held out his hand. "Pleased to meet you . . . Connor, is it?"

"Yes," he replied a bit curtly, trying to remind himself that this man whose hand he was shaking was not just Austin Ballinger's younger brother but Zoë's kin, as well.

"I want to hear all about it—everything," Julian declared, wrapping his arm around his sister and leading her and Connor to the rear deck.

"What about Ross? Have you seen him?"

"That I have, and he's fine. At least he was until that bad piece of business started up in Canton."

"What do you mean? What's wrong? Has something happened to him?"

"Slow down," he urged, squeezing her shoulder. "Why don't we sit down over there"—he indicated some benches by the stern rail—"and I'll tell you all about it. And you can tell me how you two met and managed to convince Mother and Father to let you get married—and what, for God's sake, you're doing in Java."

Zoë came to a halt halfway across the deck and looked up at her brother. "I must know—is Ross all right?"

"He's fine—he's a guest of the Catholic mission just now. And by the time I get back, I'm sure this whole thing will've blown over."

"But that could be months—a year, even."

"No. We're heading back tomorrow."

"To Canton?" Connor asked. "We'd heard you were going to England for reinforcements."

"The captain has changed our orders. Another frigate just arrived—the *Chatham*. It's shallower draft and faster, so it will carry our messages to the Crown, while we return to Canton."

"But that's our ship," Zoë told him.

"It's taking us to Sydney," Connor added.

"I'm afraid not. Our captains met a short while ago, and it's all been arranged. The *Chatham* sails for England tomorrow, and we return to Canton."

"But my father . . ." The words trailed off, and Connor shook his head and looked out at the harbor.

Eyeing the two of them closely, Julian asked Zoë, "What's all this about? What's going on?"

Zoë looked over at Connor, who gave her a hesitant nod. "Let's sit down," she said, indicating the benches by the stern rail. "There's quite a bit to tell."

Connor remained at the rail as Zoë sat beside her brother and recited the full story of how she and Connor had met and the reason for their journey, starting with the relationship between Connor's family and their own. Though she made it clear that she had seen evidence implicating Edmund Ballinger in framing his former partner, she was careful not to mention the recent acts of violence against Connor and Graham Maginnis—or their own brother and father's involvement in it all. She merely said that Graham Maginnis's sentence had been changed and he was being sent to a penal colony in New South Wales.

It was when Zoë said they were following the *Weymouth* to Sydney that Julian interrupted her: "The *Weymouth*? You mean the convict ship?"

"Yes. That's the one Connor's father is on."

"But the *Weymouth* . . . haven't you heard?"

"Heard what?" Connor asked. He went to where they were sitting.

Julian stood and faced him. "I'm afraid, Mr. Maginnis, that the *Weymouth* went down in a storm three days ago, just west of the Keeling Islands."

"Went down?" Connor whispered, his face paling with shock. "Are you sure?"

Julian grasped Connor's arm. "We got word this morning. Only one lifeboat of sailors was picked up— the captain and the rest of the crew were lost."

"The convicts—what about the convicts?"

Julian frowned. "They were chained belowdecks. I'm afraid they all went down with the ship."

"Bastards!" Connor blurted, as much at Julian and all the Ballingers as at the fates and the corrupt system that had sent Graham Maginnis and dozens of other poor, imprisoned souls to their death. Pulling his arm free, he stalked away across the deck.

Julian started after him, but Zoë held him back. "Let him be," she breathed. "He needs to be alone."

◆━━━◆━━━◆

Before dawn on the third morning following the sinking of the naval transport ship *Weymouth*, Graham Maginnis awoke to the sound of waves lapping against shore. Raising himself up on his hands and knees on the hatch cover, he cocked his head and listened. Had they truly reached land or was it just a trick of the imagination after nearly three days without food or water?

"Ridley! Listen!" he cried, jostling the leg of the young convict who shared the raft.

Groaning, the man named Ridley pushed himself up.

"Do you hear it?" Graham asked, poking him some more.

"Wha' the hell?"

"Land! I hear land!"

It was the coastline of a small island, and as dawn broke, they pulled the raft up onto it. They had drifted ashore near a large, cultivated field, and it was quite possible that they were on British soil, perhaps somewhere along the west coast of Australia.

Not wishing to be taken back into custody, they hid the raft among some brush and set out to explore the area. Almost immediately they found a small stream and for several long minutes lay on their stomachs, drinking it in. Having gone without food for almost three days—and not having been given much on board ship before that—they were starving. So when they came upon a small clapboard farmhouse, Ridley insisted they break in and take what food they could find. Graham was not eager to be seen by anyone, especially since each of them still wore an iron cuff around his right ankle, but Ridley would not be dissuaded. Realizing he could not stop the younger, bigger man, Graham reluctantly went along.

The two men crept up to the farmhouse and peered though the front window. Inside was a modestly furnished little parlor and what appeared to be a kitchen beyond it. Trying the window, they found it unlocked and pulled it open, then climbed inside.

Passing through the open doorway to the kitchen, Graham rummaged through the cupboards and shelves. Ridley found a loaf of bread in a box on the counter and tore off a hunk, jamming it into his mouth. Reluctantly he handed the loaf to Graham, who also took a piece and put it back on the counter.

Gathering some things to take with them, they heard the sound of footsteps, and then a middle-aged man appeared through the doorway dressed in long underwear and slippers and wearing gold wire-rimmed glasses. He saw Graham standing in the middle of the kitchen, but before he could say a word, Ridley jumped him from the side, knocking him to the floor and pinning his arms behind his back. "Gimme somethin' to tie him with!" he hissed up at Graham. When the older convict did not immediately comply, he blurted, "Some rope or a towel! Now!"

Graham pulled a large linen cloth from the table and tossed it to Ridley.

"Let me up!" the man shouted.

Ridley tied his hands, yanked him up off the floor, and slapped him hard across the face. "Shut up wi' you!" he yelled as he slammed the man down onto one of the chairs at the table.

The commotion brought the man's wife, and Ridley met her at the door, a kitchen knife in his hand. He didn't tie her up but pushed her back against the counter, his eyes widening at the sight of her breasts heaving beneath her nightgown as she gasped with fear. She was a big woman and not at all attractive, but she was the first woman Ridley had touched in more than five years.

"Anyone else here?" he demanded, twisting her arm cruelly.

"N-No!" she gasped, staring wide-eyed beyond him to where her husband was slumped half-conscious over the table. "No one!"

"Go check!" Ridley ordered Graham. "Go!"

Graham hurried back through the other rooms. There was only one bedroom, and sitting beside the double bed was a cradle with an infant in it. Graham looked down at the sleeping child and shook his head in dismay. Then he returned to the kitchen.

"Just the two of them," he lied, praying that the baby would not start crying.

"Good," Ridley exclaimed. He wasn't holding the woman anymore but was still threatening her with the knife. Her husband had regained his senses, and he looked on in horror.

"We've got enough food," Graham said, trying to step between Ridley and the woman. "Let's get out of here."

"We can't leave 'em," the convict grunted. "They'll just send someone after us."

"Let her alone . . . they've done nothing," Graham urged, trying to keep his voice calm.

Ridley turned on him, pressing the tip of the knife to the older man's chest. "You want a piece o' this, too?" Sneering, he raised his other hand and shoved Graham to one side. He stepped closer to the woman and declared, "I'll bet *you* want a piece."

"You can't do this," Graham protested, circling the big man. He could see that the husband, despite his hands being tied, was preparing to launch himself at Ridley. Graham signaled the man to hold off. "We can't hurt these people," he told Ridley as he eased his way toward the far counter.

"Why the hell not? What are they gonna do? Send us to Australia?" With a sneer, he grabbed the front of the woman's nightgown, held the knife to it, and slashed open the neckline several inches. "This tart is gonna taste a piece o' me, and then she and her man'll taste a piece o' this knife!"

Ridley cut away more of the material, his eyes fixing on the woman's bare breasts as he took another step closer and pulled her toward him. Suddenly he jerked upright, his back stiffening with a stab of pain. Releasing the woman, he spun around, his legs collapsing beneath him. He dropped hard to his knees.

Standing a few feet away, his right hand extended, Graham held a long-bladed knife, which was dripping blood all over the floor. Faintly in the distance, the baby started to cry.

"Damn!" Ridley blurted between short, gurgling gasps as blood dribbled from his mouth. He tried to raise his arm, to bring his own knife into play, but his fingers opened numbly, and the blade clattered to the floor. "D-Damn . . ." he sputtered a final time, then fell forward, the life going out of him in a final sigh.

Graham did not move; he stared down at the other convict for what seemed like hours. Finally someone shook him, and he looked up to see the man and woman pulling him over to the table and sitting him down. Some time had indeed passed, for the woman had put on a robe over her torn nightgown and was cradling the infant in her arms.

Graham did not try to get away; he knew that he could face the gallows or worse, but the fight was gone from him. *Whatever they do, let it be over with quickly,* he prayed. *At last let this nightmare end.*

"We've no intention of turning you in," the husband said, realizing what Graham was thinking.

"Not after what you've done for us," the woman added, gently rocking the baby. "You're welcome to stay as long as you'd like—until you figure out what you want to do and where you want to go."

"But I . . . I'm . . ." He looked up at them, his eyes revealing his long years of desperation.

"We know what you are," the man said. "You're from the *Weymouth,* aren't you?"

"How did you know?"

The man pointed at the iron cuff on Graham's right ankle. "One lifeboat was picked up. The survivors reported that all the others had drowned."

The couple introduced themselves as Jacob and Claudie Hare, and then Graham and Jacob dragged Ridley's body outside and buried him on a remote hillock down near the water. As they worked, Jacob explained that they were on one of the Keeling Islands, a pair of atolls that had been settled thirteen years ago by Jacob's uncle, Alexander Hare, and a group of Malay seamen under the command of a Scotsman named John Clunies-Ross. It was a seldom-visited outpost that survived on the production of dried coconut meat, which was shipped back to England and used to make coconut oil.

When they were finished, Jacob sat Graham down at the kitchen table and sawed off the ankle cuff, declaring him a free man. "No one will be looking for Graham Maginnis," he explained. "He died in the wreck of the *Weymouth,* the first day of April, 1839."

"But how will you explain my turning up here?"

"No one asks questions much in these parts," Jacob assured him. "You'll spend some time here with Claudie and me, and then in a few weeks or so we'll say that you're a distant relation who came to visit on one of the merchant ships that put in."

"You'll need a new name, and papers," Claudie pointed out.

"I can arrange for the papers," Jacob offered. "As for the name, we'd better still call you Graham, since that's what you're used to."

Graham shook his head. "There aren't names at Millbank Prison. I was Number Eighty-four Fourteen."

Claudie moved up behind him and laid her hand on his shoulder. "Then that's what we'll call you."

"Eighty-four Fourteen?" he said dubiously.

"No. From now on your name is Millbank. Mr. Graham Millbank." She playfully stroked his beard. "Now let's get you washed up, your hair trimmed, and that godforsaken beard shaved off. When I'm through with you, Mr. Millbank, you'll look like a West Indies trader, born and bred."

Graham grinned, then started to chuckle. "That's what I was," he declared, his eyes filling with tears. "Before I was brought down by the treachery of a friend, that's precisely what I was—a China and West Indies trader!"

That evening, Graham Maginnis stood alone on a bluff above the water, looking across the Indian Ocean to where the sun was just reaching the horizon. The water was incredibly calm, an inky blue touched with fingers of orange, yellow, and red. It was a shimmering hand that seemed to reach out to him, calling him from so many thousands of miles across the ocean, reminding him that one day he must return.

"Yes, I'll come home to you, Connor and Emeline," he vowed. Picking up a stone, he tossed it out over the water and heard it break the surface. His jaw set, and his hands clenched into fists. "And I'll come home to you, too, Edmund Ballinger. I shall return to England and have my revenge."

XXI

━━━━━━━━━━━━━━━━━━━━━━━━━━

*On shore a man's ability is measured by
his archery and his horsemanship, but a sailor's
talent by his ability to fight with and on the water.
A sailor must know the winds and the clouds, and
the lands and the lines. He must be thoroughly
versed in breaking a spear with [beating against]
the wind. He must know, like a god, how to
break through the billows, handle his ship, and
be all in regular order for action. Then, when
his spears are thrown, they will pierce, and his
guns will follow to give them effect. The spitting
tornadoes of the fire-physic [gunpowder] will all
reach truly their mark; and whenever pirates are
met with, they will be vanquished wondrously. No
aim will miss its mark. The pirate bandits will
be impoverished and crippled, and even on the
high seas, when they take to flight, they will be
followed and caught and slaughtered. Thus the
monsters of the deep and the waves will be still,
and the sea become a perfect calm, not a ripple
will be raised.*

—Emperor Tao-kuang, in the official court

record, the *Peking Gazette,* on the 17th
day, 9th moon, 13th year of his reign.

Ross Ballinger and Fray Luis Nadal stood at the bow
of the *ta-ping ch'uan,* or "large soldier-boat," a typical war
junk with its flat bottom, high stern, square bow, and large
lugsails. With a length of one hundred twenty-five feet and
width at the beam of twenty-six feet, it was one of the
larger ships in the emperor's Imperial Navy. It was painted
red and black, adorned with a pair of large eyes at the
bow, and carried three twelve-pound and three nine-pound
cannons on each side and another nine-pounder centered at
the stern.

Ross leaned against the rail and watched as a crew
of about forty sailors hoisted an enormous lugsail up the
mainmast. Narrower in the front than the back and weighing
almost three tons, it was made of tightly woven matting
and supported by horizontal bamboo battens. The foresail,
which already had been raised and was almost as large, was
suspended from an equally high mast. The smaller mizzen
sail at the rear was on a thirty-foot mast. All three masts
were made of Foochow pine, but the mainmast had the
distinction of being decorated with strips of red paper that
bore good-luck messages in flowing calligraphy, such as
"May this mast scorn the tempest," "May fair winds blow
from every side of the compass," and "This mast is like a
general commanding ten thousand soldiers."

Gazing over the water, Luis commented, "We should
make Batavia in another day. It ought to be a simple matter
to find a vessel bound for England."

"What about the women?" Ross asked, facing the rail.
"Do you think questions will be raised?"

"I've brought along a habit for Lin Mei-li; she will
be just another sister from our mission, joining me on a
pilgrimage to Rome, via London. I doubt they'll even be
noticed under their wimples."

The two men continued to speak until a Chinese officer approached them, bowed, and spoke to Luis, who nodded and thanked him. As the officer departed, Luis told Ross, "Mei-li would like to see you."

Taking his leave, Ross made his way along the deck to one of the closed galleries just forward from the stern, where quarters had been set up for the niece of the *ch'in ch'ai ta-ch'en* and her fellow travelers. Entering the outer cabin, which served as a sitting room, Ross bowed to the naval officer on guard just inside, then crossed to a grouping of black-lacquer chairs, where the two Chinese women were seated. Sister Carmelita was in her black habit, while Mei-li wore a traditional robe of blue silk with purple trim over short black trousers. They had just finished having tea, and Ross wondered if the nun had again told Mei-li's fortune.

Mei-li was clearly delighted to see him, though her eyes also betrayed a note of concern. Sensing it at once and also noticing the nun's somber expression, Ross asked if anything was wrong.

"We not going to England," Mei-li proclaimed.

Ross looked at her curiously. For a brief moment he thought that she must have been told something by the admiral of the ship, but then he said, "It's something Sister Carmelita saw, isn't it?"

She nodded. "Sister Carmelita not see us reach England."

"Something's going to happen along the way?"

Mei-li shrugged. "We will turn back, that is certain. She see us returning to Canton."

"But why? Are you sure she doesn't mean after we get to London?"

"No. She say we not even make Java. We turn back because our destiny is in China."

"*Our* destiny? Mine also?"

"I always know that, since first moment I saw you,

My uncle realize it, as well. He thought you could make this journey to England and then return to China, but Sister Carmelita say, 'To cross great water, he must first pass through darkening of the light and ascend mountain.' "

Ross remembered the conversation in the governor-general's garden with Mei-li, Lin Tse-hsü, and Fray Luis Nadal. "Your uncle also spoke of a mountain, didn't he? What mountain? Where is it?"

"It has many names. Some call it Cold Mountain, others know it as Keeping-Still Mountain. It is not on any map; you must find it yourself."

"But that's ridiculous. Surely people know—"

"It is *your* destiny, Ross, not mine."

Mei-li lowered her eyes, her expression so unsettling that he wanted to reach out and take her hand. Forcing himself to maintain the expected decorum, he asked, "And what is *your* destiny? What did she tell you?"

"Me?" She glanced nervously at the nun, who with her eyes closed seemed either asleep or deep in thought. "She not speak about me—just that we return to Canton because it not time yet for you to leave."

"She told you something about your future, didn't she?" he pressed.

"Today? No, I promise." Again she averted her eyes.

"Not today. That first day we met. She read your leaves and told you something that disturbed you, didn't she?" When Mei-li did not reply, he asked, "What did she tell you?"

The young woman drew in a breath and, closing her eyes, let it out slowly. At last she gave a faint smile and looked back up at him. "She insist I am to marry soon. But predictions not always come true. I have no suitors, and my family not yet find a suitable mate."

Ross stroked his chin thoughtfully. "Perhaps your destiny is to choose your own husband."

"He would have to meet my family's approval," she replied somewhat cautiously.

"And this husband—would he have to be Chinese?"

Looking away again, Mei-li answered in a whisper, "In China, a woman must observe three obediences: Before marriage she is subject to father, after marriage to husband, and in widowhood to son. My uncle, my family, indeed the laws of my people, all require my husband be Chinese."

"And what about you? Do you require that, as well?"

"I . . ." Unable to answer, she lowered her head sadly.

"What about Sister Carmelita? . . . Did she say whom you would marry?"

"She say—" Mei-li stopped abruptly, looking at him with a strange, questioning expression.

"What is it? Who did she say?"

"She not tell me—just that I will marry two times."

"Twice?"

"She say, 'You will have two husbands—one of the spirit and one of the flesh.' And it seem to me that a husband of the spirit need not be Chinese, since in the spirit we all one people, whether we Chinese or *fan kuei*."

Mei-li's smile was warm and genuine, and he could not help but smile, as well. Knowing that she could sense his feelings for her and that pretense was pointless, he said, "Perhaps when I discover Keeping-Still Mountain, I will ascend it a *fan kuei* and descend a *pai hsing*." He used a common name for the Chinese people: *pai hsing*, or "one hundred surnames," referring to the limited number of official surnames in China.

"Yes, Ross Ballinger, I believe that you will."

After an awkward silence, he said, "There was something else your uncle spoke about—the first time I met him. It was very cryptic, something about an earthquake coming, and sacrificial wine, and a man making his house quiet and still."

" 'Superior man make his house quiet and still and search his heart.' "

"Yes!" he exclaimed. "That was it! What was he talking about?"

"It is from *I Ching,* a revered book of thought written perhaps three thousand years ago. It is used for divination, and oracle my uncle quoted was *Chên,* which mean the Shock."

She spoke in Chinese to Sister Carmelita, who nodded briskly and scurried into the adjoining room, which served as the women's sleeping quarters.

"I always carry copy of *I Ching,*" Mei-li explained as the nun returned with a small leather-bound book. "My uncle tell me he cast your fortune before you arrive, to see how auspicious your meeting would be." She flipped through the pages until she found the right one, then translated aloud: " 'Shock bring good fortune. Earthquake come—oh, no! Laughter heard—ah, ha! Quake terrify all within a hundred miles, yet superior man does not spill sacrificial wine. Tremor follow tremor. Thus amid fear and quaking, superior man make his house quiet and still and search his heart.' " Mei-li lowered the book to her lap.

"I'm not sure I understand," Ross admitted.

"Oracle describe a cataclysm that happen within someone's life; it could be personal or some larger catastrophe, such as war. And superior man—"

"An enlightened man," Ross cut in. "An enlightened man learns how to maintain his calm and not succumb to fear—isn't that what it means when it speaks of not spilling the sacrificial wine?"

"Yes," she agreed. "But sacrificial wine also refer to his spiritual disciplines. In time of great upheaval, he maintain his discipline."

Ross pondered her words for a moment, then said, "Your uncle also spoke of the shock being mired, and something about remaining free of misfortune by taking action."

"Hmm, let's see," she murmured, searching the text. "Yes, here it is. There are sixty-four oracles, and each consist of six broken or unbroken lines. Unbroken lines are *yang,* which is male, or positive principle. Broken lines are *yin,* the female, or negative principle."

"I've heard of the *yin* and *yang.*"

"Here is what *Chên* look like," she said, tracing a row of lines on the table in front of her. Starting from the bottom, there was an unbroken line, two broken lines, another unbroken one, then two more broken ones. "*Yang, yin, yin, yang, yin, yin.* When my uncle cast your fortune, the third and fourth lines were changing lines, which mean they will transform into their opposite. Oracle say for third one, 'Though the shock confuse and distress him, he can remain free of misfortune by taking action.' Fourth one say, 'The shock is mired in the mud, and all movement is crippled.' "

"Yes, that's what your uncle told me."

Mei-li searched through the book for another hexagram. "Now we look up hexagram *Chên* will become when two lines have changed. Then it will be *yang, yin, yang, yin, yin, yin.* That oracle will reveal something of your future." She flipped a few more pages, then said, "Here it is: *Ming I,* or Darkening of the Light."

They looked at each other in surprise; that was the phrase used first by her uncle and then a little while ago by Sister Carmelita when speaking of Ross's destiny.

"What does it say?" he asked a bit hesitantly.

She scanned the Chinese characters for a moment, then translated: " 'Sun is sinking beneath the sky. Amid this darkening of the light, superior man veils his own lamp while allowing it to shine.' "

"That doesn't sound too optimistic," Ross commented.

"Perhaps not, but it suggest way you can shine in such darkness."

Mei-li turned to the front of the book and started translating other of the hexagrams. She had just gotten to *Chun*—Difficulty at the Beginning—when a muffled explosion shattered the afternoon quiet. It was followed by a second blast—the unmistakable report of a cannon being fired somewhere in the distance.

Ross started across the room and was met by Fray Luis racing in. On his heels was a Chinese sailor, who quickly spoke with the guard at the door.

"A British man-of-war!" Luis exclaimed. "It just fired two shots across our bow!"

Mei-li and Sister Carmelita rose, and Mei-li tried to follow the men from the room, but the guard blocked her way, explaining that it was improper for women to be on deck during the threat of battle. Ross looked back at her, motioned that he was just going to see what was happening, and headed outside.

There was mass confusion on the junk, the sailors rushing around the deck, arming themselves with bows and rattan shields or taking up positions at the small cannons. Ross pushed his way through the throng to the bow of the ship and immediately saw the Royal Navy frigate about three hundred yards off the starboard bow. It was a forty- or fifty-gunner, with long double rows of cannons on each side. Smoke was rising from the two foremost guns, which apparently had been fired in warning.

Several sailors raced up to the bow and unceremoniously pushed Ross to one side. They were carrying a large, ungainly gun called a *gingall*. It consisted of a pipe six feet long and one and one-half inches in diameter, attached to a short pistol-grip butt. As the men stood it on the butt end, another sailor rolled over a large cask filled with a gunpowder mixture made of two parts ground charcoal, three parts saltpeter, and ten parts sulphur, doused with *kaoliang* spirits and dried in the sun. The powderman took a large scoop of the mixture, climbed onto a stool, and poured it down the barrel, using a bamboo pole to ram it to a depth of six inches, then adding an ounce and a half of iron pellets and dried peas.

The gun barrel was lowered and positioned in a groove in the bulwark. The gunner, called a wildfowler because the gun was used primarily to shoot ducks, lit a thin stick of incense with a flint, then fitted the smoldering joss stick into a slot at the top of the cocked, S-shaped hammer. Finally, he slid a small roll of gunpowder-filled paper through the vent hole over the pan, on the right side of the gun. The other sailors stood aside, and the wildfowler took aim, waiting for the signal to fire.

Ross noticed that the British frigate, now only about two hundred yards away, was closing in fast, preparing to move alongside and perhaps fire a broadside. He glanced back at the deck of the junk and saw the men frantically readying the guns for firing. The nine- and twelve-pounders would be little match for the firepower of the man-of-war. And that ship was only a frigate, midway between a corvette and a ship of the line, whereas this *ta-ping ch'uan* was one of the premier vessels in the Imperial Navy.

Celestial Terror . . . Ross thought, shaking his head ruefully.

The commander of the war junk, Admiral Yuen, was stationed beside the rudder man on the large, raised deck at the stern. He was watching the movement of the frigate, probably trying to determine if the first shots had merely been a warning to stop and prepare for boarding. Ross doubted the admiral would allow the Englishmen to board his vessel—not when he had been entrusted with the delicate mission of delivering the niece of the *ch'in-ch'ai ta-ch'en* to Java.

Admiral Yuen got his answer from the frigate in the

form of another double volley, which landed dangerously close to the bow. It was clear that the English had decided that a Chinese war junk so far from home on the high seas was fair game, and they intended to have some sport with it.

Choosing not to wait for a direct hit, the admiral raised his arm and gave the signal. Ross stepped back a few feet as the wildfowler adjusted his aim slightly and pulled the trigger. The burning joss stick struck the pan and sparked the gunpowder. It raced through the priming paper and down the vent hole, setting off the charge. The explosion was horrific—harsher than most cannons—and the recoil knocked the wildfowler onto his back.

There was an excited shout, then the joyous cry of several dozen sailors as the blast tore through the right side of the frigate's main topsail. This got the attention of the Englishmen, for almost immediately the man-of-war turned its starboard side to the junk, not waiting to get any closer before unleashing a broadside on the small but dangerous ship.

Just then Fray Luis ran over, yelling that Admiral Yuen didn't want anything to happen to his passengers and that Ross should get away from the bow. It would surely take the brunt of the next volley, since the admiral did not want to bring his vessel about and possibly put the galleries on the quarterdeck in the line of fire.

Ross allowed himself to be led toward the stern, but halted at the mainmast, where a curious contraption was being hoisted to the masthead by one of the halyards. It was a basket loaded with a half-dozen earthen jars, each having two or more compartments that contained gunpowder, small nails, iron pellets, and chemicals that were particularly offensive-smelling and suffocating when they burned. These "stink pots," as they were called, were individually wrapped in calico cloth. When the vessels were close enough, the cloth would be set on fire by a man atop

the mast, who would then cut the halyard and send the basket
swinging out over the enemy ship. With luck, the jars would
crash on the deck and break open, and the burning calico
would set off the contents, creating a noxious explosion
that would render unconscious anyone standing nearby and
possibly set fire to the ship.

As one of the sailors climbed the mast, Ross continued
to the aft deck, where Admiral Yuen was busy directing the
rudder man and his forces. He allowed the boat to come
around partway, angling the starboard side slightly toward
the frigate. Then he directed his men to line up on the port
side, away from the frigate. He would make the bold move
of allowing the English ship to fire her full volley before
responding in kind. At the same time, he gave the order for
the drummers to sound. A moment later, the air was filled
with the booming clash of drums and gongs.

Ross saw a burst of smoke from the frigate's starboard
cannons, followed a split-second later by the thunderous
explosion of more than twenty guns discharging. Balls
smacked into the water all around the junk, with one piercing
the hull, tearing a gaping hole just above the waterline about
halfway between the bow and mainmast. The junk rocked
violently, and a shower of splintered wood rained down
on the foredeck. The sailors held their ground admirably,
protecting themselves with rattan shields, which were three
feet in diameter and so tightly woven and elastic that they
could deflect a sword or even a long-range musket shot.

As soon as the volley ended, Admiral Yuen raised his
sword, and the sailors dashed en masse across the deck to
the side nearest the frigate, some taking up places at the
six small cannons, others nocking their bows. Ross looked
to the foredeck and saw that the *gingall* had been reloaded
and was now in a slot on the starboard side.

The admiral signaled the rudder man to hold the vessel
steady, then grasped his sword with both hands and swung
the tip of the blade in a sweeping arc to the deck. The

bowmen raised their weapons high and released their arrows in unison. Ross was amazed at how far they flew. He knew the Chinese were expert and dedicated marksmen; he had even heard that China's legendary bowman, Chi Ch'ang, began his study of the art by lying under his wife's loom for three years learning not to blink, then spent the next three years gazing at a tiny louse until it appeared as large as a cartwheel. But Ross had not realized the incredible strength these bowmen possessed in their compact physiques.

As soon as the arrows were launched, the bowmen stepped back, and the cannoneers touched their smoldering joss sticks to the primed vents. The cannons discharged, knocking two of the guns off their wooden mounts and filling the deck with dark, acrid smoke. The bowmen had already nocked their bows a second time, and they stepped forward again and let another volley fly. Then they hurried over to where several vats of oil were laid out on the deck. They wound and secured strips of cloth around the tips of their next arrows, then dipped them in the oil. As soon as the two vessels were closer, they would launch an assault with fire.

The Imperial Navy made the most of fire, employing small fire junks that they would lash together and set loose upstream from an enemy flotilla—usually in the dark of night. Sailors would swim alongside and set them alight at the last moment, and the flaming vessels would go sweeping into the enemy ships.

On the high seas, fire junks were not effective, so the war junk carried another unusual weapon, called "water thunder," which was simply a tub with a lower compartment containing a charge of gunpowder and an upper compartment filled with combustibles. Several of them were brought up on deck; when the ships drew close, the slow-burning combustibles would be lit, and the tub would be set afloat in the direction of the ship. With a great deal of luck, it would drift alongside the frigate before the charge exploded.

It was clear that the junk was trying to run behind the frigate, perhaps take a final volley and then close in, so that the more primitive weapons aboard the junk could be brought into play. The Chinese vessel, however, had little hope of outrunning or outmaneuvering the English ship.

Ross looked around but didn't see Fray Luis; he hoped that the cleric was inside with Mei-li and Sister Carmelita. Realizing that he should make sure they were all right, he started for the gallery but was stopped by the deafening report of a full volley from the starboard guns of the frigate, which now was less than a hundred yards away. Ross instinctively flattened to the deck, and he felt it heave and almost explode beneath him. Several of the cannonballs had found their mark, blasting into the side of the ship and splitting the foremast, which shuddered and went crashing to the deck, the lugsail collapsing across the bow of the junk and crushing the *gingall* and the two men operating it.

Wood was falling everywhere; a huge pulley from the mainsail rigging smacked onto the deck only inches from Ross's head. He heard a shriek overhead and looked up to see that the man atop the mainmast had been hit by musket fire. As he fell from his perch, he crashed through the basket containing the stink pots, and they came raining down on the deck, about ten yards from where Ross was lying. The pots shattered and were instantly ignited, probably by the joss sticks the man had been holding. There were a series of small explosions, and Ross saw two sailors fall, struck by flying metal and clay shards. Then a billow of thick, acrid smoke spread across the deck.

Holding his breath, Ross cautiously rose to his hands and knees. He could see that the war junk was on fire—both from the cannonade and the exploding pots. The frigate seemed largely undamaged, and as it closed in fast, Ross could make out the gold lettering on the bow. In shock, he muttered, "The *Lancet*!"

Scrambling to his feet, he looked toward the quarter gallery where the women were housed. To his horror, he saw that the top of the cabin had been struck during the volley, and half the roof had collapsed.

As the little guns of the junk fired on the *Lancet,* Ross made a dash across the deck, leaping over twisted halyards, cracked battens, and charred sections of sail matting. He heard a *whoosh* to his left and glimpsed flashing streaks of flame as the bowmen released their fire arrows at the frigate's sails.

Reaching the gallery, Ross forced open the door, which had been wrenched off its hinges, and stumbled inside, rubbing his eyes against the smoke and dust. Off to his left, someone was moaning, and he clambered over downed beams and roofing planks, calling Mei-li's name.

"Ross!" a voice called back, and then he saw her dim outline, half-buried in the rubble.

"I'm here!" he shouted as he climbed over a huge round spar that must have crashed through the roof from the mainmast.

Mei-li appeared to be buried from the waist down, but as he reached her and tried to pull the debris off her, she exclaimed, "Not me! Carmelita!"

Looking down, Ross realized that Mei-li was not trapped but was kneeling beside the nun, who was unconscious, the mainmast spar pinning her at the chest. Standing, Ross grabbed hold of the spar and with great effort lifted it off the hapless woman, carefully moving it to the side and dropping it out of the way.

Cannons and muskets again were fired, but there were no more organized volleys. Praying that the cabin did not take another hit, Ross stooped over Sister Carmelita and felt for her pulse. "She's alive," he declared, gesturing for Mei-li to help him lift her free.

"No," the young woman said, tenderly touching the

nun's forehead. "Her back may be broken. Better to leave her where she is."

Together they pulled the remaining debris off the unconscious woman, making her as comfortable as possible without moving her.

It was suddenly quiet—ominously so. There were no further reports, only the sound of people moving around the deck and the hissing of fires being doused. As it became apparent that the brief battle was ending, Ross stood and lifted Mei-li to her feet.

The smoke was clearing, and the cabin was filled with a soft, dusty light. As she looked up at him, she saw that his hair was matted with blood. "You are hurt!" she gasped, tenderly touching his forehead.

"I'm fine," he assured her, not even aware that he had been injured. "So long as you're all right."

"Yes, Ross—" she started to answer, but he touched a finger to her lips, tenderly tracing her mouth, caressing her face with his eyes. She held back, her lips quivering as she saw the white heat smoldering in those startlingly blue eyes. Then her own eyes filled with tears, and she pulled him close, her lips searching, joining his, her body melting into him as he gathered her in his arms.

"What the hell were you doing?" Julian Ballinger exclaimed, pacing across the cabin in front of his cousin, who was standing at the porthole. "Those are our enemies!" He waved an arm toward the porthole; beyond it, the war junk was floating alongside the frigate, the Chinese sailors clearing up the debris and making repairs as best they could under the guns of an English detachment from the *Lancet.* The fires had been doused, and the hole in her hull was being worked on by men suspended over the side by ropes.

"You don't understand," was all Ross replied.

"Then explain it to me. You might as well, 'cause you sure as hell will have some explaining to do to the ffist!"

"That's enough," a stern voice commanded from behind Julian.

Spinning around, he found himself facing a short but imposing officer with muttonchop whiskers and small, dark eyes. "Captain ffiske . . . excuse me, but—"

"Enough," ffiske repeated, silencing him with a raised hand.

Ross examined the man his cousin had spoken of so often. The first thing that struck him was the way ffiske rested his left hand on the hilt of the most unusual and impressive sword Ross had ever seen. He recalled that Julian had described ffiske's sword as having been the gift of a Japanese samurai.

"I think we understand what your cousin is doing here," ffiske remarked, his upper lip quirking into a smile as he addressed Ross directly. "Would you like to tell us about it, or shall I?"

"I'm headed for Java, and then on to England," Ross stated simply.

"Why don't you tell Lieutenant Ballinger why you're bound for London?" He walked across the small cabin, glanced through the porthole, then turned his back on Ross.

Julian looked at him questioningly, and Ross finally said, "I'm carrying a letter to the queen."

"To the queen! Yes, I daresay you were," ffiske blurted, spinning around. He thumped his chest with his fist. "But *I've* got that letter now! And we'll see about sending it to our fair Victoria."

"It's a private communication between the Chinese government and the Crown."

"And are you the Crown's representative in Canton?" ffiske demanded, sneering. "If an official letter needs to be sent, it should be delivered to the chief superintendent, Captain Charles Elliot." He paused, then grinned smugly.

"But *he's* trapped in Canton, is he not? Made a prisoner by that same high commissioner who is using you to run his errands." He turned to Julian. "I'd say your cousin is working for the Chinese now. I'd call that treason, wouldn't you?"

Looking more than a bit perturbed, Julian replied, "I'm sure Ross had no idea how he was being used. But you've recovered the letter, so—"

"The letter *and* a far more valuable prize. Isn't that true, Mr. Ballinger?" When Ross did not reply, ffiske went on, "We not only have the high commissioner's letter, we have his niece. And when we arrive in Canton with his precious war junk in tow, we'll see just how highly he values that prize." He strode to the cabin doorway and, glancing back, said curtly, "Your young cousin will remain here, under house arrest. You may visit as you please, and so may your sister." Shutting the door, he headed down the corridor.

"Sister?" Ross asked, walking over to Julian. "What was he talking about?"

"Zoë," Julian said flatly. "We met in Java on her way to Sydney, but her plans changed, and she decided to come back with us to Canton." He chuckled. "She wanted to find you, and now you've gone and found us."

"Can I see her?" Ross asked eagerly.

"There's one other thing . . . she isn't alone."

"Who's with her? Austin?"

Julian shook his head. "I'm afraid she's got herself a husband in tow."

"Bertie's here, too?" Ross said incredulously.

"I only wish it were so. I'm afraid, little cousin, you're in for another shock. But I'll let her tell you all about that herself." He started from the cabin, but Ross caught him by the arm.

"I . . . I have to know what happened to the others."

"You mean that priest and those two Chinawomen?"

"Yes. Are they all right?"

"The nun's arm was broken, but she'll be all right. She's in the ship's infirmary, and the priest is down there watching over her."

"And the other woman?" he asked hesitantly.

"The commissioner's niece? She's fine. The captain's treating her real well; after all, she may prove valuable when we get back to Canton."

"I want to see her," Ross said flatly.

"You're kidding. It's out of the question."

He gripped Julian's arm. "I *must* see her, Julian. You've got to arrange it."

"What the hell for? She's just—"

"She's the one, Julian."

"What?"

"I told you about her. Mei-li . . . the woman I met at the mission."

Julian searched his memory, then gave a look of recognition. "So *that's* how you got caught up in this mess. A woman . . . I'd never've thought you capable of it, little cousin." He slapped Ross on the shoulder. "You may turn out a Ballinger after all—that is, if you don't get yourself hung first."

"Julian, I'm serious. You have to arrange for me to see Mei-li."

"Forget her. I'll do what I can to get you out of this mess, but don't ask me to do something that'll just get you in deeper." He pulled his arm free and stalked down the corridor.

Ten minutes later Julian ushered Zoë into the cabin, then closed the door and left her with Ross. Despite Ross's distress over what had happened, he was genuinely delighted to see his cousin, and for a long time they just held each other close.

"Oh, Ross, I missed you so!" she whispered, kissing his cheek, then holding him away to take a good look at him. "And you've grown so."

Ross forced a smile. "We English all seem a bit bigger in the Orient."

"And blonder," she noted, tousling his hair. "Now, what's going on? I've heard bits and pieces, but it doesn't make any sense."

"I could ask the same of you. Julian tells me you're married?"

Zoë drew in a breath, her eyes betraying her fear and vulnerability. Finally she said, "Ross, you know I could never lie to you."

"What is it?"

"I'm not really married, though I've let Julian believe that." Taking his hand, she led Ross to a pair of chairs, the only furnishings beside a bunk that hung from the bulkhead. Sitting beside him, she continued to hold his hand as she said, "I'll tell you all about it, but you've got to hear me through. Do you promise?"

"Of course."

Zoë began, telling each of the incidents that led up to her journey to Australia. The hardest part was describing the complicity of their own families in the wrong that had been done to the Maginnises. A few times Ross tried to interrupt, but she made him wait until she was completely done—until she described how they came upon the *Lancet* in Java, learned that Connor's father had died in the storm, and decided to join the ship on its return voyage to Canton.

"I know it's not easy thinking that our fathers might have done something like that," she said, finishing her story. "And I'm not asking you to believe me, only to say that you'll help me uncover the truth and put things right."

For a long time Ross sat without speaking. Then he

gently touched her cheek. "I don't know what to believe, Zoë, but I do know that *you* believe what you've told me, and for now, I'll accept that it may be true. And when we return to England, we'll figure this thing out together—you and me."

"And Connor," she added with a hopeful smile.

"I'll have to meet this Connor fellow first. After all, it looks as if he's won your heart away from—"

"Ross, you're not jealous, are you?" she cut in.

He grinned. "Maybe a little, but I wasn't talking about me. I was going to say Bertie. And anyone who can win you away from the likes of Bertrand Cummington has got the makings of a friend."

"Oh, Ross, I love you!" she declared, throwing her arms around his neck.

"Well, go ahead," he said, pushing her away playfully. "Bring in this man who has so terribly compromised my cousin's honor."

"I'm the one who compromised his," she declared. "He didn't have much say in the matter."

"I'm beginning to learn that with Zoë Ballinger, none of us really has the last say!"

◆◆◆

Later that night, while the *Lancet* sailed toward China with the crippled war junk under tow, Ross heard a knock and stood from the bunk as the lock was turned and the cabin door was pushed open. It was Julian, and when he entered, he looked around furtively and whispered, "I could get keelhauled f'this, but I s'pose I owe you—though I can't seem to remember why'n hell I do." Even from across the cabin, he smelled of rum, and his smile was more of a leer. "One hour, mind you. I paid off the guards for an hour; they won't allow a minute more."

He stepped away from the doorway, and Lin Mei-li entered, dressed in a black silk robe that shimmered in the lamplight as she approached the bunk.

Julian poked his head back in. "One hour," he hissed, pulling the door shut and locking it.

For a long time they just stood looking at each other. Then she came forward into his arms, and they held each other close, her hands caressing his face, his eyes revealing the depth of his love.

"I love you, too," she sighed, though he had not spoken a word.

"I want you," he breathed, kissing her neck, his hands stroking her long black hair, then circling her shoulders and sliding down the curve of her back.

She gently bit his earlobe, her fingers pressing into his neck as she felt his right hand moving across her hip, easing up along her narrow waist and cupping her breast. She gave a soft moan and leaned back in his arms, and he lifted her off her feet and lowered her to the bunk.

"I love you," she was murmuring as he lay down beside her, his hands tracing the swell of her hips and breasts beneath the thin silk robe.

As they kissed, long and deeply, she took his hand and moved it along her body, leading it to where no man had ever been. "Love me, my husband of the spirit," she whispered, gasping at the pleasure of his touch.

But then Ross drew back, his hand easing away from her, and he stammered, "I—I can't . . ."

"Love me," she urged, pulling him closer. "We may only have tonight."

"I want more than tonight. I want to be more than just your husband of the spirit. I want . . ." His words trailed off, and she saw the anguish in his eyes.

They lay there for a long time, holding each other, not moving as the ship rolled gently beneath them. Finally Mei-li leaned back from him, her eyes moist with tears, a gentle smile playing across her mouth.

"Then we must wait," she announced. "We will wait until you have asked him."

"Asked whom?"

"My uncle. When we return to Canton, you may ask for my hand in marriage."

"But I'm a *fan kuei*. He'll never—"

"Somehow we will convince him. We will find a way." She kissed him tenderly on the lips.

"We have a custom in my country," Ross said, slipping off the bunk and kneeling beside her. "Before we ask a father—or an uncle—for a woman's hand in marriage, we first ask the woman." Taking her hand, he held it to his lips, then whispered, "Mei-li, will you marry me?"

"Yes, Ross Ballinger. If my uncle will permit it, I will be your wife."

XXII

The *Lancet* sailed into Whampoa Harbor on May 1, 1839. Advance word had been sent up from Macao, and both Captain Charles Elliot and Lin Tse-hsü were aware of the presence on board of Lin's niece. In fact, the Chinese high commissioner knew of the situation even before word arrived from the English, for the *ta-ping ch'uan* war junk and its crew, including Admiral Yuen, had been released from custody in Kowloon, and they had sent a courier to Canton by land.

During the preceding month, the twenty thousand chests of opium had begun to be delivered to the agreed-upon drop-off point at Chuenpi, an island in the Bogue at the mouth of Canton River. Within two days of the initial agreement of March 27, the commissioner had arranged for the foreigners to be given two hundred fifty animals for meat, as well as permission to purchase food. On April 15, when the first 4,515 chests had been delivered, the order was given for the servants to return to the factories. But though more than half the opium had been surrendered to the Chinese authorities by April 26, Lin still had not honored his agreement to allow travel between Canton and Macao.

Upon the arrival of the *Lancet,* Captain Elliot discovered one of the reasons why the agreement had not been fully honored. Lin Tse-hsü sent word to the chief superintendent that before the travel restrictions would be lifted and the siege ended, Lin Mei-li must be delivered to him unharmed. Elliot had no intention of keeping the young woman in custody, but he felt it might be useful to meet first with the commissioner and confirm that her release would produce the desired results.

At Lin Tse-hsü's request—and over Captain Reginald ffiske's vehement objections—Ross Ballinger was allowed to attend that meeting so that he could confirm that Mei-li was in good health. Fray Luis Nadal accompanied them to serve as an interpreter.

The meeting was held in the governor-general's garden, and it was short and productive, with an agreement quickly reached. Mei-li would be released from custody the next morning, May 2, and that same day all travel restrictions would be removed. Furthermore, Captain Elliot promised that the remaining chests of opium would be turned over by mid-May, and in a conciliatory gesture Lin said that he would remove all the guards and take down the barricades on May 2, even though that was not scheduled until three-quarters of the opium was surrendered.

There was still the matter of the attack by the *Lancet* upon a ship of the Imperial Navy. Elliot argued that it had occurred during a period of hostilities between their two nations and that the captain of the *Lancet* had been incited by the siege of Canton. When Commissioner Lin pointed out that an agreement to end the siege had been worked out long before the naval attack, Elliot insisted that the *Lancet* had sailed before learning of the agreement. Though it was true the ship had left Whampoa before an official announcement was made, Elliot was careful not to mention that he had sent news of it to ffiske with Julian Ballinger.

Lin Tse-hsü was not eager to dismiss the incident between the *Lancet* and Admiral Yuen's war junk; neither

was he inclined to prolong the tensions between their
nations. In the end, the two men agreed that no intentional
attack had occurred. Instead, Captain Reginald ffiske had
wrongly identified the *ta-ping ch'uan* as a pirate vessel
and, upon realizing his mistake, had taken every measure
to assist the junk and tow it back to Kowloon. In return
for Lin's acquiescence in this matter, Elliot agreed to send
the commissioner's letters to Queen Victoria—a promise he
had no intention of fulfilling, since he was determined that
all information about the situation in Canton come from his
own pen.

At the close of the meeting, Lin Tse-hsü asked to
speak alone with Fray Luis, and Ross and Captain Elliot
were escorted from the garden. As soon as the two men
were alone, Lin asked the Spanish cleric, "I am anxious
about my niece; is she truly well?"

"She was quite distressed, to be sure, but completely
unharmed," Luis assured him in Chinese.

"And your good sister? I hear she was injured."

"Sister Carmelita is quite a soldier of the Lord. She
is already mending and will soon be able to return to her
duties at the mission."

"Excellent," Lin declared. He sat in silence for a long
time, looking at Fray Luis. His eyes were both sad and
weary, and it was apparent that the tensions of the past
weeks had been taking their toll. Finally he said, "I have
had a disturbing report that I would prefer you not share
with the young Englishman."

Luis looked at him curiously. "What is it that upsets
you?"

"Admiral Yuen sent word of ... this is most
delicate ...." The normally composed man was quite
disconcerted as he gathered his emotions and continued,
"The admiral reports a breach of etiquette aboard
his ship."

"Etiquette?"

"It was after the attack against his ship. One of his soldiers saw my niece and the Englishman, and they were behaving not as propriety would require."

"I am certain it was nothing more than their mutual relief at having survived the bombardment," Luis assured him.

"Perhaps," Lin allowed, "but understand that she is my niece and my responsibility, now that her poor father is gone. I asked you and Sister Carmelita to accompany them on the voyage because I feared that her youthful innocence might be compromised."

"I never saw any improprieties myself. And I am sure Ross Ballinger would never compromise—"

"Of course you are right," Lin cut in, waving his hand. "But they are young; they do not understand the ways of the world. And for a woman of her station to become involved in any fashion with a foreigner . . . it is simply not to be permitted."

"Do you wish me to express your concerns to Mr. Ballinger?" Luis asked.

"I would prefer that you do not," Lin stated firmly. "I am already addressing the affair in my own manner. Perhaps it is my fault for letting Mei-li reach such a delicate age without her future being secured. And now that we have resolved the crisis in Canton, I have been able to direct more of my attention to Mei-li's situation."

Lin Tse-hsü rose, and the two men said good-bye.

◆◆◆

The next afternoon, Mei-li was brought to Canton, and the siege was lifted. Ross Ballinger accompanied her to the governor-general's compound, where she was presented to her uncle, who was delighted to see her in such good health and spirits. He thanked Ross profusely and apologized for any inconvenience that he had been caused.

It was when Lin Tse-hsü was saying good-bye to the

Englishman that Mei-li cautiously said, "Uncle Tse-hsü, Ross Ballinger has come today to ask you a question."

"And what is that?" Lin asked, looking with some concern back and forth between them.

Mei-li turned to Ross. "You may ask him now."

"Lin Tse-hsü," he began, "I've come to ask that you bestow a great blessing upon me by allowing me to take your niece's hand in marriage."

Ross tried to conceal his nervousness as Mei-li translated his words. He was heartened that her uncle's expression did not immediately darken; in fact, he looked quite pleasant and composed as he spoke with Mei-li.

"I am not surprised that it has come to this," he told her, "but I am saddened, as I am sure your father would be. This foreigner is a good man, but he is *fan kuei,* and you are *pai hsing.*"

Though Ross did not understand what the man was saying in Chinese, he did know those two terms, and he felt his heart grow heavy.

"And what would your children be?" Lin continued. "It is neither proper nor permitted that you take such a husband as this."

"But I love him," Mei-li told him.

"You will love your husband. And you will obey him, as you obeyed your father and now obey me."

"But I have no husband. I want Ross—"

"I have chosen your future husband. The eldest son of the governor-general of Nanking has just completed his studies here in Canton, and tomorrow you will return with him to Nanking and be married."

"Married?" she said in shock. "But you have never spoken of a husband."

"I thought it could wait until all of this business in Canton was finished, but I see that I was wrong—just as I was wrong to entrust you to the care of foreigners. You are a good and intelligent niece, and perhaps I have treated you too much like one of my sons. But now you must become a wife and mother."

"But I wish to marry Ross Ballinger."

"And perhaps I wish to be emperor," he replied, maintaining his even tone. "But you *will* go to Nanking and marry your husband. Is that not so?"

Mei-li lowered her eyes.

Ross did not understand what had been said, yet he knew that his request had been denied and that Mei-li was not able to go against her uncle's wishes. He was about to speak, but then Lin Tse-hsü said to him in poor English, "Good day, Mister Ballinger." He smiled and bowed, then walked from the garden, leaving Ross and Mei-li to share a final good-bye.

"I've never seen him like this," Zoë said as Ross stormed out of the sitting room at the Jardine, Matheson & Company building in Creek Factory. "Do you think he was serious?"

"About finding a woman?" Connor asked.

"*Any* woman, he said."

Connor tried not to smile. "There's no telling what an Englishman scorned might do."

"Go after him," she asked.

"Me? I hardly know him."

"I don't want him out there on his own. He's already had enough to drink."

"Look, Zoë, I've been as civil to Ross as anyone could expect, given the circumstances."

"He's nothing like his father."

"I'll take your word for it. But so far all I've seen is an impetuous youngster who's been fool enough to let himself fall in love with someone he cannot hope to have."

"Isn't that what you did?" she asked, pinching his cheek playfully.

"Who said I'm in love?" he teased.

"Then don't do it for me—do it because you and Ross are a couple of kindred fools."

Connor sighed. "Anything the madam desires," he declared, kissing her forehead and snatching his jacket from the back of the chair.

Once downstairs, Connor passed quickly through the agency buildings and out onto Factory Square. The siege of the district had been lifted that morning, and he had only been ashore a few hours, but he knew enough to guess that Ross was headed for the nearby alley known as Hog Lane. When they had arrived, Julian had given a quick tour and had taken particular delight in pointing out the *samshu* bar in Hog Lane as a favorite place for him and Ross to carouse.

Moving through the crowd that filled the small lane, Connor tried to remember which of the establishments was the *samshu* bar in question. It was easy to pick out, since a half-dozen English sailors were gathered in front of it. Pushing through to the window, he gazed inside and saw a young, fair-haired man hunched over a glass at the bar, which was crowded with sailors and merchantmen.

Connor walked in and slapped Ross on the back. "Mind if I share a drink?"

Ross glanced up, then turned back to his glass of rum.

"Thanks." Connor signaled the bartender to bring him a glass. "You'll have to cover it, I'm afraid. I haven't the slightest idea how to pay for things in China."

Without speaking, Ross slipped a coin from his waistcoat pocket and tossed it on the bar.

"Thanks again." Connor took the glass from the bartender and downed it in a single gulp. He quickly realized his mistake and almost spit it all over Ross, but he managed to swallow the powerful local brew and only gagged a bit. "*Samshu*, eh? I'll have to remember to forget it exists." His dark eyes flashed mischievously.

The bartender was there instantly, ready to refill the glass, but Connor shook his head and said, "No more." That didn't stop the man, who quickly filled it back up.

Connor was about to object, when Ross said, "When you say no, they think you're just being polite. If you really don't want any more, cover the glass with your hand."

"I see." Connor raised the glass and took a sip this time; the rum did not go down any easier.

"Well, I'll be upstairs," Ross announced, downing his drink. "I don't suppose you want to come?"

"Are you sure *you* want to?"

"Why the hell not? These Chinawomen are all alike."

Connor laughed aloud.

"What's that for?" Ross asked.

"You, talking about Chinese women as if they're all some kind of harlots—just because Lin Mei-li has agreed to an arranged marriage. Their customs sure are unusual, but I doubt that at heart they're much different from the women in England or anywhere else."

Ross shifted on his seat and looked up at Connor. "They are, believe me."

"And you're an expert on women?"

"What, are you?" Ross said dubiously.

Connor took another sip. "I've known my share."

"I'll bet you have," Ross said with a smirk, turning back to the bar and calling for another drink.

"Look, I didn't come here to argue with you."

"Why exactly did you come here?"

"Your cousin—she's worried about you. We both know how hurt you must feel, but—"

"You don't know *shit*," Ross muttered, downing his drink and slapping the glass back on the bar.

"You little bastard," Connor snapped, grabbing him by the jacket sleeve and spinning him around. "I don't know what the hell your problem is, but don't go talking about Zoë like—"

"I was only referring to you."

The two men glowered at each other, then Connor let go of Ross's jacket. "Look, fellow, I've got every reason to hate your guts, but I've been trying not to, for Zoë's sake."

"Don't do me any favors." Ross got up from his stool.

"I won't," Connor promised. "You can feel sorry all by yourself. Hell, you can go find yourself a Chinese whore and prove whatever it is you're trying to prove to yourself."

"I will!" Ross blurted, stalking over to the stairs that led to the rooms above.

One of the sailors was coming down just then, and Ross was none too gentle in pushing past him.

"Watch it!" the sailor barked, grabbing Ross by the arm. Ross yanked himself free and took a swing at the man, who warded off the ineffectual blow, then rammed a fist in Ross's belly, sending him tumbling down the stairs. Rubbing his fist, the sailor continued down to where Ross was lying on his back at the foot of the stairs, grasped his jacket lapels, and lifted him off the floor so that he could strike him again.

"Enough!" a voice shouted; it was Connor.

Releasing Ross, the enraged sailor turned on Connor, taking a wild swing that Connor easily avoided. Feinting to the left, Connor followed with a quick right jab to the man's jaw, stunning him. The sailor staggered back a few feet, then growled and charged. Connor took a glancing blow to the temple but landed a more solid punch to the man's soft belly, doubling him over. Connor's knee then connected with the man's forehead, snapping back his head and sending him sprawling alongside Ross.

Several other sailors were rising from their seats and advancing on Connor now, but they were stopped in their tracks by a series of popping explosions. Thinking that guns were going off, they made a mad scramble out of the *samshu* bar and into Hog Lane.

Connor saw that smoke was rising behind the bar and the bartender was chuckling. The Chinese man winked at Connor and held up a string of firecrackers, identical to the string he had lit and dropped behind the bar.

Nodding at the barkeep, Connor stepped over the unconscious sailor and knelt beside Ross, who was struggling to catch his breath. "Are you all right?" Connor asked.

"Yes," Ross gasped.

"Here. Let me help." Connor slipped his hands under Ross's arms and lifted him to his feet.

Ross's breath slowly returned to normal, and he murmured, "Th-Thanks."

"Let's get out of here. You don't really want to go upstairs, do you?"

Cocking his head, Ross stared at him curiously.

"Do you?" Connor pressed.

"Say that again."

"What?"

" 'Let's get out of here' . . . say that."

Connor looked at Ross as if he were mad, then shrugged and repeated, "Let's get out of here."

"Damn it! I knew you looked familiar!"

"Whatever are you talking about?"

"When we met on the *Lancet,* I thought I'd seen you before, and just now it came back to me."

"What did?"

"You were the one who helped me the night of the coronation, when those two men jumped me."

Slowly the realization struck Connor, as well. "That was you?"

Ross just smiled sheepishly.

"And here I am helping you again," Connor declared. "That is, if you want my help. What d'you say we head on back to Jardine's? Zoë's really worried about you."

"Might as well." Ross glanced ruefully up the stairs.

"I guess what I'm looking for won't be found up there."

"It never is. Take it from someone who knows."

Connor clasped his arm around Ross, and the two men headed into the night.

◆━━━◆━━━◆

When Ross and Connor got back to Number Four Creek House, they found that Zoë wasn't alone; with her was Sister Carmelita, her arm splinted and bandaged and supported by a sling. As soon as they entered the sitting room, the nun hurried over to Ross, thrusting a piece of paper in his hand. Opening it, he read: *Please come at once—Mei-li.*

Ross handed the slip to Connor, then motioned for Sister Carmelita to lead the way.

"I want to come along," Zoë declared.

Ross looked back at her, then at Connor. Finally he nodded, and the three of them followed the nun downstairs and through the rear entrance of the factory to Thirteen Factory Street, then past Consoo House and down the alley to the Catholic mission.

Sister Carmelita ushered them into the chapel, where they found Mei-li standing at the altar with Fray Luis Nadal. When Mei-li saw Ross approaching down the aisle, she ran to meet him, tears streaming down her cheeks.

"My love," she whispered as he took her in his arms.

There were tears in Ross's eyes, as well, not just at seeing her again but at the thought of her leaving the next day with her husband-to-be. He was about to say something—to tell her that she could not leave him—when she lifted her fingers to his lips and said, "I know what you are thinking. I cannot leave you either—not like this." She glanced over at Luis, who nodded and smiled. "I want to marry you . . . right here, tonight. Fray Luis has agreed to perform ceremony. . . . That is, if you will marry me."

"If . . . ?" he murmured. "Oh, Mei-li, you know I will."
He pulled her close, and they kissed.

After a moment, Luis politely separated the couple,
urging them to go to the front of the chapel. He had
just positioned them kneeling at the altar, when Connor
interrupted, saying, "Fray Luis, would you consider a
double ceremony?" He took Zoë's hands and smiled at
her. Looking up at him tearfully, she nodded.

Luis seemed quite bewildered, uncertain as to the
propriety of either marriage. He did not even know if Connor
or Zoë was Catholic. But he could feel the love they shared,
and he knew that their souls were already in mortal danger.
Taking a step toward them, he said, "I must ask, is either of
you a Cath—" he hesitated, then shrugged "—a Christian?"

"Yes," they each blurted.

"Then join us!" Luis exclaimed.

The ceremony was brief and in Latin, so that neither
of the couples had any idea of what was being said. They
did not seem to care, however, for their attention was only
on their mates, and they nodded and responded as directed
by Luis. They did not even know when the ceremony
was finished, and he had to tell them in English that they
were finally married. Each couple kissed, then hugged and
congratulated one another. Finally Connor and Zoë took
their leave; Ross and Mei-li would spend the night at the
mission, where a room had been prepared for the bridal
couple.

As Connor and Zoë walked down the alley and headed
back to the room they had been given at Jardine's, she
rested her head on his shoulder and said, "Are you happy?"

"I just got married—what do you think?" He stroked
her long auburn hair.

"I mean the way everything has turned out, not just
tonight. I was thinking of your sister . . . and your father.
And my dragging you all the way to China when we could
have gone back home."

Connor was quiet for a long moment, then stopped and turned Zoë toward him. "Yes, I miss Emeline, and Mose, too. But I don't regret coming here, because I came here with you."

Reaching up, she laid her hand on his cheek. "I know how much you wanted to find your father."

"I did, Zoë. At least I found him and got to see who he was. And now it almost feels as if he isn't really gone . . . as if he's out there somewhere, looking after Emeline and me, waiting to come home again."

"You want to go home, don't you?" she asked.

"I *am* home when I'm with you," he breathed, sweeping her into his arms.

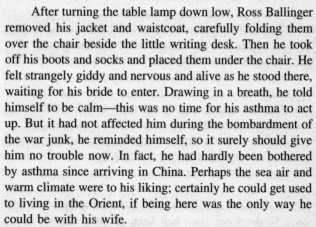

After turning the table lamp down low, Ross Ballinger removed his jacket and waistcoat, carefully folding them over the chair beside the little writing desk. Then he took off his boots and socks and placed them under the chair. He felt strangely giddy and nervous and alive as he stood there, waiting for his bride to enter. Drawing in a breath, he told himself to be calm—this was no time for his asthma to act up. But it had not affected him during the bombardment of the war junk, he reminded himself, so it surely should give him no trouble now. In fact, he had hardly been bothered by asthma since arriving in China. Perhaps the sea air and warm climate were to his liking; certainly he could get used to living in the Orient, if being here was the only way he could be with his wife.

As he walked to the narrow, single bed, he heard the click of the door unlatching, and he gazed in wonder at Lin Mei-li—at Mei-Li Ballinger—entering the room. She wore a white silk robe, embroidered with gold, draped halfway down her calves. She did not have on the traditional wide pants, nor was she wearing slippers, and Ross could not help but admire her shapely legs as she pulled the door closed and walked toward him. He wanted to tell her how much he loved her, but all he could do was smile.

As Mei-li stood in front of him, she reached up and unwound his cravat, sliding it from around his neck and letting it drop to the floor. His collar followed, and then she opened the buttons of his shirt, working slowly from the neck to his waist.

"Shh," she hushed, lifting his shirttail from his pants and pulling his shirt back off his shoulders. Her fingers traced the muscles of his upper arms and chest, sliding down around his waist to his back. She moved toward him, her head nuzzling his neck, her teeth gently nipping his ear.

Ross was almost afraid to touch her, but as he stroked her hair, his desire pushed aside any fear. He felt the curve of her back, then gripped her buttocks and pressed her close to him. Her heat drew him out, even as her hands were opening his waistband, seeking him, touching and claiming his passion.

"Yes," she whispered as his hands moved around her hips and ran up the length of her body, caressing her, pulling free the single tie at her neck. The silk rolled off her like a gentle breeze, and he lifted her in his arms, tasting each breast, reveling in her as she wrapped her legs around him and he lowered her onto the bed.

Ross felt the heat building, rising, threatening to overcome him too soon, far too soon. He started to pull back, but she drew him closer, easing him into her, whispering, "I love you, my husband of the spirit. . . ."

"And I love you, Mei-li, my heart."

The words, the abiding love, washed over and through him, and he was no longer afraid, no longer in a hurry. He was part of Mei-li. He was her husband of the spirit and of the flesh. He was home.

They moved in harmony, each one giving and receiving, each one releasing, together, to that perfect darkness.

Darkness within darkness . . . the gateway to enlightenment.

———◆———◆———◆———

The thin morning sunlight filtered through the gauzy white curtains that covered the window of the small mission room. Ross Ballinger lay alone on the narrow bed, staring up at the ceiling and smiling at the memory of his wife's exquisite touch. They had made love several times during the night, yet Mei-li had been awake before dawn. She had washed and dressed, then left the room. She had been gone for some time now, and he wondered if she was speaking with Fray Luis Nadal.

There was a rapping at the door, and Ross pulled the blanket up over him, since Mei-li would have come in without knocking. It was Sister Carmelita, and she blushed as she entered the room and placed something on the desk. Pointing at it, she walked out quickly.

Pulling the blanket around him like a robe, Ross crossed to the desk and picked up a folded piece of paper. His hand trembled as he opened it and read:

My dearest husband of the spirit,
    I not expect you to understand what I have done; I only hope in time you forgive me. I am not a warrior, nor am I a man. I must do as destiny ordains. I cannot change who I am or conditions under which I chose to be born, nor can I disavow my family or my people, even for love of my heart. But you must always know, no matter where life leads you, I am with you, in spirit and in heart.
    Since I must submit myself and my future to another man, I release you from all obligations, my love. Yet you are and shall remain my husband of the spirit. And in life to come, we

shall be together at last; I am as sure of this as
I am certain there is a China and an England
beneath the sky. Farewell, my love.

                    Your wife of the spirit, Mei-li.

Ross stared in shock at the letter crumpled in his hand.
He looked at his clothing on the chair, then at the closed
door. He saw himself running through the streets, shouting
her name, sweeping her back into his arms and into his life.

Dropping to his knees on the cold stone floor, he held
the letter against his cheek, wetting it with his tears.

◆ ◆ ◆

Mei-li looked back at Five-Story Pagoda, which towered over the north wall of Canton. Beyond it lay the
city, and near the water's edge, the husband she had left
behind.

She felt someone pat her hand, and she looked over at
the stranger beside her, a pleasant-looking young man, but
a stranger nonetheless. He must have sensed her reticence,
for he withdrew his hand and resumed staring through the
window on his side of the covered palanquin.

The sedan chair rocked gently as a retinue of twelve
bearers carried her and her future husband north, away from
the river, away from her love. Turning from the window,
she placed a hand on her belly and prayed for the gods to
allow Ross Ballinger's seed to take root inside her.

Mei-li looked back at the city a final time. "I will
always carry you within me," she whispered in the language
of her husband of the spirit. "In the darkness and in the
light."

Epilogue

◆━◆━◆━◆━◆━◆━◆━◆━◆━◆

On May 21, 1839, the last of the 20,283 chests of opium were surrendered to the Chinese authorities on the island of Chuenpi, where Commissioner Lin Tse-hsü had arranged to have them destroyed. At the same time, the foreigners started leaving Canton, heading to Macao as they did every spring to sit out the summer season.

On the first of June, Lin Tse-hsü wrote in his diary:

> Early this morning I sacrificed to the Sea Spirit, announcing that I should shortly be dissolving opium and draining it off into the great ocean and advising the Spirit to tell the creatures of the water to move away for a time, to avoid being contaminated.

The text of the address he used when performing this ceremony to *Chi Hai-shen wen,* the God of the Sea, begins:

> On the seventh day of the fourth month of the nineteenth year of Tao-kuang, the special commissioner, appointed Governor-General of Kiangnan and Kiangsi, Lin Tse-hsü, respectfully offering hard bristle [a pig] and soft down [a

sheep], together with clear wine and diverse dainties, thus ventures to address the Spirit of the Southern Sea: 'Spirit whose virtue makes you a chief of Divinities, whose deeds match the opening and closing of the doors of nature, you who wash away all stains and cleanse all impurities . . . why should you raise any barrier against a horde of foreign ships? But alas, poison has been allowed to creep in unchecked, till at last barbarian smoke fills the market. . . . At this Heaven's majesty thundered forth; a special envoy came galloping.'

On the island, three shallow basins had been prepared, each twenty-five by fifty yards, their sides braced with timbers and their bottoms covered with flagstones. They were filled with fresh water from a nearby creek. The chests were opened, and coolies carried the balls and cakes of opium onto a series of wooden platforms that traversed the basins, where they smashed them into pieces and dumped the fragments into the basins. Salt and limestone were dumped on the surface, and coolies waded into the stinking solution and stirred it all around with shovels and hoes. Finally the sludge was released into the creek and washed out to sea.

Two American missionaries who were allowed to witness the destruction of the opium were quite impressed that Lin Tse-hsü had actually done what he had set out to do, despite being surrounded by some of the most corrupt officials in all of China. One of them later wrote, "Have we anywhere on record a finer rebuke administered by Pagan integrity to Christian degeneracy?" And a printed circular from one of the American missions proclaimed:

Christian Brethren and Friends,
    For ten years past, those who ought to have introduced the gospel, with all its happy

accompaniments, have instead been bringing in a flood of desolation. This tide is now checked, but not yet entirely stopped. The destruction by the Chinese government, of twenty thousand chests of opium, which if sold would have brought into its treasury ten or fifteen millions of dollars, will long be referred to as an act, illustrative of the combined power of conscience and correct principle, operating even in pagan hearts. The novel plan by which the article fell into the hands of the Chinese may have been wrong, but when once in their possession, it seemed incredible that it should be destroyed. Yet so it was—entirely destroyed.

For his part, Lin Tse-hsü was pleased by the respectful attitude displayed by the English merchantmen, and he wrote the emperor, "Judged by their manners, it appears that they feel a sense of shame. Henceforth . . . it seems that all will reform themselves and be greatly improved."

Lin Tse-hsü was convinced that his actions had ended the crisis and that trade between the foreigners and the Chinese would return to normal once the new trading season began. He would soon learn that the English, once having left Canton and Whampoa, were not eager to return. And when they did, it would be with a Royal Navy expeditionary force determined to teach China that it could not dictate terms to the English government. Thus began what became known as the Opium War.

Author's Note

◆━━◆━━◆━━◆━━◆━━◆━━◆━━◆

While most of the major characters of *Beneath the Sky* are fictional, many others are based on historical figures. Lin Tse-hsü was, in fact, the high commissioner sent to deal with the opium problem, and much of the information regarding his activities comes from his diaries as translated by Arthur Waley. The Chinese *hong* leader, Howqua, is a composite of several, including the father and son named Howqua and two *hong* leaders named Mowqua and Powqua. Their names were actually a combination of their family name and the honorific title *qua,* which signifies that they were mandarins of the ninth, or lowest, rank.

Among the Englishmen in China, James Matheson was indeed one of the owners of Jardine, Matheson & Company, which is still in business today. Robert Thom served as a clerk and translator for Jardine's, and some of the other merchantmen, such as James Innes and Lancelot Dent, were actual traders. In his lifetime, Captain Charles Elliot was both controversial and renowned. In 1842 he served as the English chargé d'affaires to the Republic of Texas, where he became a close friend of Sam Houston's.

While the events leading up to the Opium War are recreated as faithfully as possible, some literary license has been taken. The battle between the *Lancet* and the

Chinese war junk did not take place but is based on similar encounters that happened somewhat later. And while the characters of Ross and Mei-li are fictional, it is historically accurate that Lin Tse-hsü tried to deliver his letter to Queen Victoria by sending copies of it with foreign travelers bound for England, so that it would not be intercepted and perhaps destroyed by the English representatives in Canton.

The letter exists today in two versions, the first having been reproduced in this novel. That version never made it to England but was later revised, approved by the emperor, and sent aboard the merchant ship *Thomas Coutts* to London, where it was printed in the *Times*.

Some of the books that were invaluable in researching Victorian England and China during the Opium War include:

Chang, Hsin-pao. *Commissioner Lin and the Opium War*. Cambridge: Harvard University Press, 1964.

Fay, Peter Ward. *The Opium War, 1840–1842*. The University of North Carolina Press, 1975.

Keswick, Maggie, editor. *The Thistle and the Jade: A Celebration of 150 Years of Jardine, Matheson & Co*. London: Octopus Books Ltd., 1982.

Mayhew, Henry. *London Labour and the London Poor*. London: Griffin, Bohn, and Company, 1861.

Priestley, Philip. *Victorian Prison Lives*. London: Methuen & Co. Ltd., 1985.

Waley, Arthur. *The Opium War Through Chinese Eyes*. London: George Allen & Unwin Ltd., 1958.

Worcester, G.R.G. *The Junks and Sampans of the Yangtze.* Shanghai: Statistical Department of the Inspectorate General of Customs, 1947.

◆━━◆━━◆

I would like to thank Gregory Tobin, a former associate publisher at Bantam Books and currently the editorial director of Quality Paperback Book Club, who brought me to Bantam and continues to provide unfailing encouragement. Thanks, also, to Irwyn Applebaum, Lou Aronica, Tom Dupree, Tom Beer, and the rest of the folks at Bantam Books.

A special acknowledgment is due Marla Ray Engel, George Engel, and the staff of Book Creations Inc. for their unflagging faith and support. I am particularly grateful to Senior Editor Pamela Lappies for her skillful editing on this and all my previous novels. She has played an integral role throughout the creative process, and I am fortunate that she is not only my colleague but my friend.

Finally, I am deeply grateful to my parents, who introduced me at an early age to the wonders of our multicultural world and instilled a special love for China and its people. Thanks, also, to my wife, Connie, and my children, Kiva and Ueyn, for their love and support. And a private thanks to Chung Fu, wherever he may be, for helping fan the embers all those years ago.

Foreign Words and Phrases

Note: All words are Mandarin unless otherwise noted. Most of the Mandarin spellings and definitions are from *A Mandarin-Romanized Dictionary of Chinese* by D. MacGillivray, published by the Presbyterian Mission Press, Shanghai, 1922.

Chên—"the Arousing"; one of the sixty-four hexagrams, or oracles, of the *I Ching* (Book of Changes); from *chên*, "to move, agitate"

Chi Hai-shen wen—the god of the sea

chia-ch'ang fan-ts'ai (also *pien fan*)—"pot luck" or "everyday fare"; the serving of ordinary foods, as opposed to full-course feasts

chih-tao—"to know"; from *chih*, "to know," and *tao*, "to speak, reason"

ch'in-ch'ai—"imperial envoy"; from *ch'in*, "command respect, grand," and *ch'ai*, "to send"

ch'in-ch'ai ta-ch'en—a high commissioner to the emperor who has been granted special plenipotentiary powers; from *ch'in-ch'ai*, "imperial envoy," *ta*, "great," and *ch'en*, "a minister"

chin-wên—"modern text" or "latest news"; a reform-minded school of thought, of which Lin Tse-hsü was a proponent *ching-shih chih-yung chih-hsueh*—"knowledge for the development of the state and for practical use in the world"; a progressive approach toward scholarship that incorporated a world view that was not limited to the boundaries of the Celestial Empire

chop—"stamp" (a shipment of tea marked with the same stamp is a *chop* of tea); also "quick" (pidgin)

chop-chop—"quickly" (pidgin)

chopsticks—"quick sticks" (pidgin)

Chun—"Difficulty at the Beginning"; one of the sixty-four hexagrams, or oracles, of the *I Ching* (Book of Changes)

cohong—members of guild of *hong* merchants (Cantonese)

¿cómo están?—"How are you?" (Spanish)

fan kuei—"foreign devil"; term used by Chinese to represent all foreigners

fei-hsieh—a small Chinese gunboat called a "fast crab"; from *fei*, "to fly or go swiftly," and *hsieh*, "crab"

first-chop—"first rate" (pidgin)

fu ch'uan—"official boat"; a medium-sized, double-masted junk; from *fu*, "a palace, a store," and *ch'uan*, "a boat"

gingall or *jingall*—a heavy, barrel-loaded musket fired from a rest or mounted on a swivel or carriage; used in China and India by the military and by wildfowlers to shoot ducks (from the Hindustani *janjal*) *hola*—"hello" (Spanish)

hong—"row, firm, guild"; a commercial house of foreign trade in China; also a warehouse or factory (Cantonese)

hsieh hsieh—"thank you"

Hsing luan-pang, yung chung-tien—"To rule a chaotic state, severe punishment must be imposed"; quote by the Duke of Chou, who started the Chou dynasty (1150–249 B.C.)

I Ching—Book of Changes; system of divination developed about three thousand years ago; from *i*, "to alter, change," and *ching*, "sacred book"; an alternate title is *Chou I*, or Changes of Chou, after the Duke of Chou, who added text to the hexagrams developed by his father, King Wên

kaoliang—any of a number of grain sorghums, the grain of which is used for food and the stalks for thatching, fodder, and fuel; a form of spirituous liquor made from the juice of *kaoliang* stalks; from *kao*, "high, tall," and *liang*, "grain"

koi—freshwater carp indigenous to Asia that inhabit ponds and sluggish streams and sometimes live to a great age and grow to a large size (Japanese)

kowtow or *k'o-t'ou*—to kneel and touch the forehead to the ground as an act of homage or worship; from *k'o*, "to knock, bump," and *t'ou*, "the head"

k'uai-pan—"quick plank boat"; a passenger junk designed for maximum speed; from *k'uai*, "fast, soon, sharp," and *pan*, "plank, board"; *pan* is used to denote a small ship, such as *san-pan* (or *sampan*), which means "three-planks"

k'ung-p'a—"I fear"; from *k'ung*, "fear, alarm, suspicion," and *p'a*, "to fear" *lao-hu*—"the tiger"

Lao-tzu—founder of Taoism; from *lao,* "great," and *tzu,* "son, seed"

li—measure of distance equal to about one-third mile

mah-jongg—Chinese game usually played by four players who draw and discard 144 tiles until one player attains a winning hand of four sets of three tiles and a pair; the modern name is circa 1920 from Mah-Jongg, a trademark

Mei-li—woman's name meaning "beautiful plum"; from *mei,* "beautiful," and *li,* "a plum"

Ming I—"Darkening of the Light"; one of the sixty-four hexagrams, or oracles, of the *I Ching* (Book of Changes)

p'a-lung—"scrambling dragon"; a long, multioared boat often used to transport opium from foreign vessels; from *p'a,* "to creep, crawl," and *lung,* "dragon"

pai hsing—"one hundred surnames"; a common name for the Chinese people; it refers to the limited number of official surnames in China, which are listed in the *Pai-chia-hsing* (Book of Surnames); from *pai,* "one hundred," and *hsing,* "surname"

palanquin—an enclosed litter carried on the shoulders of men by means of poles; formerly used in eastern Asia as a means of conveyance usually for one person (Portuguese *palanquim,* from the Javanese *pëlanki*)

pidgin—"business"; language used by Chinese and foreign traders that is a corruption of English, Chinese, Portuguese, and Hindustani *qua*—an honorific title added to the names of mandarins of the ninth, or lowest, rank; hence Howqua, Mowqua, Powqua

rickshaw or *ricksha*—a small covered two-wheeled vehicle usually for one passenger that is pulled by one man; originally developed in Japan (from Japanese *jinrikisha*)

samshu or *samshoo* or *san-shao*—form of rice liquor at times fortified with tobacco juice and arsenic; also called first-chop rum; from *san,* "three," and *shao,* "to boil"

ta-ping ch'uan—"large soldier-boat"; a war junk with a flat bottom, high stern, square bow, and large lugsails; from *ta-ping,* "grand army, imperial troops," and *ch'uan,* "boat"

tao—"the way"; the mystery at the heart of Taoism, which developed from the teachings of Lao-tzu, who lived in the fifth century B.C.

Tao Te Ching—Book of the Way; the teachings of Lao-tzu; from *tao,* "the way," *tê,* "virtue, kindness," and *ching,* "sacred book"

T'ien Hsia—"Beneath the Sky," "Land Under Heaven," or "Celestial Land"; name formerly used by the Chinese to refer to their empire; from *t'ien,* "sky, heaven," and *hsia,* "beneath, below"

t'o-ku kai-chih—"finding in antiquity the sanction for present-day changes"; a practice followed by *chin-wên* scholars

yang—the male, or positive principle; represented in the *I Ching* by a solid line; also "the sun, light"

yin—the female, or negative principle; represented in the *I Ching* by a broken line; also "shady, dark" *yin-yang*—"male and female" or "heaven and earth"

Ying Kuo—"Eminent Country"; the Chinese name for England; from *ying,* "eminent, brave" (chosen because it sounds like the first syllable of England), and *kuo,* "country"

yuloh—a Chinese sculling oar with a fixed fulcrum; from *iu,* "to agitate, shake," and *lo,* "oar" (Cantonese)

A Letter to the Reader

i
sit
frozen
cup of tea
stalk of yarrow
chopstick on the snow
bowing low before the garden
hearing lao-tzu ah! ha! ha! laughing
dancing twelve-point circle through the drift
upraising high the spoon and chalice
washing in the mountain well
compressing expanding
length of spine
like a bow
arched
until open
the eye in turn
is following the dawn
the rolling wind grows black
snapping ice-bent shivering branches
waiting for the shock oh! oh! it comes oh no!
laughing voices laughing ah! ha! ha!
no sacrificial chalice spoon
no snow no chopsticks
no thundershock
but ha ha!
ha ha!
ha!
!

It is a bitter cold but sunny mid-January day in upstate New York, the ground covered with a foot of newly fallen snow. I just came downstairs after rummaging through the drawers of an old dresser and finding the preceding poem, which I wrote around 1973 or 1974 when I was in my early twenties. Entitled "The Arousing (shock, thunder)," it is based on the hexagram by the same name from the *I Ching,* a sacred book of Chinese thought written about three thousand years ago.

I have always felt particularly close to this hexagram, or oracle, which comments upon how an enlightened person must maintain his or her balance even in the midst of a cataclysm. In fact, when I started writing *Beneath the Sky,* I wanted to call it *The Arousing (shock, thunder).* But the publisher was rightfully concerned that someone browsing in a bookstore might mistake it for some sort of horror book, so I chose the current title and instead put my own translation of the hexagram at the opening of the book.

◆——◆——◆——◆

Initially I intended to write a single novel that would follow three families through the early period of the British Colonial Empire during Queen Victoria's reign. I began by doing preliminary research and then creating a one-hundred-page outline. That first outline included descriptions of thirty characters (twenty-three fictional and seven historical), twenty-four of whom made it into the final book, and a detailed synopsis of the plot, which was to have covered the four years from the coronation of Queen Victoria to the signing of the 1842 treaty that ended the Opium War.

I should have realized right at the start that it would be difficult to fit such a sweeping story into the six hundred manuscript pages that the publisher was expecting. And when I had gotten halfway through the manuscript but had covered only one-sixth of the synopsis, I knew I was in serious trouble.

Fortunately the good folks at Bantam Books came to the

rescue by allowing me in *Beneath the Sky* to tell the story of Ross Ballinger, his cousin Zoë, and Connor Maginnis through the period of the initial crisis that triggered the Opium War and to cover the war years in a subsequent novel.

◆   ◆   ◆

I am currently working on that sequel, which I am calling *Darkening of the Light.* Like *The Arousing (shock, thunder),* that title comes from the *I Ching.* The thirty-sixth hexagram is *Ming I,* or Darkening of the Light, which says: "The light has sunk into the earth—the image of Darkening of the Light. Thus does the superior man live with the great mass: He veils his light, yet still shines."

In *Beneath the Sky,* Lin Mei-li recited this oracle to Ross Ballinger during their journey aboard the Chinese war junk. It embodies the theme of the sequel, which covers a time when the sun truly appeared to be setting for the Celestial Empire.

As the Opium War heats up, the key lesson to be learned by Ross Ballinger—indeed, by all the participants in the drama—is how, during such a time of disruption and strife, to influence events around him without getting so caught up in them as to lose his own center. At the opening of *Darkening of the Light,* Ross discovers that he has lost not only the woman he loves but his own self, as well. It will be his challenge during the coming years of chaos and death to discover who he is and what role he must play in the drama unfolding around him. Zoë and Connor Maginnis must share their own quest of discovery, one that threatens to tear them and their love apart.

◆   ◆   ◆

While working on *Beneath the Sky,* a number of people asked what made me decide to write about England and China. As for England, I spent much of my junior year of college traveling throughout Great Britain, and I feel a great affinity to the land and its people. While I have no British blood that I know of, my children are descendants, on their mother's side, of Mary, Queen of Scots.

China has always been a source of great fascination for me, thanks primarily to my father, Murray Block. As a youngster he was a voracious reader of anything he could find relating to China, and he always dreamed of going there one day. When he enlisted in the Army Air Corps toward the end of World War II, he was thrilled to learn that he would be stationed in China. He had not requested the assignment and is convinced that if he had, the military undoubtedly would have sent him elsewhere.

My father served first in Sichuan (Szechwan) Province and at the close of the war was stationed in Beijing, known at the time as Peip'ing and later as Peking. When he flew from India to China and arrived in the little village of Hsinching near Chengdu, he felt the eerie sensation of having been there before. The sounds, the smells, the images of the buildings and people—everything was incredibly familiar to him. Indeed, our family has long believed that if there is such a thing as reincarnation, Murray's last life was spent in China. That first stay in China lasted a year, and since then he has returned five times, traveling extensively throughout the country.

I grew up in a house that blended Chinese and American decor, and I can't remember a time when I didn't know how to use chopsticks or say *"hsieh hsieh"* to the waiters. My own love for China and its people probably began as some sort of osmosis from my father, fully manifesting itself in 1985 when I had the good fortune to spend twenty-five days traveling throughout the country with my parents.

Accompanying us on that journey were my father's army buddy, Warren "Breck" Breckenridge, Jr., and his wife, Diane. Not only did I get to see China through my father's eyes, but I got to see a bit of my father as a young man through the reminiscences of Breck, who had the dubious pleasure of teaching Murray to drive a stick shift Jeep in December 1945 on the rocky back roads between Beijing and the Great Wall.

At the time, the Chinese drove on the left-hand side of the road, like the English and Japanese. But on January 1, 1946— only a few weeks after my father learned to drive— they switched to the right. Though the government urged citizens to make the change by plastering the country with the motto "Drive Right With Chiang Kai-shek," the changeover created mass confusion, with rickshaws, carts, and motorized vehicles traveling every which way. When my father next got into their Jeep, he almost mowed down large portions of the populace, and Breck refused to let him behind the wheel ever again. I daresay Murray's driving still suffers from that early trauma.

In addition to Breck's insights during our journey to China, I owe him a debt of gratitude for providing me with a trove of information regarding the China trading firm of Jardine, Matheson & Company.

My first trip to China took me to Shanghai, Hangzhou (Hangchow), Suzhou (Soochow), Wuxi (Wu-hsi), Nanjing (Nanking), Beijing (Peking), Xi'an (Sian), Guilin (Kweilin), Kunming, and Guangzhou (Canton). While the most exciting aspect of the journey was meeting the friendly, generous people, there were also many unforgettable sights. One of my favorites was Dragon Gate, a path carved into the wall of a cliff hundreds of feet over Lake Dian near Kunming. The trail, which in several places consists of a tunnel hacked out of solid rock, connects a series of meditation caves and pavilions that afford a spectacular view of the surrounding valley and lake. It was carved between 1781 and 1843 by a Taoist monk named Wu Lai-ch'ing, assisted by several stonecutters.

The Great Wall is even more impressive, and I was

especially moved when taking a photograph of my father at the exact spot he had his picture taken in 1945. Notable also were visits to the buried terra-cotta statues of Xi'an and the Stone Forest at Kunming. But perhaps the most inspiring moments of all were spent cruising up the Li River near Guilin, where Chinese paintings come to life in the form of the most eerily beautiful mountains I've ever seen.

In a few months I am scheduled to return to China, this time retracing the Silk Road camel route from Kashi (Kashgar) near the border of Afghanistan to Xi'an. The journey may inspire me to send Ross home to England via this once-popular land route, rather than by sea, perhaps even meeting the Taoist monk Wu Lai-ch'ing along the way.

Along with a love for China, I have a deep love of history— especially for learning about the everyday life of people in other ages. When I lived in San Francisco in the mid-1970s, I began collecting old books, and later I found myself drawn to write about past times and events that intrigued me. Among the favorite books in my collection are several old encyclopedias and mail-order catalogues, which have proven invaluable in researching the past.

Although not a student of seafaring history, I've slowly been gathering information on the subject, including an unusual pair of books that describe hundreds of the junks and sampans on the inland waterways of China, complete with detailed sketches of most of them. This set of books has led me to others, which will prove invaluable in describing the naval battles between the Chinese and British.

I have a particular fascination for the healing arts of the eighteenth and nineteenth centuries and have collected numerous medical books from that era. I hope to indulge that interest in *Darkening of the Light* through two new characters—a British ship's surgeon and a Chinese herbal healer— who will provide a comparison between Eastern and Western medicine at that time.

While there are significant differences between the two medical traditions, both were at the forefront in developing new surgical techniques. As early as the fifth century A.D., the Chinese were removing cataracts, with the first published description of the operation being given in the book *Wai Tai Mi Yao,* or *Medical Secrets Held by an Official,* written by Wang Tao in 752. A remarkably similar operation is described in *A Treatise on the Operations of Surgery* by Samuel Sharpe, a book I recently purchased that was published in London in 1782. And our current interest in preventive medicine is mirrored in China's oldest and most comprehensive medical classic, *Huang Di Nei Jing,* or *The Yellow Emperor's Canon of Medicine,* an eighteen-volume compilation of treatises from the third century B.C. It places great importance on "treatment of potential diseases," and it likens waiting to treat a disease until after its onset to digging a well only after one is thirsty.

To the western world, China has always seemed a vast land of deep mystery. To me, it is a place of rich beauty and culture, its people among the warmest I have ever encountered. Writing about China and its people is proving to be both a learning experience and a great voyage of the imagination, and I thank you for sharing it with me. I will endeavor to be as true to the history and culture as possible and apologize in advance if I sometimes fall short of the mark. Most importantly, it is my sincere hope that *Beneath the Sky* and the coming sequel, *Darkening of the Light,* capture in some small measure the wonder and excitement I feel about China and the events that took place there one hundred fifty years ago.

Since I view the writing of a novel as a collaboration between author and reader, I invite you to write to me in care of Bantam Books, 1540 Broadway, New York, NY 10036. I would especially enjoy hearing your own stories of England or China . . . or of any far-flung place to which you find yourself drawn, whether in the physical world or in your imagination.

—Paul Block
January 1993

About the Author

———◆———◆———◆———◆———◆———◆———

PAUL BLOCK was born in Manhattan and raised in Glen Cove on Long Island. While attending the State University of New York, he traveled for a year in Great Britain and Spain and received his degree in creative writing in 1973. The next six years were spent in San Francisco and Los Angeles, where he worked as an apartment manager, cappuccino maker, and fish cleaner, finally becoming a newspaper editor.

In 1979, Block moved to Albany, New York, to become assistant city editor at the afternoon newspaper. Preferring fiction to reality, he took a position at Book Creations Inc., in 1981, serving as editor in chief from 1990 until earlier this year when he left to pursue his writing career. He continues his association with Book Creations as a creative consultant.

Block has had seven previous novels published. The first five were westerns published under pseudonyms, followed by *San Francisco* and its sequel, *The Deceit,* published under his own name by Lynx Books. He is currently working on a sequel to *Beneath the Sky,* entitled *Darkening of the Light.* He lives in upstate New York with his family and recently returned from his second journey to China.

CAMERON JUDD

THE CANEBRAKE MEN

Following the War of Independence against the British, a band of Tennessee settlers intends to carve out a new state. But they face the opposition of the federal government, as well as bloody resistance from the Chickamauga Indians. In this untamed land Owen Killefer will find within himself a spirit as stout and strong as that of any rough-hewn frontiersman.

From one of America's most poweful and authentic frontier storytellers comes a sweeping new saga capturing the vision, the passion, and the pain that gave rise to a glorious new nation—America. This is the unforgettable story of the bold men and women who led the way into an unexplored land and an unknown future, seeking new challenges.

It all began with
WAGONS WEST
America's best-loved series by Dana Fuller Ross

❑ *Independence!* (26822-8 $4.95/$5.95 in Canada) A saga of high adventure and passionate romance on the first wagon train to Oregon territory.

❑ *Nebraska!* (26162-2 $4.95/$5.95 in Canada) Indian raids and sabotage threaten the settlers as "Whip" Holt leads the wagon train across the Great Plains.

❑ *Wyoming!* (26242-4 $4.95/$5.95 in Canada) Facing starvation, a mysterious disease, and a romantic triangle, the expedition pushes on.

❑ *Oregon!* (26072-3 $4.50/$4.95 in Canada) Three mighty nations clash on the fertile shore of the Pacific as the weary pioneers arrive.

❑ *Texas!* (26070-7 $4.99/$5.99 in Canada) Branded as invaders by the fiery Mexican army, a band of Oregon volunteers rallies to the cause of liberty.

❑ *California!* (26377-3 $4.99/$5.99 in Canada) The new settlers' lives are threatened by unruly fortune seekers who have answered the siren song of gold.

❑ *Colorado!* (26546-6 $4.95/$5.95 in Canada) The rugged Rockies hold the promise of instant wealth for the multitudes in search of a new start.

❑ *Nevada!* (26069-3 $4.99/$5.99 in Canada) The nation's treasury awaits a shipment of silver just as the country is on the brink of Civil War.

❑ *Washington!* (26163-0 $4.50/$4.95 in Canada) Ruthless profiteers await wounded Civil War hero Toby Holt's return to challenge his landholdings.

❑ *Montana!* (26073-1 $4.95/$5.95 in Canada) The lawless, untamed territory is terrorized by a sinister gang led by a tough and heartless woman.

❑ *Dakota!* (26184-3 $4.50/$4.95 in Canada) Against the backdrop of the Badlands, fearless Indian tribes form an alliance to drive out the white man forever.

❑ *Utah!* (26521-0 $4.99/$5.99 in Canada) Chinese and Irish laborers strive to finish the transcontinental railroad before corrupt landowners sabotage it.

❑ *Idaho!* (26071-5 $4.99/$5.99 in Canada) The perilous task of making a safe homeland from an untamed wilderness is hampered by blackmail and revenge.

❑ *Missouri!* (26367-6 $4.99/$4.99 in Canada) An incredible adventure on a paddle-wheel steamboat stirs romantic passions and gambling fever.

❑ *Mississippi!* (27141-5 $4.95/$5.95 in Canada) New Orleans is home to an underworld of crime, spawned by easy money and ruthless ambitions.

❑ *Louisiana!* (25247-X $4.99/$5.99 in Canada) Smuggled shipments of opium and shanghaied Chinese workers continue to invade the country.

❑ *Tennessee!* (25622-X $4.99/$5.99 in Canada) Unscrupulous politicians lead an army of outlaws and misfits to threaten America's cherished democracy.

❑ *Illinois!* (26022-7 $4.95/$5.95 in Canada) One of the nation's most awesome catastrophes tests the courage of the tough, new immigrants to the Midwest.

❑ *Wisconsin!* (26533-4 $4.95/$5.95 in Canada) Wealthy lumber barons seek to destroy those new enterprises that dare to defy their power.

❑ *Arizona!* (27065-6 $4.99/$5.99 in Canada) The comancheros who rule this sun-scorched frontier with brutal terror are sought by the U.S. Cavalry.

❑ *New Mexico!* (27458-9 $4.95/$5.95 in Canada) Law-abiding citizens infiltrate a cutthroat renegade gang to bring law and order to the Southwest.

❏ *Oklahoma!* (27703-0 $4.95/$5.95 in Canada) Homesteaders and ranchers head toward an all-out range war that will end their dreams of a peaceful existence.

❏ *Celebration!* (28180-1 $4.50/$5.50 in Canada) As Americans prepare to honor their nation on its centennial, the enemies of democracy stand ready to move in.

And then came
THE HOLTS: AN AMERICAN DYNASTY
The future generation by Dana Fuller Ross

❏ *Oregon Legacy* (28248-4 $4.50/$5.50 in Canada) An epic adventure of a legendary family's indomitable fighting spirit and unconquerable dreams.

❏ *Oklahoma Pride* (28446-0 $4.99/$5.99 in Canada) Buckboards and wagons get ready to roll as the "Sooners" await the start of the biggest land grab in history.

❏ *Carolina Courage* (28756-7 $4.95/$5.95 in Canada) As a dread disease runs rampant, hatred and blame fall on the last great Indian tribe of America's East.

❏ *California Glory* (28970-5 $4.99/$5.99 in Canada) Riots and strikes rock America's cities as workers demand freedom, fairness, and justice for all.

❏ *Hawaii Heritage* (29414-8 $4.99/$5.99 in Canada) Seeds of revolution turn the island paradise into a land of brutal turmoil and seething unrest.

❏ *Sierra Triumph* (29750-3 $4.99/$5.99 in Canada) A battle that goes beyond that of the sexes challenges the ideals of a nation and one remarkable family.

❏ *Yukon Justice* (29763-5 $5.50/$6.50 in Canada) As gold fever sweeps the nation, a great migration north begins to the Yukon Territory of Canada.

And now
WAGONS WEST: THE FRONTIER TRILOGY
From Dana Fuller Ross

❏ *Westward!* (29402-4 $5.50/$6.50 in Canada) The clock is turned back with this early story of the Holts, men and women who lived through the most rugged era of American exploration.

❏ *Expedition!* (29403-2 $5.50/$6.50 in Canada) In the heart of a majestic land, Clay Holt leads a perilous expedition up the Yellowstone River.

JANE'S POCKET BOOK OF NAVAL ARMAMENT

Edited by Denis Archer

COLLIER BOOKS
A Division of Macmillan Publishing Co., Inc.
New York

Macmillan Publishing Co., Inc.
866 Third Avenue, New York, N.Y. 10022
Collier Macmillan Canada, Ltd.

Library of Congress Catalog Card Number: 74-10317

First Collier Books Edition 1976

Printed in the United States of America

Contents

Introduction

In compiling this book I have attempted to provide the reader with a convenient source of information on most of the surface and submarine weapons currently or imminently in naval service or available for purchase by approved customers.

Apart from omissions resulting from inadvertence or ignorance, there are three categories of weapon which I have excluded altogether and two others in which coverage has been deliberately restricted. The excluded categories are aircraft armament, mines and man-portable weapons. From the wide range of airborne weapons it was tempting to select for inclusion those that have been developed specifically for naval use: on reflection, however, it seemed that there was no valid reason for preferring them to functionally similar weapons that happen also to be used against targets on land by land-based aircraft. Since to include every weapon that is or might be carried by naval aircraft would unreasonably increase the size and dilute the contents of the book, the only reasonable course appeared to be to omit them all.

Mines present a problem of a different kind. That mine warfare is an important part of naval warfare is undeniable; and if one chooses to look on an acoustic or magnetic mine laid by a ship, submarine or aircraft as a very slow homing torpedo, the logical case for including such weapons in a book of this kind is strong. Unfortunately, while it is possible in some instances to obtain details of dimensions and general characteristics of mines that happen to be made by commercial organisations, many are made in state-controlled factories from which it may be difficult to obtain any information at all. Moreover, the really important information, that concerning mine operating systems and the ways in which they can be countered, is understandably not available for publication.

Much the same is true of one of the two categories whose share of the book has been restricted. On older and smaller craft, and notably on those that never venture far from the shore, there is to be found a great miscellany of weapons that have little relevance to the broad picture of naval armaments. Some of these are converted army weapons; others are rare survivors from an earlier era. For many such devices identification and the subsequent discovery of performance characteristics present problems which are out of keeping with the value of the information ultimetely obtained.

Among current weapons there are no deliberate omissions from the extensive list of cannon and guns having calibres of more than 30 mm. Below this calibre some small weapons and especially some varieties of mounting for widely deployed weapons have been omitted because operationally the weapons are so much alike even though they may differ widely in superficial mechanical detail.

At the other end of the scale, however, I have included brief descriptions of the submarine-launched ballistic missiles which are either currently operational or known to be in development.

Arguably, these are not naval weapons at all, but counters in the international strategic contest that happen to be transported by naval vessels; on the other hand it scarcely seemed reasonable, in a book about naval armament, to omit the most potent weapons ever installed in any naval vessel.

Purpose of the Book

In some ways it is easier to define what the purpose of the book is not than to enlarge on my opening statement of intent.

First, it is not a book on weapon recognition. To perform that function adequately the number of illustrations would have to be greatly increased; and for some weapons it would be difficult to deal adequately with the problem in this format.

Secondly it is not a "systems" book. In the weapon descriptions the emphasis is on performance rather than on construction or on the relationship between the weapon and associated radar and other systems.

Lastly it is in no sense an official guide or manufacturers' catalogue. Although help from both official and commercial sources has been willingly given, this help has been limited to the provision of information on some (by no means all) of the weapons listed herein. The selection and presentation of that information and of much additional material obtained from other sources has been strictly my responsibility.

Security

All the information used in compiling this book has been obtained from open sources. As already noted, many official bodies and commercial organisations have, directly or indirectly, supplied much of this information; but a further substantial input has been derived from the host of books, yearbooks and periodicals which deal with military affairs and with weapons.

While data on some weapons can be obtained only from such published sources or, as an example of another source, by the scrutiny of photographs obtained from press agencies or official or commercial press offices, it is also often possible to use such openly published data to supplement officially supplied information on other weapons.

This aspect of the information gathering and presentation process is extremely relevant to the question of official secrecy. All weapon data obtained from primary sources (that is, official bodies in the weapon's country of origin and any concerned commercial bodies in the same country) are subject to whatever general and particular security restrictions bear on that weapon; and this commonly results in the absence of one or more important characteristics (such as speed or range) from the primary source data.

Secondary sources, which include official bodies, commercial organisations and the press in other countries, are not similarly inhibited; and if they know, or can guess, what the missing figures should be there is nothing (except, in some instances, wider-ranging alliance security restrictions) to prevent them from making their views public. The figures they publish may or may not be correct; but until they are displaced by some more authoritative primary source pronouncement or a more convincing secondary source statement, they will be added to the general corpus of published data on weapon performance from which other writers and commentators can draw freely without infringing security regulations.

Where two or more secondary sources are independently contributing data on the same weapon system, their pronouncements on particular aspects of the system will frequently differ. If such differences are other than trivial, anyone making use of the secondary source data must either select what he regards as the most likely set of figures or accept the uncertainty as it is.

In the weapon descriptions in this book I have not distinguished between data obtained from primary or secondary sources. Where there is no obvious uncertainty involved I have set out the relevant figures without qualification: where there is a conflict of information or I am for any other reason doubtful of the accuracy of a figure I qualify it by the use of such words or phrases as "probably" "possibly" "said to be" and so forth. The milder qualifications "approximately" or "about" are used to cover such minor discrepancies as can arise from multiple metric /imperial/metric conversions or a failure to specify the precise nature of a measurement.

It is very important to realise, therefore, that although a manufacturer's name may be associated with a weapon description it is possible that none of the published data was supplied by him and quite likely that he did not supply all the figures. A specific and interesting example may make the nature of this situation clearer. In May 1971 the East German magazine *Militärtechnik* published a short description of the Blowpipe man-portable surface-to-air missile system; and in the tabulated data accompanying this description were figures for missile speed, maximum range, maximum engagement altitude and so forth, some of which still have not been published by any primary source in the UK.

Whether or not the figures given in this description were correct, therefore, I cannot say: what can be said is that, viewed against what is known or surmised concerning other missile systems the figures do not appear to be unreasonable. If Blowpipe as such were described in this book I would use these figures without qualification: in the Blowpipe-derived systems which are described here I have used them with such qualification as the change of use seems to require.

Accuracy

That secondary sources need to be used when possible to fill gaps in data supplied by primary sources will be readily appreciated: it may strike some readers as odd, however, that I should not indicate which data come from which source. To do so, however, would inevitably encourage the view that primary source data are superior to and more reliable than secondary data; and while this may often be so it is easy to invent circumstances in which the converse would be true: the primary data, for example, might simply reflect the requirements of the design specification while the secondary data might be based on an assessment of some much more recent firing trials of which details had found their way into circulation.

Few, if any, sources of information on weapons can be regarded as wholly impartial: almost all have some commercial, political or diplomatic axe to grind and standards of assessment vary widely from country to country. Moreover, there is likely to be a big difference between the performances achievable with a weapon system when, on the one hand, it is perfectly adjusted and operated by a well-drilled crew in fine weather with no enemy about; and when, on the other hand, it has been at sea for a year or two and is operated by a battle-stressed crew under fire in foul weather: since the latter performance is probably the one that matters, and since there is no simple way of inferring it from the optimum performance, another element of uncertainty and inaccuracy is added to those associated with the sources of information.

From all this it follows that no compilation of weapon data can provide more than an indication of the performance to be expected from any weapon and of the relative merits of competing weapons. In the pages that follow I have done my best to provide this indication; but the accuracy of the data is not warranted.

Arrangement

There is no uniquely logical way of arranging such a collection of information. Generally, for weapons whose calibre is a significant parameter, I have arranged them in descending order of calibre, in alphabetical order of country within each calibre division and roughly in chronological order within each country subdivision. Other weapons, such as guided missiles, are arranged in alphabetical order of the names by which they are commonly known.

Weapon Status

In most instances I have given some indication of the status of a weapon or system. Because information travels more rapidly through some channels than it does through others these status descriptions cannot be regarded as exactly contemporaneous. Most of them, however, relate to the beginning of 1975 with a tolerance of about three months in either direction.

Polaris A-3

Polaris A-3 is one of the two submarine-launched ballistic missiles currently operational in the US Navy, the earlier A-1 and A-2 models having been phased out. It has a range of some 4,600 km (2,500 nm) and was originally fitted with a single 1MT warhead but all deployed missiles now have a 3 × 200 KT MRV warhead.

Polaris A-3 is currently deployed in the *Ethan Allen* and *George Washington* classes of SSBN and in some of the *Lafayette* class. Submarines in the last-named class are being converted to carry the Poseidon C-3 missile, and early in 1975 all but eight had been converted. The two earlier classes cannot be converted to Poseidon and will continue to carry Polaris until they are withdrawn from service.

Missile Data
Length: 9.7 m
Diameter: 137 cm
Launch weight: 16 tons
Propulsion: 2-stage, solid propellants
Guidance: Inertial
Warhead: 3 × 200 KT MRV
Range: 4,600 km (2,500 nm)
Date introduced: 1964 (with single warhead)

Manufacturer
Main system contractor: Lockheed Missiles and Space Co.

Status
Production complete. Missiles in service as stated. *Lafayette* conversions should be completed in 1978.

Poseidon C-3

Poseidon is the larger and more potent of the two missiles currently deployed on US ballistic missile submarines. Nearly twice the weight of the Polaris A-3, it has the same range; but it incorporates an improved guidance system and—its most significant feature—a much more elaborate warhead arrangement. This Mk 3 (or 300) re-entry vehicle has capacity for 14 subsidiary re-entry vehicles, with or without warheads, each of which can be independently targeted (MIRV system).

Poseidon is already deployed in the majority of the 31 *Lafayette* class of submarines in which it is replacing Polaris and in which it will remain until supplanted by the C-4 Trident 1 missile now in development.

Missile Data
Length: 10.4 m
Diameter: 188 cm
Launch weight: 27 tons
Propulsion: 2-stage, solid propellants
Guidance: Improved inertial
Warhead: MIRV with 14RV capacity
Currently 10 × 50 KT + penaids
Range: 4,600 km (2,500 nm)
Date introduced: 1971

Manufacturer
System contractor: Lockheed Missiles & Space Co.

Status
Operational on an increasing scale in *Lafayette* submarines of the USN.

TRIDENT MISSILE PROGRAMME   (USA)

Currently in development as a successor to the Poseidon missile, this weapon was formerly known as the ULMS—undersea long-range missile system. The development programme has been through several revisions but now appears to divide into two fairly distinct missile development operations with one associated submarine development operation.

First, as an interim measure to improve the US strategic position vis-à-vis the USSR, a C-4 missile (also known as Trident 1) is being developed and will be deployed in place of Poseidon in at least some of the *Lafayette* class submarines of the USN. It will also probably be used as the first missile to be deployed with the new Trident submarine which is also currently being developed. The important new features of the C-4 missile will be an increase in range to 7,000 km (3,800 nm) and the introduction of the Mk 500 MARV warhead—a device which is able to manoeuvre slightly during the re-entry phase so as to confuse and evade the defences. Subsequently, as a second stage of missile development, a new missile with an even greater range (10,000 km—5,400 nm) will be introduced and used as the armament of the new heavy submarines, supplanting the C-4 missile if all goes well.

Manufacturer
Missile main contractor: Lockheed Missiles & Space Co.

Status
Development.

Comet-2 missile used for the earliest ballistic missile installations in Russian submarines

RUSSIAN SUBMARINE-LAUNCHED BALLISTIC MISSILES

There are three basic types of significant and currently operational submarine-launched ballistic missile in service with the Soviet Navy. Such brief details of these missiles as are available are given in the entries following this one; but because the place of these missiles in the general pattern of Soviet naval development is best understood by reference to the parallel submarine development programme, some brief notes on relevant submarines are appended.

Z-V Class

Diesel-powered submarine converted in 1955-57 for surface launch of ballistic missiles. First trials were with an adapted Scud-A missile system developed for the Red Army: subsequently the short range missile known by the NATO code-name Sark or the US code SS-N-4 was installed. Only one, non-operational, member of the class is known to remain.

G Class

Diesel-powered submarine built to launch ballistic missiles from the surface. Originally equipped with the SS-N-4 (Sark), about half the class were later converted to the improved SS-N-5 (Serb) missile. About twenty of these submarines are still operational but the remaining Sark missiles, which were credited with a range of only 650 km (350 nm) are no longer regarded as operationally significant—especially when mounted in a diesel-powered submarine. G-class submarines entered service around 1960 and the first Serb conversions became operational in about 1968.

H Class

These were the first nuclear-powered Russian submarines to be equipped with ballistic missiles. Like the G-class boats they were first equipped with Sark missiles in launch tubes mounted in the fin, and first became operational around 1960. All submarines in this class, however, were converted to carry the SS-N-5 Serb missile between 1963 and 1967; and it was only after these conversions were complete that the G-class conversion began. Eight of these submarines are believed to be operational.

Y Class

Similar to the US *Lafayette* class, these submarines were built to carry a much-improved ballistic missile suitable for underwater launch which is positively known as the SS-N-6 and probably bears the NATO code-name Sawfly. The nuclear-powered submarine carries 16 of these missiles. About 33 of these submarines, which entered service around 1968, are believed to be operational.

D Classes

A development of the Y-class boat, this class was designed to carry 12 larger and longer-range missiles which are positively known as the SS-N-8 but whose NATO code has not been published. The first D-class patrols began in 1974 and the submarines are still being built. Construction of a larger version of the submarine capable of carrying 16 SS-N-8 missiles has been reported and a final total deployment of 18 D-I and 12 D-II (enlarged) has been postulated.

Sark ballistic missiles—the first to be designed specifically for launching from Russian submarines—in a Moscow parade

(USSR)

The most advanced of the first generation of Russian submarine-launched ballistic missiles, the SS-N-5 is still operationally deployed although it can be launched only from the surface. It is believed to be ejected from its launch tube by cold gas generators which are jettisoned when the main motor fires. Visual identification of this missile is uncertain, however, and all data given here (with the possible exception of the range) should be viewed with suspicion.

Serb missile on parade

SS-N-5 (SERB) BALLISTIC MISSILE

Missile Data
Length: 11-13 m
Diameter: 120-150 cm
Launch weight: 13-18 tons
Propulsion: storable liquid
Guidance: inertial
Warhead: nuclear, single
Range: 1,300 km (700 nm)
Date introduced: 1963

Status
Operational in G and H class submarines. Scale of deployment is about 50 launchers of which about 24 (in H class boats) are counted in the SALT context.

First of the second-generation, dived-launch, Russian SLBM, this missile is certainly designated SS-N-6 in the US code and probably known as Sawfly to NATO. There is, however, some doubt (in the public arena at least) regarding the visual identification of this or the SS-N-8 with any missile that has ever been exhibited in a Moscow parade. All data given below—except the ranges, which are firmly quoted by US official sources—should be regarded as tentative.

According to US official statements three models of this missile have been observed. The first two are single-warhead weapons, Mod 2 having a greater range than Mod 1: the third has a 2-3-warhead MRV arrangement.

Missile Data

Length: 10-13 m

Diameter: 150-180 cm

Launch weight: 20 tons

Propulsion: storable liquid

Guidance: inertial

Warhead: Mods 1 & 2 nuclear, single
Mod 3 MRV, double or triple

Range: Mod 1 2,400 km (1,300 nm)
Mods 2 & 3 3,000 km (1,600 nm)

Date introduced: Mod 1, 1968   Mods 2 & 3 1974.

Status

Currently the most widely-deployed Russian SLBM. All three versions are operational although Mod 1 is expected to be phased out gradually. All are deployed on Y-class submarines.

Sawfly SLBM

SS-N-8 BALLISTIC MISSILE

Latest in the series of Russian-developed SLBM, the SS-N-8 has a greater range capability than any other operational submarine-launched missile. Currently deployed with a single warhead it is expected that a multiple warhead will be put into operational use before long.

As with other Russian SLBM, information available from open sources does not present a clear picture of the dimensions and configuration of this missile. The following data must therefore be regarded as provisional except, once again, that the achievable range has been positively stated by the US authorities.

Missile Data

Length: 13-15 m
Diameter: 150-180 cm
Launch weight: 28-30 tons
Propulsion: storable liquid
Guidance: inertial
Warhead: nuclear, single at present
Range: 7,800 km (4,200 nm)
Date introduced: 1973

Status
Operational in D-class nuclear submarines of the Soviet Navy.

(UK)

RN POLARIS MISSILES

The Royal Navy has an operational fleet of four ballistic missile submarines equipped with a British version of the American A-3 Polaris missile. The *Resolution* class submarines were built in the UK (by Vickers and Cammell Laird) between 1964 and 1969: a plan for a fifth submarine was cancelled in 1965. The hulls and machinery are of British design but the whole of the missile launching complex and the nuclear power plant is of American design. The associated Polaris missiles were also designed, and are made, in the USA except for the nuclear warhead, re-entry vehicle and fuzing and arming devices which were designed and are made and fitted in the UK. Each submarine carries 16 missiles.

Status
Operational in the Royal Navy.

RN Polaris missile in flight

24

(FRANCE)

A programme covering the development of submarine-launched ballistic missiles and their associated nuclear-powered submarines has been running now for more than a decade. Four submarines have been launched and three are operational, each with sixteen ballistic missiles. A fourth submarine, *(L'Indomptable,* launched in 1974) was due to become operational at the end of 1975 by which time the fifth submarine, *Le Tonnant,* should have been launched.

The parallel ballistic missile development programme has been conducted in two phases with a third and possibly a fourth to follow. The first phase resulted in the M-1 missile which has a range of some 2,500 km (1,350 nm) and this equips the first two submarines *(Le Redoutable* and *Le Terrible)*. The second phase resulted in the M-2 missile to equip the third *(Le Foudroyant)* and succeeding submarines: this missile has a range of some 3,400 km (1,825 nm) but the same nuclear warhead (believed to be 500 KT) as the earlier missile. M-2 missiles will be retrofitted to the first two submarines in due course.

The third stage of the programme is scheduled to involve the fitting of a thermonuclear warhead, in the megaton range, equipped with penetration aids. The fourth and fairly remote stage involves upgrading the system to some 5,500 km (3,000 nm) range and adding MRV or MIRV warhead arrangements.

Missile Data (Current weapons)
Length: 10.4 m
Diameter: 150 cm
Launch weight: M-1 18 tons
M-2 20 tons
Propulsion: 2-stage, solid propellants
Guidance: inertial
Warhead: nuclear, probably 500 KT
Range: M-1 2,500 km (1,350 nm)
M-2 3,400 km (1,825 nm)
Date introduced: M-1: 1971
M-2: 1975

Manufacturer
Missile System contractor: Aérospatiale.

Status
Operational as described above.

SUBMARINE-LAUNCHED BALLISTIC MISSILE

Apart from one Russian-type G-class submarine capable of launching ballistic missiles only when surfaced and for which there may well be no functioning missiles, the People's Republic of China has no deployed SLBM force at present.

Military authorities in the USA, however, are firmly of the opinion that nuclear-powered ballistic missile submarines and missiles for them will be developed in China. They expect the first missile to be similar to the early US Polaris missile and to use solid propellants. It is known that the Chinese are working on solid propellant systems, but the currently and imminently operational Chinese land-based ballistic missiles all use liquid propellants.

DUAL-PURPOSE MISSILES

The missiles described in this section have all been designed primarily for surface-to-surface applications and cannot in general be used against aerial targets. Missiles that have been designed primarily for anti-aircraft and anti-missile purposes, however, can often be pressed into service to attack surface targets; and some missile systems have a genuine dual-purpose capability.

Missile systems for which useful surface-to-surface capability has been claimed, and which are not otherwise described in this section, are listed below.

Basic, Improved and Advanced Point Defence Missile Systems **(USA)**
NATO Sea Sparrow **(International)**
Sea Dart **(UK)**
Seaslug **(UK)**

It should also be noted that the Canadian Sea Sparrow system, described in this section, was designed from the outset as a dual purpose system.

This is an extended-range surface-to-surface missile system suitable for installation in fast patrol boats or larger vessels. The system comprises a container-launched inertially-guided missile, with automatic altitude control and with an active radar homing system for the terminal phase, backed up by a shipborne target location and fire control system. The missile has a cylindrical body with a pointed ogival nose and cruciform wings indexed in line with cruciform tail control surfaces. It is powered by a tandem two-stage solid-propellant motor giving it a high subsonic speed.

Computed future target position data are programmed into the missile guidance system before launching and the missile flies on this programmed course to within about 10 km of the target after which the active radar homing system takes control. During flight the missile height is maintained at 2-3 metres above the sea surface by a radio altimeter system.

Missile Data

Length: 512 cm
Body diameter: 344 mm
Wing span: 100 cm
Launch weight: 720 kg
Warhead: At least 150 kg HE
Cruising speed: High subsonic
Maximum range: 37 km (20 nm)

Manufacturers

Aérospatiale (System manufacturer)

Status

In production and in service with, or on order for, the French Navy and several Western European and South American Navies. Further development of the system is in hand for shipborne (MM39, and MM40 and possibly MM100) submarine (SM39) and airborne use (AM38, AM39). The airborne applications are not further discussed in this book.

Exocet MM38 launch

29

EXOCET MM39

This is a shipborne derivative of the AM 39 airborne version of the original Exocet missile. Dimensions, weight and propulsion details are the same as for the airborne missile; but the MM39 has folding wings to enable it to be accommodated in small glass-fibre container-launchers. Four of these tubular containers can be accommodated in the space required for an MM38 launcher.

Missile Data
Length: 469 cm
Body diameter: 35 cm
Wing span: 100 cm
Launch weight: 650 kg
Warhead: believed to be the same as for MM38
Max range: 50 km (27 nm)

Manufacturer
Aérospatiale.

Status
Advanced development. Expected to be ready for service before 1977.

Exocet MM 38 (below) and AM 39

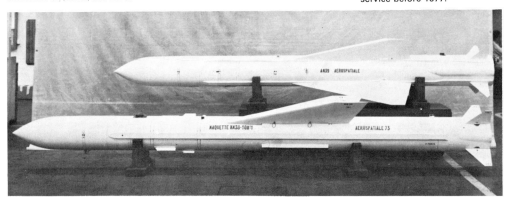

30

(FRANCE)   EXOCET MM40

This designation is believed to have been earmarked for a very long range version of the Exocet missile. No details are available except that a range of 50-100 nm is believed to be contemplated and that this would be covered at a speed probably in excess of Mach 2. It is also understood that the project would be a joint Franco-German (Euromissile) programme.

(FRANCE/GERMANY)   EXOCET MM100

This is an upgraded version of the original MM38. It has the same weight and dimensions and is launched from the same launcher-container. Propulsion improvements, however, give a boost phase of 2.4 seconds followed by a sustainer burn of 220 seconds—nearly double that of the MM38. This is expected to extend the maximum range of the missile to about 70 km (38 nm).

Status
Development—with completion expected before 1977. Coastal defence application under consideration.

Gabriel launcher/container

This medium-range surface-to-surface missile system is suitable for installation in fast patrol boats or larger vessels. The system comprises a container-launched radar command-guided missile with autopilot/altimeter flight control backed up by a shipborne target location and fire control system. Terminal guidance is believed to be (probably semi-active) radar with infra-red alternative for ECM conditions. Also for use in conditions unfavourable to command guidance is a shipborne manual/optical missile control system. The missile has a cylindrical body with a pointed nose and cruciform wings indexed in line with cruciform tail control surfaces. It is powered by tandem solid-propellant motors providing a 3-second boost of some 3,600 kg st and a sustained thrust of some 77 kg st for 100 seconds. The missile, pre-packaged in its glass-fibre container, is mounted on a swivelling launch platform but launched at a fixed elevation. After an initial climb it descends to within a few metres of the sea-surface under altimeter control.

Missile Data
Length: 335 cm
Body diameter: 32 cm
Wing span: 138 cm
Launch weight: 400 kg
Range: 22 km (14 nm)
Speed: about Mach 0.7
Warhead: 160 kg HE
Manufacturers
Israel Aircraft Industries.
Status
In service in Israel and supplied to at least four other countries. A longer-range version with a longer-duration (200 sec) sustained motor is believed to be entering service. It is credited with a range of 41 km (26 nm). Gabriel was used operationally in the 1973 war and performed better than the Russian Styx.

Gabriel missile in flight

Long-range all-weather, anti-ship cruise missile system. Three systems—air-launched, surface-launched and submarine-launched—all based on the same missile are being developed. The surface-launched version comprises an inertially-guided missile, with an active radar search and homing system for the terminal phase, and a command and launch subsystem which can be used with various launchers backed up by either own ship's or third-party data acquisition devices. This flexibility will enable the weapon to be installed on a wide variety of naval vessels ranging upwards in size from patrol hydrofoils. The cylindrical missile has an ogival nose and is fitted with cruciform wings indexed in line with cruciform tail control fins for the main missile and with cruciform fins on the booster assembly which provides initial propulsion; cruise propulsion is by turbojet. During the boost phase the missile executes an unguided climb; after booster separation it is brought on course by the on-board computer and inertial system operating on target data inserted immediately before launch. It then cruises at a low altitude under altimeter control; when it nears the target the active radar homing system is switched on to seek, locate and lock on the target. In the final phase the missile executes a rapid climb-and-dive manoeuvre. The homing radar is frequency agile for ECCM purposes. Suitable missile launchers include those used for ASROC, Tartar and Terrier and a special canister launcher for patrol hydrofoils or other ships not fitted with one of the other launchers.

Missile Data

Length: 475 cm (384 cm without booster)
Body diameter: 34 cm
Wing span: 83 cm
Launch weight: 635 kg (500 kg without booster)
Warhead: HE, possibly nuclear
Range: in excess of 55 km (30 nm)

Manufacturers

McDonnell Douglas Astronautics Company.

Status

Advanced development. Service entry planned for 1975.

Harpoon fired from a surface launcher

NATO LONG-RANGE ANTI-SHIP MISSILE

An attempt has been made to establish a common requirement for a long-range surface-to-surface ship-launched missile which NATO navies could adopt as a standard weapon for the 1980s. As yet no firm agreement has been promulgated, but it is thought that the current US cruise missile development programme probably covers most of the likely requirements. Much depends on what is ultimately regarded as a reasonably "long" range: if it is upwards of about 150 nm all current NATO developments other than the USN cruise missile would be eliminated; if it is between 100 nm and 150 nm weapons like Otomat or conceivably the proposed MM100 are possible candidates.

A long-range surface-to-surface missile system, Otomat is suitable for installation in fast patrol boats or larger vessels. The system comprises a container-launched autopilot-guided missile with automatic altitude control and with an active radar homing system for the terminal phase, backed up by a shipborne target location and fire control system. The missile has a cylindrical body and pointed nose; its cruciform wings are indexed in line with cruciform tail control surfaces and each carries an air inlet for the turbojet cruise motor at its root. For launching, two lateral jettisonable solid-propellant boosters are mounted in the angles of the wings.

Launched at an angle of 20°, the missile initially climbs to about 150 m then descends, within a distance of about 2 nm (4 km), to its cruising height of 15 m. In this phase it is flying under turbojet power with autopilot navigation and radio altimeter control. When about 6.5 nm (12 km) from the target the active radar homing system takes control and within the last 3.75 nm (7 km) or so the missile executes a programmed climb and steep terminal dive.

Missile Data
Length: 438 cm
Body diameters: 40 cm (forward), 46 cm (over turbo-jet)
Wing span: 138 cm
Launch weight: 700 kg
Warhead: 210 kg semi-AP, HE
Cruising speed: high subsonic
Range: 80 km (43 nm)

Manufacturers
Engins Matra and OTO Melara.

Status
Ordered by three countries including Italy and Venezuela. Further development in hand.

OTOMAT MK II

A Mk II version has been developed. Its principal features are increased range (about 100 km) and a new homing head which permits the missile to follow a sea-skimming trajectory to the target instead of executing the pull-up and dive manoeuvre of the Mk 1.

TÉSEO

A third version is in development for the Italian forces under the name Téseo. Range is said to be 200 km and it is probably intended for coastal defence.

Otomat launch

Penguin is a medium-range surface-to-surface missile system intended primarily for installation on fast patrol boats but suitable also for other applications. The system comprises a container-launched, inertially-guided missile, fitted with an infra-red search and homing system for the terminal phase, and requires a back-up data-acquisition and fire-control system. The missile has a cylindrical body with swept cruciform wings which control the flight and which are indexed in line with small swept fins mounted on the tapered nose. It is powered by a two-stage solid-propellant rocket motor. Missiles are supplied pre-packaged in glass-fibre launch containers: these are mounted on fixed launch platforms and connected to the fire-control system by an umbilical connector. After launch the missile follows a predetermined but variable trajectory until within infra-red seeker range of the target; at which point the homing system searches for, locates and locks onto the target, providing terminal guidance for the missile.

Missile Data
Length: 300 cm
Body diameter: 28 cm
Wing span: 140 cm
Launch weight: 330 kg (500 kg including launch container)
Warhead: 120 kg semi-AP, HE. Impact fuse
Cruising speed: Mach 0.7
Range: at least 26 km (14 nm)

Manufacturer
A/S Kongsberg Vaapenfabrikk.

Status
In service in Royal Norwegian Navy and supplied to Sweden. A Mk II version with a range of about 30 km (15 nm) is in development. Possible helicopter-launched applications are under consideration.

Penguin missile launchers on *Storm* class FPB

This long-range surface-to-surface cruise missile system is intended for coastal defence or shipborne use on destroyers or larger vessels. The system is based on the French (Aérospatiale, formerly Nord-Aviation) CT20 target drone and comprises a rocket-launched turbojet-powered monoplane with autopilot guidance and (probably) radar homing. The autopilot is programmed with target data up to the moment of launch and maintains course at a constant altitude (after an initial climb) until the homing system takes over for the terminal phase. Although the system has been in service for many years, performance data and details of the homing system have never been revealed. It may be assumed, however, that the range of the system is limited more by the accuracy with which future target position can be predicted and by the system guidance accuracy than by the missile's flight endurance.

Missile Data

Length: 572 cm

Wing span: 301 cm

Launch weight: 1,215 kg including 315 kg for rocket booster unit

Warhead: said to be large enough to destroy an average freighter

Cruising speed: probably not more than Mach 0.8

Range: potentially some hundreds of kilometres, but see above

Date introduced: 1967

Manufacturers

SAAB Aktiebolag

Status

Production ceased in 1970. System is now deployed on two *Halland*-class destroyers of the Royal Swedish Navy and for coastal defence.

RB 08 launch

SEA KILLER Mk 1   (ITALY)

Formerly, known as Nettuno, this is a short-range surface-to-surface missile system suitable for installation in fast patrol boats or larger vessels. The system comprises a multiple launcher which can be remotely trained and which carries five missiles prepacked in launch containers. Missile control is by beam-riding in azimuth and by radio commanded radio altimeter in elevation. If interference precludes beam-riding, optical tracking and radio command can be substituted. The system is designed for use with an X-band gunfire control system modified to provide the radio command and optical (TV) tracking facilities. The missile has a cylindrical light alloy body with an ogival nose section. Control is by movable wings which are indexed in line with the cruciform tail stabilising fins. It is powered by a solid-propellant rocket motor which develops 2,000 kg st and burns for five seconds. After an initial climb the missile descends to within a few metres of the sea surface for the final stages of its flight.

Missile Data
Length: 373 cm
Body diameter: 21 cm
Wing span: 86 cm
Launch weight: 170 kg
Warhead: 35 kg HE
Cruising speed: subsonic after burn-out
Range: over 10 km (5 nm)
Date introduced: 1969

Manufacturer
Sistel SpA

Status
In service with the Italian Navy on the FPB *Saetta,* otherwise superseded by Sea Killer Mk 2 for shipborne use. The missile is used in the Marte helicopter anti-ship system.

Sea Killer Mk I

SEA KILLER Mk 2

(ITALY)

Formerly known as Vulcano this medium-range surface-to-surface missile system is suitable for installation in fast patrol boats, hydrofoils, gun motor-boats or larger vessels. The system is similar to the earlier Sea Killer Mk 1 but the missile is powered by two solid propellant motors—a 4,000 kg st booster and a 100 kg st sustainer—and carries a larger warhead. The boost motor is contained in a rear section which is jettisoned after burn-out (about 1.7 secs) and which is fitted with large cruciform wings to stabilise the missile which is unguided during the boost phase. After the boost meter has been jettisoned the sustainer motor is ignited, the missile is gathered to the fire-control radar beam and guided to the target by the same procedures as are used for Sea Killer Mk 1. The missile can be launched from fixed launchers or the quintuple launcher designed for Sea Killer Mk 1.

Missile Data
Length: 470 cm (364 cm without booster)
Body diameter: 21 cm
Wing span: 100 cm
Launch weight: 270 kg
Warhead: 75 kg semi-armour-piercing HE
Cruising speed: more than 250 m/sec after booster burn-out
Range: more than 25 km (13 nm)

Manufacturer
Sistel SpA

Status
In service with the Iranian Navy on the *Saam*-class frigates. Like Sea Killer Mk 1 the Mk 2 missile can also be used in the Marte helicopter anti-ship system.

Launching a Sea Killer Mk 2

Quintuple trainable launcher for Sea Killer Mk 2

This extended-range surface-to-surface automatic homing missile will have a performance superior to that of Sea Killer Mk 1 or Mk 2 (qq.v.). Differences from the earlier missiles include a second cruise motor to give extended range, a larger warhead and an active radar terminal homing system. The system can use target data from own ship's radar or from other ships or aircraft: these data are converted into coordinates relative to own ship's stabilised platform by a launch computer in the missile control console and programmed into the missile. After launching the missile climbs under boost on a fixed trajectory: the booster then separates and the missile is brought under autopilot control to the correct heading on a descending cruise path. It continues under autopilot control until approximately 6 km (3 nm) from the target at which point the active radar homing system is switched on: this radar searches for, locates and locks on the target, providing guidance for the missile in the terminal attack phase. The shipboard installation comprises only two (single or double) launchers and a missile control console. The missile configuration is similar to that of Sea Killer Mk 2 and it is powered by a solid-propellant booster giving 10,000 kg st for 1.6 sec and two solid-propellant sustainers each giving 100 kg st for 70 secs.

Missile Data

Length: 530 cm (410 cm without booster)
Body diameter: 32 cm (at wing roots)
Wing span: 109 cm (control wings)
Launch weight: about 548 kg reducing to 335 kg
Warhead: 150 kg semi-armour-piercing HE: impact/proximity fuze
Cruising speed: 280 m/sec after booster burn-out
Flight height: 10 m cruising; 3-5 m attack
Range: more than 45 km (24 nm)

Manufacturer

Sistel SpA

Status

Advanced development.

SEA SPARROW

(CANADA)

This system is intended for use in both surface-to-surface and surface-to-air engagements. It uses the AIM-7E2 version of the Sparrow III missile (Raytheon) which is operational in other systems in various countries. In the Canadian system the missile is launched from a four-missile support pylon on an extendable cantilever beam.

Missiles can be fired singly or in rapid succession, automatic pre-launch commands being supplied electrically. Semi-automatic power loading provides rapid recycling and launching.

A Signaal radar and fire control system capable of handling surface and airborne targets simultaneously is an integral part of the missile system.

Manufacturer
System contractor, Raytheon Canada Ltd.

Status
Operational as a dual installation in *Iroquois* class destroyers and as a single installation in the replenishment ships *Preserver* and *Protector* of the Canadian Armed Forces.

SS.11 is a small wire-guided missile developed initially as an anti-tank weapon but suitable as a general-purpose assault weapon and used in some marine installations. The current version is the SS.11 B.1.

Missile Data
Length: 120 cm
Body diameter: 16 cm
Wing span: 50 cm
Launch weight: 30 kg
Warhead: HE, armour-piercing or fragmentation
Guidance: wire guidance command to line-of-sight by joystick controller. Visual tracking
Cruising speed: 580 km/h
Range: 500-3,000 m

Manufacturer
Aérospatiale.

Status
In service.

Canadian *Iroquois* class helicopter-carrying destroyer armed with Sea Sparrow missiles. The twin fire-control and radar turrets can be seen immediately before the mast

The earliest of the Russian surface-to-surface shipborne cruise missiles, the SS-N-1—whose NATO code-name is believed to be Scrubber—has been operational since 1958. It is a long-range, radio-command-guided, subsonic missile with an infra-red homing head and a high-explosive warhead. It is powered by a ramjet motor with a solid-propellant launch booster and is launched from a long (about 17 metres) trainable launcher. 8-9 reloads are carried for each launcher. Estimates of the performance of this missile have varied widely; and it may be that more than one mark of the missile has been deployed during its long operational history. Estimates of maximum range, in particular, have varied from as little as 60 nm to as much as 130 nm (about 110-240 km). Estimated dimensions also vary, though less importantly.

Missile Data

Length: about 800 cm
Body diameter: about 125 cm
Wing span: about 400 cm
Launch weight: about 4,500 kg
Warhead: HE
Cruising speed: subsonic, possibly Mach 0.9
Range: see above

Status

Obsolescent. Deployed on 2 *Kildin*-class destroyers (one launcher each) and 2 *Krupny*-class destroyers (two launchers each). The *Kildin*-class destroyers are being converted to carry the SS-N-11 Missile (see below).

SS-N-1 launcher on a *Krupny* class destroyer

Developed by a scaling-up process from the highly-successful SS.11 missile, the SS.12 carries a warhead weighing about four times as much as the earlier missile. The marine version, SS.12 M, was first successfully demonstrated in 1966.

Missile Data
Length: 187 cm
Body diameter: 18 cm (warhead 21 cm)
Span: 65 cm
Launch weight: 75 kg
Warhead: 30 kg HE
Guidance: Wire-guided command to line-of-sight by joystick controller. Visual tracking
Maximum speed: 940 km/h
Range: 6 km (3.2 nm) reached in 32 sec.

Manufacturer
Aérospatiale.

Status
Operational in several navies.

SS 12M launch

SS-N-2 missile being loaded into its launcher

A medium-range surface-to-surface subsonic cruise weapon, also known by the NATO code-name Styx, the SS-N-2 is the most widely-used of the Russian ship-borne missiles. It has been operational since 1960, is carried by small fast attack craft and has been supplied to all the navies of the Warsaw Pact and to those of many other countries. Constructed in the form of a small aircraft, the missile is powered by a solid-propellant jettisonable booster and a sustainer motor which also probably uses a solid propellant. It is launched from an enclosed launcher but differs from some other cell-launched missiles in that the launcher is a re-usable fixture into which the missile is loaded. Several different (but apparently functionally similar) launchers have been observed; and it is believed that two versions of the missile exist. Apart from a suggestion of a slight difference in range performance no differences between these 'A' and 'B' versions have been reported; but it is thought that the 'B' version is the one used (now, at least) by the Warsaw Pact forces. The missile is command-guided and has an active radar homing system.

Missile Data

Length: about 650 cm
Wing span: about 275 cm
Launch weight: about 2,000 kg
Warhead: HE
Cruising speed: subsonic, possibly Mach 0.9
Range: minimum about 11 km (6 nm), maximum about 43 km (23 nm)

Status

Operational in *Komar* (2-launcher) and *Osa* (4-launcher) missile boats throughout the Warsaw Pact and in the navies of Algeria, Cuba, Egypt, India, Indonesia, Korea (North), Syria and Yugoslavia. The missiles were also supplied to China where they are probably now made for the Hola and Hoku missile boats. Styx missiles are also carried by the Isku missile boats of the Finnish Navy. They were used successfully by Egyptian forces in the 1967 war with Israel and by Indian ships against Pakistan vessels in December 1971. In the 1973 war, however, Styx appears to have been convincingly out-performed by Gabriel.

Russian *Osa* class FPB with SS-N-2 launchers

Quadruple trainable SS-N-3 launchers on a *Kynda* class GM cruiser

(USSR)

A long-range surface-to-surface cruise missile, the SS-N-3 is sometimes referred to as Shaddock, although this NATO code-name may be more appropriate to a road-mobile version. The missile, of which there is probably more than one shipborne version, is extensively deployed in cruisers and submarines of the Soviet Navy. The launcher is a large reloadable cylindrical device which is mounted in single, twin or quadruple installations, fixed or trainable, in the various vessels. The missile appears to have an aeroplane-type configuration and to be propelled by two JATO boosters and a sustainer motor which may be a ramjet or a turbojet. A steep climb after launching appears to be typical of the missile's trajectory and short-range guidance is thought to be pre-programmed with active radar terminal homing. For longer ranges external guidance—eg from aircraft—is assumed to be necessary. Early versions of the missile may have been subsonic: those carried on Echo-class submarines are thought to be supersonic. The missile has been operational since 1961-2. Range data given below are those generally accepted; but the missile's ability to hit anything at the maximum range is not known to have been demonstrated.

Missile Data

All data subject to wide variations in published estimates.

Length: about 1,100 cm

Diameter: about 100 cm

Wing span: not known—wings probably folded in launcher

Launch weight: estimated around 5,000 kg

Warhead: believed nuclear, kilotons range

Cruising speed: estimated from Mach 0.9-1.5 (see above)

Range: minimum 22 km (12 nm); maximum 830 km (450 nm)

Status

Operational only in Soviet Navy. Fitted to Kynda cruisers (2 × 4 launchers), Kresta I cruisers (1 × 4), E-1 submarines (experimental 6 × 1), E-2 (8 × 1), J (2 × 2), W Long Bin (1 × 4) and W Twin Cylinder (2 × 1).

SS-N-7

This medium-range sub-surface-to-surface cruise missile is installed on Charlie-class submarines of the Soviet Navy and capable of being launched below the surface. Few details are available, but the missile and submarine have evidently been the subjects of a comprehensive weapon system design programme. The missile is believed to be supersonic and probably has an active radar homing system: initial guidance is presumably a programmed inertial system linked to the submarine's navigation system.

Missile Data

All data tentative.

Length: about 700 cm

Cruising speed: Mach 1.5 suggested

Range: about 30 nm (56 km)

Status

Operational since 1969-70 in C-class nuclear submarines each of which carries 8 launching tubes for the missiles in addition to 8 21-inch torpedo tubes.

Long-range surface-to-surface cruise missile installed in triple mountings on the Nanuchka-class missile corvettes. Apparently intermediate in size between the SS-N-2 and SS-N-3 missile types, the SS-N-9 is believed to be supersonic in flight and to have a maximum range in the region of 150 nm. This is a surprisingly long range for a missile deployed on an 800-ton ship and the estimate should be viewed with caution: mid-course guidance would be needed if the estimated maximum range were to be achieved. Command guidance is likely and radar homing probable. Launchers are cylindrical fixed in position and reloadable.

Missile Data
All data tentative.
Length: about 850 cm
Cruising speed: in excess of Mach 1.0
Range: minimum about 74 km (40 nm); maximum about 278 km (150 nm)

Status
Operational since about 1970 in *Nanuchka* corvettes (2 triple launchers) of the Soviet Navy.

A medium-range surface-to-surface missile, the SS-N-11 is believed to be an improved version of the SS-N-2 Styx missile described above. The missiles themselves have not yet been publicly displayed but the launchers have been seen in the latest *Osa II*-class missile boats and, more recently, on a modified version of the Kildin-class destroyer from which the SS-N-1 missiles previously carried have been removed. In this installation the large SS-N-1 launcher has been replaced by two twin gun turrets and the SS-N-11 launchers mounted two on each side of the after funnel and pointing aft.

Range and speed of the SS-N-11 are assumed to be similar to those of the SS-N-2 but the guidance system is thought to be better.

Status

In service as noted above.

Further Development

Development of additional Russian surface-to-surface weapons has been reported from time to time, including a long-range (circa 400 nm) device provisionally entitled SS-NX-13. It is very likely that the USSR authorities have a series of development programmes in hand; but it is perhaps worth noting that, to judge by their past performance in the development of all kinds of guided missile, their common practice is apparently one of periodic introduction into service of a model representative of the latest stage in a continuing development process whereas NATO practice tends to be to develop one complete article and then stop.

SS-N-11 launcher on an *Osa-II* class FPB. Although little can be seen of the missile it seems probable that it has folded wings

(USSR)

A medium-range surface-to-surface cruise missile, the SS-N-10 is deployed on modern cruisers and destroyers of the Soviet Navy as the principal surface armament. As with most other recently-introduced Russian shipborne missiles, only limited and tentative data are available; but it appears to be generally accepted that the missile is supersonic in flight and has a range of some 30 nm. The launchers are apparently cylindrical and have so far been seen in two configurations—a "flat four" trainable version and a 2 × 2 fixed version.

SS-N-10 "flat four" mounting on a *Krivak* class GM destroyer

(USA)

Formerly known as the Interim Surface-to-Surface Missile (ISSM) the Standard SSM programme was initiated to meet an urgent need for surface-to-surface missiles on USN ships pending the development of Harpoon. The immediate objective was attained by installing modified versions of the Standard medium-range anti-aircraft missile on ships already designated for Standard missile installations; the modification giving the missile an horizon-limited surface-to-surface capability in addition to its surface-to-air capability. This missile is known as Standard-1 and has a semi-active radar homing head. A second stage of the programme involved adapting the Standard ARM airborne radiation-seeking anti-ship missile for launching from specially-designed shipborne box-launchers. Being a radiation-seeking weapon, this version has the advantage of not being limited in range by the radar horizon. As

a parallel part of the programme, Standard-1 missiles were installed in other ships using modified ASROC launchers. Finally, a development project, aimed at producing a version of the Standard missile with an active radar homing system (Active Standard), was initiated as a third stage of the programme. Development delays made it seem, in 1974, less appropriate as an interim substitute for Harpoon; but the programme was continued for a time, as an insurance against delays in the Harpoon programme until terminated by Congress.

Manufacturer
General Dynamics Corporation.
Status
Both Standard-1 (SM-1-MR) and modified Standard ARM are in service with the USN.

(FRANCE)

SUBMARINE-LAUNCHED EXOCET SM39

The possibility of launching an Exocet missile from a submarine has been under consideration for some years. With the development of the MM39 folded-wing tube-launched shipborne version the possibility of developing a submarine version is brought a stage nearer.
Status
Project.

Standard (MR) missile fired from a USN gunboat

The basic Harpoon ship-to-ship concept has been extended to a submerged launch by placing the missile in a capsule which is compatible with standard submarine torpedo tubes and torpedo loading and handling equipment. The capsule, with its booster motor, is expelled from the tube pneumatically or hydraulically and rises to the surface by its own buoyancy. A broach sensor signals when the surface is reached and initiates a sequence in which the capsule ends are discarded and the booster ignited. Thereafter the missile follows the same flight plan as the ship-launched version. Targeting is accomplished by inserting into the missile computer data obtained either from own ship's sources or from external observers.

Status
Advanced development. Service entry planned for the mid-1970s.

Submarine-launched Harpoon missile

Primarily intended as a submarine-launched weapon to provide USN submarines with a long-range cruise missile comparable in performance with those used by the Russian Navy, this weapon is likely also to be installed in some surface vessels.

Both strategic and tactical versions are envisaged for the submarine-launched missile (SLCM). Both are to be suitable for launching from standard torpedo tubes (21-inch: 533 mm): the tactical model will have a range of some 300 nm (555 km) and the strategic version a range of around 1,500 nm (2,780 km). Cruising speed will be subsonic: guidance will be by terrain contour com-parison or similar techniques (eg magnetic field comparison) supplemented by inertial navigation. Terminal guidance for the tactical version at least will probably be by active radar homing. Since terrain contour comparison (TERCOM) is not effective over water and since the magnetic field comparison technique is believed to be at an earlier development stage than TERCOM, it is likely that the version installed for ship-to-ship use will carry an inertial-plus-radar guidance package generally similar to that used in Harpoon.

Manufacturer
LTV Aerospace.

Status
Development.

This description relates to a weapon conceived as the main future armament of the nuclear hunter-killer submarines of the Royal Navy. Conceptually it is similar to the submarine-launched Harpoon being developed in the USA and the little information that has so far been released suggests that it is proposed to base the design on a derivative of the HSD/Matra Martel air-ground missile. To this will have to be added a booster and the whole will have to be encapsulated for launch from a torpedo tube. The USGW (or Sub-Martel) has much in common with a 1970 proposal for a SSM Martel derivative (Ship Martel) which was passed over by the Royal Navy in favour of Exocet. The main differences between the USGW and Sub-Harpoon are that the British missile is under power from the moment of launch and is sea skimming throughout its air flight.

Status
Study and experimental contract placed with Hawker Siddeley Dynamics Ltd. as prime contractors. Project vulnerable in present British economic climate.

Mock-up of the UK underwater-to-surface guided weapon exhibited by Hawker Siddeley Dynamics at Farnborough in 1974

Aegis is a shipborne area defence system primarily concerned with ship defence against anti-ship cruise missiles and high-performance aircraft. Its special feature is its elaborate multi-function multiple phased-array radar (AN/SPY-1) and associated computer-controlled data handling and fire control system.

The detailed operation of this system is outside the scope of this book, however, and it is sufficient to note the capability of the system to launch and control the SM-2 surface-to-air missile from the fully-automatic Mk 26 dual-purpose launcher which can also be used to launch ASROC.

SM-2 is a special Aegis version of the Standard missile and is a semi-active radar homing device with provision for mid-course command guidance. Available details of this missile will be found under the Standard heading. A more advanced missile is expected to be added to Aegis in due course. When this happens the Talos system, in particular, will be retired from service.

Manufacturers

System contractor for Aegis is RCA Government and Commercial Systems.

Status

Development. The AN/SPY-1 radar is being tested aboard the USS *Norton Sound*. At least one successful anti-missile interception has been carried out.

USS *Norton Sound*. The white polygonal shape is one of the two phased arrays of the AN/SPY-1 radar

ALBATROS

Albatros is an all-weather missile and gun system comprising a missile and gun fire control system, a missile launching system involving either the Sparrow III or Aspide missile and up to three groups of guns. It is thus essentially a control and handling system capable of incorporating various weapons—not a specific weapon system. This note is included here because references to the system (which is being supplied for installation in Italian ships) sometimes appear to suggest that there is a specific Albatros missile.

(ITALY)

ASPIDE

Aspide is a high-performance multi-purpose missile. It is being developed for use both in an air-to-air role and in such shipborne weapon systems as Albatros—there being slight differences in dimensions between the two versions. The following brief data apply to the surface-launched version.

Missile Data
Length: 370 cm
Body diameter: 203 mm
Wing span: 80 cm
Fin span: 64 cm
Launch weight: 220 kg
Propulsion: single-stage solid-propellant rocket motor
Guidance: semi-active radar homing
Speed; Mach 2.5
Warhead: 35 kg HE

Manufacturers
Selenia—Industrie Elettroniche Associate.

Status
Development virtually complete. Service entry planned for 1977-78 when Aspide will replace the Sparrow III missile in Italian Navy systems.

Aspide missile mounted on an aircraft wing for dynamic testing

(USA)

BASIC POINT DEFENCE MISSILE SYSTEM

One of several shipborne anti-aircraft systems based on versions of the Sparrow air-to-air missile, the BPDMS was assembled as a working system from existing hardware with a minimum of new development. The AIM-7D Sparrow III missile is launched from a modified 8-cell ASROC launcher mounted on a 3-inch gun mounting. Missile guidance is by CW semi-active radar homing; target data from the ship's combat information centre are supplied to a manually-operated fire control system; and the target is acquired and illuminated for homing guidance by a director/illuminator radar controlled manually by handlebar controls. Low-angle engagements are possible and the weapon can be used against surface targets.

Manufacturer
System Contractor: Raytheon Company.

Status
In service in the USN since 1972.

A Sea Sparrow missile blast test vehicle launched from a BPDMS launcher

Foilborne launch of a Sparrow missile from the hydrofoil *Plainview*

Four container fits for the Blowpipe missile system have been developed by the manufacturers for use on surface craft. One of these is a simple manually operated twin launcher which can be bolted to the deck of any vessel and includes a 10-missile ready-use locker: the other three use a 10-round remotely-controlled pedestal launcher with a variety of director systems. One of these is the pedestal director sight originally developed for the lightweight version of Seacat; a second is a stabilised periscope director system based on the integration of the Kollmorgen Mk 35 gun director with the 10-missile launcher; and the third is a TV auto-tracking system based on the Saab-Scania TVT 300/1 aiming system.

Missile Data (Blowpipe)
Length: 140 cm
Diameter: 76 mm
Span: 274 mm
Weight: 18 kg with its container-launcher
Propulsion: two-stage solid-propellant motor
Warhead: HE 2.2 kg with proximity fuze
Guidance: radio command with optical tracking
Range: at least 3 km: probably 4 km
Altitude: maximum interception believed to be 2,500 m

Manufacturers
Short Bros. & Harland Ltd.

Status
Proposal.

Multiple laurcher for Blowpipe missiles

Catulle is the naval equivalent of a land-mobile surface-to-air weapon system called Javelot which has been in development for some years. The system comprises a multitube, gun-effect rocket launcher capable of firing salvoes of rockets with a predetermined dispersion, an acquisition radar, a fire control radar and a digital computer.

Detailed information is in short supply, but the launcher is believed to consist of a roughly rectangular array of 96 launch tubes from which numerous salvoes of rockets can be fired, before reloading is necessary, with a gap of 2-4 seconds between salvoes. Effective range is believed to be about 1,500 metres and calibre is 40 mm.

Manufacturer

System: Thomson-CSF.

Status

Development of the Javelot weapon has been financed by the French and US Governments and is believed to be nearing completion. Status of Catulle is not definitely known.

Multiple launcher for Blowpipe missiles (see previous page)

Based on the US Army Vulcan low-level anti-aircraft system the CIWS, also known as Vulcan/Phalanx, is being developed as a "last-ditch" device to stop incoming missiles by means of an intense obstructive barrage. Success obviously depends on exceptionally short reaction times and the CIWS is intended to be fully automatic in the entire process of target location, threat evaluation, identification and attack if necessary. The system at its present stage of development incorporates high performance radar and computing devices for this purpose: further improvements contemplated include the addition of a forward-looking infra-red (FLIR) system and a laser rangefinder to improve target acquisition in darkness or bad weather.

At present a standard 6-barrel Vulcan gun is used with its standard ammunition: in its Army role this gun fires either 1,000 or 3,000 rounds of 20 mm ammunition per minute (airborne versions can fire at rates up to 6,000 rounds per minute). Which rate will be chosen for the CIWS is not yet certain because there is a proposal to introduce a significantly heavier bullet containing depleted uranium which will obviously influence the decision.

It was originally intended, and probably still is, that the Vulcan/Phalanx gun system should be associated with a short-range surface-to-air missile system. Possible candidates are an improved version (CHIMP) of the Chaparral missile which is associated with Vulcan in the land-mobile system or an adaptation (RAM—rolling airframe missile) of the Stinger man-portable AA missile—possibly along lines similar to those proposed for Blowpipe in the UK.

Manufacturers
CIWS system contractor: General Dynamics/Pomona. Gun: General Electric.

Status
Vulcan/Phalanx is being developed at high priority. A decision on the associated missile was to have been during 1975. A non-radar system is described in the section on guns.

Vulcan-Phalanx close-in weapon system

Pairs of small barbette mountings abaft the SS-N-10 missile launchers on Kresta II class cruisers of the Russian Navy are believed to be a close-in or "last ditch" anti-missile system similar in concept to the US Vulcan-Phalanx systems.

No details of dimensions or performance are available.

Status
Operational as stated above.

Russian close-in weapon system

Formerly known as Murène in the proposed Murène/Mureca shipborne air defence system, a naval version of the land-mobile Crotale surface-to-air missile system has now been ordered for the French Navy and is under development. It is a highly automated system requiring only one operator to handle the director and control two banks of four canister-launched missiles.

The Crotale missile has a slim cylindrical body with cruciform wings on the nose cone indexed in line with cruciform tail control surfaces. It is command-guided by signals from a fire control radar system which can track and command two missiles simultaneously. Surveillance and target acquisition will be provided in the naval version by ship's radar working in conjunction with the system's real-time computer. The following data apply to the land version but are probably also true of the naval version.

Missile Data

Length: 289 cm
Diameter: 15 cm
Span: 54 cm
Launch weight: about 80 kg
Propulsion: single-stage solid-propellant motor
Speed: Mach 2.3 (in 2.3 sec). 16 sec to 8 km
Guidance: Infra-red gathering; secondary radar tracking; digital radio command to missile autopilot
Range: 500 m-8.5 km
Date introduced: Series production began in 1968.

Manufacturers
Thomson-CSF and Engins Matra

Status
Development for the French Navy at least 20 systems have been ordered.

Photo-montage showing Crotale Naval

HIRONDELLE WEAPON SYSTEM

Based on the Matra Super 530 air-to-air missile, Hirondelle is a proposal for a surface-to-air weapon system for small fighting ships. The Super 530 would be launched from a small (probably 4-cell) trainable launcher and would be associated with a sophisticated radar and fire control system which would operate in conjunction with the semi-active homing system of the missile.

Manufacturer

System proponent: Electronique Marcel Dassault.

Status

Proposal. The Super 530 missile is due to become operational in its airborne role in 1977.

Similar in principle to the Basic Point Defence Missile System, the IPDMS is a developed version using new or substantially modified components to produce a fast-reaction system. The missile is still a member of the Sparrow family but is a new version, RIM-7H, which has wings which fold to enable a smaller launcher to be used: like the ASROC launcher used with BPDMS, this has eight cells but weighs much less. Like the BPDMS, the IPDMS is intended for anti-ship as well as anti-aircraft use.

Missile Data
Length: 365 cm
Diameter: 20 cm
Span: 100 cm (extended)
Launch weight: 200 kg
Warhead: HE 30 kg
Guidance: CW semi-active radar homing
Range: about 22 km (12 nm)

IPDMS is also known as the NATO Sea Sparrow system because it was decided in 1968 that Belgium, Denmark, Italy, Norway and (subsequently in 1970) the Netherlands would adopt the system, would share in the production operation and would contribute to the development costs. The initials NSSMS (NATO Sea Sparrow Surface Missile System) are sometimes used.

Manufacturer
System contractor: Raytheon Company.

Status
Sea trials using various NATO ships (including high-latitude trials on KNM *Bergen)* were completed successfully in 1974 and the system is in production.

ADVANCED POINT DEFENCE MISSILE SYSTEM

Representing a further advance in the BPDMS-IPDMS progression, the Advanced PDMS is being developed independently of the NATO system and will include a new missile. An important feature of the system concept is vertical launching coupled with a rapid pitch-over operation, using thrust deflection, in the direction of the target. This does away with the need for launcher training and provides a fast reaction for anti-missile operation.

VELARC

VELARC—Vertical Ejection Launch Aero Reaction Control— is a projected PDM system for high-speed hovercraft and hydrofoils. It will employ a pop-up pneumatic ejector to lift the missile from a below-deck launcher before the motor is ignited. Otherwise it is believed to be conceptually similar to Advanced PDMS.

Status
Raytheon are developing both Advanced PDMS and VELARC. The former is at an advanced development stage.

Masurca is a long-range tandem two-stage anti-aircraft weapon deployed on some French naval vessels. The missile has a cylindrical body with a pointed nose and pivoted cruciform tail control surfaces indexed in line with long-chord narrow wings. Powered by solid-propellant booster and sustainer motors, it is launched from a twin launcher and carries a proximity-fused high-explosive warhead. It can intercept supersonic targets at ranges of 40 km or more.

Two types of guidance are employed: the Mk 2 Mod 2 missile is guided by radio command and the Mk 2 Mod 3 uses semi-active radar homing. Externally the two versions are virtually identical and the complete shipboard installation—which includes an independent fire control system for each twin launcher and a three-dimensional radar system—is designed to handle the two types simultaneously: it can also track and control two radio command missiles simultaneously, long-range tracking being aided by a missile-borne transponder.

Missile Data

Length: 8.6 m

Body diameter: 40 cm

Wing span: 77 cm

Launch weight: Mod 2 1,850 kg

Mod 3 2,080 kg

Propulsion: solid-propellant booster and sustainer motors

Guidance: Mod 2 radio command

Mod 3 semi-active radar homing

Range: Mod 2 40 km

Mod 3 45 km

Warhead: 48 kg HE

Manufacturer

DTCN/ECAN Ruelle

Status

Both types operational in the cruiser *Colbert* and the *Suffren* class destroyers of the French Navy. Other vessels will be fitted.

Masurca missile on launcher

MURENE/MURECA

Murene and Mureca are the names which were applied to two versions (which could also be combined) of an anti-aircraft weapon system for the protection of small ships against low-flying supersonic aircraft. Murene was the naval version of the Crotale landmobile AA missile system: Mureca is the name given to a similar system in which the Crotale missile launcher is replaced by a device called Catulle, which is a multitube launcher firing salvoes of 40 mm rockets. The name Murene is believed now to have been dropped in favour of Crotale Navalisè.

Manufacturer
System: Thomson-CSF

Status
Advanced development. Apart from the French involvement the US authorities are interested in at least the land-mobile version (Javelot) of Catulle. Crotale Navalisè has been ordered by the French Navy.

Rafale is a multiple rocket launcher currently proposed for naval use and especially for ship defence against sea-skimming missiles. It depends for its operation on the saturation of a volume of airspace with small high-velocity projectiles moving in all directions. This effect is achieved by firing a salvo of three rockets, each of which has a payload of 35 grenades, each of which contains 160 metal balls, each of which is capable of piercing 8 mm of high-resistance light alloy (such as might form the airframe of a missile) at a range of about 40 m. The dispersion of the resultant 16,800 balls is adjusted for maximum effect by very careful timing within the rockets.

The launcher is remotely controlled and consists of three units, each of six launching tubes, pivoted in two axes and mounted on a magazine containing 90 rockets. The system can thus discharge six salvoes before reloading. Reloading is also possible after three salvoes if time permits.

The Rafale system is assumed to be associated with a ship's radar and fire control system but is otherwise completely self-contained, remotely-controlled and fully mechanised.

Rocket Data

Length: 320 cm
Diamater: 147 mm
Weight: 78 kg
Launch velocity: 110 m/sec
Maximum velocity: 1,100 m/sec
Warhead: 19 kg
Maximum range: 30 km
Sea skimmer engagement range: 1-4 km

Manufacturers

Joint venture by Creusot-Loire, SEP and CSEE.

Status

Development.

ROLAND II M

(FRANCE/WEST GERMANY)

Roland II M is a proposal based on the all-weather variant of the land-mobile surface-to-air weapon system developed jointly by Aérospatiale and Messerschmitt-Bolkow-Blohm. The system comprises target acquisition and tracking radars and optics, command guidance link, launcher and magazine all in a single self-contained assembly requiring only power supplies from outside.

Target detection in azimuth and IFF identification is performed by the search radar. After selection of the target by the system commander the target is tracked by the tracking radar or optically and after launch the missile is gathered automatically to this line of sight and maintained thereon by an infra-red missile tracking system and a radio command link.

Missile Data

Length: 240 cm
Diameter: 16 cm
Span: 50 cm
Launch weight: 63 kg
Warhead: HE with proximity fuze
Guidance: Command—see text
Cruising speed: about Mach 1.6
Range: 500-6,500 m

Manufacturers
Aérospatiale and MBB who jointly own Euromissile.

Status
Land-mobile system in service. II M marine system proposed. Other systems being studied.

A third-generation shipborne anti-missile system, derived from Roland and provisionally named Jason, has been proposed. A missile similar to Roland, but having a greater maximum range and the performance required for missile interception, is envisaged and it is thought that a five-year programme—or thereabouts—would be appropriate. The Euromissile partners might require a third company to join them.

This missile is also known by the NATO code-name Goa and is well-known as the SA-3 land-mobile missile which has figured largely in the Arab-Israeli wars. The missile is installed in many of the larger warships of the Soviet Navy on roll-stabilised twin launchers mounted on top of magazines from which they are reloaded vertically.

Powered by a booster and sustainer, the missile proper is cylindrical and slim with relatively large cruciform fixed wings at the rear and small cropped-delta control surfaces on the tapered nose. The booster is short, larger in diameter and furnished with rectangular fins indexed in line with the other control surfaces. Some missiles have an additional set of small tail fins between the booster and the second-stage wings which appear to be furnished with trailing-edge control surfaces: it is thought that this is the more modern version of the missile.

Associated with all installations is the radar complex known as Peel Group.

Missile Data
Length: 590 cm
Diameters: 45 cm and 70 cm (booster)
Wing span: 122 cm
Propulsion: solid-propellant booster: sustainer probably solid-propellant also
Warhead: HE
Guidance: Command
Range: believed to be about 15 km
Ceiling: believed to be about 12,000 m
Date introduced: 1961-62

Status
Well over 100 Goa launchers are installed in ships of the Soviet Navy.

SA-N-1 missiles on launcher

SA-N-2

SA-N-2 is the US alphanumeric code for the shipborne version of the missile known by the NATO code-name Guideline.

This long-range anti-aircraft missile, which has for many years been the principal field AA weapon of the Soviet forces and has been used in action extensively in Vietnam and the Middle East, has been installed in only one Russian ship, the cruiser *Dzerzhinski,* on a twin mounting.

Since in order to make this installation a triple 6-inch gun turret (X position) was removed it is scarcely surprising that the SA-N-3 installation has been left in position: the absence of other installations of what is clearly otherwise a well-regarded missile, however, makes it fairly clear that the experiment was a failure. The most probable reason for this is that, even when fired from a stable structure on land, the Guideline missile is difficult to gather to the desired flight path: it is said, indeed, that if it is not brought into the radar beam in the first six seconds it will not be acquired at all. Clearly, the motion of a ship in a heavy sea would make this process even more difficult. The associated Fan Song E radar must also present installation difficulties—especially on smaller ships.

Missile Data

Length: 10.7 m overall
Body diameter: 50 cm and 70 cm (booster)
Wing span: 170 cm
Launch weight: about 2,300 kg
Propulsion: solid-propellant booster and liquid-propellant sustainer
Warhead: 130 kg HE
Guidance: radio command
Range: 40-50 km
Ceiling: about 18,000 m

Status
In service but possibly non-operational

(USSR)　　　　　　　　SA-N-3

Little information on this missile system has emerged since attention was first drawn to the existence of a new type of launcher on the *Moskva* class helicopter-carriers. This twin launcher which, unlike that for the SA-N-1, appears not to be roll-stabilised, is associated with a radar complex known as Head Lights in the NATO code and the missile launched from it is believed to be called Goblet.

It is generally agreed by the authorities that the missile is a larger and longer-range successor to the SA-N-1 but there the positive information ends. One plausible suggestion is that the SA-N-3 Goblet is the naval equivalent of the SA-6 Gainful missile which has been in the Soviet military inventory for several years and was used against the Israelis in the 1973 war. Gainful certainly has a higher performance than the SA-N-1 and there is no obvious reason why it should not be adopted for naval purposes.

Status

In service with the *Moskva* class and with the *Kara* and *Kresta II* class cruisers and entering service with the *Kuril* class aircraft carriers.

SA-N-3 launcher a *Kresta II* class cruiser

(USSR)

Even less is known about this recent addition to the Soviet naval weapons inventory than is known about the SA-N-3. One difficulty is that the missile and launcher assembly is normally concealed within a large cylindrical container from which it can be raised (but has not so far been raised very often in public) to fire its missiles.

First seen in the *Nanuchka* class missile boats but now fitted to at least six classes of Soviet warship the SA-N-4 is evidently thought to be an important naval weapon. It has been suggested that it is a close-in defensive weapon—a suggestion which is certainly consistent with the observed widespread deployment and with the increasing popularity of anti-ship missiles among many Western navies—and it could be that the silo protection is to ensure maximum missile readiness in cold weather conditions.

Status
Operational on an increasing scale in the Soviet Navy.

In this picture the "dustbin-lid" cover of the SA-N-4 weapon system can be seen immediately forward of the guns. The ship is a *Krivak*-class GM destroyer.

This close-range surface-to-air missile system is in widespread naval use in various configurations with a variety of fire control systems. The missile is radio command guided and can be visually tracked and controlled by two men in a director unit using binoculars and joystick controls or handled by some sophisticated radar or TV tracking systems. The standard launcher carries four rounds but the manufacturers have also made a lightweight three-round system for installation, with a simplified optical director, on small vessels. A proposal to combine a Seacat missile with a Bofors 40 mm gun was dropped.

Aerodynamic control is by cruciform pivoted swept-back wings indexed at 45 deg. to the fixed tail fins. Two of the latter carry flares at their tips to aid visual tracking.

Missile Data
Length: 148 cm
Body diameter 19 cm
Wing span: 64 cm
Launch weight: about 65 kg
Propulsion: two-stage solid-propellant motor
Warhead: HE with contact and proximity fuzes
Guidance: radio command with visual, TV or radar
tracking
Range: 4,750 m

Manufacturer
Short Bros. & Harland Ltd.

Status
Operational in or on order for at least fifteen navies.

Seacat launch from standard four-round launcher

This is a long-range area defence weapon launched from a twin launcher and powered by a solid-propellant booster and a ramjet sustainer. Guidance is by semi-active radar homing, tracking and illumination being provided by the Type 909 target illuminator radar with which is associated a fire control computer. The launcher is automatically loaded and computer-controlled. The possibility of using it against surface targets has been suggested.

The missile has four guidance interferometer aerials round the ramjet air intake in the nose and fixed long-chord wings, towards the rear of the slightly tapered body, indexed in line with cruciform tail control surfaces.

Missile Data
Length: 436 cm
Body diameter: 42 cm
Span: 91 cm
Launch weight: 550 kg
Propulsion: solid-propellant booster and ramjet sustainer
Warhead: HE fragmentation with proximity fuze
Guidance: semi-active radar homing with radar tracking
Range: at least 80 km

Manufacturers
System contractor: Hawker Siddeley Dynamics Ltd.

Status
In service with the RN on HMS *Bristol* and entering service with the *Sheffield* class destroyers. On order for Armada Republica Argentina and for HMS *Invincible.*

Sea Dart missiles on launcher

SEA INDIGO   (ITALY)

This is a naval version of a short-range surface-to-air missile originally developed as a land weapon. It is intended for installation in various configurations on large or small vessels, including a combined installation with surface-to-surface Sea Killer missiles sharing a common fire control system.

The missile is cylindrical with an ogival nose cone and is controlled by movable mid-body cruciform wings indexed in line with the fixed tail fins. Radio command guidance with radar tracking is standard with optical IR tracking as a standby for ECM conditions. The system has a fast reaction: standard delay from target detection alarm to launch sequence initiation is six seconds and 10.5 seconds to motor burn-out. These figures apply to the land version with Superfledermaus fire control but the Sea Hunter fire control system used in the naval version should produce similar results.

Missile Data
Length: 320 cm
Body diameter: 19 cm
Wing span: 79 cm
Launch weight: 97 kg
Propulsion: single stage solid-propellant motor
Speed: Mach 2.5 at burn-out
Warhead: HE with proximity fuze
Guidance: Radio command and radar with standby optical tracking
Range: 1-10 km

Manufacturer
Sistel SpA.

Status
Land version in service. Naval system status under review.

(UK)

SEASLUG

This long-range beam-riding surface-to-air missile system has been in service with the Royal Navy since 1961. It is fitted in the County class destroyers, and is launched from a twin-ramp launcher which is commanded by the fire control system and reloaded from a between-decks magazine.

There are two versions of the missile, the Mark 2 having a longer range and better low-altitude performance. Both missiles can be used against surface targets; but again the performance of the Mark 2 is superior to that of the Mark 1.

The unconventional appearance of this missile results from the forward mounting of four wrap-around solid-propellant boosters. The missile proper is cylindrical with a pointed ogival nose-cone and cruciform fixed mid-body wings indexed in line with cruciform pivoted tail control surfaces.

Missile Data

Length: 610 cm
Body diameter: 41 cm
Span: 144 cm
Launch weight: about 1,000 kg
Propulsion: 4 solid propellant boosters and single solid-propellant sustainer
Warhead: HE with proximity fuze
Guidance: beam-riding using Type 901 M shipborne radar with coded transmissions
Range: probably better than 45 km

Manufacturer

System contractor: Hawker Siddeley Dynamics Ltd.

Status

In service with RN since 1961. Mark 2 in HM Ships *Glamorgan, Fife, Norfolk* and *Antrim.* Mark 1 originally fitted in other ships being replaced by Mark 2.

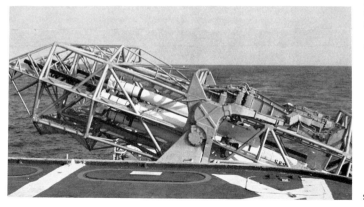

Seaslug missile in its launcher

Several shipborne surface-to-air weapon systems are based on versions of the Sparrow III missile originally developed in the USA as an air-to-air weapon. Current programmes are the Canadian Sea Sparrow, the Italian Albatros and the Basic and Improved Point Defence Missile Systems of the US Navy: the last-named programme is also known as the NATO Sea Sparrow and is being developed and produced as a co-operative effort by the USA, Belgium, Denmark, Italy, the Netherlands and Norway: it will use a special version of the Sparrow missile which will have folding wings and will be launched from a new lightweight 8-cell launcher. The Basic Point Defence System, however, uses a fixed-wing Sparrow which is launched from a modified 8-cell ASROC launcher. Albatros uses either a Sparrow or an Aspide missile launched from an Italian-developed multi-cell launcher.

The Canadian Sea Sparrow, being a dual-purpose missile system is described in Section Two.

Sparrow missile launched from an Albatros launcher

Seawolf is being developed as the missile of the Royal Navy's GWS 25 short-range self-defence system. Its special feature is a very short reaction time to enable it to intercept high-speed aircraft or anti-ship missiles. In addition to the main maximum-performance system, which is at a very late stage of development, simpler systems are being studied for possible use in smaller vessels. One of these, Seawolf-Omega, is a lightweight visually-directed system; another, Seawolf-Delta, is a lightweight darkfire version. The maximum-performance system employs line-of-sight guidance by microwave radio command with differential radar or TV tracking. Its ability to intercept a small missile target travelling at Mach 2 has been demonstrated.

Main units of the system are the surveillance radar, the radar tracker and command guidance complex, the data handling and control system and the launcher with its missiles. All these have been designed with an eye to the possibility of retrofitting the system to older vessels as well as installing it in new ones.

The Seawolf missile is about 2 m long and has four fixed (but possibly folding) wings indexed in line with movable tail control, but control may not be wholly aerodynamic. The launcher carries six rounds and is a low-inertia system capable of high pointing accelerations. To keep weight down, reloading is manual.

Once an interception is initiated all subsequent operations are automatic. Normal missile tracking is by radar with TV as standby for low-angle or otherwise difficult radar interceptions. The missile has a high-explosive warhead with both contact and proximity fuzes.

Manufacturers
System contractor: British Aircraft Corporation.

Status
Advanced development. Sea trials of system units in progress.

Seawolf in flight during development trials.

SLAM denotes Submarine (or Surface) Launched Air Missile System. It has been developed by Vickers to provide submarines or light craft with an effective short-range defence against other surface craft and helicopters.

The missile chosen as the basis of the system is Blowpipe, which was originally developed as a man-portable AA missile. Vickers have developed a special launcher for SLAM comprising six missiles grouped round a central electronics and TV unit which is used as the 'eye' of the system for missile guidance. For submarine installation this unit is raised into action from a pressure vessel in which it is housed when submerged. Target acquisition is by means of the submarine's attack periscope with the azimuth of which the launcher unit is automatically aligned when its mast is raised. This brings the target into the view of a remote operator by means of the TV system; whereafter the operator tracks the target and fires and guides the missile (which is automatically gathered to the line of sight) by remote control.

Missile Data (Blowpipe)

Length: 140 cm
Diameter: 76 mm
Span: 274 mm
Weight: 18 kg with container launcher
Propulsion: two-stage solid-propellant motor
Warhead: HE with proximity fuze (2.2 kg)
Guidance: radio command with optical tracking. Twist and steer by nose-mounted control surfaces
Range: at least 3 km: possibly as much as 4 km
Altitude: believed to be about 2,500 m

Manufacturers
System: Vickers Ltd.

Status
Submarine system development complete and successfully demonstrated. Surface ship systems exist as detailed proposals.

SLAM launcher (left) installed in a trials modification of a submarine bridge fin

SPARROW III (USA)

Designed primarily as a long-range air-to-air guided missile and produced in several versions, the Sparrow III missile is now also used in a variety of other roles. Relevant systems are described elsewhere but the following basic data for the missile may be helpful.

Missile Data
Length: 366 cm
Body diameter: 20 cm
Wing span: 102 cm
Launch weight: about 200 kg
Propulsion: single-stage solid-propellant rocket motor
Guidance: semi-active radar homing
Speed: more than Mach 3.5
Warhead: 27 kg HE
Range (airborne): 25 km (13.5 nm)

Manufacturer
Raytheon Company

Status
In widespread operational use

Stern-mounting for Standard 1 missile for SSM use

Standard 1 (MR) missile launched from normal twin launcher

Originally developed in two versions as medium-range (MR) and long-range (ER) anti-aircraft weapons, the Standard family of missiles has since been considerably extended to include surface-to-surface and air-to-surface missiles. The additional versions so far announced are listed below.

Standard 1 (SM-1) An improved replacement of the original missile. Also used in the Standard SSM (formerly ISSM) surface-to-surface project.

Standard 2 (SM-2) A further improved version being developed for the Aegis system. It has a greater range (more than 48 km in the MR version and nearly 100 km in the ER version) an improved inertial reference and provision for mid-course command guidance.

Standard ARM An airborne anti-radiation missile.

Standard Active An anti-ship version with an active radar homing head. Now discontinued in favour of Harpoon.

In its basic AA configuration the SM-1 missile is launched from a two-round electrically driven launcher commanded by the fire control system and automatically loaded from a magazine. Guidance is by semi-active radar homing.

Missile Data (SM-1 MR and ER)
Length; 457 cm (mr), 823 cm (ER)
Diameter: 30.5 cm
Launch weight: about 600 kg (MR), about 1,350 kg (ER)
Propulsion: dual-thrust solid-propellant motor (MR), tandem solid-propellant booster and sustainer (ER)
Warhead: HE with impact and proximity fuzes
Range: more than 18 km (MR), more than 55 km (ER)
Date introduced: (original versions) 1968

Manufacturer
Pomona Division, General Dynamics Corporation.

Status
Standard 1 in widespread USN service and in some Spanish ships.
Standard 2 nearing production.

(USA)

One of the few NATO shipborne surface-to-air missiles to have been used in action, successfully intercepting targets at a range of some 110 km, Talos is a large long-range missile installed on some cruisers of the USN. The basic missile employs beam-riding guidance with semi-active terminal homing: in recent versions the semi-active CW guidance uses an interferometer technique and in another version an anti-radiation homing head is fitted—possibly for surface-to-surface applications.

The missile comprises a solid-propellant jettisonable booster and a ramjet sustainer, the whole being contained in a cylindrical body tapered slightly towards the ramjet air intake in the nose in which is mounted a conical centre body. Control is by pivoted cruciform wings indexed in line with cruciform tail fins, which in turn are in line with the fins on the booster. The missile is launched from a twin launcher which is electrically operated and comanded by the fire control system.

Missile Data
Length: 640 cm + 313 cm for the booster
Body diameter: 76 cm
Span: 290 cm
Launch weight: 3,175 kg
Warhead: HE or nuclear
Speed: Mach 2.5
Range: over 120 km
Ceiling: over 26,500 m
Date introduced: 1959

Manufacturer
System contractor: Bendix Corporation

Status
In service in the USN and expected to remain in service until replaced by Aegis when when the latter has a longer-range missile than the SM-2.

Talos long-range missiles on their launcher

TARTAR

This medium-range missile is in widespread service in NATO navies and elsewhere providing primary air defence for ships of destroyer size and secondary defence for some larger vessels. A fully-automatic magazine handling and loading system is employed and missiles are fired from an electrically-driven remotely-commanded twin launcher. Guidance is by semi-automatic radar homing.

The Tartar missile has a cylindrical body with an ogival nose and long narrow cruciform fixed wings almost touching the wider tail control surfaces.

Missile Data
Length: 460 cm
Body diameter: 30 cm
Launch weight: 680 kg
Propulsion: dual-thrust, solid-propellant motor
Speed: above Mach 2.5
Range: more than 25 km
Date introduced: 1961

Manufacturer
System contractor: Pomona Division, General Dynamics Corporation.

Status
No longer in production and being replaced by Standard-1 (MR), Tartar is still in service with the USN and with the Australian, French, Italian, Japanese, Netherlands and West German navies.

Tartar missile

Operational since 1956, Terrier has been the subject of almost continuous development and improvement and is still in widespread service. Current systems are generally those known as Advanced Terrier which is visually distinguishable from the early versions by the change of wing planform from the original cropped-delta shape to the current strake-like outline.

Structurally the missile is of tandem two-stage design with a cylindrical body and ogival nose. The booster stage is of larger diameter than the main missile and has cruciform fins indexed in line with the missile tail control surfaces which in turn lie immediately to the rear of the missile wings.

Guidance is by a beam-riding system with semi-active radar terminal homing and the missile is launched from an electrically-operated remotely-controlled twin launcher which in some installations is shared with ASROC.

Missile Data

Length: 460 cm + 363 for booster

Body diameter: 30 cm

Launch weight: about 1,350 kg

Propulsion: tandem two-stage solid propellant rocket motors

Warhead: HE with impact and proximity fuze. Can be nuclear

Speed: Mach 2.5

Range: over 32 km

Ceiling: over 20,000 m

Date introduced: 1956

Manufacturer

General Dynamics Corporation.

Status

In service with the USN and in the navies of Italy and the Netherlands.

(overleaf) Terrier missiles and launcher

TRIPLE 16-inch GUN MOUNTING

These 16-inch 50-calibre guns were the main armament of the *Iowa* class battleships of the US Navy. The individual guns weighed about 125 tons and the complete triple mounting some 2,000 tons. Bagged charges were used for the propellant of which 300 kg was used in 6 bags at a time.

16-inch guns of the USS *New Jersey*

Gun Data
Calibre: 406 mm (16 in)
Barrel length: 50 calibres (67 ft)
Projectile weight: 935 kg
Muzzle velocity: 850 m/sec
Rate of fire: 2 rounds/min
Maximum range: 42 km (23 nm)
Date introduced: 1936

Status
The last of the *Iowa* class to be in service—and indeed the last battleship in the world to be in action—was the USS *New Jersey* whose guns are illustrated here. She was last decommissioned in December 1969 and placed in the Pacific reserve.

(UK/SPAIN)

Fitted as four twin turrets in the heavy cruiser *Canarias,* these 50-calibre guns are of a design that was first introduced by Vickers in 1924. The *Canarias* was built by the Sociedad Española de Construction Naval, El Ferrol, was laid down in 1928, launched in 1931 and completed in 1936. Her design was basically that of the contemporary British *Kent* class cruisers.

A notable feature of the gun at the time of its construction was the maximum elevation capability of 70 degrees—comparing favourably with the contemporary US 8-inch gun of only 40 degrees. The later US 55-calibre gun (1944 model) had an elevation capability of 80 degrees.

Gun Data
Calibre: 203 mm (8-in)
Barrel length: 50 calibres
Elevation: to 70 deg
Projectile weight: 113 kg
Muzzle velocity: 840 m/sec
Rate of fire: 6 rounds/min
Maximum range: 30 km (16 nm)
Date introduced: 1924

Manufacturer
Vickers

Status
Operational but no longer made.

(USA) TRIPLE 8-inch MARK 15 MOUNTING

This 8-inch 55-calibre mount is remotely controlled and guns are independently laid. The projectile is propelled by separate bagged charges to a maximum range of about 28 km (15 nm) and the rate of fire is 5 rounds per barrel per minute. The barrels weigh 37,000 lbs (16,800 kg), and the turret probably about 500 tons. The original design of the turret dates from 1935, but modifications since then have considerably improved laying accuracy and reliability. The barrel is of two piece design featuring a radially expanded tube and a shrunk-on jacket.

Gun Data

Calibre: 203 mm (8 in)
Barrel length: 55 calibres
Projectile weight: 125 kg
Muzzle velocity: approx 900 m/sec
Rate of fire: 5 rounds/min
Maximum range: approx 28 km (15 nm)
Date introduced: 1927

Status

Installed in some of the older US heavy cruisers now in reserve.

MARK 16 MOUNTING

In the *Salem* class heavy cruisers of the US Navy an 8-inch 55-calibre gun designed to fire cased ammunition was installed in triple turrets. Apart from the modification to fire the new ammunition fully automatically the gun characteristics were generally similar to those of the earlier 8-inch semi-automatic guns. The turrets were larger, however, and the rate of fire was 10 rounds per barrel per minute instead of five. The gun was first introduced in 1944.

Status

There were three heavy cruisers in the "Salem" class. The last of these to be in service was the *Newport News,* now in reserve.

8-inch Mk 15 mountings of the USS *Boston*

An eight-inch (203 mm) gun is proposed for use with destroyer-size ships of the US Navy. So far described as the "Major Calibre Light Weight Gun" (MCLWG), it is believed to be intended primarily for shore bombardment, and to be destined in the first instance for the *Spruance*-class destroyers.

Manufacturer
FMC/NOD

Status
Development. Successful test firings have taken place under USN auspices.

GUIDED PROJECTILES
Also under development for the US Navy are two guided projec-

tiles, one of which is an eight-inch round for use with the light-weight gun (the calibre of the other is five inches). Although experimental firings have taken place, neither projectile is believed to be near operational service. A laser designator plus marked targe seeker is used.

The US Navy also carried out operational shore bombardment experiments with 8-inch rocket-assisted projectiles during the war in Vietnam, modifying the 8-inch 55-calibre Mark 15 guns of the cruiser *Saint Paul* (which was decommissioned in 1971). Using projectiles weighing about 51 kg a surface range of about 55 km (30 nm) is believed to have been achieved.

New 8-inch major calibre lightweight gun

TRIPLE 180 mm GUN MOUNTING

(USSR)

Now the largest carried by Russian ships, the 180 mm gun is found only on the two surviving members, *Kirov* and *Slava,* of the *Kirov* class cruisers. Both ships were launched before the Second World War, although *Slava* (formerly *Molotov)* was not completed until 1944.

Each cruiser carries the 180 mm guns in three triple mountings. The three guns in each mounting are mounted in a single sleeve and are thus not capable of individual elevation.

Gun Data

Calibre: 180 mm
Barrel length: 57 calibres
Elevation: to 40 deg
Projectile weight: 100 kg
Muzzle velocity: 920 m/sec
Rate of fire: 6 rounds/min
Maximum range: about 35 km (19 nm)
Date introduced: 1933

Status

Operational but obsolescent.

180 mm guns of the cruiser *Slava*

(SWEDEN)

These 6-inch (152 mm) Bofors guns were first introduced in 1942 and are now to be found as a triple mounting only in the cruiser *Latorre* of the Chilean Navy (formerly the *Göta Lejon* of the Royal Swedish Navy.

Gun Data

Calibre: 152 mm (6 in)
Barrel length: 53 calibres
Elevation: 60 deg
Projectile weight: 46 kg
Muzzle velocity: 900 m/sec
Rate of fire: 10 rounds/min
Maximum range: 26 km (14 nm)
Date introduced: 1942

Twin and Single Mountings

The same guns are also installed in twin mountings in the *Latorre* and in the cruisers *Almirante Grau* of the Peruvian Navy and *De Zeven Provincien* of the Royal Netherlands Navy. The single 6-inch guns of the minelayer *Alvsnabben* of the Royal Swedish Navy are believed to be of the same pattern.

Manufacturer

Bofors.

Status

Operational but no longer manufactured.

152 mm guns of R Neth N *De Zeven Provincien*

DP TWIN 6-INCH MOUNTING MK 26

This twin automatic dual-purpose mount is remotely radar-controlled and electrically traversed and elevated. It is also fitted with local sighting equipment and joystick control. It is notable for the high rate of fire that can be achieved. Weight of the twin-gun turret is about 163 tons and the gun crew is 16.

Gun Data
Calibre: 152 mm (6 in)
Elevation: to 80 deg
Rate of fire: 20 rounds/min
Date introduced: 1951

Manufacturer
Vickers.

Status
Operational on *Tiger* class cruisers of the Royal Navy but no longer made.

(UK/INDIA)   TRIPLE 6-inch GUN MOUNTING

This 1934 pattern Vickers gun is no longer in service with the Royal Navy, though the guns may be seen on the cruiser *Belfast* now preserved as a floating museum in London. The triple 6-inch gun mounting on the Indian cruiser *Mysore* (formerly HMS *Nigeria*) is, however, believed to use the 1934 gun. The mounting weighs about 135 tons but can be traversed by hand if power fails.

Gun Data
Calibre: 152 mm (6 in)
Barrel length: 50 calibres
Elevation: to 45 deg
Traverse: 240 deg. total
Projectile weight: 50 kg
Muzzle velocity: 820 m/sec
Rate of fire: 8 rounds/min
Maximum range: 23 km (12 nm)
Date introduced: 1934

Manufacturer
Vickers

Status
Believed to be in service in only one ship.

(UK/ARGENTINA)   TRIPLE 6-inch MOUNTING

Main armament of the Argentine cruiser *La Argentina* are three triple 6-inch turrets. These were originally built by Vickers in the UK.

Gun Data
Calibre: 152 mm (6 in)
Barrel length: 50 calibres
Projectile weight: 45 kg
Muzzle velocity: 850 m/sec
Rate of fire: 5 rounds/min
Maximum range: 20 km (11 nm)
Date introduced: 1923

Status
Operational but no longer made.

TRIPLE 6-inch MARK 16 MOUNTING

(USA)

This 6-inch 47-calibre gun mounting in a triple turret is of an old semi-automatic design but is still in service in a few light cruisers of the US Navy. The turrets are remotely controlled but have local sighting and ranging facilities. The guns are independently laid and the turret weighs 154 tons.

Gun Data

Calibre: 152 mm (6 in)
Barrel length: 47 calibres
Projectile weight: 46.5 kg
Muzzle velocity: approx 900 m/sec
Rate of fire: 10 rounds/min
Maximum range: approx 23.5 km (13 nm)
Date introduced: 1933

Status

As noted above, these guns are in service in operational light cruisers and in cruisers in the US reserve fleet. It is believed that they are the same as the guns on the ex-US Navy cruisers now serving in various South American navies.

A later version of this gun adapted to fire cased ammunition and to be used as a dual-purpose weapon was mounted in twin turrets on the large *Worcester* class light cruisers. The ships concerned have now been scrapped, however.

Mk 16 6-inch gun mounting on USS *Little Rock*

(USSR)

These guns are in service with several of the older cruisers of the Russian fleet. The *Sverdlov* class cruisers each carry 12 guns in four triple mountings, except for the *Dzerzhinski* which has had one of its turrets replaced by a launcher for the SAM-2 Guideline missile. The older *Tchapaev*-class cruisers also carry four triple turrets.

Guns in the turrets are mounted in separate sleeves, thus permitting individual elevation to at least 50 degrees. An 8-metre range-finder is incorporated in each turret and the guns are semi-automatic.

Gun Data
Calibre: 152 mm (6 in)
Barrel length: 50 calibres
Elevation: to 50 deg
Projectile weight: 50 kg
Muzzle velocity: 915 m/sec
Rate of fire: 10 rounds/min
Maximum range: about 27.5 km (15 nm)
Date introduced: 1938

Status
Operational as noted.

Triple 152 mm mounting

TWIN 130 mm MOUNTING   (USSR)

These mountings are to be found on the older destroyers of Russian and client navies, notably the *Skory*, *Tallin* and *Kotlin* classes. The mountings are semi-automatic and said to be fully stabilised. There appear to be some external differences between the mountings on the earlier and later vessels and it is possible that there may be an earlier, unstabilised mounting on some.

Gun Data
Calibre: 130 mm
Barrel length: 50 calibres
Projectile weight: 27 kg
Muzzle velocity: 875 m/sec
Rate of fire: 10 rounds/min
Maximum range: 25 km (13.5 nm)
Date introduced: 1936

Status
Operational, as noted above.

TWIN AND SINGLE   (CHINA)
130 mm MOUNTINGS

Twin 130 mm mountings are being incorporated in the new *Luta* class destroyers of the Chinese (PRC) Navy. Externally they look very much like the elderly Russian weapons of the same calibre; but it is reasonable to assume that the design will have been modernised in details.

Gun data are assumed to be broadly similar to those of the Russian weapon; but again it may be assumed that performance will have been upgraded to some extent.

Single Mountings
Single mountings of what is probably the same gun have been installed during refit in several of the old naval vessels inherited by the PRC from their predecessors.

Status
Operational in new destroyers and old escorts.

Russian twin 130 mm mounting

Although this 127 mm gun is of French design and manufacture it was designed to use standard American 5-inch gun ammunition, and for that reason it has here been described by its Imperial measure calibre.

Now fitted only in some *Surcouf* class destroyers these guns have elsewhere been replaced by the new single 100 mm gun. The twin-gun turret weighs about 45 tons.

Gun Data
Calibre: 127 mm
Barrel length: 54 calibres
Elevation: to 80 deg
Projectile weight: 32 kg
Muzzle velocity: 850 m/sec
Rate of fire: 15 rounds/min
Maximum range: 22 km (12 nm)
Maximum altitude: 13,000 m
Date introduced: 1953
Status
Operational as stated above.

DP SINGLE 127/54 GUN MOUNTING   (ITALY)

This is a dual purpose gun mount intended as a main armament for frigates and destroyers.

Ready use ammunition is held in three drums just below the turret. A central elevator hoists the ammunition, chosen from one drum, and delivers it to the turret where two oscillating arms perform the final movement to the loading trays.

OTO 127/54 mounting

The drums are automatically reloaded through two hoists manually loaded in the magazine. The layout permits storage of three different types of ammunition in the ready use magazine. Remote controlled fuse setters are provided in the oscillating arms.

The reloading, feeding, loading and firing sequence is controlled by a control console operated by a single man. Optionally, the mount can also be fitted with a stabilised line of sight local control system.

The barrel is fitted with a multi-muzzle brake. The shield is of fibreglass and is watertight. The complete mounting weighs 54 tons.

Gun Data

Calibre: 127 mm
Barrel length: 54 calibres
Elevation: −15 to +85 deg
Traverse: 330 deg
Elevation speed: 30 deg/sec
Traverse speed: 40 deg/sec
Projectile weight: probably about 32 kg
Muzzle velocity: probably about 850 m/sec
Rate of fire: 45 rounds/min
Ready-use ammunition: 66 rounds
Maximum range: probably about 22 km (12 nm)
Date introduced: 1969

Manufacturer

OTO Melara

Status

In service with the Italian Navy and others.

This is the oldest design of 5-inch mounting still in service in the US Navy, but it is also one of the most widely used. The 5-inch 38 calibre gun has indeed been described as "the prototype of the conventional US naval gun".

The Mark 32 mounting contains two Mark 12 guns and an enclosed mounting with ammunition-handling room beneath. Remotely-controlled, semi-automatic, dual-purpose it also has local laying facilities on the mounting. Fire angle limits are good but angular velocity and acceleration are significantly lower than those of the later 5-inch mountings.

Semi-fixed ammunition is used, consisting of a projectile weighing about 25 kg (varying according to type) and a case assembly weighing about 13 kg including a full powder charge of 6.8 kg. The ammunition is raised to the gun house by hydraulically powered hoists. The complete mounting weighs about 53 tons.

Gun Data

Calibre: 127 mm (5 in)
Barrel length: 38 calibres
Traverse: 300 deg.
Elevation: −15 to +85 deg.
Projectile weight: about 25 kg
Muzzle velocity: 792·5 m/sec max.
Rate of fire: 15 rounds/min normal, 22 rounds/min emergency
Maximum range: 16.5 km (9 nm)
Maximum altitude: 11,400 m
Date introduced: 1935

Status

Twin mountings were installed in battleships, heavy cruisers and destroyers. Some of these are still in service in both the active and reserve fleets of the US Navy as well as in ex-US ships of other navies. They are also in service with Spanish-built ships of the Spanish Navy.

SINGLE MOUNTINGS

In addition to the enclosed twin mounting of the 5-inch 38 calibre gun there have been three other general types of mounting—
(a) Enclosed single mount with ammunition-handling room below. Originally on destroyers, destroyer escorts and aux-

Five-inch 38-calibre gun mounting

iliaries. Now mainly found in auxiliary vessels of the US Navy, these single mounts are also the main surface armament of the *Lepanto* class destroyers and *Legazpi* class frigates of the Spanish Navy.

(b) Open single mount with ammunition-handling room below. Auxiliary vessels.

(c) Open single mount without ammunition hoists or handling room. Converted merchant vessels.

In performance there is essentially no difference between the first two of these and one gun of the enclosed twin mounting. The third arrangement is necessarily less efficient in terms of ammunition handling; but otherwise the gun characteristics are the same.

MARK 39 MOUNTING

This mounting is an intermediate stage between the 5 in/38 mountings and the 5 in/54 Mark 42 mountings. It can be regarded as a 5 in/38 single enclosed mounting Mark 30 with the Mark 12 38-calibre gun replaced by a Mark 16 54-calibre gun. This gun fires a heavier shell (about 32 kg instead of about 25 kg) with a slightly higher muzzle velocity and thus a longer range.

It may be noted that in this mounting an amplidyne all-electric power drive is used, whereas in both the 5 in/38 mountings and the 5 in/54 Mark 42 mountings the drive is electro/hydraulic. The gun was first introduced in 1944.

Status

Installed as a single enclosed mounting in *Midway* class aircraft carriers.

Five-inch Mk 42 Mod 9 lightweight mounting

This widely-adopted mounting had several advantages over both the 5-inch 38 calibre mountings and the 5-inch 54 calibre Mark 39 mounting. It uses the Mark 18 54-calibre gun, and it is capable of very much higher rates of fire. Mod 7, which is the most widely used operationally of the earlier versions, is a dual-purpose single enclosed mounting fitted with automatic ammunition feed mechanisms. Driven by electric-hydraulic power units, it can be operated in local or automatic control.

The gun housing slide and breech mechanism are quite different from those of the semi-automatic 5-inch 54-calibre and 5-inch 38-calibre designs, as also is the ammunition feed system which involves manual operations only in loading the cylindrical, power-driven loading drums. As a result the single gun can achieve a continuous firing rate equal to that achieved only in short bursts by an expert crew on the two guns of the 5-inch 38-calibre Mark 32 mounting. The complete turret weighs about 60 tons.

Gun Data

Calibre: 127 mm (5 in)
Barrel length: 54 calibres
Elevation: to 85 deg.
Projectile weight: about 32 kg
Muzzle velocity: about 810 m/sec
Rate of fire: 45 rounds/min
Maximum range: approx 24 km (13 nm)
Maximum altitude: 13,600 m
Date introduced: 1953

Status
Operational in ships of the US Navy and elsewhere. To be mounted on the new *Andalucia* class frigates of the Spanish Navy.

MODIFIED MOD 7 MOUNTING

In some installations of the Mk 42 the starboard "bubble" or "frog-eye" on the mount has been removed. This dome is normally used for local anti-aircraft control; the port dome, which is retained in these installations, is for local anti-surface control.

LIGHTWEIGHT MOD 9 MOUNTING

Functionally similar to the Mod 7 mount described above, the Mod 9 is an improved design featuring lower mount weight (58,700 kg), nearly 10% lower power consumption and a smaller crew requirement. Improvements incorporated included replacement of all electronic components of the earlier mount by solid-state devices. Only two men are needed on the mount as against four for the Mod 7, and the total crew requirement is 12 men instead of 14. The only respect in which the Mod 7 performance is known to be superior is that of elevation acceleration (60 deg/sec² against 40 deg/sec²).

Status
51 units of the above-decks portion of the mount were manufactured by FMC/NOD and supplied for use on DE-1052 class ships. The below-decks portion was produced by the US Navy Naval Ordnance Station, Louisville.

DP SINGLE 5-inch 54 CALIBRE (USA)
LIGHTWEIGHT MARK 45 MOUNTING

This new gun mounting was designed primarily for installation in new ships, was required to embody all relevant improvements developed over some 30 years since the 5-inch/38 was first introduced and was required to be light, easily maintained and exceptionally reliable. The result requires only one-third of the crew of a 5-inch/38 and with it a single man in a control centre can fire a drum load of 20 shells without help.

Developed by FMC/NOD the mount offers a crew reduction from 14 to 6 with none on the mount and a weight reduction from 60 to 25 tons. To achieve these reductions, however, the upper elevation limit has been reduced to 65°, the rate of fire to 20 rounds/min and the number of ready service rounds from 40 to 20. Gun characteristics otherwise are believed to be the same as described for the Mk 42 mounting.

Manufacturers

FMC—development and first 25 production models. General Electric—at least 56 production models.

Status

In production. Deliveries commenced in 1974. To be fitted to the *Spruance* class destroyers and some other vessels of the USN.

Guided Projectile

A 5-inch guided projectile is under development for the US Navy as part of a programe which also includes an 8-inch round for the new lightweight 8-inch gun. No operational date is known.

Five-inch 54-calibre Mk 45 mounting

(US/ARGENTINA ETC)   DP SINGLE 5-inch MOUNTING

A 5-inch (127 mm) gun is mounted on the ex-USS *Brooklyn* class cruisers of the Argentine Navy—and on similar vessels in the Chilean Navy. The gun is a short 25-calibre weapon and is mounted as eight single installations.

These weapons are assumed to be of American manufacture, but 5-inch guns of this type are no longer in service in the US Navy.

Status
Operational but no longer made.

(SPAIN)   TWIN 120 mm MOUNTING

These 50-calibre semi-automatic 120 mm guns are fitted in the *Oquendo* type anti-submarine destroyers. They are of Spanish manufacture. Some of the *Oquendo* class were modified before completion to take 5-inch (127 mm) 38 calibre American guns and it is likely that the remainder will be converted in due course.

Details of construction and performance are not available. Reasonable figures, however, would be a projectile weight in the region of 25 kg, a muzzle velocity of perhaps 850 m/sec, a rate of fire of about 15 rounds/min and a range of some 20 km (11 nm).

Status
Operational but obsolescent.

DP SINGLE 120 mm MOUNTING (SWEDEN)

Found now only on the *Karlskrona* and two of the *Visby* class frigates of the Royal Swedish Navy, this gun was designed before the 1939-45 war and has long been superseded by more modern weapons.

Gun Data
Calibre: 120 mm
Barrel length: 50 calibres
Elevation: to 70 deg
Projectile weight: 24 kg
Muzzle velocity: 900 m/sec
Rate of fire: 12 rounds/min
Maximum range: 24 km (13 nm)
Date introduced: 1934

Manufacturer
AB Bofors

Status
Operational but obsolescent.

DP TWIN 120 mm SEMI-AUTOMATIC MOUNTING (SWEDEN)

These guns were introduced at the end of the Second World War and are to be found mounted in lightly-armoured turrets on the *Oland* and *Ostergötland* class destroyers of the Royal Swedish Navy. The twin turret weighs about 67 tons.

Gun Data
Calibre: 120 mm
Barrel length: 45 calibres
Elevation: to 80 deg
Projectile weight: 23.5 kg
Muzzle velocity: 850 m/sec
Rate of fire: 20 rounds/min
Maximum range: 19 km (10 nm)
Maximum altitude: 13,000 m
Date introduced: 1945

Manufacturer
AB Bofors

Status
Operational but no longer made.

(SWEDEN)

DP TWIN 120 mm AUTOMATIC MOUNTING

These 50-calibre Bofors 120 mm guns are mounted in twin mounts on the *Halland* class destroyers of the Royal Swedish Navy and on the *Halland* and *Friesland* class anti-submarine escorts of the Royal Netherlands Navy. They are fully automatic and radar controlled and the complete twin mounting weighs 67 tons.

Gun Data

Calibre: 120 mm
Barrel length: 50 calibres
Elevation: to 85 deg
Projectile weight: 23.5 kg
Muzzle velocity: 850 m/sec
Rate of fire: 40 rounds/min
Maximum range: 20.5 km (11 nm)
Maximum altitude: 12,500 m
Date introduced: 1950

Manufacturer

AB Bofors

Status

Operational as stated.

Swedish 120 mm DP twin automatic mounting

(SWEDEN)
DP SINGLE 120/46 AUTOMATIC MOUNTING

The Bofors L/46 120 mm Automatic Gun is designed for use against both surface and airborne targets and has a very high rate of fire.

Housed in a 4 mm steel turret mount the gun has two magazines, mounted on the elevating cradle, which are manually filled from a fixed-structure motor-driven rod hoist. Electro-hydraulic remote control is standard with the alternative of gyro-stabilised one-man local control. Telescopic sights are also fitted and the hoist and the elevation and traverse mechanisms can be operated by hand. The gun barrel is liquid cooled and has an exchangeable liner. The complete mounting (less ammunition) weighs 28.5 tons. 52 rounds are carried in the magazine.

Gun Data
Calibre: 120 mm
Barrel length: 46 calibres
Elevation: −10 to +80 deg
Projectile weight: 21 kg (round 35 kg)
Muzzle velocity: 1,800 m/sec
Rate of fire: 80 rounds/min
Maximum range: 18.5 km (10 nm)
Maximum altitude: 11,800 m
Date introduced: 1967

Manufacturer
AB Bofors

Status
Bofors started work on this gun as a private venture in 1963 and the prototype was test-fired in 1967. It is not in regular production but is supplied to special order. It has been manufactured for the Finnish Navy for use in their *Turanmaa* class frigates, in which it has been in service since 1968.

(UK/ARGENTINA)
SINGLE 4.7-inch MOUNTING

The three surviving *Buenos Aires* class destroyers of the Argentine Navy carry either three or four 4.7-in guns. These destroyers were built in the United Kingdom in the 1930s and the mountings were made by Vickers.

Gun Data
Calibre: 120 mm (4.7-in)
Barrel length: 31 calibres
Projectile weight: 28 kg
Muzzle velocity: 850 m/sec
Rate of fire: 8 rounds/min
Maximum range: 16.5 km (9 nm)
Date introduced: 1931

Status
Operational but no longer in production and not available.

(UK/SPAIN)
DP SINGLE 4.7-inch MOUNTING

Eight single 120 mm 45 calibre guns are mounted on the heavy cruiser *Canarias*. Like the Spanish cruiser's 8-inch guns, these are of Vickers design, and date from 1923.

Gun Data
Calibre: 120 mm (4.7 in)
Barrel length: 45 calibres
Elevation: 80 deg
Projectile weight: 22 kg
Muzzle velocity: 825 m/sec
Rate of fire: 9 rounds/min
Maximum range: 16 km (8.5 nm)
Maximum altitude: 10,000 m
Date introduced: 1923

Manufacturer
Vickers

Status
In service but no longer made.

SINGLE 4.5-inch MOUNTING MK 5 (UK)

This single mounting is to be found in the *Tribal* class frigates of the
Royal Navy and in similar vessels elsewhere. It is manually loaded
and normally remotely controlled but can be controlled locally by
joystick. Charge and shell are separate and automatically rammed.

Gun Data
Calibre: 114 mm (4.5 in)
Barrel length: 45 calibres
Elevation: to about 50 deg
Projectile weight: about 25 kg
Muzzle velocity: about 840 m/sec
Rate of fire: up to 14 rounds/min
Maximum range: about 19 km (10 nm)
Date introduced: 1937

Manufacturer
Vickers Ltd.

Status
Operational as noted but no longer made.

4.5-inch Mk 5 mounting

146

(UK)   DP TWIN 4.5-inch MOUNTING MK 6

This twin-barrelled remotely-controlled power-operated mounting is in operational use in many ships of the Royal Navy and others. Normally remotely-controlled electro-hydraulically it can also be controlled locally by a joystick. The loading cycle is semi-automatic, shell and cartridge being separately hoisted and manually loaded into the loading tray. The turret weighs about 50 tons.

Gun Data

Calibre: 114 mm (4.5 in)
Barrel length: about 50 calibres
Elevation: to about 80 deg
Projectile weight: about 25 kg
Muzzle velocity: about 850 m/sec
Rate of fire: 20 rounds/min
Maximum range: about 19 km (10 nm)
Date introduced: 1946

Manufacturer

Vickers Ltd.

Status

In widespread operational use.

Twin 4.5-inch mountings on HMS *Kent*

This fully-automatic gun is modelled on the British Army's Abbot gun and is fitted with muzzle brake and fume extractor. A completely new range of fixed ammunition has also been designed.

Major features of design of the mounting are a simple ammunition feed system and a remote power control system with large stability margins. The revolving structure has been kept light and a sandwich-construction glass-reinforced plastic gun-shield fitted.

The loading system is hydraulically operated and employs only four transfer points between the gun bay (ready use magazine) and the gun, and the type of ammunition may be changed without unloading or firing out a large number of rounds. A stockpile of ammunition may be accommodated at the mounting and fired remotely from the Operations Room with no crew closed up at the mounting.

Gun Data
Calibre: 114 mm (4.5 in)
Barrel length: 55 calibres
Elevation: to 55 deg
Rate of fire: 20 rounds/min
Date introduced: 1971

Manufacturer
Vickers Ltd.

Status
In production and service with Royal Navy and elsewhere.

Vickers 4.5-inch Mk 8 mounting on HMS *Amazon*

DP TWIN 4-inch MOUNTING MK 19

Designed by Vickers, this is a twin-barrelled, hand loaded, remotely-controlled naval gun mount. Electrically trained and elevated, laid by remote control, but can be locally controlled using joysticks. Fuse setting alongside each trunnion support. A good gun crew can achieve a rate of fire of up to about 16 rounds per barrel per minute.

Gun Data

Calibre: 120 mm (4 in)
Elevation: to 80 deg
Projectile weight: 15.9 kg
Muzzle velocity: 760 m/sec
Rate of fire: up to 16 rounds/min
Maximum range: 19.5 km (10.5 nm)
Maximum altitude: 13,500 m
Date introduced: 1935

Manufacturer

Vickers Ltd.

Status

Operational in British, Commonwealth and many other navies. No longer in production.

Main armament of the Nigerian corvette NNS *Dorina* (Vosper Thornycroft) is a twin 4-inch Mk 19 gun mounting

(UK/CHILE) DP SINGLE 4-inch MOUNTING

This fully-automatic 60-calibre weapon is mounted as four single mounts on the two *Almirante* class destroyers of the Chilean Navy.

Built by Vickers (as were the destroyers) and introduced in 1955, the gun and turret weigh a little over 26 tons.

Gun Data
Calibre: 102 mm
Barrel length: 60 calibres
Elevation: to 75 deg
Projectile weight: 16 kg
Muzzle velocity: 900 m/sec
Rate of fire: 40 rounds/min
Maximum range: 18.5 km (10 nm)
Maximum altitude: 12,000 m
Date introduced: 1955

Status
Operational but no longer in production.

(CHINA) DP TWIN AND SINGLE 100 mm MOUNTINGS

Twin and single dual-purpose guns of Chinese manufacture have been installed in some of the refitted escorts of the miscellaneous fleet inherited by the PRC from their predecessors.

No details of construction or performance are available but the weapons are assumed to be broadly similar to the more modern 100 mm Russian weapons on which the Chinese designs are probably based.

Status
Operational in older vessels of the Chinese Navy.

DP SINGLE 100 mm MOUNTING

(FRANCE)

This single gun is the medium-calibre weapon on which the French Navy has now standardised for new gun installations. It is fitted in most of the larger new and refitted vessels.

The gun is entirely automatic and operates with an unmanned turret. The complete mounting weighs 24.5 tons.

Gun Data

Calibre: 100 mm
Barrel Length: 55 calibres
Elevation: to 80 deg
Projectile weight: 13.5 kg (round 23.2 kg)
Muzzle velocity: 870 m/sec
Rate of fire: 60 rounds/min
Maximum altitude: 11,000 m
AA engagement: 6-8,000 m
Date introduced: 1959

Status

Operational in the French Navy and in those of Portugal and West Germany.

French 100 mm guns

(USSR)

DP TWIN 100 mm MOUNTING

Guns of this type are in service with the Russian Navy on the *Sverdlov* class cruisers (including the *Dzerjinski*) and the *Tchapaev* class cruisers, on which they are associated with Wackeltopf stabilised directors with radar. The turret is stabilised and has been said to weigh 35 tons.

Gun Data
Calibre: 100 mm
Barrel length: 60 calibres
Elevation: to 80 deg
Projectile weight: 16 kg
Muzzle velocity: 900 m/sec
Rate of fire: 20 rounds/min
Maximum range: 18 km (10 nm)
Maximum altitude: 12,000 m
Date introduced: 1942

Status
Operational as noted.

Russian 100 mm twin DP mounting

DP SINGLE 100 mm MOUNTING

(USSR)

This mounting is to be found on the two *Kirov* class cruisers, on the many *Riga* and *Kola* class destroyers that are to be found in the navies of both Russia and its client countries, and on the *Don* class support ships.

Although the guns are believed to be of more recent design than those in the twin mountings on the *Sverdlov* and *Tchapaev* cruisers they are manually operated and inferior in performance.

Gun Data
Calibre: 100 mm
Barrel length: 50 calibres
Elevation: to 80 deg
Projectile weight: 13.5 kg
Muzzle velocity: 850 m/sec
Rate of fire: 15 rounds/min
Maximum range: 16 km (8.5 nm)
Maximum altitude: 6,000 m
Date introduced: 1947

Status
Operational but obsolescent.

Single 100 mm gun mountings on a *Riga*-class destroyer

(USSR)   DP 85 mm MOUNTINGS

Two elderly mountings, one single and one twin, are still to be found on some *Kronstadt* class coastal patrol vessels and *Skory* class destroyers respectively. The same gun is probably used in both.

Gun Data

Calibre: about 85 mm
Barrel length: about 50 calibres
Elevation: to 75 deg
Projectile weight: 9.5 kg
Muzzle velocity: about 800 m/sec
Rate of fire: 15-20 rounds/min
Maximum range: 14 km (7.5 nm)
Maximum altitude: 9,000 m
Date introduced: 1943

Status

Operational but obsolescent.

(CANADA)   AA TWIN 3-inch MOUNTING

Some frigates of the Canadian fleet are fitted with twin 76 mm AA mountings of Canadian manufacture. In the *Mackenzie* class there is a 70-calibre Canadian twin forward and a 50-calibre twin of US manufacture aft: in the *Restigouche* class there is either a similar arrangement or just the 70-calibre Canadian twin.

Performance details are assumed to be similar to the UK (Vickers) Mk 6 70-calibre twin 76 mm weapon.

Status

Operational as stated.

DP SINGLE 76/62 mm MOUNTING

The 76/62 OTO M.M.I. single barrel automatic gun was developed as secondary armament for frigates and corvettes as a dual-purpose weapon system.

The gun is a single barrel, water-spray cooled, on a powered mounting. It is protected by a watertight splinterproof shield, which also houses the one man required to direct the gun.

The feed system can vary in length from a minimum of 2.50 metres to a maximum of 11 metres from loading tray to magazine. Ammunition is fixed and empty cases ejected automatically. Three men are required to reload the ammunition system.

Elevation and traverse are electrically and hydraulically controlled and there is provision for emergency manual operation. Either local or remote control is possible. The complete mounting weighs about 12 tons.

Gun Data
Calibre: 76 mm
Barrel length: 62 calibres
Elevation: −15 to +85 deg
Traverse: 360 deg
Elevation speed: 40 deg/sec
Traverse speed: 70 deg/sec
Projectile weight: about 6 kg
Muzzle velocity: about 900 m/sec
Rate of fire: 60 rounds/min
Maximum range: about 16 km (8.5 nm)
Date introduced: 1962

Manufacturer
OTO Melara.

Status
In service in many Italian ships. No longer in production and superseded by the 76/62 Compact.

OTO 76/62 MMI mountings

Developed from the 76/62 M.M.I. mounting this fully-automatic OTO mount is designed for dual-purpose use on ships of any type from hydrofoils and motor gunboats upwards.

The ammunition system is designed to sustain a high rate of fire. Rounds are hoisted from the magazine in a series of short movements to reduce acceleration forces on moving parts and on the ammunition.

Primarily the mount is designed for remote control but there is emergency local control and a stabilised line-of-sight local control system can be fitted. Normal control is electrical.

The gun is fitted with a small-hole muzzle brake and fume extractor; the gunhouse shield is made of fibreglass and the complete mounting weighs 7.5 tons.

Gun Data

Calibre: 76 mm
Barrel length: 62 calibres
Elevation: −15 to +85 deg
Traverse: unlimited
Elevation speed: 35 deg/sec
Traverse speed: 60 deg/sec
Projectile weight: 6.2 kg
Muzzle velocity: 925 m/sec
Rate of fire: 85 rounds/min
Maximum range: about 16 km (9 nm)
Maximum altitude: about 11,500 m
Date introduced: 1964

Manufacturer
OTO Melara.

Status
In current production for the Italian Navy and many others.

OTO 76/62 Compact

DP SINGLE 3-inch 50-CALIBRE MOUNTING MARK 34   (SPAIN)

This is an American designed weapon built in Spain and mounted on destroyers and frigates of the Spanish Navy. Details of this mounting and of the American designed and built twin Mk 33 mountings, which are also mounted on Spanish destroyers and frigates, will be found in the US entries below, but the main data for the Mk 34 are recapitulated here.

Gun Data

Calibre: 76 mm (3-in)
Barrel length: 50 calibres
Elevation: to 85 deg
Projectile weight: approx 6 kg
Muzzle velocity: about 825 m/sec
Rate of fire: 50 rounds/min
Maximum range: about 13 km (7 nm)

Manufacturer

Fabrica de Artilleria, Sociedad Española de Construccion Naval.

Status

Operational.

DP TWIN 3-inch MOUNTING MK 6   (UK)

This is an automatic remotely-controlled electrically-driven mounting normally operated unmanned but with provision for local control. The turret weighs about 38 tons.

Gun Data

Calibre: 76 mm (3 in)
Barrel length: 70 calibres
Elevation: to 80 deg
Projectile weight: probably about 7 kg
Muzzle velocity: probably about 1,000 m/sec
Rate of fire: 60 rounds/min
Maximum range: probably about 17 km (9 nm)
Date introduced: 1951

Manufacturer

Vickers Ltd.

Status

Operational in British and Canadian warships.

(SWEDEN/NORWAY)

This is a sturdy, simple, remotely-controlled single gun designed for surface fire. Weighing only 6,500 kg and requiring only two loaders in the ammunition room, it is suitable for installation in small ships and is currently in service on *Storm* class fast patrol boats of the Norwegian Navy.

Electro-hydraulic remote control is used. The gun is mounted in a 6 mm steel gun house and has a fixed motor-driven hoist with lifting link levers and 5-round feed device. 100 rounds are carried in the magazine and hoist. The gun has a monobloc barrel.

Gun Data

Calibre: 76 mm (3 in)
Barrel length: 50 calibres
Elevation: −10 to +30 deg
Projectile weight: 5-9 kg (round 11.3 kg)
Muzzle velocity: 825 m/sec
Rate of fire: 30 rounds/min
Maximum range: 12.6 km (7 nm)
Date introduced: 1965

Manufacturer
AB Bofors and Kongsberg Weapon Factory.

Status
Designed and developed as a private venture by Bofors, this gun was first conceived in 1962 and went into service with the Norwegian Navy in 1965.

Bofors 3 inch mounting on RSS *Sovereignty* (Singapore)

DP 3-inch 50 CALIBRE MOUNTINGS MARKS 27, 33 and 34 (USA)

These 3-inch (76 mm) 50 calibre gun mounts are primarily intended for air defence but can be used also against surface targets. Planned during the Second World War but not completed in time for combat use in that conflict, the mounts have since proved themselves so effective that they have virtually displaced their predecessors—40 mm twin and quadruple mounts—on combat vessels.

Mks 27 and 33 are twin mounts and Mk 34 a single. Mks 27 and 33 are identical in almost all respects, the main difference being in the slide. All marks use the same gun and similar backing mechanisms, except that in the twin mounts the assemblies are of opposite hand. Some models of the Mk 33 are enclosed twin mounts with an aluminium or glass-fibre reinforced plastic shield, and others again are twins with modifications for installation of a fire control radar antenna. The Mk 34 mount is an open single with a right-hand slide and loader assembly. Some models of the Mk 34 also are FRP shielded. Mount weights are in the region of 14.5 tons for the twins and 7.5 tons for the Mk 34.

Obsolescent Types

In a few vessels completed at or soon after the end of the 1939-45 war a 70-calibre gun was installed in twin mounts. Fully automatic and credited with a rate of fire of 90 or more rounds/min, this weapon also had a significantly larger range than the 50-calibre guns. In all save one instance *(Norfolk)* however these guns were subsequently replaced by 5-inch weapons and it is believed that there are now none in service anywhere.

A much earlier (circa 1936) 3-inch weapon is still to be found in a variety of US auxiliary vessels. Performance is similar to the later weapons except that the achievable rate of fire is much lower.

Gun Data

Calibre: 76 mm (3 in)
Barrel length: 50 calibres (see above)
Elevation: to 85 deg
Projectile weight: approx 6 kg
Muzzle velocity: about 825 m/sec
Rate of fire: 50 rounds/min
Maximum range: about 13 km (7 nm)
Maximum altitude: about 9,000 m

Status

50-calibre weapons are operational in many ships of the US and other navies.

Single 3-inch mounting on a GW frigate of the US Navy

(USSR)

DP TWIN 76 mm MOUNTING

This is a relatively modern mounting which can be found on the *Kynda* class cruisers, the *Kashin* class destroyers and the *Mirka* and *Petya* class frigates of the Soviet Navy. The mountings are stabilised.

Gun Data

Calibre: 76 mm (3 in)
Barrel length: 60 calibres
Elevation: to about 85 deg
Projectile weight: about 6 kg
Muzzle velocity: about 900 m/sec
Rate of fire: 60 rounds/min
Maximum range: 15 km (8 nm)
Maximum altitude: 14,000 m
Date introduced: probably late 1950s

Status

In widespread operational use.

Twin 76 mm mounting used in many Russian ships

DP TWIN 57 mm MOUNTING   (CHINA)

Twin 57 mm mountings are installed in the new *Luta* class destroyers of the Chinese (PRC) Navy. No details of construction or performance are available, but it is reasonable to assume that the designs of both gun and mounting are based on Russian designs—but probably not the latest Russian design since this entered service after the estrangement between the two countries.

Status
Operational in new destroyers of the Chinese Navy.

AA TWIN 57 mm MOUNTING   (FRANCE)

This 57 mm Bofors gun is still widely used in the French Navy but it is no longer being fitted. It is still to be found on *Surcouf* class destroyers and the *Le Normand* and *Le Corse* class frigates. On one of the latter, the after turret was replaced experimentally by a single 100 mm gun and the vessel in question still retains this gun.

The fully-automatic guns are mounted in pairs in turrets weighing some 15 tons.

Gun Data
Calibre: 57 mm
Barrel length: 60 calibres
Elevation: to 80 deg
Projectile weight: 2.6 kg
Muzzle velocity: 920 m/sec
Rate of fire: 130 rounds/min
Maximum range: 14.5 km (8 nm)
Maximum altitude: 9,000 m
Date introduced: 1950
Status
Operational as stated.

(SWEDEN)

DP TWIN 57 mm AA GUN MOUNTING

Introduced in 1950 these 60-calibre guns were at one time widely fitted. Now, however, they are to be found in the cruiser *Latorre* (formerly Göta Lejon) of the Chilean Navy and the *Halland* class destroyers of the Royal Swedish Navy. The same gun in a slightly different twin mounting is still in service in the French Navy. The complete turret of the Swedish installations weighs some 24 tons.

Gun Data

Calibre: 57 mm
Barrel length: 60 calibres
Elevation: to 90 deg
Projectile weight: 2.6 kg
Muzzle velocity: 900 m/sec
Rate of fire: 130 rounds/min
Maximum range: 14.5 km
Maximum altitude: 9,000 m
Date introduced: 1950

Manufacturer

AB Bofors.

Status

Operational but no longer in production.

57 mm AA guns on the Royal Swedish Navy destroyer *Halland*

DP SINGLE 57 mm L-70 AUTOMATIC MOUNTING

(SWEDEN)

This 57 mm Bofors single gun in a plastic gun house is designed for both surface and anti-aircraft fire.

Alternatives of electro-hydraulic remote control or gyro-stabilised one-man local control are available. The gunfeed system contains 40 rounds of ready-use ammunition, with 128 rounds stowed in racks within the gunhouse, and there are dual step-by-step fixed supply hoists. The barrel is liquid-cooled.

Two types of ammunition are available: one is a proximity-fused and pre-fragmented shell for use against aerial targets; the other is a special surface target shelf which penetrates the target and is detonated after a short delay.

The gun can be equipped with rocket-launching rails for 2-inch (51 mm) rockets.

Gun Data
Calibre: 57 mm
Barrel length: 70 calibres
Elevation: −10 to +75 deg
Projectile weight: 2-4 kg (round 5.9 kg)
Muzzle velocity: 1,025 m/sec
Rate of fire: 200 rounds/min
Maximum range: 14 km (7.5 nm)
Date introduced: 1971

Manufacturer
AB Bofors

Status
Operational in the Royal Swedish Navy and other navies, and is the only defensive weapon on the second series of *Spica* boats of the Swedish Navy.

Swedish *Jagaren* class FPB with 57/70 gun

Quadruple 57 mm AA mountings are installed in the *Kanin* and *Krupny* classes of Russian destroyer and the *Lama* class supply ships. It is believed that the guns, which in these mountings are arranged as two pairs mounted vertically one above the other, are of similar pattern to those in the twin open mountings seen in many modern or modernised Russian naval vessels. It does, however, appear that the guns in the twin mountings are usually fitted with muzzle brakes. A single mounting, probably of a similar gun (but without muzzle brake) is installed in the modified *Skory* class destroyers and the *Sasha* class coastal minesweepers.

Gun Data

Calibre: 57 mm
Barrel length: 70 calibres
Elevation: probably 85 deg
Projectile weight: 2.8 kg
Muzzle velocity: about 950 m/sec
Rate of fire: 120 rounds/min
Maximum range: about 9 km (5 nm)
Maximum altitude: about 6,000 m
Date introduced: early 1960s

Status

In widespread operational use.

Quadruple 57/70 AA guns on a *Krupny* class destroyer

AA TWIN 57 mm AUTOMATIC MOUNTING (USSR)

Several of the most modern Russian warships are equipped with fully-enclosed, fully-automatic 57 mm guns in twin mountings. They are found in the *Moskva, Kresta, Grisha, Nanuchka, Poti, Ugra* and *Chilikin* classes and are radar controlled.

Gun Data

Calibre: 57 mm
Barrel length: 80 calibres
Elevation: about 85 deg
Projectile weight: 2.7 kg
Muzzle velocity: about 1,000 m/sec
Rate of fire: 120 rounds/min
Maximum range: 12 km (6.5 nm)
Maximum altitude: 5,000 m
Date introduced: 1960s

Status

Current operational weapon, probably still in production.

AA QUADRUPLE 45 mm MOUNTING (USSR)

These Russian mountings are very similar in appearance to the quadruple 57 mm AA gun mounts described above. They are fitted to some of the older destroyers of the fleet—the *Kildin, Kotlin* (unmodified) and *Tallin* classes. They are semi-automatic in operation.

Gun Data

Calibre: 45 mm
Barrel length: 85 calibres
Projectile weight: about 1.5 kg
Muzzle velocity: about 900 m/sec
Rate of fire: about 160 rounds/min
Maximum range: 9 km (5 nm)
Maximum altitude: about 6,000 m
Date introduced: early 1950s

Status

Still operational but obsolescent.

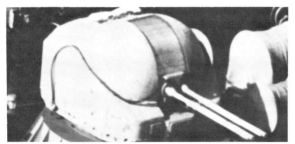

Twin 57 mm automatic mounting

The Breda Compact Twin 40 mm 70-calibre naval mounting is particularly intended for point defence against aircraft or anti-ship missiles. It is fully automatic and uses high performance remote-controlled servo systems which, with low-inertia design of the gun mounting arrangements, gives the weapon a high-quality mechanical performance.

Two versions of the mounting provide alternatives of 736 or 444 rounds in the magazine. Normally the magazine will be mounted below deck but it is sufficiently compact for an above deck mounting to be constructed if necessary. In their normal configuration the two alternative mounts weigh 5,200 kg (Type A) plus 1,800 kg for 736 rounds or 4,900 kg (Type B) plus 1,100 kg for 444 rounds.

Gun characteristics are generally similar to the Bofors L/70 except that angular velocities are 90 deg/sec in both angles and accelerations are 120 deg/sec/sec.

Manufacturer

Breda Meccanica Bresciana.

Status

In production.

Breda Compact Twin 40/70 mounting

AA SINGLE 40/60 MOUNTING

(SWEDEN)

This 60-calibre version of the well-known Bofors 40 mm AA gun was introduced in 1942 and is still in service in many places. Its performance is, as one would expect, somewhat inferior to that of the modern 70-calibre weapon.

Gun Data
Calibre: 40 mm
Barrel length: 60 calibres
Elevation: to 80 deg
Projectile weight: 0.9 kg
Muzzle velocity: 830 m/sec
Rate of fire: 120 rounds/min
Maximum range: 10 km
Tactical range: 3 km
Maximum altitude: 5,600 m
Date introduced: 1942

Manufacturer
AB Bofors.

Status
In service and still fitted in reconditioned form but obsolescent and no longer in production.

BRITISH TWIN MOUNTING MK 5

A twin mounting of the Bofors 40/60 gun is in service in many British and Commonwealth naval vessels. Gun characteristics are the same as above and the twin mounting weighs approximately 3 tons. Single mounts are also in service.

The later Mk 7 British mounting uses the 40/70 Bofors gun.

Single 40/60 mounting on HMS *Hubberston*

Bofors make a number of different mountings for their 40 mm 70-calibre naval guns, which can be used against both surface and aerial targets.

Current models have electro-hydraulic laying equipment and can be fitted for remote or local control. In local control such guns are gyro-stabilised and have reflex sights with speed rings for aiming. There are also unpowered mounts.

Manually loaded guns are made with open mountings or equipped with a light plastic cupola for weather protection. Automatically loaded guns are also made using automatic feed devices built by Breda.

Basic Gun Data

Calibre: 40 mm
Barrel length: 70 calibres
Elevation: −10 to +90 deg
Traverse: unlimited
Elevation speed: 45 deg/sec (powered mounts)
Traverse speed: 85 deg/sec (powered mounts)
Projectile weight: 0.96 kg (HE): round 2.4 kg
Muzzle velocity: approx 1,000 m/sec
Rate of fire: 300 rounds/min
Tactical range: 4,000 m (maximum about 12 km)
Mount weight: (single mounts) 2.8-3.3 tons according to type.
Date introduced: 1946 but continuously improved. Current basic design dates from late 1950s

Manufacturer
In Sweden, AB Bofors.

Status
In widespread service in the Royal Swedish Navy and many others.

---

40 mm BOFORS VARIANTS

Bofors 40 mm 70-calibre guns, like their 60-calibre predecessors, are made or adapted under licence in many countries. In particular, a series of variants on the basic mounting has been engineered by Breda Meccanica Bresciana, in Italy, with special reference to automatic feed systems. Except that the loading system clearly influences the capacity of the installation for sustained fire, the basic characteristics of the gun are unaltered in these different configurations: visually, however, the mountings are very different and some of them are illustrated here.

Status
Like the basic gun the Breda variants are in widespread service use.

BREDA/BOFORS TWIN MOUNTING
TYPE 106

(ITALY)

Special Characteristics
Magazine capacity: 32 rounds/barrel
Weight: 6,510 kg without ammunition plus 100 kg for battery
Angular speeds: 95 deg/sec
Angular accelerations: 125 deg/sec/sec

Status
Production and service.

TYPE 64

Special Characteristics
Magazine capacity: 100 rounds/barrel
Control: local or remote
Weight: 7,900 kg without ammunition +150 kg for battery
Elevation speed: 95 deg/sec
Traverse speed: 85 deg/sec
Elevation acceleration: 125 deg/sec/sec
Traverse acceleration: 110 deg/sec/sec

Status
Production and service.

Breda/Bofors Type 106

Breda/Bofors Type 64

(ITALY)
TYPE 107

Special Characteristics
Magazine capacity: 32 rounds
Control: local or remote
Weight: 3,610 kg without ammunition +100 kg for battery
Angular speeds: 95 deg/sec
Angular accelerations: 125 deg/sec/sec

Status
In production and service.

BREDA/BOFORS SINGLE MOUNTING
TYPE 564

Special Characteristics
Magazine capacity: 144 rounds
Control: local or remote
Weight: 3,300 kg without ammunition +100 kg for battery
Crew: normally two on the mount with a third at standby. A version requiring only one on the mount is available.
Elevation speed: 45 deg/sec
Traverse speed: 80 deg/sec
Elevation acceleration: 130 deg/sec/sec
Traverse acceleration: 120 deg/sec/sec

Status
In production and service.

Breda/Bofors Type 107

Breda/Bofors Type 564

AA SINGLE 40 mm 70-CALIBRE MOUNTING (SPAIN)

This version of the Bofors L-70 40 mm AA gun is built under licence in Spain and installed in Spanish warships. The mounting weighs 2.5 tons.

Gun Data
Calibre: 40 mm
Barrel length: 70 calibres
Elevation: −10 to +90 deg
Elevation speed: 45 deg/sec
Traverse: 85 deg/sec unlimited
Projectile weight: 0.95 kg
Muzzle velocity: about 1,000 m/sec
Rate of fire: 240 rounds/min
Tactical range: 4,000 m (12 km max)

Manufacturer
Empresa Nacional Bazan.

Status
Operational.

AA 40 mm MOUNTINGS (USA)

There are single, twin and quadruple barrelled versions of the 40 mm automatic recoil operated gun in service in the US Navy. The gun has a range of approx 5,000 metres and a rate of fire of 160 rounds per minute. Most mounts can be either locally or remotely controlled, and are power operated, with emergency hand operation. The gun is derived from the Bofors design.

Status
Operational as noted.

US-built 40 mm AA gun

172

(CHINA) AA TWIN 37 mm MOUNTING (USSR) AA 37 mm MOUNTINGS

Twin 37 mm AA mountings which are fairly certainly made in China are installed in several of the light craft built in Chinese yards in recent years.

No details of construction or performance are available but the weapons are apparently copies of the side-by-side twin 37 mm Russian mountings and are probably essentially similar in performance.

Status

Operational in modern light vessels of the Chinese Navy.

Twin 37 mm mountings

Twin 63-calibre AA mountings of various types are found on many of the older cruisers, destroyers and auxiliaries of the Russian Navy. The 37 mm AA calibre was first introduced for naval use, adapted from the army weapon in 1943, but the twin mountings for which data are given here are considerably more modern and are semi-automatic in operation.

Gun Data

Calibre: 37 mm
Barrel length: 63 calibres
Projectile weight: 0.7 kg
Muzzle velocity: 875 m/sec
Rate of fire: 150 rounds/min
Maximum range: about 8 km (4 nm)
Maximum altitude: about 5,000 m

Status

Operational in many Russian naval vessels. Probably no longer in production.

SINGLE MOUNTINGS

Single mountings incorporating the earlier version of this weapon are installed in open mountings in the earlier *Skory* class destroyers and *Kronstadt* class submarine chasers, and in enclosed mountings on the T-301 coastal minesweepers.

DP TWIN 35 mm OE/OTO GUN MOUNTING

(ITALY)

The 35 mm OE/OTO mounting has been produced as a private venture and is intended for use in any type of ship. It is primarily for close anti-aircraft defence, with a secondary anti-ship and anti-shore role.

Two types of turret have been designed, the first for installation above the weather deck; and the second for installation with the shank below deck level. For each type there are three fire control systems—remote control, local control with sight for optical tracking, and an integrated radar and computer system with a sight for optical tracking.

The Oerlikon gun has a high rate of fire and is belt fed. An interesting feature is that two belts are fed to each gun, and either may be selected in about 2 seconds. Thus the mounting can switch very rapidly from firing, say, anti-aircraft ammunition to armour-piercing. Each gun is provided with EVA at the muzzle to measure muzzle velocity, and this information is fed back into the computer to permit corrections in laying to be applied.

Gun Data
Calibre: 35 mm
Barrel length: 90 calibres
Elevation: −15 deg to +85 deg
Traverse: unlimited
Elevating speed: maximum: 70 deg/sec
Traversing speed: maximum: 120 deg/sec
Elevating acceleration: 130 deg/sec/sec
Traversing acceleration: 160 deg/sec/sec
Crew: 3 (2 loaders, 1 layer, if not remotely controlled)
Muzzle velocity: 1,175 m/sec
Rate of fire: 550 rounds/min
Maximum range: 6 km (3 nm)
Maximum altitude: 5,000 m
Date introduced: 1972 (gun)

Manufacturer
OTO Melara.

Status
Production.

Twin 35 mm OE/OTO mounting

(SWITZERLAND)

AA TWIN 35 mm MOUNTING TYPE GDM-A

Type GDM-A is an electrically-controlled, stabilised twin gun that can function either with radar fire control equipment or with an optical director equipment with auxiliary computer. In addition the gun is equipped with locally stabilised column control and a gunsight. The gun can also be controlled manually by handwheel.

The two weapons are completely interchangeable and can be assembled for left or right feed. The hand cocking devices and barrels belonging to each weapon are also completely interchangeable.

Gun Data
Type: KDC
Calibre: 35 mm
Barrel length: 90 calibres
Muzzle velocity: 1,175 m/sec
Rate of fire: 550 rounds/min
Date introduced: 1972

Manufacturer
Oerlikon-Bührle.

Status
In service in at least the Greek Navy.

GDM-A twin 35 mm mounting

AA SINGLE 30 mm
REMOTE-CONTROLLED MOUNTING

This French-designed mounting incorporates the Oerlikon (formerly Hispano-Suiza) HSS 831A gun and is a remotely-controlled turret mount which can be operated from an external aiming post or aimed by one or two gun layera. Primarily an anti-aircraft mounting it can be used to engage surface targets. 215 rounds are carried on a belt feed on the mounting which weighs 3.6 tons.

Gun Data
Calibre: 30 mm
Barrel length: 70 calibres
Elevation: −18 to +83 deg
Traverse: 350 deg
Elevation speed: 40 deg/sec
Traverse speed: 50 deg/sec
Projectile weight: 0.42 kg
Muzzle velocity: 1,000 m/sec
Rate of fire: 600 rounds/min
Tactical range: 2,800 m (max 10 km)

Manufacturer
Mounting: S.A.A.M.   Gun: Oerlikon- Bührle.

Status
Operational.

OLDER 30 mm MOUNTINGS

Numerous mountings of Hispano 30 mm guns are to be found in the French Navy, as in many others, on a variety of ships. Performances of such weapons differ in detail from the figures given above but the broad picture is similar.

(SWITZERLAND/UK)

TWIN 30 mm GUN MOUNTING GCM-AOI

This 30 mm Twin Naval Mounting was developed by Hispano-Suiza (now Oerlikon Hispano) to provide close anti-aircraft defence for ships of all classes.

Under local control, the mounting is operated by a gunner who is housed in a cabin on the front right hand side.

Simple reflector sights are fitted as standard, and manual traverse, elevation, and firing gear are fitted for emergency use.

Optionally, the weapon can be used wholly under fire director control—in which case it is installed without cabin, sights or manual controls—or arrangements can be made for a gunner in a manned mounting to control a second, unmanned, mounting.

Two types of ammunition supply are available. Type A utilises twin 80 round magazines with the ammunition in coupled 20 round belts. Type B utilises twin magazines which have a continuous 140 round belt.

Gun Data
Type: Oerlikon Type KCB (formerly known as HS 831 SLM)
Calibre: 30 mm
Elevation: −15 to +85 deg
Traverse: unlimited
Elevation velocity: 60 deg/sec
Traverse velocity: 90 deg/sec
Projectile weight: 0.36 kg
Muzzle velocity: 1,080 m/sec
Rate of fire: 600-650 rounds/min

Manufacturer
Oerlikon Bührle Ltd., British Manufacture & Research Co. Ltd.

Status
Production.

GCM-ACI twin 30 mm mounting

AA TWIN 30 mm MOUNTING

A fully-automatic, remote-controlled twin 30 mm AA mounting is installed in missile boats and other small craft in the Russian Navy and in the navies of the many countries to which such vessels have been supplied.

Gun Data

Calibre: 30 mm
Barrel length: 65 calibres
Elevation: to 85 deg
Muzzle velocity: about 1,000 m/sec
Rate of fire: about 500 rounds/min
Maximum range: 3-4,000 m
Date introduced: 1960

Status

In widespread operational use.

Twin 30 mm mounting on a Russian missile boat

178

(CHINA) AA TWIN 25 mm MOUNTING

Twin 25 mm AA mountings are installed in various light craft of the Chinese (PRC) Navy. Many of these weapons were undoubtedly made in Russia and are of the same designs as those installed in similar vessels in that country: it is believed, however, that new weapons are being built in China—presumably to similar standards.

Status
Operational.

Open 25 mm AA mounting

(USSR) AA TWIN 25 mm MOUNTINGS

LAA guns of this type are installed in open, semi-enclosed or enclosed mountings in many of the smaller ships of the Russian Navy. The two guns are mounted vertically one above the other.

Gun Data
Calibre: 25 mm
Barrel length: 70 calibres
Elevation: at least 85 deg
Muzzle velocity: 900 m/sec
Rate of fire: 350 rounds/min
Maximum range: about 4 km (2 nm)
Date introduced: probably early 1950s

Status
Operational. Some mountings are probably to be regarded as obsolescent.

Enclosed 25 mm AA mounting

20 mm MOUNTING TYPE A41/804

(SWITZERLAND)

This widely used Oerlikon mounting incorporates the type 804 drum-fed cannon. Suitable for small and very small naval vessels it is operated entirely by one man and can be used for either AA or surface fire. Sighting is by ring and bead. The complete mount weighs 240 kg.

Gun Data
Calibre: 20 mm
Muzzle velocity: 835 m/sec
Rate of fire: 800 rounds/min
Ready rounds: 60 in drum magazine

Manufacturer
Oerlikon and associated companies.

Status
Weapon operational but no longer made.

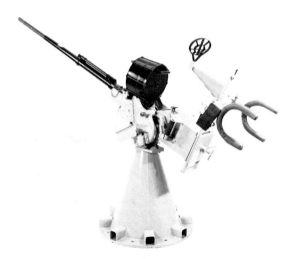

A41/804 mounting

(SWITZERLAND)

20 mm MOUNTING TYPE GAM/204 GK

This is a simple, but modern and efficient, 20 mm naval mounting embodying the 204 GK cannon.

All-up weight at 480 kg is low enough to permit installation on any type of naval vessel and the gun can be used for either AA or surface fire. No electrical power is needed: the gun is laid by the gunner using a shoulder-harness and sighting is by simple ring and bead.

Gun Data
Calibre: 20 mm
Elevation: −15 to +60 deg
Muzzle velocity: 1,050 m/sec
Rate of fire: 1,000 rounds/min
Ready Rounds: 200
Feed system: link belt

Manufacturer
Oerlikon-Bührle.

Status
Production.

EARLIER MODELS

Very large numbers of manually-operated single 20 mm cannon of earlier types are to be found in very many navies. The modern weapon described above is typical of current practice: the earlier weapons are too numerous to list but it may be assumed that their performance is generally inferior to that of the GAM/204GK.

GAM/204 GK pedestal mounting

20 mm NAVAL VULCAN AIR DEFENCE SYSTEM (USA)

Naval VADS is a system derived from the US Army Vulcan Air Defence System for close-in anti-aircraft defence. The basic system consists of a lead-computing sight, a range update computer and a control panel all associated with the M-168 gun, a modification of the M61A1 Vulcan gun, which has alternative firing rates of 1,000 or 3,000 rounds/min. Local, local with external range and remote control modes are available.

The gun and its feed system are also the basis of the Phalanx close-in defence combined radar and gun system.

Manufacturer
General Electric

20 mm THREE BARREL DECK MOUNT (USA)

This system comprises an M 197 three-barrel 20 mm gun and ancillary equipment mounted on a US Navy Mk 10 stand. The gun and its associated delinking feeder (M-89) are used by the USMC in helicopters and in US naval aircraft.

The M 197 weapon is electrically operated and power is supplied by a battery mounted on the gun stand.

The three barrel gun is derived from the six-barrel M-61 (Vulcan) gun and has alternative rates of fire of 600 and 1,200 rounds/min.

Pintle mounting of the weapon is also possible using a flexible chute to connect the gun to the ammunition box.

Gun Data
Calibre: 20 mm
Elevation: −15 to +75 deg
Traverse: unlimited
Ammunition: M-50 Series
Muzzle velocity: 1,030 m/sec
Rate of fire: 600 or 1,200 rounds/min
Ready rounds: 300
Weight on Mk 10 mounting: approx 500 kg
Date introduced: 1969 (airborne weapon)

Manufacturer
General Electric.
Status
Production.

MISCELLANEOUS ARTILLERY

Most shipborne guns of more than about 40 mm calibre, even though in some instances they may be derived from earlier land force weapons, are unmistakably naval weapons both in the design of their mountings and in the way in which they are operated.

There are, however, some exceptions, of which three examples are 105 mm howitzers (Vietnam), 3.7 inch howitzers (Iraq) and a 76 mm tank gun and turret (USSR). It is not, of course, suggested that the existence of such weapons (and many other instances could have been quoted) is important when viewed against the background of the world's total naval armament: it does, however, reflect the remarkable longevity of well-designed weapons—despite all the pressures generated by the insistent development of new and usually much more elaborate devices.

BOMBARDMENT ROCKETS

Although the bombardment rocket has a long history as a naval weapon, and despite the growing popularity of multiple rocket launchers among land forces in recent years, there is little apparent enthusiasm for such weapons in the world's navies at present. Even the Russians, who have led the field in this department of warfare for more than three decades, have done little to develop their many launchers as naval bombardment weapons.

For anti-submarine purposes, of course, there have been numerous rocket weapon developments, and these are described in the section on ASW weapons. Illuminating flare rockets and, more recently, ECM chaff-dispensing rockets are also to be found, but these are scarcely to be described as weapons.

In Western Europe the only recent naval bombardment rocket developments have been the French Rafale and RAP 14 systems, the Swiss twin-rocket launcher and the Italian SCLAR system which, although designed primarily for ECM and illuminating rockets, can also be used with bombardment rockets. All these weapons are described below. Systems, such as the British Corvus, believed to be intended only for ECM or signalling purposes are not included.

Outside Europe the only positive information relates to a Brazilian development of two shipborne rockets which was current a few years ago but has not been heard of recently.

RAP 14 BOMBARDMENT ROCKET SYSTEM

(FRANCE)

The multiple unguided rocket system known as RAP 14 has been proposed for naval applications. As can be seen from the accompanying picture of a model of the system, the naval version will have a 2 × 9 rocket launcher on a remotely controlled mounting with provision for automatic reloading from below deck with the launcher in the vertical position. Each of the two magazine drums will contain 36 rockets, giving a total capacity, with a full launcher and full magazine, of 90 rockets. The model shown here is of an installation suitable for ships of the *La Combattante II* type; other configurations are possible.

Weapon Data
Calibre: 140 mm
Launch weight: 54 kg
Warhead: 19 kg HE standard
Speed: Mach 2 maximum
Rate of fire: 9 seconds for 18-round salvo, single rounds or smaller salvoes may be fired
Range: 16 km (8.5 nm) standard maximum
CEP: 90 m

Manufacturers
Systems C.N.I.M. and in cooperation with Creusot-Loire for the mounting.

Status
Land version fully developed. Naval version proposed.

Model of RAP14 naval launcher

(USSR) 140 mm ROCKET LAUNCHER

For the past thirty years and more the Russian Army has been using and arranging for the development of a wide range of unguided barrage rockets. It is not surprising, therefore, that the Russian Navy should also use these weapons: indeed it is surprising that they have not made greater use of them.

So far as is known at present the only confirmed installation is on the *Polnocny* class landing ship. This carries a trainable launcher with a capacity for 18 rounds of 140 mm rockets. These are credited with a range of some 9 km.

(ITALY) MULTI-PURPOSE ROCKET LAUNCHER

Designed primarily for electronic warfare applications, but capable of being used for other purposes, and described as a third-generation device, this is a servo-controlled mounting which can be trained and elevated by remote control and on which is mounted a multi-tube launcher assembly for 105 mm rockets.

Both the mounting and the individual launch-tubes are remotely controlled from a console of sophisticated design. The twenty rockets can be fired in various sequences or in accordance with a fixed programme. Either chaff or flare rockets are normally used: the launcher could, of course, also fire similar rockets with HE warheads but so far as is known this has not been done.

Manufacturer
Breda Meccanica Bresciana.

Status
In production and service.

SCLAR MULTI-PURPOSE ROCKET SYSTEM

SCLAR is a shipboard system for launching illuminating rockets and long-range or short-range chaff dispensing rockets. It can also be used for rockets with HE warheads.

Rockets are launched from tubes mounted in a 20-tube launcher which can be elevated and trained by remote control. The complete SCLAR system includes the Elsag fire control sub-system from which this remote control is exercised.

The rockets are fin-stabilised, the fins being folded for insertion in the launcher and opening and locking when discharged from it.

Two types of chaff rocket are available for short and long-range operation, their lengths being 1,142 mm and 1,849 mm and weights 18.4 kg and 27.0 kg respectively, and one type of illuminating rocket (long) is used. HE rockets are not available as standard but can be supplied if required and the warhead weight for all rockets is 10.2 kg. Rockets are fired electrically by remote control. Maximum ranges are 2,100 m and 11,600 m.

Manufacturers
Rockets: Snia Viscosa—BPD Division-SpA.
Launcher: Breda Meccanica Bresciana SpA.
Fire Control: Elettronica San Georgio SpA.

Breda rocket launcher

(SWITZERLAND)

81 mm ROCKET LAUNCHER

This Oerlikon unguided rocket launcher has been developed for installation on FPBs and other light naval vessels.

The complete mounting comprises two single barrel-launchers, each of which has a 9-rocket magazine, mounted on a turntable. The mounting is power-operated and remotely controlled.

Characteristics
Rocket calibre: 81 mm
Elevation: −10 deg to +50 deg
Traverse: unlimited
Rate of fire: about 80 rounds/min/launcher
Length overall: about 3 m
Weight: (without rockets) about 900 kg

Manufacturer
Oerlikon-Bührle.

Oerlikon 81 mm rocket launcher

MORTARS

Apart from ASW depth-charge mortars, which are described in the ASW section, a variety of mortars and mortar mountings may be found among small craft—notably riverine craft and certain vessels of the US Coastguard.

By far the commonest calibre among these weapons is 81 mm, but there are some 60 mm US mortars in service and Thompson-Brandt, in France, have recently proposed a naval mounting of their 60 mm vehicle mortar. There is also at least one family of 3-inch mortars in service.

These weapons differ from conventional land-based mortars in that they are customarily mounted on trainable mountings: otherwise they are functionally similar to the land force weapon. Typical ranges are 2.5 km and 5 km maximum ranges for 60 mm and 81 mm mortars respectively, with corresponding direct-fire ranges of about 300 m and 600 m.

It should be noted that the Swedish/French 4-barrelled anti-submarine mortar system can also be used for shore bombardment.

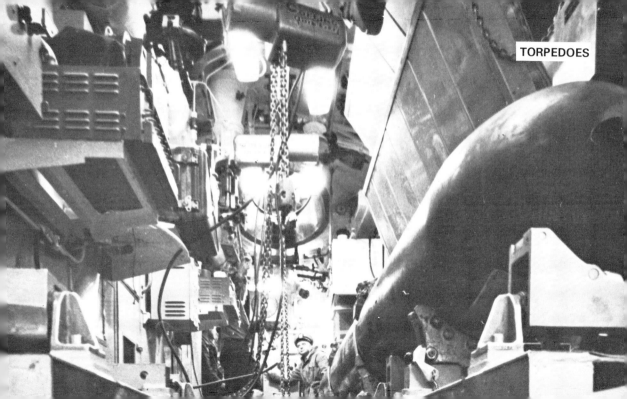

TORPEDOES

550 mm TYPE E14   (FRANCE)

Submarine-launched anti-ship (or anti-submarine) torpedo.

Data

Target: 0-20 kt ship or submarine near surface
Guidance: acoustic, 500 m range, with autopilot approach
Length: 429 cm
Weight: 900 kg
Propulsion: electric
Speed: 25 knots
Range: 5,500 m (3 nm)
Submersion: preset 6-18 m
Warhead: 200 kg HE
Fuze: contact and electromagnetic

Manufacturer

CIT-Alcatel for DTCN.

Status

Quantity production: French Navy service.

550 mm TYPE E15   (FRANCE)

Submarine-launched anti-ship (or anti-submarine) torpedo.

Data

Target: 0-20 kt ship or submarine near surface
Guidance: acoustic, medium range, with autopilot approach
Length: 600 cm
Weight: 1,350 kg
Propulsion: electric
Speed: 25 knots
Range: 12,000 m (6.5 nm)
Submersion: preset 6-18 m
Warhead: 300 kg HE
Fuze: contact and electromagnetic

Manufacturer

CIT-Alcatel for DTCN.

Status

Quantity production: French Navy service.

E14 torpedo

(FRANCE) 21-inch TYPE L3

Ship-launched or submarine-launched anti-submarine torpedo.

Data
Target: submarine up to 20 kt and down to 300 m
Guidance: acoustic, active, 600 m range in good conditions. Pre-programmed circular or helical (deep water) search pattern if target not detected after predicted time.
Length: 432 cm
Weight: 900 kg
Propulsion: electric
Speed: 25 knots
Range: 5,500 m (3 nm)
Submersion: max 300 m
Warhead: 200 kg HE
Fuze: contact and acoustic proximity

Manufacturer
DTCN.

Status
Available for manufacture but not in production.

(FRANCE) 21-inch TYPE L4

Anti-submarine torpedo designed to be launched from aircraft or the Malafon ASW missile. Special devices to ensure smooth entry into the water.

Data
Target: submerged submarines up to 20 kt
Guidance: active acoustic homing preceded by circular search
Length: 313 cm including parachute-stabiliser
Weight: 540 kg
Propulsion: electric
Speed: 30 kt
Fuze: impact and acoustic proximity

Manufacturer
DTCN.

Status
In service with the French Navy.

L4 torpedo

21-inch TYPE L5

Ship-launched (Mod 1) or submarine-launched (Mod 3) anti-submarine torpedo.

Data

Target: submerged submarine
Guidance: active/passive acoustic homing with choice of direct attack or programmed search with either
Weight: Mod 1, 1,000 kg; Mod 3, 1,300 kg
Speed: 35 knots

Manufacturer
DTCN.

Status
Operational in the French Navy.

550 mm TYPE L3

Ship-launched or submarine-launched anti-submarine torpedo.

Data

Target: submarine up to 20 kt and down to 300 m
Guidance: acoustic, active, 600 m range in good conditions. Pre-programmed circular or helical (deep water) search pattern if target not detected after predicted time
Length: 430 cm
Weight: 910 kg

Propulsion: electric
Speed: 25 knots
Range: 5,500 m (3 nm)
Submersion: max 300 m
Warhead: 200 kg HE
Fuze: contact and acoustic proximity

Manufacturer
DTCN.

Status
Quantity production and service with the French Navy.

550 mm TYPE Z16

Submarine-launched anti-ship (or anti-submarine) torpedo

Data

Target: surface vessels or submarines near the surface
Guidance: pre-set gyro running angle and depth. Zig-zag search if no target encountered after preset time
Length: 720 cm

Weight: 1,700 kg
Speed: 30 kt
Range: 10 km (5.5 nm)
Submersion: to 18 m
Propulsion: electric
Warhead: 300 kg HE
Fuze: contact or magnetic proximity

Status
Obsolescent.

(GERMANY-FGR)

21-inch SEEAL

Ship-launched or submarine-launched anti-ship torpedo.

Data
Target: surface vessel
Guidance: active/passive acoustic homing
Propulsion: electric

Manufacturer
AEG.

Status
Developed in parallel with Seeschlange in the 1960s. Now obsolescent and replaced by SUT.

21-inch SEESCHLANGE

Ship-launched or submarine-launched anti-submarine torpedo.

Data
Target: submarine down to 300 m
Guidance: active/passive acoustic homing
Propulsion: electric

Manufacturer
AEG.

Status
Developed in parallel with Seeal in the 1960s. Now obsolescent and replaced by SUT.

21-inch SST 4

Dual-purpose ship-launched or submarine-launched torpedo. It is the internationally available version of the German Navy's SUT torpedo.

Data
Target: surface vessels or submerged submarines
Guidance: wire-guided with double dispenser arrangement: a dispenser casket left in the torpedo tube allows for ship movement and a torpedo-borne dispenser allows for torpedo movement. Active/passive homing sonar
Length: 639 cm including dispenser casket
Propulsion: electric
Submersion: 300 m
Warhead: 260 kg HE
Fuze: contact and magnetic

Manufacturer
AEG.

Status
Believed to be in service with Argentina and Turkey.

21-inch SUT

Dual-purpose ship-launched or submarine-launched torpedo. Detailed data not available but believed to be substantially similar to SST 4 and presumably superior in some respects because the SST 4 is the non-secret, internationally available version.

Generally, it is an electrically-propelled, wire-guided torpedo with active/passive acoustic homing and combines the advantageous characteristics of the Seeal and Seeschlange torpedoes which it replaces.

Manufacturer
AEG.

Status
In service in the Federal German Navy.

21-inch TYPE A184

Dual purpose ship-launched or submarine-launched torpedo.

Data
Target: surface vessels or submerged submarines
Guidance: wire-guided with active/passive acoustic homing controlling course as well as depth in the homing phase
Length: 600 cm
Propulsion: electric

Manufacturer
Whitehead-Moto-Fides SpA.

Status
Developed to replace both G6e and G62ef torpedoes. Probably now operational.

21-inch TYPE G6e

Ship-launched or submarine-launched anti-ship torpedo.

Data
Target: surface vessels
Guidance: wire-guided with passive acoustic homing
Length: 600 cm
Propulsion: electric
Warhead: 300 kg HE
Fuze: contact

Manufacturer
Whitehead-Moto-Fides SpA.

Status
Certainly obsolescent and probably obsolete.

21-inch TYPE G62ef   (ITALY)

Submarine-launched anti-submarine device comprising the main body of the (obsolete) Whitehead G6E 21-inch wire-guided torpedo with an American Mk 44 lightweight 12.75-inch (324 mm) torpedo in place of the G6E warhead and homing device. The combination is known as the G62ef or Kangaroo torpedo.

Data
Target: submerged submarines
Guidance: wire-guided run-out of G6E followed by Mk 44 ejection and search-and-homing by active sonar
Length: 620 cm including the Mk 44 payload
Propulsion: electric

Manufacturer
System: Whitehead-Moto/Fides SpA.

Status
Obsolescent. Will be replaced by Type A 184—presumably when existing stocks are used up. Meanwhile the torpedo is in service with the Italian Navy.

(SWEDEN)   21-inch TYPE 61

Ship-launched or submarine-launched long-range anti-ship torpedo.

Data

Target: surface vessels
Guidance: wire-guided
Length: 702.5 cm
Launch weight: 1,765 kg
Propulsion: Thermal, low wake, using hydrogen peroxide as oxidizer
Warhead: 250 kg HE
Fuze: impact and proximity

Manufacturer

Forenade Fabriksverken.

Status

Produced in large numbers for the Royal Swedish Navy and for some NATO navies. Operational.

(UK)   21-inch MARK 8

Ship-launched or submarine-launched free-running anti-ship torpedo.

Data

Target: surface vessels
Guidance: free-running with mechanically preset depth and course angles
Length: 670 cm
Weight: 1,535 kg
Propulsion: compressed air
Speed: 45 kt
Range: 4.5 km (2 nm)
Submersion: to 18 m

Status

Obsolescent. Replaced in RN service by Tigerfish torpedo.

21-inch MARK 20

Submarine-launched anti-submarine (or anti-ship) torpedo.

Data

Target: submarines: limited anti-ship capability
Guidance: preset depth and course angles plus passive sonar homing in depth and azimuth
Length: 411 cm
Weight: approx 820 kg
Propulsion: electric: perchloric acid battery
Speed: 20 kt
Running depth: 3—64 m
Range: 11 km (6 nm)
Submersion: max homing depth 244 m
Warhead: 91 kg HE

Status

This torpedo has been the subject of a modernisation programme to make it compatible with modern control systems. A major element in this programme was the replacement of the mechanical depth and course angle setting method by an electrical remote setting arrangement using a standard NATO 'A' link umbilical cable. Submarine trials of the modified weapon were completed in 1971 and the modified torpedoes are available to order. The modification was developed and modification kits are made by Vickers Ltd.

Submarine-launched anti-submarine torpedo of sophisticated design.

Data

Target: submarines
Guidance: initial wire guidance (dual wire dispenser system) followed by active sonar homing. Computer in torpedo linked to submarine's torpedo fire control system computer throughout engagement
Length: 646.4 cm
Weight: 1,550 kg
Propulsion: electrically driven contra-rotating propellers
Speed: dual high/low selectable
Fuze: impact and proximity

Manufacturer

System contractor Marconi Space and Defence Systems Ltd.

Status

In service with the Royal Navy.

Tigerfish

21-inch MARK 14

Submarine-launched anti-ship torpedo which has been in service for some 40 years. Current model is Mk 14 Mod 5.

Data (Mod 5)
Target: surface vessels
Guidance: preset depth and course angles
Length: 525 cm
Weight: 1,780 kg
Propulsion: alcohol-burning thermal engine/compressed air
Speed: 32—46 kt
Range: 4.6—9 km (2.58—5 nm)
Submersion: to 18 m
Warhead: 230 kg

Status
Operational in the USN and elsewhere.

(USA)   21-inch MARK 48

Submarine-launched dual-purpose torpedo of highly sophisticated design. The subject of a competitive development with a change of operational intention, about half-way through the programme, from ASW only to dual-purpose, the selected Mod 1 design entered service in 1974—twelve years after invitations to tender were issued.

Data
Target: surface vessels and submarines
Guidance: free-running or wire-guided run-out; active, passive or active/passive homing; multiple re-attack capability
Length: 580 cm
Weight: about 1,600 kg
Propulsion: pump-jet propulsors powered by liquid momo-propellant (Otto) motor
Speed: 50 kt
Range: 46 km
Submersion: max sonar homing depth over 900 m
Manufacturer
Gould Inc.
Status
In service with USN.

Mk 48 torpedo

(USA)   DEXTOR

DEXTOR—deep experimental torpedo—is a project name reported to relate to a development programme for a deep-diving torpedo (presumably a successor to the Mark 48) for use against nuclear submarines at great depths.

21-inch M-57

A calibre of 21 inches appears to have been the standard for Russian anti-ship torpedoes since 1945. A smaller, 18-inch, calibre was in use before the Second World War and may still be in use as an air-launched weapon; but it is likely that the post-war designs were based on the wartime German 21-inch torpedoes—which were also used as the basis of some developments in the UK and USA.

The M-57 is a very large torpedo carried by submarines and fast torpedo-boats. It is 825 cm long.

Status

Operational in navies of Warsaw Pact countries at least.

Torpedo loading;

Ship-launched or submarine-launched dual-purpose (but see below) torpedo. Can be deck-launched using Mark 23 and Mark 25 torpedo launchers; and for submarine launching the torpedo is fitted with guides which enable it to fit into, and swim out from, a standard 21-inch tube.

Two distinct versions of the torpedo have been built, of which has had two model numbers. Mods 0 and 3 are free-running torpedoes with active and passive sonar homing: Mods 1 and 2 are wire-guided.

Although intended for use against both surface and submerged targets, the Mk 37 has been used primarily in an anti-submarine role because of the difficulties associated with sonar homing against surface targets. A modified version of the torpedo, the Northrop Torpedo 37C, has been developed to overcome this difficulty and improve the weapon in various other ways.

Data—Mods 0 and 3

Target: mainly submarines

Guidance: preset depth and course angle for run-out followed by active, passive or active/passive sonar homing with or without preliminary search pattern

Length: 352 cm

Weight: 648 kg

Propulsion: electric (silver-zinc battery)

Speed: 30 kt

Range: 7 km (4 nm)

Submersion: max homing depth 370 m

Warhead: 150 kg HE

Fuze: impact

Date introduced: 1952

Mods 1 and 2 as Mods 0 and 3 except—

Guidance: wire-guided run-out

Length: 409 cm

Weight: 766 kg

Date introduced: 1961

Status

Obsolescent in USN service. Replacement torpedo is Mk 48.

19-inch NORTHROP 37C

Ship-launched or submarine-launched dual-purpose torpedo. Derived directly from the standard US Mk 37 (mods 2 and 3) torpedoes by modification, the 37C is also made in free-running and wire-guided versions.

Major elements of the modification are the replacement of the battery-electric propulsion system by an Otto fuel motor of the type used in the Mk 46/1 torpedo, improvements to the acoustics system to increase sonar detection probability and modification of the logic to give three attack modes—A, straight run anti-ship without homing; B, as A but with delayed search-and-home for lost target; C, full anti-submarine search-and-home.

Performance data have not been published but the following are estimated.

Data

Target: submarines or surface vessels
Guidance: modified Mk 37 (see text)
Dimensions: believed to be substantially the same as Mk 37
Propulsion: liquid mono-propellant (Otto) motor
Speed: 42 kt
Range: 14 km (7.5 nm)
Submersion: max homing depth 370 m
Warhead: 150 kg HE
Fuze: impact

Manufacturer
Northrop Corporation.

Status
In production and in service in Canada and the Netherlands.

Freedom torpedo

(USA)

FREEDOM TORPEDO

This is a 19-inch weapon which is compatible with 21-inch launch tubes and with many fire control systems. Two models are available, Mod 0 having programmed terminal patterns and Mod 1 having a long-range homing system. Both are wire-guided. An anti-circular run protection device is fitted.

Data
Target: surface vessels
Guidance: wire with terminal pattern (Mod 0) or long-range homing (Mod 1)
Length: 572 cm
Weight: 1,237 kg warshot; 950 kg exercise
Propulsion: electric from 9-minute seawater battery
Speed: 40 kt
Range: 10.9 km (5.9 nm)
Submersion: 2-15 m
Warhead: 295 kg minimum
Fuze: contact

Manufacturer
Westinghouse Defence and Electronic Systems.

Status
Private venture.

(USSR)

18-inch TORPEDOES

18-inch torpedoes were standard anti-ship weapons in the Soviet Navy before the Second World War. Since the war, however, the 21-inch calibre has been adopted—as it has in almost every other country—for large anti-ship weapons; and it is believed that the 18-inch calibre is no longer used by any Russian surface vessel or submarine.

The Russian Naval Air Force, however, uses a torpedo which is smaller than the standard 21-inch weapon; and it has been suggested that this is the old 18-inch device. The suggestion is plausible but there is no definite information on the subject.

400 mm TYPE 41

Ship-launched or submarine-launched lightweight dual-purpose torpedo with special ability to operate in shallow water or in otherwise acoustically difficult conditions. Simple to operate and easily installed in almost any vessel from a fishing boat upwards.

Data
Target: ships or submarines
Guidance: active homing sonar giving both azimuth and depth guidance
Length: 250 cm
Weight: 250 kg
Propulsion: electric
Fuze: impact and proximity

Manufacturer
Forenade Fabriksverken.

Status
In service with the Royal Swedish Navy.

400 mm TYPE 42 (SWEDEN)

Lightweight all-purpose torpedo generally similar in concept to the Type 41 but with the additional facility of launching from helicopters and with the option of add-on wire guidance.

Data
Target: ships or submarines
Guidance: active homing sonar giving both azimuth and depth guidance. Optional added wire guidance
Length: 244 cm (plus 18 cm for optional wire section)
Weight: 250 kg (without wire section)
Propulsion: electric
Fuze: impact and proximity

Manufacturer
Forenade Fabriksverken.

Status
In production (after extensive proving trials) for the Royal Swedish Navy.

Type 42 torpedo

(USSR)

Ship-launched or submarine-launched anti-submarine torpedoes, said to be of 400 mm calibre and capable of being fired from trainable tubes mounted either singly or in groups of up to five, were introduced in the Soviet Navy probably during the 1960s.

No details of these weapons are known except that the launch tubes are only about 5 metres in length. Aft-mounted torpedo tubes, also said to be of 400 mm calibre, are to be found in some Russian submarines and probably fire similar torpedoes.

12.75-inch TYPE A. 244 (ITALY)

Ship-launched or air-launched lightweight anti-submarine torpedo. Generally similar to the US Mk 44 Mod 2 but with more modern electronics.

Data

Target: submerged submarines
Guidance: programmed search and active acoustic homing. Depth and course settings by umbilical cable
Length: 256 cm
Weight: about 230 kg
Propulsion: electric

Manufacturer

Whitehead Moto Fides SpA

Status

In service in the Italian Navy.

12.75-inch PROJECT 7511 (UK)

This project covers the development of a new lightweight anti-submarine torpedo for use on surface ships or by helicopters or other aircraft. It replaces the cancelled Mark 31 development and the torpedo will replace the US Mark 46 torpedo in RN service.

Status

Study contract with Marconi Space & Defence Systems Ltd.

(USA)

Ship-launched or air-launched lightweight anti-submarine torpedo. Has been used as the payload of the ASROC missile and in the G62ef Kangaroo torpedo combination by the Italian Navy. Deck launching is from Mk 32 tubes.

Data
Target: submarines
Guidance: depth and course settings by umbilical cable; active acoustic homing
Length: 256 cm
Weight: 233 kg
Propulsion: electric
Speed: about 30 kt
Range: 5 km (2.5 nm)
Submersion: max homing depth 300 m
Warhead: 40 kg HE
Date introduced: 1960

Status
Obsolescent. Replaced by Mk 46 in US and UK and generally being replaced in other countries.

MW 30 practice torpedo (made by Plessey) externally identical with the Mark 44 torpedo

12.75-inch MARK 46

Ship-launched or air-launched lightweight anti-submarine torpedo. Successor to the Mark 44 in general USN service it has also replaced it as the ASROC payload and is used in CAPTOR. Two versions were developed, one (Mod 0) using a solid-fuel motor and the other (Mod 1) using a liquid mono-propellant (Otto) motor. Mod 0 did not become operational because the Mod 1 motor was preferred. The following data refer to Mod 1: Mod 0 was a little heavier.

Data
Target: submarine
Guidance: active/passive acoustic homing. Multiple re-attack capability
Length: 267 cm
Weight: about 250 kg
Propulsion: liquid mono-propellant (Otto) motor
Speed: about 40 kt
Range: 11 km (6 nm)
Submersion: max homing depth 450 m
Warhead: 40 kg
Date introduced: 1964

Status
In widespread operational use in the USA, UK and elsewhere.

CAPTOR

Captor—"encapsulated torpedo"—comprises a US Mk 46 torpedo inserted into a mine casing with some additional apparatus. The combination can be laid in deep water by ships or aircraft, and the operational plan is believed to involve sowing the mines in narrow seas to attack and destroy enemy submarines as they attempt to pass through on their way to or from their operational stations. If desired, the torpedo could be fitted with a nuclear warhead.

The system is said to be able to discriminate between submarines and surface vessels. Presumably, also, there is some means whereby a friendly submarine (or other vessel) can inhibit or neutralize the system.

Manufacturer
Goodyear Aerospace Corporation.

Status
Scheduled to enter service in mid-1975.

NEARTIP

This is the name given to a "near-term improvement" programme currently in hand in the USA. The purpose of the programme is the improvement of the Mk 46 lightweight torpedo. The programme is believed to involve the development of a retrofit package but no details of its nature have been released.

Status
Project, understood to be aimed at a service entry date of about 1978.

ADVANCED LIGHTWEIGHT TORPEDO

AWLT—advanced lightweight torpedo—is the project designation so far applied to a programme for the development of a new, presumably 12.75-inch, lightweight torpedo to succeed the Mk 46. No details of this programme have been released, but it is presumably long enough to justify the NEARTIP Mk 46 improvement exercise.

ANTI-SUBMARINE ROCKET SYSTEM

On the *Moskva* class helicopter carriers of the Soviet Navy there is a twin missile launcher, forward of the two surface-to-air missile launchers, which is widely believed to be for some kind of anti-submarine missile—possibly of the ASROC type.

If anything further is known, other than in Russian and allied military circles, concerning the nature of performance of these missiles, it has not so far publicly emerged.

ASROC launch

214

This long-range anti-submarine weapon consists of a ship-launched ballistic missile with alternative payloads of an acoustic homing torpedo (Mk 46) or a nuclear depth charge. Associated with the missile and the various launchers that can be used with it are a sonar system and a computer to process the sonar data and missile ballistics to determine the missile launch angles. After the initial boost by its solid-fuel motor the missile sheds the booster and follows a ballistic trajectory to a predetermined distance from the predicted target position. At this point the payload is separated from the missile body and either parachuted to the surface, if it is a torpedo, or allowed to plunge into the sea if it is a depth charge.

Various launchers can be used, the standard being an eight-cell device and recognised alternatives a combined ASROC/Terrier launcher and the Mk 26 dual-purpose launcher of the Aegis system.

Missile Data
Length: 460 cm
Diameter: 325 mm
Fin span: 845 mm
Launch weight: 450 kg
Range: believed to be from about 2 km to about 11 km (1-6 nm)
Date introduced: 1961

Manufacturer
Honeywell Inc.

Status
Operational in the USN and in the Canadian, Japanese and West German navies.

IKARA

A long-range anti-submarine weapon system comprising a guided, powered vehicle and an acoustic homing torpedo. The vehicle is launched from a surface vessel and is powered by a dual-thrust solid-propellant rocket motor. It has short cropped-delta wings, elevon control surfaces and upper and lower vertical tail fins. The payload is a lightweight torpedo (typically the American Mk 44).

Target data, from own ship's sonar or elsewhere, is computed to determine target position; the vehicle is launched from its trainable launcher and radar tracked and radio guided to a torpedo dropping position near the target. The torpedo is dropped by parachute on receipt of a command signed from the launching vessel: on entering the water it executes a search pattern to locate the target and then homes on it.

Initial design was by the Australian Department of Supply and Department of the Navy; and the version installed in Australian ships has its own autonomous digital computer. *RN Ikara* is a version adopted by the Royal Navy in which computer service is provided by the ship's Action Data Automation System. *Branik* is a version developed in the US for the Brazilian *Niteroi*-class Mk 10 frigates with a different method of providing computer service.

Vehicle Data
Length: 335 cm
Wing span: 150 cm
Range: Not disclosed, but in excess of maximum sonar range

Manufacturers etc.
Australian Department of Supply
Hawker Siddeley Dynamics Ltd. (RN Ikara & Branik)
Ferranti Ltd. (Branik)
Vosper Thornycroft Ltd. (Branik)

1974 Status
Ikara and RN Ikara in service. First *Niteroi*-class frigate launched January 1974.

Ikara on its launcher

(FRANCE)

MALAFON ANTI-SUBMARINE DRONE SYSTEM

Torpedo-carrying winged drone system primarily designed for use from surface vessels against submarines but suitable also for use against surface targets.

The missile is ramp-launched from a trainable launcher and is propelled by two solid-fuel boosters for the first few seconds of flight. Subsequent flight is unpowered but radio-command guided and controlled in altitude by a radio altimeter to maintain a nearly flat trajectory.

At about 800 metres from the estimated target position a tail parachute is deployed to decelerate the missile and eject the torpedo payload to complete its mission by acoustic homing.

The drone and launcher are associated with a suitable fire control system and appropriate target sensors. Flares on the drone wingtips aid tracking for guidance.

Development started in 1956, and although final evaluation and operational trials did not take place until 1964-65 some installations (referred to as Malafon Mk 1) were made before this.

Missile Data
Length: 615 cm
Body diameter: 65 cm
Wing span: 330 cm
Launch weight: 1,500 kg
Maximum range: about 13 km (7 nm)

Manufacturer
Société Industrielle d'Aviation Latécoère.

Status
Operational in the French Navy.

Malafon torpedo-carrying drone on its trainable launcher

SUBROC

SUBROC is a submarine-launched anti-submarine rocket carrying a nuclear depth bomb and forming part of an advanced system designed for deployment in nuclear-powered attack submarines operating against nuclear-powered ballistic missile submarines.

Associated with the missile is an elaborate sonar and fire control system which programmes the missile's inertial navigation system. The missile is launched conventionally and horizontally from the submarine's 21-inch torpedo tubes and at a safe distance from the submarine the solid-fuel missile motor is ignited. After a short continuation of its horizontal motion it is steered upwards and clear of the water.

Throughout its powered flight, both in the water and in the air, the missile is guided by jet deflectors controlled by its inertial navigator. At a predetermined point, however, the rocket is separated from the bomb and the latter continues on an unpowered trajectory towards the water re-entry point. During this part of the flight the bomb is guided aerodynamically by vanes. Impact with the water is cushioned, to protect the arming and detonation devices, and the bomb is detonated at a pre-determined depth in the vicinity of the target.

Missile Data
Length: 640 cm
Diameter: 533 mm (21-inch) max
Launch weight: about 1,800 kg
Warhead: nuclear depth bomb
Range: 55 km (30 nm)
Date introduced: 1965

Manufacturer
Goodyear Aerospace Corporation.

Status
Operational in USN nuclear attack submarines.

Subroc missile on test

This system comprises a shipborne rocket launcher having two or more launch tubes, shipborne sonar and a fire control system. Sonar data on submarine position are used to determine the launcher elevation and bearing angles and the firing system permits the launching of rockets either singly or in salvoes. A special design of missile nose ensures a predictable and accurate under-water trajectory. The launcher is reloaded by automatic means from the magazine which is disposed directly below the launcher.

Missiles have three types of rocket motor giving differing range brackets. The missile trajectory is flat thus giving a short time of flight to minimise target evasive action. Fuses are fitted with hydro-static and DA devices.

The initial version of the system, comprising a four-tube launcher and the M/50 rocket, was developed by AB Bofors in the early 1950s, and became operational about 1956. A two-tube launcher was developed in 1969-73. A version made in France by Creusot-Loire under licence from Bofors has a six-tube launcher and entered service with the French Navy in 1967.

Data

2-tube Launcher

Weight, excluding rockets: 3.2 tons
Traverse: unlimited
Elevation: 0-60 deg (firing), 0-90 deg (loading)
Angular speed: 30 deg/sec

4-tube Launcher

Weight, excluding rockets: 7.3 tons
Traverse: ±130 deg
Elevation: 15-60 deg (firing), 15-90 deg (loading)
Angular speed: 18 deg/sec

Rockets

M/50: 250 kg: range 300-830 m
Erika: 250 kg: range 600-1,600 m
Nelli: 230 kg: range 1,520-3,600 m

Manufacturers

Design and manufacture of basic system by AB Bofors. French version of the system designed and built by Creusot-Loire.

Status

In widespread use in the Swedish, French and many other navies.

Bofors 2-tube rocket launcher

375 mm ANTI-SUBMARINE ROCKET SYSTEM

(FRANCE)

A French version of the Swedish Bofors AS rocket system has been developed and produced by Creusot-Loire and is installed in many French warships

Mechanically, the main innovation is the extension of the system to a six-tube remotely-controlled, automatically-reloaded launcher. With this is associated a CIT-Alcatel sonar and a Thomson-CSF computer to predict future submarine position and calculate the current launcher attitude. The system can use the complete range of Bofors 375 mm AS rockets (brief details of which are listed in the description of the Bofors system) and the computer calculates ballistics for initial velocities of 70, 90, 100 and 130 m/sec as required by the various rockets to give ranges from about 260 m to about 3,600 m.

Launcher Data
Weight, excluding rockets but including remote control: approx 16 tons
Traverse: 350 deg
Elevation: 0 to 92.5 deg
Rate of fire: 1 round/sec

Manufacturer
Launcher: Creusot-Loire SA.

Status
In service with the French Navy.

Creusot-Loire 6-tube launcher

WEAPON ALPHA ANTI-SUBMARINE ROCKET

This American-designed weapon is no longer in service with the USN but still equips at least the *Akizuki* class destroyers and *Isuzu* class frigates of the Japanese Navy.

It consists of a turret-mounted 324 mm diameter launch tube (Mk 108) from which is projected an anti-submarine rocket weighing 227 kg. The launcher is automatically reloaded, is capable of a high repetition rate and has an almost circular field of fire.

Weapon Data
Calibre: 324 mm (12.75 in)
Rocket weight: 227 kg (500 lb)
Rate of fire: 15 rounds/min
Maximum range: about 800 m

Status
Obsolescent. Still in service but surpassed by more recent developments. "Weapon Alpha" was formerly known as "Weapon Able", the progression in title reflecting the change in the phonetic spelling of the letter A.

4-tube launcher on Japanese *Mogami* class frigate

RUSSIAN ANTI-SUBMARINE ROCKET LAUNCHERS

The Russians do not appear to have adopted the streamlined depth charge of the kind introduced by the Americans in the 1940s. Instead they appear to have leap-frogged a development stage and proceeded directly from the slow-sinking depth-charge to the medium range anti-submarine rocket.

The development of this type of weapon by the Russians was first noticed by outside observers around 1960. The earliest installation appears to have a small (150 cm long) twin launcher for rockets with a range of 6-800 m. This may still be found on the old *Kola* class frigates, and *Kronstadt* class submarine chasers. More recently a range of more powerful weapons has been introduced: these are described in the entries below.

Status

It is not definitely known that these weapons are still in service.

12-barrel 250 mm launcher

16-barrel 250 mm rocket launcher

(USSR) 250 mm ANTI-SUBMARINE ROCKET LAUNCHERS

Three different types of mounting for 250 mm calibre anti-submarine rockets have been observed; and it is believed that the performance of rockets launched from one of these—the earliest in service—is inferior to that of rockets launched from the other two.

This "inferior" model is the five-barrel launcher. The range of these rockets is said to be some 1,800 m: launch tube length is 180 cm—as also is that of the other two launchers.

The more recent models are the 12-barrel and 16-barrel launchers. Range of rockets launched from these launchers is said to be about 2,500 m.

Status

Weapons of these three types are very extensively deployed in the Soviet Navy. The 1,800 metre launchers are mainly deployed on small craft of Warsaw Pact naval forces.

5-barrel 250 mm launcher

(USSR) 300 mm ANTI-SUBMARINE ROCKET LAUNCHERS

These long-range Russian anti-submarine rocket launchers have been reported in two slightly different forms. Both are 6-barrel, pedestal-mounted, remotely-controlled mechanisms but in one configuration the two columns of three barrels are parallel whereas in the other the top two barrels are closer together than the other two pairs.

The range of the rockets used with these launchers has been reported as 4,500 m. If correct this figure compares favourably with that of systems of this type made in other countries.

Status

Operational in the Soviet Navy.

6-barrel 300 mm AS rocket launcher

TERNE III ANTI-SUBMARINE ROCKET SYSTEM

This system uses a rocket-propelled depth charge fired from a remotely-controlled, automatically-loaded 6-round launcher. The launcher is controlled by a fire control system which accepts sonar date for the prediction of the target's future position and computes the rocket ballistics to determine the launcher attitude. The launch rails are pivoted about two axes to give an all-round launch cone. The launcher design provides special protection to enable the weapon to be used in arctic conditions.

Weapon Data
Rocket calibre: 200 mm
Length: 200 cm
Weight: 120 kg
Rate of fire: 6-round salvo in 5 sec
Reload: automatic from magazine: 40 sec
Firing sector: 360 deg
Range: probably about 3,000 m
Date introduced: 1961

Manufacturer
Kongsberg Vaapenfabrikk.

Status
Operational in the Royal Norwegian Navy and the USN.

Terne rockets on their launcher

Depth charge launched from a Russian SO-1 submarine chaser.

DEPTH CHARGES AND LAUNCHERS

Since the introduction of the anti-submarine depth charge by the Royal Navy in 1916 many devices have been used to create a pattern of underwater explosions having a reasonable chance of critically damaging a submarine.

Fixed Launchers

The modern equivalents of the original simple cylindrical depth charge and their fixed launchers are still widely deployed; and although in some quarters this type of anti-submarine warfare is regarded as obsolescent—because the depth charges must be launched from a moving ship and because the necessarily long interval between launch and explosion (to enable the launching ship to get clear) increases the submarine's chances of escape—they are likely to remain in service for some years yet.

Fixed launching arrangements for depth charges of this sort consist of simple rails, from which the charges are dropped into the sea, and fixed spigot mortars, catapults or similar devices, operated by small explosive charges or compressed air, whereby the charge can be projected 100 metres or more from the ship. A combination of rails and launchers with suitable timing can produce a pattern of explosions of predetermined shape and dimensions.

Typical Characteristics

Depth charge calibre: 305 mm (12 in)
Weight: 150 kg
Explosive: 134 kg
Fuze: Hydrostatic
Depth limit: down to about 90 m (50 fathoms)
Maximum projected range: 160 m
Date introduced: 1940 for these characteristics

Status

Operational in various forms throughout the world.

Trainable Launchers

Beginning in the Second World War and continuing to the present day there have been sporadic outbursts of development activity resulting in a variety of ASW mortars whose direction and angle of fire can be controlled and which fire a streamlined depth charge with a higher sinking rate to a greater distance from a ship which need not be in motion. Currently operational weapons of this type are described individually in the entries that follow, which deal with weapons developed or manufactured in Australia, Britain, France, Italy and Sweden. So far as is known, no weapon of this type has been developed in the USSR: both there and in the USA the preference, in longer-range anti-submarine weapon technology, has been for rocket-propelled charges.

This was the first of the trainable anti-submarine depth-charge mortars. It was developed by the British Admiralty Underwater Weapon Establishment during the 1940s and is still in service in older ships of many navies.

Position data from the ship's sonar are used by a predictor to compute the mortar aiming position. The 3-barrel mortar then fires its depth charges which are programmed to give a three-dimensional explosion pattern ahead of the target. The charges can be set to explode at variable depths using hydrostatic and delayed-action fuzes.

Weapon Data
Calibre: 305 mm (12 in)
Projectile weight: 200 kg
Range: about 400 m
Date introduced: about 1948

Status
Obsolescent but still in widespread use. The obsolescence stems primarily from its lack of operational flexibility compared with later devices.

LIMBO ANTI-SUBMARINE MORTAR SYSTEM

(UK)

Limbo is the successor to the Squid anti-submarine mortar and was developed during the 1950s—also at the Admiralty Underwater Weapons Establishment. Designated AS Mk 10 it is currently the standard anti-submarine mortar of the Royal Navy and several others (reference should be made also, however, to the Australian modification of the system).

The principle of operation is the same as that of the earlier system but Limbo is a more highly mechanical device and thus more flexible operationally. The mortar is stabilised in pitch and roll, loading is pneumatic and the fuzes are set by remote control. The weapon also has a longer range than Squid.

Weapon Data
Calibre: 305 mm (12 in)
Projectile weight: 200 kg
Range: 800-2,000 m
Date introduced: 1955

Status
In widespread operational use.

Limbo

An improved version of the AS Mk 10 (Limbo) system has been developed in Australia. The new development eliminates the use of rotating electric machinery in the pitch and roll servo loops—with consequent saving in power, deck-level weight and noise—reduces the weight and noise level of the loading mechanisms (pneumatic for Limbo) and eliminates the mechanical problems that can arise from the use of uniselectors in the fuse-setting system.

In the new design the metadyne servo control system for pitch and roll has been replaced by an electric system using silicon-controlled rectifiers to control the launcher drive motors; the pneumatic rammer has been replaced by a smaller and lighter electrical device; and the fuse setting system has been redesigned to use solid-state logic circuits with which have been incorporated additional supervisory circuits that permit checking of the setting before launch.

One effect of all these changes—apart from reduction in cost, weight and noise—is a manning reduction from seven to three.

Manufacturers

Sponsoring Organisation: Department of Manufacturing Industry—Weapons Research Establishment.

Status

Production equipments are being delivered to the Royal Australian Navy.

MENON ANTI-SUBMARINE MORTAR SYSTEM

This is the earlier of two Italian anti-submarine mortar systems and is currently in service in various destroyers and frigates of the Italian Navy.

It is a turret-mounted device which is generally mounted so that it has an arc of fire extending something like 150 degrees on either side of the forward direction. The mortar is programmed by an anti-submarine weapon control system which in turn derives its information from sonar and own ship data.

Weapon Data
Calibre: 305 mm
Projectile weight: 160 kg
Range: 1,500 m
Date introduced: 1956

Status
Operational but no longer in production.

(SWEDEN/FRANCE)
FOUR-BARREL ANTI-SUBMARINE MORTAR SYSTEM

This system was developed by Bofors in Sweden, subsequently taken up by their licensees, CAFL, and is now regarded as more a French than a Swedish system.

Unlike other AS mortar systems, this one is also intended for use as a shore bombardment mortar, firing a smaller bomb over a longer range. In its anti-submarine role it functions, like other modern mortar systems, in conjunction with a sonar-plus-computer system; and like the Italian system it is turret-mounted with a good forward field of fire and is automatically loaded. As can be seen from the following data, it has the longest range and the heaviest projectile of all current AS mortar systems.

Weapon Data

Calibre: 305 mm

Projectile weights: 230 kg anti-submarine; 100 kg bombardment

Range: 400 to 2,750 m anti-submarine; 6,000 m bombardment

Date introduced: 1959

Status

Operational in the destroyer *Aconit* and some frigates of the French Navy and on a small scale elsewhere.

SINGLE BARREL ANTI-SUBMARINE MORTAR

More recently introduced than the three-barrelled Menon mortar, these Whitehead weapons equip the more modern frigates of the Italian Navy. They are noted for their high rate of fire.

Like the three-barrelled weapon, they are turret-mounted with a good forward field of fire. Fire control is by an Elsag DLB-1 FCS.

There are believed to be two models of this mortar, designated K112 and K113: the following data are believed to relate to the K113.

Weapon Data
Calibre: 305 mm
Projectile weight: 160 kg
Range: about 1,000 m
Rate of fire: 15 rounds/min
Date introduced: 1960

Manufacturer
Whitehead Moto-Fides SpA.

Status
In service as stated.

"Hedgehog" is a name given generally to a family of multiple ahead-throwing spigot mortars designed to produce a patterned fall of shot in an area believed to contain a submarine. The projectiles are small bombs with a high sinking rate and contact fuzes and are intended to disable the submarine by striking it—one or two bombs being sufficient to do this.

The system was originally developed in the USA during the Second World War and has since been taken up by many other countries. The original design was a fixed system giving a single oval pattern of 24 bombs directly ahead of the launcher, and fixed launchers of subsequent marks are widely deployed today. In the meantime, however, more elaborate trainable launchers associated with more sophisticated fire control systems have been developed.

The term "Hedgehog" should strictly be confined to 24-bomb launchers: a smaller device using only eight bombs is known as "Mousetrap". The term is, however, often misapplied to a variety of multiple bomb launching devices.

Weapon Data
Calibre: 127 mm (5 in)
Projectile weight: 26 kg
Range: 350 m
Date introduced: 1943 onwards

Status
In widespread operational use in many different versions.

Hedgehog

MOUSETRAP ANTI-SUBMARINE SPIGOT MORTARS

"Mousetrap" was the name given to a multiple spigot mortar weapon similar in principle to, but smaller than, the Hedgehog. It used the same bomb as Hedgehog but had a shorter range and fired a pattern of 8 instead of 24 bombs.

Weapon Data

Calibre: 127 mm (5 in)
Projectile weight: 26 kg
Range: about 200 m
Date introduced: 1944

Status

Various marks of this weapon and similar weapons
are to be found in many navies.

INDEX